ABU

THE
BREAKER

THE
BREAKER

NICK PETRIE

G. P. PUTNAM'S SONS   NEW YORK

PUTNAM
— EST. 1838 —

G. P. Putnam's Sons
Publishers Since 1838
An imprint of Penguin Random House LLC
penguinrandomhouse.com

ISBN 9780525535478
ebook ISBN 9780525535485

Printed in the United States of America
10 9 8 7 6 5 4 3 2 1

Book design by Nancy Resnick

This is a work of fiction. Names, characters, places, and incidents either are the product of the
author's imagination or are used fictitiously, and any resemblance to actual persons, living or dead,
businesses, companies, events, or locales is entirely coincidental.

For all those who strive to make new things

"The future has arrived—it's just not evenly distributed yet."

—William Gibson

THE
BREAKER

1

PETER

The flatbed Toyota was too big for tight city parking, so Peter and Lewis left it behind a gas station and walked up St. Paul and across the river toward the Milwaukee Public Market, four blocks away. It was lunchtime on a blue-sky October day, and they were dirty and cheerful from a morning of demolition on a property Lewis owned in the city.

Peter Ash was tall and bony in a faded gray T-shirt and double-front work pants torn at the knees, a blue hooded sweatshirt slung over one shoulder. He hadn't cut his hair since a large-animal veterinarian had shaved his head the year before and it now hung in a dark surfer's shag streaked with premature gray.

He didn't like dealing with all that hair, but it changed the shape of his face, which was helpful. Most of the pictures they had of him were from his old Marine Corps ID, with the classic jarhead cut that revealed the shape of the skull beneath.

June Cassidy liked to tease him by saying he'd be cute with a man bun.

He found her seated on the far side of a table outside Colectivo Coffee, across the street from the Public Market. She sat sideways in her chair, looking in the opposite direction. He tossed the blue sweatshirt onto the table. "Hey, toots," he said. "You order yet?"

June held up her hand, still staring up the street. "Hang on." She wore a black Pussy Riot shirt under a running pullover and crisp mountain pants. Her bike was chained to a meter twenty feet away. She did not seem relaxed.

Lewis eased onto a stool like a lion into a crouch, following her gaze. He had coffee-brown skin and tight-cropped hair, black Levi's and an NWA sweatshirt with the sleeves cut off. "Lemme guess," he said. "Weird-looking dude with the beard, coming our way?"

June nodded. "Red hat and jacket. Something's wrong with him, but I can't figure it out."

Searching the sidewalk, Peter walked around the table and took the seat next to June, his back against the building's brick. Old habits weren't always bad habits.

The weird-looking dude was a quarter-block away. His baseball cap was pulled down tight over mirrored sunglasses and a heavy beard. The black strap of some kind of bag, probably a backpack, showed over his right shoulder.

Peter couldn't figure out what was wrong with him, either. But June was right, there was definitely something strange. Maybe it was the way he walked? Fast, but without swinging his arms, his elbows tight at his sides.

The guy wasn't clocking them at all. He stared across St. Paul toward the glass-walled Public Market with its rows of sidewalk benches and umbrella tables packed with office workers soaking up the autumn sun on their lunch break.

As the guy got closer, Peter could see the Cardinals logo on his cap and across the chest of his jacket, two birds on a baseball bat. The day was sunny and warm, so the hat and sunglasses made sense. But the baggy jacket didn't, especially zipped to the neck. It was hard to tell the size of him underneath it, but Peter could see some bulk in the torso. Maybe he was a gym rat, trying to sweat off some weight.

The ball cap and razor shades told Peter something else. Some of his Marines had worn that look overseas, and many more after they mustered out. It was a way to project toughness, to make yourself unreadable, and also a way to hide the rawness of your emotions, even from yourself.

As traffic slowed for the light, the guy left the sidewalk to angle across the street. He jogged a few steps, as if eager for an appointment. The backpack bounced on his shoulder and his jacket rode up on his left side. Forty feet away, Peter saw something slim and dark poke out beneath it.

The black barrel of a rifle. The jacket hem had snagged on the front sight. Nothing else it could be. Peter had seen enough of them to know.

"Shit," he said.

"Uh-huh." Lewis had seen it, too. He was on his feet now, ready. Lewis was always ready.

"What," June said. She was an investigative journalist, a good one, but she'd honed her instincts in a newsroom. Lewis had done a single tour in the army, deployed twice for a total of thirty months of combat. Peter had spent eight years as a Recon Marine, the tip of the spear, deployed more times than he cared to remember.

Now he was standing, too. He put his fingertips on June's back and stepped beside her. "Our guy's got some kind of rifle under his jacket. See the barrel showing at his hip?"

Which explained why he walked with his elbows locked, to keep the rifle from swinging on its sling. Although the jacket was baggy, the fabric was thin enough that the motion would betray the weapon's angular shape.

Then June saw it. She blinked twice. "Goddamn it."

It was too short to be a hunting rifle. It would be something with a shorter barrel and a collapsing stock, an M4 or AR-15 or any of two dozen guns like it. An assault rifle designed for war, with a magazine that held twenty to thirty rounds. He probably had more magazines in his pockets or his pack.

Lewis turned and scanned up and down the street, fingers tapping a drumbeat on his thigh. "Never a cop when you need one." He turned to Peter with a tilted smile bright on his dark face. "So much for lunch."

June put a warm hand on Peter's bare arm. She didn't say anything, but she didn't have to. She knew who he was, the man the war had made. Wound up and restless and hardwired to make himself useful. She'd seen what that could mean, in moments like this. She still didn't like it.

She tightened her grip on his arm and picked up her phone. "I'm calling 911. The police will handle it."

"Great idea," Peter said. "Lewis and I will just go into the market and wait for them to show up."

June looked at him like she could see the marrow of his bones, down to each individual molecule. Down to the werewolf that lived inside of him. Softly, she said, "Can't it be someone else's turn? Just this once?"

Peter knew she didn't mean it, not really. He leaned in, pressed his lips to her freckled cheek, and breathed in her summery smell, the clean athletic tang of fresh sweat combined with some complex, exotic scent he'd never been able to resist and could no longer live without.

"Is that who you want me to be?" he asked. "Someone who doesn't step up when something bad is about to happen?"

Muscles flexed in her jaw. "Goddamn it, you know it isn't," she said. "I just wish you'd wait for the fucking police."

Lewis had his eyes on the red jacket. "If we doin' this, Jarhead, it's time to move."

Peter straightened and looked over his shoulder. The guy with the gun had passed the streetcar stop and was almost at the market's corner entrance. As he reached one hand toward the door, his other hand reached for his jacket's zipper pull.

Peter put his hand on June's. He kept his voice soft. "You know how much damage he can do before the police get here. I'm sorry, but right now there is nobody else. Right now, we're it."

Lewis stepped into the street. "Time to go, Jarhead."

Peter walked backward after Lewis, eyes still locked on hers. "I'll see you in a few minutes. As soon as the cops show up, we're gone."

Then he turned and caught up to Lewis. Side by side, they loped across the street toward the busy market. At lunchtime, the place would be packed.

Lewis said, "The cops won't get here in time." There was no trace of strain in his voice. As if he were standing in a field watching butterflies, instead of chasing down a guy with a gun.

"I know," Peter said. His chest rose easily, pulling in oxygen, and his legs felt strong and sure. He tasted copper on his tongue and felt the familiar lift of adrenaline in his blood.

Alive, alive, I am alive.

Neither man carried any kind of weapon.

2

The Public Market was a pleasing block-long arrangement of concrete and glass and steel trusses at the edge of Milwaukee's Historic Third Ward, a former manufacturing and warehouse district that now held mostly restaurants, condos, and art galleries, with just a few of the old industrial businesses remaining.

Peter and June went to the market at least once a week. The crowded, noisy environment was a good place for Peter to push the limits of his post-traumatic stress, an acute claustrophobia that was the only souvenir of his many combat deployments overseas. It came from kicking in doors in Fallujah, he figured. All those weeks of fighting house to house, room to room, clearing insurgents one doorway at a time.

He called it the white static, and it didn't like crowds or enclosed spaces. It began with jangling nerves that sparked up his brainstem like naked electrodes under the skin, calculating firing angles, searching for exits, his fight-or-flight reflex gone into overdrive. When he first mustered out, he could only handle twenty minutes indoors before the static turned into a full-blown panic attack, bad enough to make living outside seem like a good idea. For more than a year, he'd slept alone under the stars or under a rain fly, high above the tree line of one mountain range or another, barely able to manage resupply in small-town grocery stores.

The static had gotten better, until it got much worse, bad enough to make him think seriously about dying. Then it had changed again, and now it lived in his head like a low-grade fever, a heavy hum just below the level of his conscious mind. Until his old combat instincts woke up and the hum revealed itself for what it really was, the deep rumble of a high-performance engine just waiting for someone to step on the gas.

He could feel it now, wide awake and focused. Ready to go.

The corner entrance was a natural choke point. Flanked by concrete pillars, two single doors opened to a small glass vestibule, where a double door allowed entry to the market proper. Five people were stacked up in the vestibule, their arms loaded with lunch.

Peter stood on his toes and spotted the red Cardinals cap inside the market, moving away. The guy with the gun was shorter than average, which made it harder to see him.

Lewis held the door for the shoppers, calm and cool, waiting for an opening. Peter stepped sideways to peek around the corner, hoping to see a police car parked on Water Street. No luck.

"They got cameras all over this place," Lewis said. "No matter what happens, somebody gonna be watching that footage. You prepared for that?"

"No," Peter said. "But I don't want to live with the consequences of doing nothing, either."

Peter's name and picture were in multiple federal databases and posted on police bulletin boards all over the U.S., with several warrants issued for his arrest. Because of his background and training, he was assumed to be armed and dangerous. It was a reasonable enough assumption.

Interpol and the FBI believed that he'd murdered a government employee in Iceland the previous December, which was not true. He had killed several other people, however, to save his own life and the lives of others, although that fact wouldn't help his case with the feds. At least those bodies were buried where nobody would find them.

The FBI had no clue where Peter was now, although scrutiny of video footage might change that. He'd been living under the radar and minding his own business for nine months. The outstanding warrants helped him keep his promise to June Cassidy, too. Peter didn't blame her for being pissed. He'd lied to her about going to Iceland. He'd taken unnecessary risks. He hadn't asked for help when he needed it most. He'd almost died because of it. She'd let him know in no uncertain terms that this behavior was unacceptable.

Peter's deal with June wasn't complicated. She wanted him to stop diving headfirst into trouble, and he agreed. She wanted him to put himself into something more constructive, and he agreed. She felt—and Peter's therapist felt—that the best way to put his war in the past was to work toward the future. He agreed. They were right.

But sometimes the world had other plans.

A man came out of the entrance vestibule and pushed past them, glaring. He wore a plaid western-style shirt and a straw cowboy hat. Peter smiled at him. "Can I borrow your hat?" Without waiting for an answer, he plucked it off the man's head, then settled it on his own. Not a perfect fit, but good enough. He looked at Lewis. "Let's go."

The hat's owner turned back, sputtering, and cocked a fist. He was younger than Peter, and thick through the neck and shoulders. Peter gave him a flat stare and the other man took a step back, probably without even realizing he'd done it.

"Call 911," Peter said. "I mean it. Right now. Tell them you saw a guy with a gun walking into the market." A second call would help the cops take the threat more seriously.

Lewis floated into the vestibule, with Peter right behind him.

The white static flared, that internal engine revving up high.

The market ran the length of the block along St. Paul. Behind it, a loading dock and large crowded parking lot filled the space under the low ceiling of the freeway overpass. The interior floorplan was a figure eight of aisles, with another wider aisle extending off the end like the tail of a tadpole. Vendors and food stalls with refrigerated glass display cases were crammed into both sides of every walkway.

Peter and Lewis entered at the top left of the figure eight. There was another entrance at the top right, two more near the bottom of the eight leading to the street and the parking lot, and one entrance at the bottom of the tail. The aisles were packed with people. The white static crackled like Frankenstein's machinery, and Peter felt something ancient inside him coming back to life. Hello, old friend. It's been too long.

He was on the left, facing a narrow path between a Mexican food counter and a kitchen supply and spice shop. Lewis was on the right, where a wider path ran between the spice shop and the hissing espresso machines of Anodyne Coffee.

The guy with the gun was nowhere to be seen.

Past Anodyne, stairs wrapped around an elevator shaft toward the open second level with its scatter of tables and views of the market below. It was a good place to see the whole picture. It was also the logical place for a shooter to set up if he wanted to do the most damage. Not that mass shooters were logical.

"I'm going up." Lewis took out his phone and veered right. "Stay on comms."

"Roger that." As Peter went left, eyes searching the crowd, his phone rang and he put it to his ear.

"Top of the stairs, peeking past the corner now." Even through the cell connection, Lewis's low voice sounded like motor oil, slippery and dark.

"Moving clockwise below you." Peter eased between a woman in a pink blazer and a skinny hipster in a bowling shirt. His eyes searched the crowd of diners and shoppers for a red hat and rain jacket, but saw nothing. The kitchen shop had thick wooden cutting boards, and Peter almost took one for a shield or a club, but decided against it. With one hand on the phone, he needed his remaining hand free. To the left of the Middle Eastern deli was another entrance, but he saw only new people coming in. He turned right and kept moving through the market. The cowboy straw felt strange on his head, but it was a good reminder not to look up for cameras.

"All clear at the tables," Lewis said. "Going to check the bathrooms and the market office." The guy with the gun wouldn't be the first shooter needing to take a hot greasy adrenaline dump. Peter knew plenty of Marines who'd stunk up the latrines before going outside the wire. Or else the guy wanted a private place to amp himself up for mass murder, or maybe just one last solitary minute to try to reason with the voices screaming in his head.

Peter kept moving down the aisle, trying unsuccessfully to thread his way through lazy clusters of men and women dressed for work, talking to each other and the workers behind the counters. Way too many people.

The second floor was much less crowded, and Peter knew Lewis would be moving faster. He didn't have to deal with people who couldn't decide between an espresso truffle and a sea salt caramel.

Lewis said, "At the bathrooms now."

Over the phone, Peter heard the quality of the sound change as Lewis entered the small space with its hard surfaces. Then a loud *bang*. Not the sharp crack of a firearm, but the dull metallic rattle of a stall door slamming open.

"Damn, my bad." Lewis's voice was distant, the phone down from his mouth. "Sorry, brother, I thought it was stuck." A low chuckle, and the sound changed again as he stepped back into the open. "All clear in the can 'cept for a pissed-off UPS driver taking a moment. Okay, I'm looking through the glass at the market office, everything normal there. Now I'm at the railing, looking down. I got you, but no red hat."

Peter had reached the middle of the figure eight. The aisle below him was a traffic jam, but the aisle that crossed the figure eight was relatively open. He took the open path at the wine bar, scanned the center exit to the street, then looked left and right down the aisles. "I don't see him. Anything?"

"Nothing. I'm moving back toward the stairs, I'll get a long view that way."

"Maybe he took off his fucking hat."

"Didn't take off that bright red coat, though," Lewis said. "We'd have heard the screams."

Peter saw an opening and jogged past the polished wood of the wine bar toward the Brew City stall at the bottom of the eight. June had recently given him one of their more stylish T-shirts, trying to up his clothing game. No sign of the guy with the gun.

Down the tail of the tadpole now, head on a swivel, Peter slipped through the clotted crowd at the soup place. At the end was the St. Paul Fish Company, where a giant inflatable crab stood guard over the oyster bar and bubbling tanks of live lobsters.

No red cap or jacket.

Still no police, either. What was taking them so long?

More than anything, he didn't want June to come after them. It would be just like her to follow the story into a goddamn fire-fight. They weren't so different, Peter and June.

"Lewis?"

"I got nothing. Maybe he went out that first exit at the top. Maybe this is just a trial run. Or maybe he's headed for downtown."

Peter turned and looked back over the throngs of people. He was tall enough to see over the heads of most of them. "Maybe he stopped moving." Peter reversed course. "Look to your left, down by the salad and sandwich place." Peter had skipped that crowded leg of the figure eight. The popular shop across from the parking lot entrance was busy enough to clog the aisle during the lunch rush. "See anything?"

"No. Wait. I can't see the doors, but I just caught got a flash of red walking out of sight."

The white static soared. "On my way." Peter pushed his way past a South Asian couple browsing at the meat counter. "Excuse me," he said. "Sorry." He rounded the corner to the exit and found himself blocked by a curved line of chattering schoolchildren headed into the market, holding hands in a chain with their teachers at each end. Through the wide glass doors, he saw a big yellow bus double-parked with more kids climbing down to line up on the walkway.

Right beside them, the guy with the gun. His face invisible behind the glossy beard and sunglasses.

"Lewis, I see him. He's outside. Get down here."

But the chain of children had caught Peter in an open loop, and he couldn't move forward. He smiled at two girls, one in braided black pigtails, the other with a thin yellow scarf in an ornate knot, eight or nine years old at most. "Hi there. Can you please let me through?"

The girl in the pigtails gave Peter major side-eye. "Mrs. Grundl," she said. "Mrs. Grundl!"

The teacher, red-faced and clearly focused on managing her students, turned to Peter. "Excuse me," she said. "Don't talk to my children."

"Ma'am, I just need to get through," Peter said. "I'm stuck. Please."

Mrs. Grundl was ten or fifteen years older than Peter. "Sir, these are children and you're on camera." She pointed toward a black dome mounted overhead. "Behave yourself." Behind him, the South Asian couple had turned to watch, at the same time blocking Peter's rear escape route from the string of curious children who were now all staring at him.

Outside, the guy with the gun stood at an angle to the glass doors. His right hand gripped the shoulder of a bald man in a cream-colored suit. His left hand was on the zipper of his half-open rain jacket. His head turned to survey the children swirling around him, not nervous but clearly calculating. His plan had hit the fan, and he was revising on the fly.

Peter said, "I'm sorry, ma'am, this is an emergency."

She put her free hand on her hip and glared. "Oh, really. What kind of emergency?"

"Trust me, you don't want to know." Peter raised his foot to high-step over the girls' linked arms. They shrieked and released each other's hands, the line split apart, and Peter stepped through.

Mrs. Grundl opened her mouth to speak. Peter beat her to it.

"Ma'am, there's a situation in the parking lot." He pointed down the tadpole tail toward the far exit. "Get your kids out of here now and call 911."

Then he reached a long arm into the nearby produce stall and grabbed three fat apples in one wide, knuckly hand. He still had his phone to his ear. "I'm going to the parking lot," he told Lewis. "There's a busload of kids. Get them someplace safe." He jammed the phone into his back pocket and strode toward the glass doors.

Outside, the teachers were still gathering the unruly children.

The guy with the gun was gone.

3

Peter jogged down the walkway into the parking lot and looked left and right. He saw plenty of people headed away from him, toward downtown or their cars, but none of them wore a red cap and jacket.

He jogged past the school bus, hoping it had blocked his view. Nothing. His right hand held all three apples. With the freeway like a high ceiling overhead, sound echoed strangely.

The bus driver leaned out his window, blowing smoke from a slim e-cigarette. He wore a wispy mustache and a Brewers jersey, with a Brewers tattoo peeking out from under the sleeve. "You lose track of somebody?"

"A guy with a red baseball hat and jacket," Peter said. "Beard and sunglasses. You see him?"

"That Cardinals-cap-wearing motherfucker?" For some fans, it wasn't enough to love a team. They also wanted someone to hate. With his e-cig, the bus driver pointed toward the end of the divider between the parking lot and the market's loading dock. "Went over that way with some other guy."

Peter was on the move before the bus driver finished talking.

The divider began as a six-foot brick wall that transitioned to a three-foot metal fence lined with an assortment of vinyl sheds and short shipping containers used as auxiliary storage. Behind it, the first vehicle lane was wide and flat, designed for vans and smaller box trucks. On the far side of a concrete freeway pylon, the second two lanes were a true loading dock with a parking ramp descending to put the semi-trailer decks at the same level as the market's apron.

Peter rounded the fence and the outermost container. The farthest loading bay held a big white Freightliner, its trailer tucked tight against the platform. The middle bay was empty but for a haphazard stack of empty pallets waiting for pickup. In the flat bay, a few dozen feet out from the dock, someone had parked a white Isuzu box truck, nose-out.

On the far side of the Isuzu's square glass-filled cab, Peter caught a vanishing glimpse of red.

Taking one of the apples in his left hand, he slowed to peek around the front corner of the Isuzu. He saw a red sleeve, gesticulating. On the freeway above them, tires hit the expansion joints with resonant staccato booms. He crept down the side of the truck until he could see two men standing in the empty space behind it, maybe five feet apart. The guy in the Cardinals jacket had his backpack slung sideways off one shoulder and his gun out, held one-handed and pointed directly at the chest of a man in a cream-colored suit.

The weapon had the distinctive long curved magazine and wooden handguard of a vintage AK-74, some close-quarters eastern bloc variant with a steel-frame shoulder stock folded up under the barrel. With the stock folded, it would be difficult to aim, a truly indiscriminate killing machine.

The man in the suit, hands jangling out from his sides, was backed against a rickety picnic table that filled a gap between two

17

storage sheds. His shaved head gleamed with panic sweat, his face rigid with fear. Behind him, Peter saw the parking lot and the tangle of schoolchildren just beginning to form a line.

Peter knew that this was the moment June was afraid of. That he would find himself in this position, caught between self-preservation and the need to act. They both knew which impulse would win.

Not that Peter wanted to be here. He'd been shot before, and hadn't enjoyed it. He definitely didn't want to get killed. June would never forgive him.

The guy jabbed the gun toward the other man's chest, said something Peter couldn't quite hear, then held out his free hand in demand. The man in the suit dipped into his pocket and brought out his phone.

The guy with the gun said something else. The man in the suit did something to his phone and held it out again.

The gunman leaned in to take the phone, then backed off and glanced down at it, his thumb flying across the screen for a few seconds. Then he dropped the phone into his side-slung pack and took hold of the rifle's handguard with his free hand, to better control the muzzle's tendency to fly upward from recoil while firing.

Behind the man in the suit was a busload of schoolkids. Behind Peter was a parking lot full of empty cars and the wide concrete pylon that carried the freeway overhead.

He wasn't going to get a better chance.

He cocked his arm, took a single step forward, and threw his first apple.

Peter had played catcher on his high school team, liking the intensity and focus the position required. With his Recon platoon, he'd organized pickup games between deployments, but he couldn't remember the last time he'd held a baseball.

He'd aimed for the gunman's center mass, just trying to get him to change his focus. With the way the guy held the AK, low and close like Scarface rather than raised to his shoulder like a trained shooter, Peter figured the odds of the guy finding a specific target to be somewhere south of zero. But if he fired into the gap between the containers, especially on full auto, he'd injure or kill at least one person, probably more.

From forty feet, Peter missed the guy completely. The apple flew past his shoulder and splattered off the loading dock wall.

The guy's head snapped around, his face hidden behind the shiny beard and sunglasses, and the muzzle of the gun followed.

Peter was already moving forward, his second apple raised in his left hand. He locked on to his target, dropped his elbow, and threw right at the guy's head with a nice follow-through. The apple hit him square on the chest. It wasn't a regulation Rawlings, but the fat honeycrisp still punched like a fist.

The gunman rocked back a step, then caught himself and raised the rifle in line with his sunglasses, his mouth set hard inside the glossy snarl of beard.

Still accelerating, too late to change plans, Peter fired his last apple like a rocket to second, the start of a double play. He'd always been better in motion. The honeycrisp glanced off the guy's cheekbone, knocking his hat up and his sunglasses sideways.

It wasn't the hard hit Peter wanted, but the guy jerked his head away in instinctive response. His skewed glasses would limit his vision.

He pulled the trigger anyway.

4

Everything slowed down.

The AK clattered with each round, the muzzle flash a bright orange flare. On full automatic, it took real training and practice to control a decent weapon like an M4, let alone a stamped-metal spray-and-pray vintage AK with the shoulder stock folded.

Peter dove to the ground as the barrel rose. He felt the rounds part the air above him as he rolled to his feet and converted that forward motion into a sprint. He knew he was too far away. He saw the gunman release the trigger and bump his sunglasses into place with the back of his wrist, coolly resetting himself. Peter wondered abstractly where the bullets had gone, how many innocents wounded or dead.

Then he was airborne, arms wide for maximum capture, but the gunman had somehow slipped sideways. Peter didn't even get a hand on him. All he managed was the tip of a finger hooked inside the sunglasses before a slim, strong hand scooped up Peter's ankle and flipped him, flying ass over teakettle to land hard on the concrete, flat on his back.

He lay momentarily stunned, all breath knocked away, waiting for a bullet. The gunman was somewhere behind him.

The moment hung there, suspended. The smell of spent powder in the air. The strange ringing silence that came after gunshots.

Until the children in the parking lot began to scream.

Peter rolled over looking for the shooter and saw Lewis appear in the gap between the storage sheds. With a predatory grace, he leaped the low fence and landed atop the rickety picnic table, which yawed wildly beneath his weight. Rather than try to stabilize himself, Lewis just bent his knees and kept his momentum, flying over the fetal form of the man in the suit to land in a three-point stance as if he'd planned it that way all along.

But the gunman had hit reverse and already doubled the distance between them, past the freeway pylon and headed toward the Freightliner with the AK now aimed directly at Lewis's chest. "Stop," he said.

With no alternative, Lewis caught himself.

The gunman's eyes flicked from Lewis to Peter and back. His pupils were enormous but his hands were steady. "Move and you're dead."

His voice was rough and strange, like he had something stuck in his throat. With the Cardinals cap bumped upward and his sunglasses gone, his upper face was fine-boned and delicate above the thick beard, at odds with the voice and the ballistic vest under the open jacket.

By now, the gunman had drifted all the way back to the semi's trailer, the chassis frame level with his chest. On the other side of the fence, shouts and cries of fear and panic.

Then, without seeming to move at all, the gunman slung the AK under his arm, elbowed the open, side-slung pack around to his back, and floated under the low semi-trailer like a leaf on the wind. Peter blinked and the guy was gone. The only sign he'd ever been there was the stolen phone, fallen from the pack.

Lewis knelt beside Peter. "You hit?"

"Embarrassed." Peter pushed himself up. "You coming?"

He ran left toward the nose of the Freightliner. He wasn't going to follow the gunman under the trailer, where any pursuer would be an easy target. Lewis headed toward the loading dock and the back of the rig.

Peter peeked past the front bumper and saw a red-coated figure run between two parked cars into traffic, where he sideslipped across the low hood of a startled sedan, the backpack airborne like a balloon on a string. Lewis came around the trailer end. Peter ran forward, waving Lewis on.

They sprinted into the street and skirted the now-honking sedan to see the gunman stopped at a parking meter, where he threw his leg over a funky-looking bicycle. It had wide knobby tires and an angular black frame with long silver boxes strapped to the bars.

The gunman tugged down his cap, zipped the gun under the red jacket, and pulled the pack onto his second shoulder. Then he smiled at them through that beard and flipped a switch on the handlebars. The bike leaped forward, accelerated across St. Paul, and flew down the wrong side of Broadway faster than any man could run. The guy barely touched the pedals.

They stopped chasing after three blocks, although they'd lost sight of the gunman long before that. Peter had no idea if he'd turned a corner or simply vanished around the curve of the earth.

Breathing hard, hands on his knees, Lewis said, "What the fuck was that?"

Peter had lost his cowboy hat at the loading dock. Behind them, finally, rose a distant duet of sirens.

"Come on." Peter turned toward the market. "We need to talk to that guy in the suit. This wasn't some random stickup. You don't steal a phone with an AK-74."

"You don't want to go back there," Lewis said. "All those cameras, remember?"

The cameras. The police.

Peter sighed.

June was going to be *pissed*.

5

Three blocks from the market and just moments after the staccato rattle of an automatic weapon, nobody on the street seemed to have noticed. They jogged back toward the coffee shop where they'd left June.

Two blocks out, lunchtime walkers were still rooted to their shadows like startled sheep, uncertain of what they'd heard or what to do next. One block out, they met the first frantic people running in the opposite direction. By the time they made it to the coffee shop, they saw shoppers shoving their way out of the market.

June was gone. Peter's blue sweatshirt lay abandoned on their table. Peter pulled his phone from his pocket and texted her. All okay here. Where are you?

No answer.

"You know where she is," Lewis said.

Peter felt the answer like a pit in his stomach. June was a journalist to her bones, hardwired to get after it. Which would put her inside the market, chasing the story.

The pit in Peter's stomach got deeper. How long had she waited before going after them? If she'd been hurt or killed by the gunman's stray rounds, Peter would never have forgiven himself. He'd hunt that fucker to the ends of the earth.

The pair of sirens sang louder.

Peter pulled the hoodie over his gray T-shirt as he slipped into the coffee shop, where he took a mesh-backed trucker's cap off the display shelf, dropped a twenty in front of the clerk, and left without his change. Lewis was already on the move. Peter caught up and together they ran around the east end of the market building, past the outdoor tiki bar, and toward the delivery area.

Five minutes after the gunman had opened fire, Peter stepped over the crushed cowboy straw and looked across the low metal fence, afraid of what he might see on the other side. The parking lot was emptying out. Dazed bystanders hugged themselves and each other. June stood beside them with her phone out, asking questions and taking pictures.

With the sight of her, Peter felt his heart begin to beat again.

She hadn't been a straight newspaper reporter for years, but he could see her as she might have been at twenty-one, fresh out of J-school, lit up by the action and the hunt for the truth of what had happened.

Peter raised a hand and called out. "June."

She turned and saw him. A wave of relief washed across her face. "You're okay? Lewis is okay?" Peter nodded. She glared at him. "You are such an asshole."

"Better than the alternative," he said. The schoolkids were clumped together by the bus under the fierce gaze of their teachers. They looked scared but unharmed. "Did anyone get hurt?"

"Nobody that I've seen," she said. "What happened?"

Peter told her about the gunman taking the phone, then preparing to execute the victim. "Did you see a guy in a cream-colored suit? Shaved head, scared as hell?"

June cocked her head and pushed her mouth sideways and squinted into space. Peter knew this meant she was running her mental fingers through the giant filing cabinet of her brain. "Yeah. He climbed the picnic table to get over the fence. But he had his phone in his hand." The squint got sharper as she focused inward. "Actually, he looked familiar." June met a lot of people in the course of her work. A keen memory for faces was a crucial tool in her kit.

The sirens blatted, getting close. Peter was running out of time. He didn't want to be inside their perimeter when they finally arrived. But he should have heard a lot more than two cars. "Where the hell are the cops?"

She made a face. "Chasing phantoms. I texted Zedler and he said some dickhead called in a half-dozen bomb threats all over town." Dean Zedler was a coworker at the *Milwaukee Journal Sentinel*, another investigative reporter she'd worked with in Chicago, years ago.

Over her shoulder, Peter saw two cruisers come to a stop on Water Street, lights flashing, sirens now mercifully silent. The patrolmen climbed out, thick in their body armor, hands on their holstered weapons, heads turning like gun turrets. In their hats and sunglasses, they didn't look that different from the gunman.

Peter said, "Tell them they're looking for a guy with a big beard and a red cap and jacket riding a crazy-fast electric bike, headed south on Broadway. He's probably in Ohio by now."

She shooed him away with the back of her hand. "Get the fuck out of here before some rookie recognizes you from a wanted poster."

Peter blew her a kiss and turned to go.

Behind a shipping container, Lewis stood amidst scattered brass, staring at the Isuzu box truck. The front was stitched with a row of bullet holes. "Cuttin' it close."

"We got lucky," Peter said. Past the truck was a clear line of fire to the parking lot and a busy street and a cluster of office buildings a block away. He thought of how the gunman had stood with his AK on full automatic, glasses askew, firing indiscriminately. He wondered how many other people weren't so lucky.

"Found something." Lewis held up his open pocketknife. A pair of razor shades hung balanced on the blade.

"You don't want to leave those for the police?"

The tilted smile. "They never caught me with all those years of trying. Figure we got as good a chance as anyone." He raised a shoulder in an elegant shrug. "We find anything useful, we mail 'em to June at the paper. She'll get 'em to the cops."

Peter looked at him. "You're going to dust for prints?"

Years back, for professional reasons, Lewis had taken a couple of criminology classes at the community college. He had once been a very successful armed robber.

The tilted smile got wider. He offered Peter the knife handle. "That ain't half of it. Take a look."

Peter raised the glasses closer and saw a green light above the right lens. Then he noticed nearly invisible buttons in the plastic of the temple. And a pin-sized dot in the center of the bridge.

He looked at Lewis. "Camera glasses?"

"I figure that green light means they're still recording. I'm guessing they're wireless, streaming to the guy's phone or laptop, anything with enough memory to hold all that video. Prob'ly got some nice footage of your face, too."

Peter hit the button with a fingernail and the green light turned off.

The cops would be turning over every rock in six counties to find the gunman. When they did, they'd get his electronics, too.

If Peter wanted to stay free, he'd better find the guy first.

6

I n the nine months since he'd come back from Iceland with his face on a wanted poster, Peter had tried to keep his head down. He'd stayed out of bars and bad neighborhoods and other places where trouble might find him.

The problem was that Peter liked trouble. In a way, he needed it.

On nights when he couldn't sleep, when the werewolf began to howl inside the cage of his mind, he'd lace up his old combat boots and go for a long run through the city. Sometimes he'd push himself hard along the lakeshore and let the cool breeze blow through him. Sometimes that was enough.

Other times, he ran the darker ways, putting himself in the path of predators. Occasionally, he got lucky. Once he'd found three young men wrestling an overserved young woman into a car. It wasn't exactly a fair fight, but Peter had held himself in check. No permanent damage. That wasn't the point. The point was to be useful.

And to let the werewolf out of its cage, if only for a few minutes.

As Peter pulled the flatbed Toyota into the driveway, his phone lit up with a call. "Hi, Franny. What's up?"

Fran Anderson was a rail-thin ninety-seven-year-old widow who lived across the street. As far as Peter could tell, she spent her days on her screened porch or at her front window, talking back to the radio as she glared at the drivers of passing cars, smoked Marlboro Lights, and made a list of chores for Peter. She had an avocado-green wall-mounted phone with a forty-foot cord for the handset so she could call from anywhere in the house.

"You're home early, kiddo." Part concern, part accusation. Fran had a clear position on lazy people. "Did you get that replacement burner for my stove?" She'd slammed a cast-iron frying pan onto her stove in frustration after the Cubs fell out of the pennant race.

"Special order," Peter said. "It should come next week." Like almost everything else in her house, the stove was older than Peter's dad. "Everything else okay?"

"Still vertical," she said. "Are you going to rake my leaves? And maybe clean my gutters?"

"I hope so," Peter said. "I might have to take a trip, and I don't know how long I'll be gone. I'll let you know."

The previous January, after Peter and June had moved in, he noticed that his neighbor's walk went unshoveled after a snow, so he took care of it. Several snows later, she beckoned him to her front door, where she waited with a box of Thin Mints in one hand and an envelope in the other.

The cookies had been expired for three years and the box was cold to the touch. Inside the envelope was her name, phone number, and the key to her house.

"If my porch light is still on at seven in the morning, you better come look for me." She tapped the frosty box with a bony finger. "You play your cards right, kiddo, you'll get another box. I got a freezer full of 'em."

"Ma'am, you don't even know me," Peter had said. "You sure you want to give me a key?"

"You have a good face," she'd said.

Now he stood in his kitchen in the fading afternoon light, checking the contents of the backpack he'd put together nine months ago, in case he had to run. That old tension inside him like a spring wound too tight, the need to take action.

He wanted to be somewhere else when the U.S. Marshals found him. He wasn't going to let June get charged with aiding and abetting or harboring a fugitive.

The charge would be righteous, too. Because for Peter, June was his safe harbor from the storms of the world. Wherever she lived, that was home. He just had to hope he could find his way back to her. And that he'd still be welcome when he got there.

He had to admit, he'd grown attached to the house. It was one of Lewis's rentals, a basic 1950s colonial that backed onto the Milwaukee River Greenway, a half-wild tree-filled steep-walled ravine with the river running through the bottom, eighty feet below. The Greenway had miles of trails and linked a half-dozen parks. Peter could step out his back door and walk for hours on narrow, winding trails and see very few people. The street was only one block long, but part of a larger quirky network of streets aligned to the contours of the ravine. There was a giant old elm in the front yard. Lewis and Dinah and their boys, Charlie and Miles, lived three doors down.

When Peter moved in, he and Lewis had replaced the walls in the back half of the house with floor-to-ceiling windows on both floors that looked out on the ravine. In the spring and summer, with the sun filtered green through windblown leaves, it had felt like a treehouse. In the fall, with the maples and oaks and birches changing colors, it was like living inside a painting.

He'd been looking forward to seeing the leaves drop entirely, when the bare trees would stand like sculptures along the steep slopes of the ravine. He'd wanted to see the winter's first frost on the branches, the first fallen snow on the bones of the land.

The illusion of living outside had helped the static fade, at least most of the time. He felt like he was making progress. He and June had shared a bed consistently for the first time since they'd met. They'd shared a life.

June had landed a journalism fellowship at Marquette University so she could work on her book about the Washington insider who had almost started a war. The fellowship came with a desk at the *Milwaukee Journal Sentinel*, where she'd found the lively camaraderie that she'd been missing since she joined the virtual newsroom of Public Investigations.

Peter spent his days working with Lewis, first renovating the rental, then expanding Dinah's kitchen down the block, then beginning the rescue of a severely neglected bungalow in Washington Heights. Peter always finished the day tired, hungry, and dirty, feeling like he'd done something useful. He'd found a weekly veterans' group. He'd gotten back to yoga and meditation, which his shrink recommended to help the post-traumatic stress. The war still lived inside him, as it always would, but the static had softened and the tightness behind his eyes had begun to ease.

Now that life was over.

Peter had done the right thing, he knew that. He couldn't

watch a man carry a rifle into a crowded building and do nothing. He had plenty of regrets, but going into that market wasn't one of them.

And none of those kids had died.

Peter would count that as a win.

7

The side door banged open and June walked her bike into the kitchen, her work bag slung over one shoulder and her face flushed pink from the ride. She often said that one of the best things about living in Milwaukee was the fact that everything was within bicycle distance.

She hung her helmet on the handlebars and bent to remove the Velcro band that kept her pant leg out of the bike chain, all while keeping her eyes locked on Peter at the table, his open go-bag in front of him.

It was an oversized daypack that carried a change of clothes, a fresh burner phone, a multi-tool, a liter of water and a handful of granola bars, a backpacker's hammock and rain fly, a decent first aid kit, twenty thousand dollars in small bills, and three sets of false documents that included driver's licenses, birth certificates, and credit cards. It also held a Vietnam-era Colt Commander that Lewis had given him. It wasn't a great weapon by modern standards, but Peter only kept it to calm his nerves. If push came to shove, he told himself he'd go to jail rather than hurt another policeman.

The documents were easier to obtain than he'd thought they would be. Lewis had kept in touch with his contacts from his former life, including a friend at the DMV and a printer in Wauwatosa who was a genius with Photoshop. Lewis didn't mind helping. Sometimes he missed the old days, too.

"That's it?" Her face was expressionless, her green eyes cool. "You're leaving?"

"Just for a few days," Peter said. "Until we're sure they haven't run that market security video through facial recognition."

"Where will you go?"

"Better you don't know," he said. "I don't want you to get in trouble. I won't go far."

June dropped her bag on the side table with a thump, then combed her fingers through her red pixie cut, smoothing out her helmet hair.

"I spent the whole afternoon chasing down the Public Market story." Her voice sounded casual, but Peter knew better. "It's a big deal because of the location, but otherwise, there's not much to it. Aside from some flying glass in an office on Michigan Street, nobody got hurt. It's really just attempted robbery and discharge of a weapon. The shooter vanished without a trace. The victim's gone, and he even got his phone back. The market cameras aren't exactly cutting-edge. The police don't know a damn thing. Plus some lunatic carved up two guys with a machete on Hampton and Teutonia this afternoon. So unless something new happens to make the Public Market a priority again, this story will be gone in a couple of days."

She looked him right in the face. "Or is there something else you're planning to do?"

She knew him so well.

"Lewis found a pair of sunglasses," Peter said. "The gunman's. They're video glasses, and they were recording the whole time, streaming to his phone or laptop."

He'd researched the glasses on the way home and learned that they connected to a device via Wi-Fi, but thankfully had no GPS. Lewis had already dusted them and found no fingerprints. Now they sat on the kitchen counter beside a jar of loose change.

"And what," June said. "You're leaving here and going after him? That's not your damn job. Turn those glasses over to the cops. Fucking stand down, Marine." June's vocabulary would make a drill sergeant blush. "You stopped a massacre, you don't need to be the police, too."

"That sunglasses footage has my face in it. It won't be crappy public security footage, either. If they catch him, they'll be able to catch me, too. Then they'll start looking at Lewis."

Except for his time in the army, Lewis had been a career criminal from the age of thirteen until he and Peter had come into a financial windfall several years before. Lewis had washed the money through various investments, but anyone looking closely could find hints of his past. Peter was afraid that his carefully rebuilt life, which now included Dinah and the boys, might not withstand prolonged scrutiny.

"Then throw the damn glasses away. Or better yet, put them somewhere safe in case you need to hand them over later. This is not your fight, okay? Your current mission is your own damn life."

"If I get caught," he said, "you'll get charged, too. I'm not letting my bad decision to go to Iceland ruin your career, ruin your life."

She put her hands on her hips. Freckles flared bright on her face. For a slim woman, she took up a lot of space in the room.

"You dumb fuck," she said. "Don't you know a goddamn thing about women? I'm not mad about your decision to go to Iceland. In retrospect, it was the right thing to do. I'm not even mad about you ending up on the FBI's Wanted list. I'm mad—no, I'm royally pissed—that you lied to me about going. Because I was scared to death, okay? Scared not knowing where you were, or what was happening, or whether you were okay. And I don't *ever* want to *not know* again."

She took the go-bag from his hand and flung it against the wall, where it slid down behind a big leafy plant. She was stronger than she looked.

"We have a good thing here," she said. "It works for both of us. Don't you want to be happy? Fixing houses with Lewis seems to make you happy. At least I think it makes you happy."

"Living with you makes me happy," he said quietly. "Unless you're yelling at me."

"Then stay, goddamn it." She took a bottle of wine out of her backpack and waved a hand at his dusty work clothes. "Get cleaned up and I'll call Dinah and see if they want to come for dinner. We'll order Thai food." June didn't cook, but she was an expert at takeout.

He heard her on the phone as he stripped naked and climbed into the shower. Two minutes later, she pulled back the curtain with a rattle. Water streamed down his long, lean body and splashed onto the bathroom floor.

She stared at him as she undressed. Her eyes shimmered with tears. She stepped over the rim of the tub and into his arms. He picked her up and she wrapped herself around him and they stayed that way, each holding the other in that most ancient sacrament, for a long, long time.

——

As it turned out, Dinah and Lewis had parent–teacher conferences, so Peter built a scrap-lumber blaze in the fire pit and they sat together on the big deck that he'd cantilevered over the steep edge of the ravine. With the lights off in the house behind them and open space all around, they drank Lucky Buddha beer and handed the white takeout cartons back and forth like urban primitives, soaking up the last warmth of the day while the night grew dark around them.

After the fingernail moon rose over the trees, the wind changed direction and they heard a dog's deep bark. Riverwest was full of dogs, but the only big mutt on the block was Mingus, the huge high-energy stray that Dinah's boys had adopted after he took up residence under the porch at their old house.

Mingus was an escape artist and a rambler. Over the summer, he'd learned to tear the pickets off Dinah's back fence, causing an arms race between Lewis's growing carpentry skills and relentless canine ingenuity. Canine ingenuity usually won. As a result, Mingus pretty much kept his own schedule. But he was crazy about June, and often her calls were the only thing that brought him home. He never seemed to mind getting caught as long as June would rub his belly.

She got up and walked into the side yard and toward the front with its enormous old elm. "Mingus, where are you?"

A moment later she reappeared at the corner of the darkened house. "Peter," she whispered. "Come here."

Before she finished talking, Peter was out of his chair and moving. Mingus barked again. Standing beside June, Peter could tell that the dog wasn't on the loose, he was still inside his fence.

Mingus couldn't be bothered to bark at a passing stranger. He barked when someone came up the front walk of Dinah's house. Or June's.

"It's the side door," June said quietly. "It's standing open."

"Are you sure you locked it?"

"I always lock it," she said. "Always."

They never used the front door. The only time they used the side door was when June came home on her bike. Peter had installed a third door in the back wall, for direct access to the deck and the detached garage.

The house was still dark inside. With the floor-to-ceiling windows, if someone had turned on even a single lamp, the yard would have lit up. They wouldn't have missed it.

He grabbed the pitchfork he used to turn the compost heap, then opened the back door, reached inside, and flipped the switch for the big kitchen's overheads.

Nobody there.

He floated through the first floor, pitchfork at the ready, then slipped upstairs, turning on more lights as he went, until the house blazed bright as day. Not a soul. In the basement, he found only spiders.

The side door still stood open six inches. He closed it and threw the deadbolt. "All clear," he called.

He found June in the kitchen with her softball bat and a grim face.

"They took my goddamn bag," she said. "It had my laptop in it, my wallet, my biking gloves, everything." She gestured at the little white side table where she stacked her notebooks and charged her gear every night. It was empty. "Peter, they took all my shit." She waved at his backpack, still behind the plant where she'd thrown it a few hours before. "Why didn't they take *your* goddamn shit?"

Peter pulled her into his arms. Her whole body vibrated with emotion. "It's only stuff," he said. "We'll get you new stuff."

She beat on his chest with her fists, then buried her face in his shoulder. "And change all the locks," she said with a muffled voice.

"And change all the locks." Peter rubbed her back as he scanned the room for what else might be missing. The jar of loose change still sat on the kitchen counter. But not the gunman's sunglasses that had sat beside it. "First thing in the morning."

8

While Peter poked around outside with a flashlight, trying to figure out how the thief had gotten in, June borrowed his phone and called her bank to freeze her accounts and order new cards. The service rep seemed surprised that there were no new charges. Apparently the first step for most credit card thieves was to fill their gas tank, then go buy a bunch of expensive stuff they could resell for cash.

She didn't bother calling the Milwaukee police. Peter's legal status aside, the cops would probably take two days to show up for a simple B and E. They had enough on their plate. Besides, she wasn't going to file a claim and they weren't going to beat the bushes for her burglar, so why waste everyone's time?

But June was a reporter and plenty pissed, so she used her iPad, which she kept under her pillow, to log on to her account, hoping she could track down her stuff using the location app. But the system couldn't find either the laptop or the phone.

She wasn't surprised about the laptop, because it needed Wi-Fi to get online, but her phone should have been visible anywhere it had a cell signal, even if it was asleep. Which meant either the thief had turned it off, or he was somewhere underground, probably relaxing on the dirty mattress behind the boiler in his mom's basement while he pawed through her things. Grrrr.

She really hated to lose the electronics. Her phone and her laptop were cutting-edge gear set up for security with a virtual private network and a wide array of specialized research software, along with a lifetime of professional contacts and every draft of every piece of writing she'd ever done. She'd spent countless hours tuning her equipment, and large chunks of each day working with them. She knew they were just tools, but they felt more like trusted friends.

Yes, she had multiple backups in place, so all her information was intact in the cloud, but still. Ordering new gear would not heal the hole in her heart.

Worse yet was losing her reporter's notebook. Again, because she transcribed her messy shorthand into her laptop at every opportunity, she hadn't lost any of the day's field notes. She even took photos of each page, because seeing her actual notes sometimes knocked new ideas loose, and because redundant backups were not paranoia but good practice. So it wasn't the notebook itself, but the leather cover, which was a gift from her first editor at the *Chicago Tribune*. It was warped and worn and had fit her hand perfectly.

Too wired to sit down, let alone go to bed, she stayed up late cleaning, which really was not like her at all. When she ran out of things to tidy or sweep or mop or scrub, she sat awake with a biography of Marie Colvin, alert to every creak of the old house, while Peter prowled the yard as if the burglar was coming back for their mismatched thrift-store silverware.

By two a.m., she'd had enough.

She stepped out of the side door bare-ass naked with her hands on her hips. She felt the cool night air raising goose bumps. "Hey, Marine," she called quietly.

Peter jogged around the corner of the house. His eyes got wide when he saw her, and his mouth curved into a wolfish grin, demonstrating once again why she was crazy about him. She'd tried to tone herself down for every other guy, but Peter liked her wild side, and he had the energy to keep up.

"Again?" he asked.

She gave him a catwalk strut, putting on a show, then turned on her heel. "Hey, if you're not up for it . . ."

He laughed and scooped her up, threw her over his shoulder, and carried her inside.

Eventually, they got tired enough to sleep.

On her bike in the rain the next morning, headed north with Peter's emergency credit card to pick up her new laptop and phone, June thought about the Public Market shooting. She couldn't help herself. It was automatic. She'd woken up with a list of questions fully formed in her reporter's mind.

For example: Who was the man with the assault rifle and the electric getaway bike? When she and Peter and Lewis had watched the gunman approach the market, they had all thought he was a mass shooter. But he'd walked through the whole place and bypassed many possible targets to go after one guy and his phone.

Why?

It wasn't for the value of the phone. Even the latest and greatest model was only worth a few hundred bucks on the black market. The gun itself was worth much more than that, at least according to Lewis. Assuming the shooter was even semi-rational, the risk of armed robbery in a public place was too large to justify the profit. Which meant the shooter wanted something on that particular phone.

Next, why use an actual assault rifle? Pistols were smaller, cheaper, and easier to get. Was it the thrill of the weapon? Was it personal? Was he making some kind of larger point?

He'd shot up the market afterward, but hadn't killed a single person. And unlike most mass shooters, who often made elaborate attack plans that ended with suicide or suicide by cop, this guy had an exit strategy, his electric bike.

Still, Peter told her that the shooter had seemed ready to kill his victim. Which implied some personal connection between the shooter and the victim. Murder was almost always personal.

When she thought about the victim, another thought arose. If someone held you up at gunpoint and appeared ready to kill you, someone you had a personal connection with, why on earth would you leave before the police arrived?

The only reason she could imagine was that the victim had done something he wanted to keep secret. Something he thought was worse than the threat of murder.

June had to admit this was all terribly interesting. But what really stuck in her head was something else. She kept thinking she'd seen the victim's face before. Which was strange, because she'd spent most of her career covering tech in Silicon Valley, so her mental filing system was full of West Coast hotshots, not Milwaukee suits.

Back on her bike with her new equipment protected from the drizzle by her stylish new commuter bag, she told herself that she wasn't going to get answers to any of those questions. If she could ask Peter to stand down from the hunt for the guy with the video glasses and the electric bike, she'd better apply that same logic to herself. Let it go, chill out, relax already.

Because if she dug deeper into this thing, if she turned over the wrong damn rock, she ran the risk of the police deciding to take another look at the security footage. She didn't want them to run facial recognition on the good Samaritan in the cowboy hat, not when she and Peter were finally finding their groove.

Besides, June had a book to write and a deadline to meet. Even if she'd already done the fun part, which was chasing down the original story. The job now was to put new meat on the bones with additional sources and experts to put the story into larger context. Painstaking work. It would be a good book, and her agent assured her it would sell like hotcakes. But right now, she was fucking bored to tears. It was so much more fun to be on the hunt for something new.

Usually, she went to her borrowed desk at the paper to pound out some pages in the blissful noise of the newsroom. Today, though, she knew she'd get pulled into the market story follow-up, so she decided to stay home and finish her goddamn chapter.

Just as soon as she figured out why the guy in the suit looked so familiar. She'd gotten a decent look. Bald, egg-shaped head, deep-set eyes over slab cheeks, with fleshy lips and prominent ears. Like a movie robot from the fifties, made of bent tin and molded rubber.

She'd find him.

June's facial recognition was better than any goddamn computer.

une plugged in her new laptop and started downloading updates, then fired up the coffeemaker. She told herself that she'd only look at her iPad until the caffeine was ready.

She thought that she might know his face if he'd been in the *Journal Sentinel* in the last few months, so she went to their site and clicked through past stories, looking at pictures. There was plenty on the county exec and the governor and various business and government debacles, but no sign of the man from the market. She did the same thing with the *Milwaukee Business Journal* and got the same result. Nothing.

Maybe he wasn't local. Maybe he was in her mental file because he actually was a tech hotshot from out West who'd come to Milwaukee for some conference. But she found no conferences this week in Milwaukee or Madison, which was a tech hub, or even in Chicago, which was ninety miles away. Crap.

Was he with one of the Big Five? She knew their top people well enough, could pull up their faces in her mind, but they were called the Big Five for a reason—they were big, and had a lot of people. She went through their corporate sites and found head shots of executive teams and leaders of top departments. No luck. Industry sites like TechHub had the usual PR cheese, but those photos got her nowhere, either.

Maybe if she could remember his place in tech, that would narrow the search.

Was he an enterprise guy, with Oracle or Salesforce or Slack? An infrastructure guy, with Intel or Sysco? Social media? Venture cap? An academic hotshot? Nothing rang a bell. She sighed and poured herself a cup of coffee.

With the first sip, she had a new thought. She put his age somewhere between fifty or sixty. What if he looked familiar because he'd been a big deal in the past? Time would have changed his face just enough to mess with her memory. If that was the case, and he was still on her radar, he'd have been a very big deal indeed.

If he was sixty, she reasoned, he was old enough to go all the way back to the first Internet boom in the late nineties, Netscape and AOL and all those first-generation companies, most of them now gone or greatly diminished. It was before her time as a tech journalist, but she knew the history. Her laptop was still downloading and updating software, so she didn't have access to her Public Investigations database subscriptions yet. But she had other resources. She went back to TechHub and ran a few searches and clicked through an endless photo feed.

It was full of self-satisfied white guys in blue button-down shirts and power ties and pleated khakis. Very few women among them. Jesus, if she really drilled down, she could spend a week at this, or a month. She picked up her coffee but it had gone cold. The exciting life of an investigative reporter. And this wasn't even her story; she was just curious. Although curiosity was a big part of what drove the work, maybe the most important part. Who knew what you might come up with?

While the microwave warmed her mug, she thought about the business cycle. When the dot-com bubble burst in 2000, it weeded out companies with catchy domain names and slick websites but no real business plan or paying customers. By the end of the decade, innovative survivors like eBay and Amazon had roared back, along with the next generation of companies, fueled by the emerging mobile Internet, which was then followed by the social media boom, which led to the unfortunate rise of the tech bro and hoodie as fashion statement. If her guy was fifty, he might have been in one of those groups.

Back to TechHub. Another search, another feed of photos. The enormity of the task was clear now, and she clicked faster. A few brown faces this time, a few more women, but still mostly white guys. Which didn't matter, because that's who she was looking for.

She was a half-dozen clicks past the picture before it registered. She missed it again going the other way before she finally slowed down and found it. There. In a corporate photo taken more than a decade ago, five men posed on a winding glass staircase, wearing matching polo shirts and Ritalin smiles.

According to the attached article, they were the top five people at Sense Logic, a privately held company that did innovative things with electronic hardware, including energy and power management modules, accelerometers, magnetometers, gyroscopes, and a suite of other real-world sensors. Important stuff, but not exactly sexy.

Except for the fact that the photo was taken to commemorate the company's sale to a multinational industrial behemoth for well north of two billion dollars, part of a pre-recession tech spending spree that would not end well for the multinational giant.

No wonder everyone looked so cheerful.

June's guy was on the second step from the top. At least she *thought* it was him. In the picture, he had a dirty blond ponytail and an extra hundred pounds that was the opposite of muscle. A former Caltech professor and the cofounder of Sense Logic, his name was Vincent Holloway.

Now she remembered him. Right after she'd left the *Tribune*, she'd written her first freelance piece for the *Mercury News* about why a sensor company was worth two billion dollars. And of the dozen or more people she talked with, Vincent Holloway was the best interview.

He spoke in complete paragraphs and spun out a vision of advanced robotic manufacturing and complex industrial equipment that would notify a technician when it needed service.

This was a full decade before the automation revolution was on the cover of *Newsweek* and the Internet of Things was featured in the *New York Times Magazine*.

She remembered Holloway as being driven and arrogant, but with moderately better people skills than the typical undersocialized engineer. At the time, she'd been certain Vince Holloway would soon be running the next big thing. Now, she wondered why she hadn't heard more about him. She plugged his name into the search bar.

She found a lot of information from the time Sense Logic was sold, including her own piece. That corporate photo had been used in all of them. But newer stuff? Almost nothing.

There was a short, flattering Wikipedia entry, clearly written by a paid publicist, with a photo of Holloway at a big glass desk wearing the same polo shirt as in the corporate shot, probably taken on the same day. And an archival Sense Logic website maintained by some tech history geek with too much free time. Sense Logic itself no longer existed, its people and technology absorbed into the new parent company, which was still selling off its unprofitable divisions to survive its earlier irrational exuberance. Capitalism was a bitch.

Which meant, all told, she had only two pictures of Holloway, and they both showed the same overweight man with the blond ponytail. Maybe he wasn't her guy after all.

According to his Wikipedia page, he'd earned 452 million from the sale. But there was nothing more recent.

So he'd had a really big payday, but what was he doing now? In June's experience of the tech world, high achievers like Holloway rarely quit working, and each new venture would require *some* public presence to attract outside funding. Plus these guys usually had fingers in many pies, so it was doubly strange that there were no publicity shots for a board membership or venture fund, not even a charity event. And no social media. In the modern world, it took a lot of effort for a successful person to stay invisible.

She'd dig deeper when she got her laptop's databases up and running.

Maybe his former partners knew how to find him. The other four guys were all over the Internet, which made Holloway's absence all the more stark. She found them on social media and sent each one a private message with her email and phone number, saying she had a quick background question for an article she was writing. Who knows if they'd ever reach out to her, but she had to start somewhere.

In the meantime, she went back to Holloway's Wikipedia page and clicked on the photo, then on the Details tab. The photo credit was listed as "Pinnacle." She scrolled down to the metadata. The photo copyright was owned by Pinnacle Technologies. She scrolled back up to the file history and looked for Pinnacle's other Wikipedia contributions. There were none.

So Pinnacle Technologies was not a Wikipedia regular. It didn't exactly sound like a name for a freelance photographer. And wouldn't Holloway have kept the copyright for himself? Maybe he hadn't paid a PR flack after all. Maybe he'd written it himself. Maybe Pinnacle Technologies was Holloway.

A simple web search for the company came back with too many results to be useful. Holloway had lived in California, so June went to the State of California's business portal and plugged "pinnacle technologies" into the search box. Twenty-six results, a much smaller group. Probably not Pinnacle Technologies Orthodontia in Escondido, or Pinnacle Technologies Custom Hot Rods, which had closed in 1988. The only real candidate was Pinnacle Technologies, registered a decade before and still listed as active, with a Sacramento incorporating service listed as the Agent. She knew through long experience that the incorporating service wouldn't tell her anything without a court order.

She sighed. All this to track down a random photo credit on a Wikipedia entry. A waste of time. She set the iPad aside. Then picked it up again, and went to a phone directory where she had an account. Sometimes she forgot the simple stuff.

Still no Holloway, but Pinnacle Technologies had a listing. The address was the same as the Sacramento incorporating service. But the phone number was different.

June was a reporter, so she did what reporters do. She called the number.

There was the strange ring rhythm of call forwarding. Finally, she heard a man's voice. "Hello. How may I help you?" He was neither young nor old, with no detectable regional accent. Like a D.C. newscaster.

"Hi, is this Pinnacle Technologies?"

"This is reception. I'm Gary. How can I help you?"

"Hi, Gary. I'd like to speak with Vincent Holloway, please."

"What is your name, please?"

"My name is June Cassidy. I'm a reporter, working on a story about an incident at the Milwaukee Public Market yesterday. I just have a few quick questions on background, nothing for publication."

"Who do you represent?"

"I'm a technology fellow at Public Investigations, a national nonprofit news organization."

"Please hold."

The line went quiet. No music, no nothing. Apparently Pinnacle Technologies was a bare-bones outfit. Or maybe it was a philosophical thing, one less distraction for the high-achieving tech professional.

June's stomach rumbled. She glanced at the clock and was surprised to discover it was after one. She'd wasted way too much time on this thing. And now she was on a strange silent hold.

With the phone clamped between her shoulder and her ear, she rummaged through the fridge, looking for something to eat. They'd ordered all that Thai food last night, and the only thing left was half a container of drunken noodles. She opened the microwave and took out her coffee, which was cold again, then dumped the noodles into a bowl and put the bowl in to reheat. When she moved to put the phone on speaker, she realized that Gary had hung up on her.

Huh. June called back.

"Hello. How may I help you?" The same even, neutral voice.

"Hi, Gary. My name is June Cassidy with Public Investigations. I think we got disconnected. I'm holding for Vince Holloway? About the Milwaukee Public Market? Off the record?"

Pause. "There is no person here by that name."

"Then why did you ask me to hold when I called for Vincent Holloway? Mr. Holloway is the owner of Pinnacle Technologies, correct?"

Another pause. She was afraid he'd hang up again. "Wait, Gary, wait. Please, just one more question, off the record. Can you describe Mr. Holloway? For example, what color hair does he have?" But she got no answer. The line was dead.

Seriously, Gary needed to work on his people skills.

June was willing to admit that it might be a wrong number, an artifact of the Internet scrape. Plus she'd basically pulled Pinnacle out of her ass anyway. And it wasn't unusual at all for people to hang up on June. People who actually wanted to talk to a reporter usually had an axe to grind. Which was fine with June, as long as they answered her questions. She didn't even mind if they lied. That was part of the job, to sort the bullshit from the truth.

She reviewed the conversation in her head. What had Gary actually said? Had he even acknowledged that the number was for Pinnacle? Or that Holloway was even associated with that number?

Honestly, she didn't even mind if they dodged her questions. She usually learned something from the pattern of their evasions.

The only way she didn't learn something was if there was no conversation at all.

Maybe Gary was good at his job after all.

10

PETER

Peter walked out to his truck at dawn, still thinking about the break-in the night before, and the missing video sunglasses. His phone rang in his pocket.

"What's up, Franny?" His elderly neighbor had probably seen him from her post at her front window. Peter set his alarm for seven every morning just to check her porch light.

"Can you stop at Otto's on your way home?" Otto's was a local chain of liquor stores.

"Already?" As far as Peter could tell, Fran subsisted entirely on scotch and Girl Scout cookies. He'd bought her a liter bottle of the Famous Grouse just last week.

"Don't get smart with me, kiddo. And get the good stuff, not that cheap crap you bought last time. I'm almost ninety-eight, you know."

"Yes, ma'am. Anything else? Maybe some vegetables? A can of soup?"

"Oh, no. Just grab some of those spicy Cheetos I like."

"Sure thing, Fran." She'd made it this far, she must be doing something right. Or else she was some kind of medical marvel, held together by alcohol and preservatives.

He got to Bliffert Lumber just as they opened. He picked up new heavy-duty deadbolts and jamb plates for the house, as well as a few 2x10s to replace the rotten floor framing in the Washington Heights project. The heavy planks were too long for the truck, and they hung off the back farther than he liked, but he didn't have far to go.

The Toyota was a work in progress. He'd gotten a deal on it because the steel cargo box was rusted out. After stripping the cargo box down to the chassis, he built a new wooden bed, then wired in fresh taillights to replace the old, although he hadn't gotten around to welding up the overhead rack.

He returned home to replace the deadbolts on all three doors, as he'd promised June the night before. It still bothered him that he couldn't find any tool marks where the thief had gotten in. If June hadn't left the door unlocked, then the guy was a real pro. That wasn't good.

The rain began as he drove west toward Washington Heights, feeling the long 2x10s bounce with every pothole. On the Vliet Street bridge, police cars lined both rails, overflow parking for the Third District station on the far side. It was just after shift change and uniformed officers clanked out to their cruisers, carrying their duty bags and coffee, shoulders up against the weather. Peter faced front and tried to look like an upstanding citizen, the kind of man who went to church twice a week and paid his taxes early.

He had no claim to any of that.

When he and Lewis had chosen the project house on 53rd Street, proximity to the cop shop had been a plus. Statistically,

Lewis said, neighborhoods were safest near a police station. The single woman or young couple who were the most likely eventual buyers of the renovated house would like that.

Peter had driven across that bridge every day for a month with no real concern. Even the most dedicated police officers had more important things to do than compare every person they met to the faces on the FBI's email bulletins and wanted posters tacked to the station's bulletin board. They didn't even know Peter was in the state, let alone the country. And with every month that passed, new criminals would do new stupid things, new posters would get layered over the old, and Peter would become even more invisible. A normal day carried zero risk for a wanted man, as long as he stayed out of trouble.

Peter reminded himself of this again now, as a uniformed sergeant eyeballed him from the curb. Peter nodded at the man, showing respect for the law as he braked for the light. All around him, cruiser doors thumped shut. In the rearview, he watched the sergeant's Crown Vic pull out and roll up behind him.

Peter's wipers went back and forth. Finally the light changed and Peter stepped on the gas, hoping the Crown Vic would turn left or right. It stayed right behind him. Past the station, Peter thumped through yet another pothole and felt the boards bounce on the flatbed. He touched the brakes again and glanced at his mirror at the exact moment the sergeant turned on his overheads.

Shit, shit, shit.

He pulled into the parking lane with the Crown Vic thirty feet back, feeling his heart thump in his chest. He rolled down his window and waited while the sergeant sat in the cruiser and punched Peter's plate into the computer.

Peter had been worried about this moment for nine long

months. His driver's license was supposed to be clean and legiti-mate, straight from Lewis's contact at the DMV. But the only way to know was to put it to the test. Which was going to happen any minute now.

The static began to hum louder.

Peter had gotten pretty good at spending time inside. The pros-pect of prison was something else entirely.

He was acutely aware that most fugitives were caught not committing new crimes, but during a routine traffic stop or a background check for a new job. If the license wasn't legit, the sergeant would almost certainly escort Peter to the station, take his prints, and plug them into the system. Federal alarm bells would ring loud enough to hear on the moon.

None of these thoughts damped down the static rising into his brain. Left unchecked, the crackle of nerves would escalate his war-wired fight-or-flight reflex into overdrive. Which would not help Peter look like a respectable citizen. It didn't matter how legit the license if the sergeant thought he was a meth-head.

Or if they'd run facial recognition on the low-res market video and the software had somehow spit out his name. And the ser-geant's morning briefing had included Peter's picture.

He focused on his breath, slow and deep, in and out. This was one of the tools he'd learned to try to calm his revved-up limbic system. Hello, old friend. We can do this. Just hang on to your shit a little longer. Or things will get a whole lot worse.

11

By the time the sergeant finally stepped out of his car and adjusted his equipment belt, Peter's muscles were tight as bridge cables, but the white sparks were holding steady.

The sergeant stopped just behind Peter's left shoulder. It gave him a full view of Peter's body and the interior of the truck, but Peter couldn't make any offensive moves without twisting awkwardly in his seat and telegraphing the whole thing. Not that he would go kinetic on this guy, a block from the District Three station. Definitely not. Breathe in, breathe out.

"Sir, do you know why I pulled you over?"

"No, Sergeant."

"You have a brake light out."

"Really?" Peter turned to get a better look at the officer. He had a square head and a mustache like a push broom. Peter had never had good luck with mustache cops. "I just replaced them when I built the flatbed. Maybe the rain got into the wiring, or the potholes knocked something loose. You mind if I get out and take a look?"

He hoped his DIY attitude would help. Law enforcement was a blue-collar job, and the police were often sympathetic to guys who worked with their hands.

The sergeant shook his head, but his eyes stayed locked on Peter's face, as if he wasn't sure what he was looking at. "Stay in your seat, sir. License, registration, and proof of insurance, please."

"You bet." Peter's wallet was in the open forward console. He took out his fake license and handed it over. "The paperwork's in the glove box. I'm going to reach for it now." Peter had been on the other side of this kind of work, manning checkpoints in Baghdad. He knew how to keep the temperature down. Not that it helped with the static right now.

"Slowly, sir." Maybe the sergeant had been over there, too. At least he didn't have his hand on his pistol.

Peter pulled the paperwork and held it out, speckling in the rain.

The sergeant took a long moment to examine Peter's license, then compared the photo with the face in front of him. "Sit tight, Mr. Murphy." He walked back to the Crown Vic in the rain while the lightbar flashed red and blue.

Why had Peter driven past the cop shop, today of all days? Just to show his big brass Marine Corps balls? It didn't have to be the crappy market security cameras that got him. What if they'd caught the gunman overnight? Along with his computer and the high-def footage streamed from the video sunglasses?

If they'd found Peter in the federal database, it wasn't just a problem for Peter. It was a problem for June, too. And Lewis. The static sparked higher, threatening to fill his head. Breathe, goddamn it.

He told himself that he'd go quietly. He'd get a good lawyer and do it the right way, serve the time he had coming. That's what he told himself.

But then, he'd said the same thing the last time, before he'd kicked his way out of an Icelandic police car and taken down four Icelandic cops with a baton because he couldn't keep the werewolf under control.

Even the idea of prison, of years in a concrete cube without sight of sun or sky, under the control of a system designed to break the souls of even the hardest men, was enough to set the werewolf growling and turn the static's sparks into frantic lightning.

No matter what he told himself, Peter knew the truth.

He was one of those wolves who'd chew off their own leg to get free of the trap.

Finally the sergeant returned with his paperwork. "Mr. Murphy, do you own this vehicle?"

Oh, crap. Lewis liked to make fun of the beater truck by calling it the Redneck Cadillac, so it was easy to forget it was registered in Lewis's name, or rather in the name of the corporation that owned his rental properties. "Actually, Sergeant, it's a company truck. Let me call my boss. Or you can call him, obviously."

The mustache twitched. "Let's see if you can solve your brake light problem first. I'll give you five minutes."

Peter felt the flush of relief and grabbed a multi-tool and a roll of electrical tape from the console. "Thank you, Sergeant."

The light assembly wasn't loose or damaged. He popped the cover, but the inside was dry and the gasket looked intact. He squirmed under the back bumper and followed the wires toward the rear harness where they met the wires from the good side. In the light of his phone, he saw that the plastic harness had cracked, either opening the circuit or shorting it with water. Maybe a stone from the road, maybe just a bad part. Bad luck.

He unplugged the prongs and wiped them on his shirt, then wiped the harness and blew out the sockets. He plugged the prongs in again and wrapped the cracked case tight with electrical tape. With rust flakes on his face and his clothes damp from the pavement, he climbed to his feet, opened his door, and bent to check the fuse. Somehow not tripped.

When he put his wet butt on the driver's seat and touched the brake pedal, the sergeant walked up to meet him. "You got it."

"Great," Peter said. "Thank you."

Again the sergeant looked Peter full in the face. "I keep thinking we've met somewhere."

"I don't get out much," Peter said. "Unless I worked on your house?"

"Pretty sure I'd remember that," the sergeant said. "You have a safe day, sir. Better double-check that taillight when you get home tonight."

When the sergeant walked back to his cruiser, Peter finally let out the breath he didn't know he'd been holding.

At the project house, Peter found Lewis pushing a wheelbarrow full of broken plaster toward the dumpster in the driveway. He saw Peter's face and dropped the handles. "What happened?"

"I got pulled over by the police. A brake light was out."

"Bad couple minutes while he ran your license?"

"Yeah." Peter stared at the 1924 bungalow. Taken by the city for back taxes, it was so damaged that no normal person would ever want to own it. The windows were rotting in their frames and the front porch was sinking like a ship. The roof had leaked for years, ruining the ornate plaster and hardwood floors. Mold bloomed in every room. It was a gut job, a labor of love, a new beginning.

Lewis said, "You're rattled, man. What ain't you telling me?"

Peter looked at his hands. He couldn't just go back to work. Not now, not with this noose around his neck.

"Someone broke into our house last night. They took all June's work stuff, her electronics and notebooks. Whoever it was, they were total pros, because I have no idea how they got in. Plus they left my go-bag behind, with laptop and phone and twenty grand in cash. The only other thing they took were the gunman's sunglasses."

Lewis put his hands on his hips. "And when the fuck were you planning to tell me this?"

"I didn't want to get you involved. Once they start looking into your life, what will they find? Plus I promised June I'd stay out of it. She didn't notice the sunglasses were gone, and I didn't tell her."

"Brother, they broke into your *house*," Lewis said. "Whatever this is, you're in it whether you like it or not. We all are."

No matter how hard he tried, Peter couldn't find a flaw in that logic.

He sighed. "What do I tell June?"

Lewis clapped him on the shoulder with a hard hand. "Man, you way too smart to be this dumb. Let your uncle Lewis school you. When it comes to women, you can't never go wrong with the truth."

"June might have mentioned that before," Peter admitted. "I'm a slow learner." He waved at the wheelbarrow full of plaster. "Let's clean this shit up and find an auto parts store so I don't get pulled over again. Then see if we can find out where somebody might buy one of those crazy custom electric bikes."

With the video glasses gone, the bike was the only lead they had.

12

They dropped the Toyota at the house and took Lewis's black Yukon to a shop called The Fix, the closest place that offered custom bikes. Located on Humboldt in Riverwest, it occupied the south end of a funky brick and concrete building designed to look like an old industrial space, down to the exposed and rusting metal beams.

Inside, the theme continued with polished concrete floors, plywood furnishings, and rows of racks made of bent rebar and sheet metal. The static hummed softly, not liking the flickering fluorescent lights, but otherwise it didn't mind being indoors the way it used to. There were no employees in sight.

Most of the bikes on display were radically simple, with elegant triangular frames, flat handlebars, and just a single speed. They looked like a hundred and fifty years of bicycle history put into a pot on high heat until everything extraneous had boiled away and only the most elemental design remained. They had multispeed models, but just for cargo, with stretched frames to accommodate a half-dozen bags of groceries or an insulated pizza delivery case.

A sign on the wall read ALL BICYCLES MUST COME WITH BRAKES.

Lewis eyed a matte-black model and ran a finger across the handlebars. "Man, I haven't owned a bike since I was ten years old."

"Really? June has three, and that's just in Milwaukee." Peter had found a good used Rockhopper and tuned it up to ride the root-rutted trails in the Kettle Moraine.

He left Lewis to fondle the merchandise and walked to the service window in the back. Behind a high counter was a pair of empty repair stands, a rackful of bikes awaiting work, and a long tool bench with a wheel-truing machine bolted to one end. In the far corner, a reedlike young man pedaled an exercise bike no-handed while he noodled on his phone and drank something green from a clear plastic cup. He wore a tangled ponytail, starter sideburns, and stainless-steel grommets in his ears. His T-shirt had the stylized sprocket logo of the Wisconsin Bike Federation.

The plywood countertop was dented and stained from a thousand greasy bike parts. A sleek computer monitor shared space with an intricate metal business-card holder in the shape of a bicycle, a service-order-form pad, and a tooth-chewed pencil taped to a piece of twine. Peter knocked on the counter and the hipster's head popped up. "Hey. What do you need?"

Peter smiled. "Hi. I saw on your website that you do custom work. Do you build electric bikes?"

The hipster kept pedaling. "Uh, no." He looked back to his phone.

Peter resisted the urge to jump the counter. He reminded himself he'd catch more flies with honey and kept smiling. "Really? I see them everywhere."

"Electrics are for your grandmother, man. Our customers are people who pedal. Saving the planet one bike at a time."

Peter wasn't crazy about idealists of any stripe. He waved at the rows of bikes behind him. "Tell me something. What's with the single-speed thing?"

"Fixed-gear," the hipster corrected. "The rear gear is fixed to the wheel, so you can slow using your leg muscles. It started with bike messengers, who stripped off everything unnecessary. Fixies are simpler, cheaper, lighter, and lower-maintenance. Although every bike we sell comes with at least one hand brake. 'Company policy.'" He made air quotes and rolled his eyes. "For the newbies, I guess. First thing I did was take mine off."

"People really want to buy a bike with just one speed?"

"Like you wouldn't believe, especially in the city. Do you pay any attention to the world? Climate change, environmental disasters, income inequality? Bikes are the future, man. The world's most elegant machine. Simpler, cleaner, cheaper than cars. Plus I get my exercise getting to work. No carbon, no sitting in traffic, no need to join a gym."

Peter raised his eyebrows. "Even in January?" Wisconsin winters were brutal.

"Studded tires and good gloves. Fifteen miles each way, every day. Makes me strong. Life is a fight, right? Besides, I can't really afford a car, not with my student loans. Same with most people my age. I'm never going to be able to buy a house, not the way things are going."

The hipster swung himself off the exercise bike without using his hands. His arms were thin, but his thighs were like tree trunks. When he set his drink and phone on the workbench, Peter noticed that the phone was plugged into an electrical outlet set into the top of a cardboard shoebox, along with a rechargeable handlebar light and a laptop. A wire from the side of the box went to the exercise bike. It looked like the bike's wheel had been repurposed into a generator, charging the hipster's electronics.

Peter said, "You clearly know a lot about this stuff. I saw this crazy electric bike, and it looked custom. I figured your shop was the place to go." He put out his hand. "I'm Peter, by the way."

They shook. "Carson. Like I told you, we don't do custom electrics. Not enough demand, not in Milwaukee anyway. Try one of the big shops. Wheel and Sprocket will have a bunch of factory models."

"Not like this," Peter said. "Really fast. Like nothing I've ever seen."

"Like bike-racer fast? The rider standing on the pedals, cranking hard?" Carson the bike fanatic was interested in spite of himself. Maybe electrics weren't entirely for your grandmother.

Lewis had been floating in the background, listening to the conversation. Now he stepped to the counter beside Peter and smiled pleasantly. "Man wasn't pedaling at all. He took off like a rocket."

"Well, you do have to pedal an electric bike," Carson said. "Technically, they're called electric-assist. Otherwise it's not a bike, it's an electric motorcycle, and you need a special license. People do bypass those controls, go full-on outlaw electric. But if you get busted, it's a big fine."

"This was not a regular bike. It was something different." Peter moved the bicycle-shaped business-card holder aside and pulled the order form and pencil across the counter, talking as he drew. "It was very basic, with none of the curved tubes of a modern bike. Kind of like the fixed-gear frames you have here."

He sketched a big rough triangle with the long frame and high crossbar of an old Schwinn, then added the fork, the seat and chain stays, and the tires. He was no artist, but he'd drawn up his share of building plans, and he managed to get the proportions right. "More like an early motorcycle than a bike, actually. The rear hub was thicker than usual, kind of weird-looking."

Lewis leaned in, pointing. "And it had these long silver boxes strapped inside the frame, with wires coming out of them, maybe spare batteries? But nothing that looked like a motor. You ever see anything like that?"

Carson's eyes were wide. "No, no, sorry." He retrieved the business-card holder and put it back behind the computer keyboard, then abruptly jammed his hands into his armpits. "You know, lots of people modify their bikes. Stretch the frame, tweak the fork. It's not that complicated. Any welder could do it."

His ear grommets were quivering. Peter smiled. "Carson, what aren't you telling me?"

The grommets quivered more violently. Carson looked from Peter to Lewis. "Who are you guys? From the city? Police?"

"Oh, no." Lewis smiled, his voice a low purr. "We are mos' definitely not police."

Peter said, "Why would you think we're police?"

"Well, uh, if someone has a full electric bike without a license, that would be illegal, right?"

"We're not here for that," Peter said. "We're just interested in the bike."

"Well." Carson turned away and lifted a bike onto one of the repair stands. "I wish I could help you guys, but like I said, that's not what we do. Now, uh, I got a couple of tune-ups this afternoon, so, you know."

Lewis looked at Peter, tipped his chin toward the hipster, and raised his eyebrows in an unspoken question. Carson definitely knew something. It wouldn't take much to get him to talk.

But Peter just shook his head, stretched his long arm across the counter, and picked up the little metal business-card holder. The cards had the name and information for The Fix, but Peter wasn't interested in that. He was interested in the intricate bicycle-shaped holder.

It was beautiful work, an old-school banana-seat low-rider on a polished steel baseplate. Peter turned it over. On the underside, someone had engraved the words KIKO'S WELDING AND CUSTOM FRAMES in crisp freehand letters, with a website and phone number.

Carson's face fell. Peter gave him a smile. "Thanks for your time, Carson. We'll get out of your hair." He tore another sheet off the order form and wrote down his cell number. "If you think of anything else, give me a call."

Lewis held up a hand. "Actually, gimme one minute." He stepped into the showroom and came back wheeling the matte-black fixed-gear model he'd been admiring. "I'll take this one."

13

According to its aggressively basic website, Kiko's Welding was owned by Kiko Tomczak, with an address on South Fifth. The location was good, a block from Bradley Tech and down the street from the Iron Horse Hotel and Mobcraft Brewing. But when they got there, they found a former streetfront industrial building converted into a glossy modern art gallery. It was closed until Friday, with the lights off and nobody home.

They stood in the drizzle while Lewis pulled up the gallery on his phone and paged through the site. "Looks like they rent space, too. That address is on Pierce, right around the corner."

It turned out to be in the same sprawling building. Right before a lumpy cobblestone alley, they found a reinforced steel door. Someone had taped up a laminated sign that read DUE TO NEIGHBORHOOD THEFTS, PLEASE KEEP DOOR LOCKED AT ALL TIMES. The knob and deadbolt were high-end Medeco models. A wide-angle security camera perched out of reach on the wall above. The door was propped open with a block of wood.

Lewis shook his head. "Can't do nothin' with stupid."

"It's not nice to call people stupid." Peter pulled the door open. "Didn't you learn anything in kindergarten?"

Lewis chuckled, low and dark. "Brother, I think we went to different kindergartens."

Inside, they found a small informal entry with a high white ceiling and ancient pine floors painted a cool modern gray that hid everything and competed with nothing. Bright art hung on three walls, giant portraits made with many-colored bottle caps glued to sheets of plywood. Peter admired the level of obsession required.

There was no directory of tenants. To the right was a steep narrow stairway leading up. The static hummed low in his blood, letting him know it was ready.

Lewis said, "Would you run a welding business on the second floor?"

"Not if I had to carry steel up and down those skinny stairs all day. Unless there's a freight elevator somewhere."

A faint pulse of music came from the far side of the lobby where a wide corridor led away into the building. The drywall was punctuated by double doors inset at long intervals, all closed. They were decorated with taped cartoons and sketches and watercolors and other demonstrations of wit and talent. It reminded Peter of his college dorm.

The hallway came to a T at a large corkboard covered with announcements for upcoming exhibitions, workshops, and classes all over the city. The music came from the left. Peter followed. It grew louder and louder until they came to a plywood partition, twelve feet wide and hung like a barn door on a steel track. Screwed to the partition was a rough rectangle of metal, engraved with the same crisp freehand copperplate writing as the baseplate of the little banana-seat bike sculpture.

It read I'M ALREADY DISTURBED. FOR YOUR OWN SAFETY, DON'T MAKE THINGS WORSE.

The music thumped through the plywood, a light fixture visibly vibrating on the wall beside it. A bass-heavy REO Speedwagon remix, rolling with the changes. The static hummed higher.

Lewis said, "How we doing this?"

Peter shrugged. "Smile, be friendly, ask questions."

"That works for you?"

"It will if you stand there and look like the muscle."

Lewis snorted. "Brother, I am the muscle." He pulled the door open.

Inside, the music was louder still, nearly overpowering the buzz of a MIG welder on a rolling cart, its thick cable looping a thick-bodied man who labored at a rough steel table, his back to the door.

His shoulders were broad and powerful under the heavy suede welder's jacket. His salt-and-pepper hair poked through the straps of the welder's mask on his massive head. The MIG's bright spark cast flickering shadows on the walls.

He was surrounded on three sides by a strange steel frame that came up to the middle of his back. It was mostly scrap pieces tacked together with spot-welds, but it looked supremely functional. Wheels sized for a bicycle were mounted on the left and right, with hard rubber tires scarred by flying sparks. Above each wheel hung a pivoting steel tool rack that held an orderly array of hammers and punches and pliers and other metalworking tools. On the back of the frame, twin tanks of oxygen and acetylene stood chained to a stout shelf, the hoses and torch slung for easy access. Below sat a greasy cube the size of a milk crate, surrounded by a network of thin stainless tubes leading to hydraulic pistons whose purpose wasn't clear.

The bike maker had built himself a rolling work platform, everything he needed within arm's reach.

The big man hadn't noticed his visitors, the MIG still buzzing away. Peter wasn't going to walk up and tap the guy on the shoulder. He'd learned long ago not to distract anybody with a live power tool, for their protection and his own. So he found the sound system on a high shelf, a vintage Pioneer tuner with a cool green glow, analog dials, and a smartphone plugged into the input jack. As REO Speedwagon gave way to Dick Dale's booming surf guitar, he picked up the phone, then held it so Lewis could see the screen. It showed four missed calls, all from the same number.

Lewis leaned in to be heard over the music. "You think our friend from the bike shop tried to warn him?"

Peter nodded, set down the phone, and dropped the volume on the Pioneer. After a moment, the MIG went silent.

"Sorry," the metalworker called over his shoulder. "I didn't think anyone was here." He pulled off the welder's mask and hung it on one of the pivoting tool racks, then popped out a set of foam earplugs. On the other rack, he flipped a switch and the hydraulic platform began to shift. While they watched, the frame sank down between the wheels. When the metal stopped moving, he put his hand on a joystick and spun the platform to face them.

Peter saw his withered legs and realized that the metalworker was partially paralyzed. The work platform was actually a homemade hydraulic wheelchair. The man had turned a physical challenge into an asset.

"Pretty cool rig." Peter smiled. "Are you Kiko Tomczak?"

"Yeah, that's me." Kiko's craggy face looked like a relief map of some harsh, bony desert, lines carved deep by wind and time, eyes disturbingly clear behind steel-framed glasses. "What do you need?"

Peter put out his hand to shake. "I'm Peter, this is Lewis. We got your name from The Fix, the bike shop on Humboldt."

Peter had big hands, but Tomczak's were meatier, like T-bones cut from an escaped longhorn that had been struck by a train. He was even bigger from the front. A heavy suede welder's jacket covered his arms and chest and lap to protect him from flying sparks, and suede chaps protected his thin legs. His steel-toed boots had leather flaps over the laces so they wouldn't burn.

He reached behind his back to unfasten the jacket, then pulled it from his arms. He was shirtless and sweating, with a Milwaukee Fire Department logo tattooed on one massive bicep and a clock without hands on the other, the second tattoo done in the Bic blue of a jailhouse artist. His grizzled hair stuck up in random clumps.

He mopped his forehead with a black bandanna, then eyed his visitors in their stained work clothes. "You're not here for a custom bike frame. What do you want? How the hell did you get in here, anyway?"

"Someone left the door open," Peter said.

Tomczak rolled his eyes. "Artists," he said. "You're looking for architectural work, right? Stairs or railings? You won't find better work for better prices anywhere in town." He spread his hands to encompass his work space. "I can build anything you need."

The shop was the size of a three-car garage. The welding table took up the center of the space, flanked by rolling racks that held rough-cut steel and partially finished components. Shining finished bicycle frames hung from the unpainted Sheetrock like butterflies pinned to a collector's cabinet. The walls were lined with heavy equipment, including a big drill press, lathe, bandsaw, and hydraulic press, along with a workstation with fine tools for delicate work. Above the door, lengths of raw steel bars and tubes sat stacked across reinforced brackets ten feet in the air. Although how a guy in a wheelchair got those down, Peter had no idea.

"Actually," he said, "we're looking for a particular bicycle that you may have built." He held out the sketch he'd made at the bike shop. "It's electric, and totally unique. I saw somebody riding it the other day. Faster than anything I've ever seen. I think there's a real market for something like that."

Kiko shook his head. "I don't build electrics, that's specialty stuff. I can make anything from a blueprint, I'm real good with structure, but circuits and motors aren't my thing."

"What about your chair?"

Kiko shook his head. "I swapped work with somebody for the complicated stuff. Hydraulics for custom pressure tanks."

"But you do know who owns that bike," Peter said. "Can you put us in touch?"

The metalworker reached over his shoulder, pulled the oxy-acetylene torch from its place on the back of his chair and rolled the tool idly in one sausage-fingered hand. An old-fashioned spark igniter had somehow appeared in the other. He sucked on his teeth and looked at them over the top of his glasses.

"I'm supposed to believe, what, you're some kinda bicycle big shots? Vice presidents from Trek come down from Waterloo, in your torn-up Carhartts and dirty sweatshirts? 'Cause I know for damn sure you ain't cops."

Usually Peter could read people pretty well, but Kiko's weathered face was locked down tight, probably a survival skill he'd learned in prison. Still, the muscles in his forearms bunched and flexed, an involuntary stress reaction. He knew something. But how to get to it?

"You're right," Peter said. "I'm sorry we lied to you. We don't build bikes and we're definitely not cops. Here's the truth. You heard about the shooting at the Public Market yesterday, right? The place was full of kids. It's a miracle nobody got killed. Well, the shooter got away on a custom electric bike." He raised the rough drawing. "This bike right here."

Kiko eyeballed Peter, then Lewis. "Why are you here instead of the cops?"

Peter wasn't going to get into the video sunglasses or his legal issues. "It's personal. That shooter could have killed us, too."

"You're the goddamn Samaritans from the paper," Kiko said. His face tightened and the lines deepened into canyons. He turned the thumbwheel with one hand and sparked the igniter with the other. A foot-long flame leaped out of the head, the torch adjusted for maximum length. Heat came off the orange and blue jet like a furnace blast. One pass across human skin would scorch flesh into black blisters. "Who the hell do you work for?"

Peter raised a hand and took a step back. "Hold up, hold up. I'm telling the truth. We don't work for anybody. We were just at the market by dumb luck. But we'll go to the cops if we have to."

Kiko considered them for a moment, then turned the thumbwheel again. The flame vanished. "Listen, I didn't make any damn electric bike and that's the God's truth. I don't do motors or circuits or any of that. The only bike work I do is frames, and I got customers all over the Midwest. Besides, you think I remember every custom job I do?"

"This was a slim guy with a big beard and mirror shades," Peter said. "Wore a red Cardinals jacket and hat, if that helps. Ring any bells?"

Kiko's face eased, just slightly. If Peter didn't know better, he'd say the man looked relieved.

"Doesn't sound like anyone I know. Anyway, most of my customers I deal with over the phone."

"What about your files," Lewis said. "Billing records, technical drawings. Maybe we find our shooter that way."

Kiko waved the torch at the shop. "I look like an accountant to you? I don't do paperwork. People pay me cash. They want a receipt, I write one by hand."

Lewis raised his eyebrows. "How do you run a business without records?"

"I'm old-school like that." Kiko looked at them. "Let me spell this out for you two. Back in the day, Milwaukee was called the Machine Shop of the World. Most of that manufacturing is gone now, but you know how many skilled welders and machinists still live in this town? Not to mention retirees with a shop in their garage, making stuff for the fun of it? A couple thousand, at least. Any one of them could have made something as simple as a bike frame. So good luck finding your guy."

Lewis said, "Lemme ask a different question." He pointed at the big machines against the wall. "You have everything you need to be a gunsmith, too. You ever make a receiver for an automatic rifle? One of those old AK variants?"

Lewis was thinking of the shooter's weapon. But Kiko didn't bite.

"Dude, I'm a damn felon, okay? I don't touch guns. I don't need them." He stowed the torch on the rack behind his back, then reached into a pouch hung off the side of his chair and pulled out a Y-shaped metal frame. A loop of surgical tubing hung loose from the arms of the Y, with a leather pouch in the middle. He unfolded the brace and settled the thing in his hand.

It was a shop-made version of a wrist rocket, a high-powered slingshot outlawed in several states and many more cities. Peter had one as a kid. Some Internet fanatic had tested its power against various pistols and found that only the .357 Magnum did more damage at close range.

Kiko straightened his arm with the slingshot in one hand and pulled back the sling with the other, aiming directly at Lewis's face. "I can bull's-eye the O in a stop sign at fifty yards, make a hole you can put your thumb through. I can throw a deer slug a quarter mile and crack a damn cinder block. You do not want to be messing with me, you hear?"

Peter couldn't tell whether there was a slug in the sling. Lewis gave no sign that he might be bothered. He just gave Kiko that cool tilted smile. "You gonna keep flexing or you gonna tell us why you so worried about who we might work for?"

Kiko relaxed the slingshot and returned it to its pouch, then pulled the welder's jacket onto his big arms and torso. "That's a different thing," he said. "I got my own problems. Now get the hell out of here so I can get back to work."

He flipped a switch on his chair and it began to elongate, rising to work height.

"Kiko," Peter said. "If you know something, talk to us. This shooter is dangerous."

Tomczak flipped another switch. The hydraulics hissed as the platform rose higher still. Now he towered over them, arms thick as pythons in the heavy suede welder's jacket. Peter no longer wondered how he managed to get the heavy steel tubing down off the storage rack overhead.

"Don't make me mess you boys up, all right? I don't want to go back to prison." He plucked a five-pound sledge off the tool shelf and pointed it like an extension of his hand. "Close the door on your way out."

He twisted the volume knob on the Pioneer and an electric

guitar blared through the speakers, the opening riff from Tom Petty's "Runnin' Down a Dream." It was loud enough to drown out a shout. Then he pushed the joystick and the metal monster powered forward, crowding them backward out of the shop.

Lewis looked at Peter, who shook his head and let it happen. They could put Tomczak down, but not without taking some damage from that sledgehammer. And there was nothing to be gained by a fight, at least not now. Peter had met plenty of guys like Kiko, more than enough to understand that, no matter what Kiko knew, he wouldn't tell them shit.

In the hallway again, with the door closed behind them, Lewis looked at Peter. "You are truly a master of interrogation."

"You're supposed to be a tough guy," Peter said. "Why don't you go back in there and talk some sense into him?"

"I ain't gonna hit no dude in a wheelchair. Who the hell you think I am? A man's got to have a code, motherfucker."

"That big hammer didn't have anything to do with it?"

"Hell, no. And definitely not the fact that he's strapped into some crazy machine makes him nine feet tall. That ain't freaky at all."

Peter said, "You saw that, right? How he felt better once I told him what the guy looked like?"

Lewis nodded. "He knew something, though. Until you told him what the guy looked like, he had somebody in mind. Maybe on both sides of that fight. Remember how he asked who we worked for?"

"Uh-huh. Then he changed the subject," Peter said. "Hey, what's with that question about the AK receiver?"

"The shooter's weapon was a cold-war variant, the AKSM with the underfolding stock. Originally designed for Russian paratroopers." Lewis had a ridiculous collection of firearms, although he was most partial to a 10-gauge shotgun. "Last time I looked, it was easiest to find the Polish and Romanian models. You can buy kits on the Internet for a few hundred bucks, but they don't come with the receiver."

The receiver was the central component of the gun, housing the trigger and firing mechanism that made the weapon function as designed. Because firearms had interchangeable parts, the receiver was the component that the U.S. government restricted, with every purchase monitored by law.

"The cops will look into everything registered," Lewis said. "But if our guy has the tooling to make and bend the receiver himself, and the expertise to assemble the gun, he'll have a fully operable and completely untraceable assault rifle." He flashed Peter a grin. "But he'd have to be a real gun nut to do that."

Peter laughed. Lewis had two big Sportsman Steel safes in his basement. "How many firearms do you own?"

Lewis looked at him sideways. "That's a very personal question, motherfucker." They were walking out the way they'd come in. When they came to the bulletin board, Lewis paused to scan the display and plucked a sheet of paper from its pin. "Tell you what, though. I think I found our next stop."

It was a flyer for something called the South Side MakerSpace. A shared workshop with a wide variety of tools available to members, and classes in how to use them. Lewis tapped the page. "Kiko Tomczak, owner of Kiko's Welding and Custom Frames, returns with his popular course, How to Make Your Own Bicycle Frame in a Weekend."

Right below that was a scheduled orientation for the Maker-Space's Electronics Shop, featuring the basics of motor design, battery power, and electrical diagnostics.

14

JUNE

June's stomach growled as she scribbled the last of her notes on what she'd learned about Vince Holloway and Pinnacle Technologies, including her non-conversation with Gary the receptionist. It was almost two in the afternoon, and the left-over noodles barely made a dent in her hunger.

Her head suggested riding to Beans and Barley for a spinach salad, but her heart cried out for a grilled Turkenstein with spicy fries at the Comet. She'd camp out in one of their booths, turn off her phone, and knock out the end of her damn chapter. If she didn't finish this book soon, it was going to kill her.

She threw her new laptop in her new bag, pulled on her rain-coat, and wheeled her bike out the side door into the softly falling rain, pausing to double-check the knob to make sure it had locked behind her. She put her weight on the pedal and pushed off to get the bike rolling, then swung her leg over the seat and began to ride. A smile came to her face as it almost always did at this moment. The daily miracle of the bicycle.

At the end of the block, a big white van came around the corner. The street was narrow with cars parked on both sides, so she hopped up to the sidewalk until the van passed, then bumped down the curb again and turned into the city.

Riverwest was a funky old neighborhood of modest houses, duplexes, and small apartment buildings. It had a nice mix of people, working-class folks and students, creative hipsters and retired people, black and white and every shade of brown. Milwaukee was a more interesting city than she'd expected, with a buzzing art and music and film scene. Although with Peter's face on a wanted poster, they didn't go out as much as she'd like.

The rain on her face reminded her of Seattle, where she'd lived when they met. Biking in the rain made her feel strong and capable and virtuous. She was a firm believer that there was no such thing as bad weather, just bad gear, and June was all about good gear. The real problem with wet days was the damn drivers, who sat all cozy inside their heated bubbles with their wipers on and seemed to forget cyclists even existed. At least Humboldt Boulevard had a bike lane.

Midafternoon traffic was light enough that she wasn't worried. She only had to slam on the brakes once, when another van passed her with the passenger-side tires riding the white line of the bike lane, the driver looking at his phone, oblivious to her and everyone else. This was why she didn't clip into her pedals in the city.

Still, her legs felt good, and the thought of a Turkenstein and fries made her ride harder. She saw the unwritten end of her chapter laid out like a schematic in her mind. The line of parked cars scrolled past on her right. She was going twenty-one miles an hour.

Directly in front of her, a car door flew open. Without

thinking, she leaned left and hit the brakes with both hands. But she was too late.

Her front wheel hit the lower edge of the door, which flexed back slightly on its hinge but not enough to make a difference. She had strong arms and a good grip on the brakes, so when her momentum threw her weight forward, the back tire rose off the ground.

She had just enough time to hunch her right shoulder and tuck her head to take the hit on her helmet so the window frame didn't break her face. She bounced off the metal and rolled sideways with the bike turning beneath her until her legs got tangled and she fell onto her butt on the wet asphalt.

A man climbed out of the big white van that had doored her. "Oh, jeez, I'm sorry." He smiled at her. "I bet that hurts, huh?"

Did she hurt? She didn't know yet. Mostly she was embarrassed. She scrambled up and pulled her bike out of traffic. The impact had turned her front wheel nearly parallel to the handlebars, which explained the sideways roll. She gave the wheel a spin and it turned just fine. She was lucky the stem hadn't been fully torqued down. Otherwise the rim would be bent and unrideable.

Standing in the bike lane, she took a quick inventory of her body. Nothing broken, no serious blood. Her neck turned without pain. She'd find the scrapes and bruises when she undressed for the shower. Her left butt cheek would be six shades of purple in the morning. She didn't think her backpack had hit the ground, so her new laptop should be fine.

Cars drove past as if nothing had happened. It could have been worse, she told herself. She could have missed the door and veered into traffic. Three tons of implacable steel would have made a much bigger impact. She'd gotten off easy.

The man said, "Good thing you wear a helmet, huh?"

She glared at the idiot. "Did you even think to look before you opened that door?"

He raised his eyebrows. "I did look." His voice was earnest. He walked toward her. "But I didn't see anything. You must have been going pretty fast. Sorry if you got hurt."

But he didn't seem particularly sorry. He still wore that cheerful smile on a fleshy face over a big round body made rounder by the starched white dress shirt untucked over unfashionable jeans. The raindrops on his shirt were translucent dots that showed the pale, hairy skin beneath. June wanted to get out of there.

Instead she pulled out her phone and took a quick video of her bike. Aside from the misaligned wheel, a torn grip, and a few scrapes, the old girl didn't look too bad. She wasn't some fancy carbon-fiber hothouse flower, she was a sturdy steel workhorse that wasn't taking any shit from some asshole passenger van. She was still rideable.

"Gosh, I really wish I could do something to help." The man grinned like he was hearing an internal laugh track. His hands roved aimlessly at the end of his meaty arms. He wore a pair of black sunglasses folded into the open neck of his shirt.

His van was still running, too, although its engine had an odd, off-center rattle, something definitely wrong with it. He hadn't even closed his door.

"Oh, you'll help." June raised her phone again, video still running, and captured his face, then caught the car and the license plate, too. "I'll get myself checked out and send you the bill."

"Let me give you my information." He stepped closer. "Where are you headed? Wow, it's really raining now. Can I take you somewhere?" Happy as a fucking clam.

"I don't think so." He seemed harmless, although a little off. Maybe not so bright, or not so good at social cues. She hauled her bike away from him, and behind his van onto the grass parking strip. She trapped her front wheel between her knees and pulled the handlebars back into rough alignment. Both rims still spun freely against the brakes and the quick-release hubs were locked tight, so she was safe to ride at least a short distance. She'd give everything a closer look when she got to the paper.

He was closing in again. "Hey, I'm an Uber driver." He pointed at the sticker on his windshield. "My name is Edgar. Let me take you. It's the least I can do." Why was he so damn cheerful?

She backed away. "Jesus, no." There was no way in hell she was getting in his car. She'd been through that before and it hadn't gone well.

"At least let me give you my information. Come on over, my wallet's in the van."

She tucked her phone into her pocket and threw one leg over her bike. "Edgar, I'm a journalist. I have your license plate. If I need you, I'll find you."

He turned to look at the steady flow of oncoming traffic, then back at her. His white shirt had become entirely translucent from the rain. Droplets streamed down his forehead. He still smiled, but his face had changed. He didn't look harmless anymore. Not even a little bit.

He kept walking toward her. "Lady, get in the van." He didn't seem to notice the rain at all.

"Excuse me?"

She saw him clearly now, knew exactly what he was. She still straddled the crossbar of her bike, shifting her weight.

That strange smile got wider. "You heard me, reporter lady. Get in the van." He was maybe twelve feet away. He took another step toward her, then another. Nine feet away. "I don't want to hurt you. I just want to talk."

She didn't believe that for a second. "I don't want to fucking talk to you, Edgar." It was June's turn to grin. "But I do have your picture."

Now he came for her, hands outstretched, but June was already in motion. Weight on her left foot, she swung her right leg clear of the seat and continued the pivot with strong arms and an easy grip on the handlebars to pop the front wheel off the ground. The back wheel quickly followed, and in just a quarter-turn, she had the whole bike flying in a horizontal arc. She shifted her weight and leaned into the spin, hauling the bike through the air as she widened her stance, the lugs of her hiking shoes giving her a solid grip on the wet grass.

He thought she was running, and kept coming.

But June wasn't running.

A hundred and eighty degrees into her turn, she pulled the handlebars toward her chest, which swung the back wheel outward, where it came to an abrupt halt when the tire slammed into the side of his smiling face. She felt the satisfying thump all the way up to her shoulders. The accumulated speed and power of the blow, half the weight of the steel bike moving fast, knocked him sideways and stumbling to the ground.

She didn't wait to see what happened next. She landed the bike and jumped aboard and stood on the pedals to pump hard up the sidewalk against traffic.

Leaving Edgar behind, eating her dust, hopefully with a big fucking headache.

15

She pushed hard down alleys and back avenues toward the reservoir until she reached the bike trail, which she took to Commerce Street and into the loose chain of parking lots that kept her off streets until the Bucks' new arena, two blocks from the *Milwaukee Journal Sentinel*. Lunch would have to wait.

She'd swing by Dean Zedler's desk. Dean always had good snacks.

She'd already decided not to tell Peter about the cheerful psychopath in the white van, not until she figured out what the hell was going on. Which was the opposite of what she'd just demanded of Peter. This made her a hypocrite, she knew. But her years as a reporter had reinforced the reflex to keep information close until she knew the whole story. And Peter's reflex was to do anything to keep her safe, which would get in the way of her learning what she needed to know.

Relationships were hard, right?

Feeling every ache and scrape of her fall to the pavement, she unlocked the loading dock gate with her ID, then chained her bike to the lonely yellow rack. Inside, she waved to Ernie at the security station and rode the elevator up to the fourth floor. Back when she was a beat reporter in Chicago, she'd never ridden her bike to the paper, because she never knew where the day might take her. That variability was one of the pleasures of the work. This book project, with most of her time spent on the phone and computer, was different. She supposed that meant she was moving up in the world.

She walked into the vast, high-ceilinged newsroom, then turned left toward her borrowed cubicle, feeling the hushed energy of the place soaking into her bones as it did every morning. This was why, after years of working from home, she'd talked her way into a desk at the *Journal Sentinel*. The feeling of a working newsroom never got old, even in this age of shrinking staffs and declining subscriptions.

She'd only had the cube for six months, but her desk looked like she'd been there for years. Every horizontal surface was covered with stacks of books and scholarly articles she'd used for background research, along with tall, shaggy mounds of manila folders filled with notes and outlines and drafts for each chapter.

The only open space surrounded two framed photos, like ringed ripples around thrown stones. One was a photo of her mom, who'd been an IT professor at Stanford. The other was her dad, who'd been a tech entrepreneur and bleeding-edge researcher before his mind had gone tangled and strange. It was no mystery why June had become an investigative journalist. She'd spent most of her childhood and teens trying to decipher their odd, troubled marriage and the disastrous divorce that had followed.

She found the morning's print edition on the seat of her chair. The story of the market shooting was on the front page, above the fold, along with a grainy security-camera photo of the bearded gunman in his red hat and jacket and sunglasses. Dean had stuck a sticky note to the masthead. "See me if you want a piece of the follow-up—DIZ."

Zedler's middle name was Ignatius, and he'd been trying to cultivate the nickname Diz, without success, since the day they'd met more than a decade ago.

She scanned the story about yesterday's Hampton Avenue machete murders, which was below the fold, probably because they couldn't print photos of the mutilated bodies, then put the paper aside. Usually she scanned at least four newspapers a day, to check their coverage and to see if there were any unexpected developments in her areas of professional interest. But now she had bigger fish to fry. Forget about Vincent Holloway and Pinnacle Technologies. She was in hot pursuit of Mr. Cheerful and his white passenger van.

First, she emailed herself the video from her phone, then threw it up on her big desk monitor where she could get a better look. She fired up some video editing software, pulled out the best stills of his face, both from the front and the side, then skipped ahead to the footage of the truck. Because the driver's door was still open, she found a half-dozen frames she could stitch together to grab the complete VIN number from the manufacturer's sticker on the outside edge. This was why she'd sprung for the fancy phone with the good camera, so she could zoom in and capture these kinds of details. She'd also gotten the plate, no-brainer, which was from Texas.

She knew somebody in the Lone Star State, right? She flipped through her mental file and came up with Christina Willis, a Chicago street cop who'd moved to Houston to escape the Midwestern winters. Now she was a detective with a talent for sifting through giant heaps of data in pursuit of organized crime.

June fired off an email to her friend's personal account. "I was riding my bike to work and some jerk with Texas plates almost killed me. I know you're not supposed to do this, but can you get me a name? You know I'm good for the favor." She attached the photos of the face, plate, and VIN.

Then, just for grins, she ran a Google image search using his face, even though the only time she ever got a half-decent result was with mug shots or celebrities. She scrolled down through the results, but this time was no different, just a bunch of random middle-aged guys, none of them her attacker. No surprise that he didn't have a big social media presence or website advertising his services as a freelance fuckhead. But she didn't mind. Once she had a name, the face would help her narrow down the candidates to her guy.

Once she found him, she could begin to figure out who sent him. And why.

She assumed his plan had been to get her into the van, then make her disappear. A missing adult was not usually a police priority. No body meant no murder.

Despite the warm newsroom, she shivered.

After putting her computer to sleep, because she worked in a roomful of good reporters who were both sneaky and competitive by nature, she went to the now-defunct cafeteria for some truly terrible vending-machine coffee, taking the morning's paper with her. She wanted to see what updates had been made to the market story since the online version she'd read the night before.

Like most reporters, the first thing she looked at was the byline. When the story was first published, Dean's name had been before hers. June didn't mind. She'd done the on-scene reporting, but Dean had worked his many city contacts to dig into the police response, and he'd also written the copy. Not to mention that June wasn't even an actual employee of the paper.

But in the byline for the print edition, June's name was now first. It might have seemed like generosity, but she was well aware of his other motives. He was trying to rope her into the story and, by extension, the *Journal Sentinel*. He'd been sending her charming and flirty recruitment emails for years.

As she scanned the story now, however, she saw that Dean had added several new paragraphs, asking readers to contact the paper if they had any information about the good Samaritans who'd intervened in the shooting, including photographs. It meant that the police were more interested than she'd previously thought. Or else Dean himself was.

Either way, not a good development.

16

Dean's cube was in the middle of the newsroom, with a view of his editor's office and easy access to the long file cabinets that lined the center aisle. The next pod held the cops reporters, although the squawking police scanners were long gone, made obsolete by radio encryption and the Internet.

She found him slouched in his chair, chewing his lip and two-finger tapping into the LexisNexis search bar. Instead of the usual unofficial reporter's uniform of a rumpled blue button-down and coffee-stained khakis, Dean wore a fine black V-neck sweater over fitted blue jeans with handsome Italian driving shoes. A cashmere blazer hung from a hanger on a file cabinet. Not a clotheshorse, not really, just someone who'd long ago learned to dress himself. Like an adult.

She tried not to compare Dean's outfit to Peter's dirty work clothes. Totally unfair. Different job entirely.

"Hey." She plopped herself into his guest chair, the queen of casual. Not at all worried at what Dean might have uncovered. "You got something new on our market shooter?"

He turned to look at her, smiling like a kid on a particularly good Christmas morning, as he often did when he saw her. He had a gap between his two front teeth that was just large enough to notice. She always felt badly when she found herself staring at it. She'd known him a long time.

"Nothing on the shooter, but my source at the cop shop finally sent me security cam pics of the Samaritans this morning. It'd be a great feature if we could find these guys." He clicked a few times and brought up a photo. "This is the guy who jumped the fence to the loading dock."

The face was fuzzy from the zoom, the features vague and indistinct. In person, Lewis made a major impression, but aside from the dark intensity of the eyes, this photo could have been anybody. For someone with Lewis's past, the ability to fade out of a photograph was a kind of superpower.

Dean clicked again. "And this is the guy who told the schoolteacher to get her kids out of the market right before the shooting started. The loading dock camera has him rushing the guy unarmed. He's lucky he didn't get killed." The image showed a large blurry cowboy hat with only the lower corner of the face exposed below the brim. June recognized the angle of Peter's cheekbone and the line of his jaw.

"Wow, lousy art." Just seeing the crappy photos, June felt better. "Is this the best you've got?"

"Unfortunately. But that neighborhood is full of businesses with their own cameras. I'm headed there this afternoon, to knock on doors and see if they'll give me access. Maybe I'll find something better."

Why hadn't June thought of that? Crap. "Didn't the cops do that already?"

"Not according to my source downtown. Nobody died at the

market, and that ugly double homicide on Hampton is where they're putting the manpower." He gave her a sunny smile. "But not me. I've got nothing but time."

Which wasn't true at all. Dean had plenty to do, but he clearly smelled something, and he was too good of a reporter to let it go. He didn't know what the story was yet, but that didn't mean he wouldn't find out. Getting access to those private cameras could get him closer. After all, Peter and Lewis had sat outside the coffee shop as the shooter walked past.

With June at the same table.

Her mouth felt dry. "But the police aren't after these two guys, are they? Didn't they help stop the shooter?"

"That's what eyewitnesses say. But why did they intervene? Were they really good Samaritans, or were they somehow involved? What kind of person doesn't step forward for his moment of glory? Maybe they know something about the shooter. Plus if they're actual heroes, the mayor will want to honor them somehow."

"What about the guy the shooter tried to rob," she said. "Any art showing his face?" Thinking of Vincent Holloway, the tech entrepreneur she thought she'd recognized. A decent picture might help her find him.

Dean shook his head. "Guy's a blur. The only clear shots are of the back of his head. But he's a question mark, too. Why did he walk? Maybe he knew the shooter? Why else would someone come after him with an assault rifle?"

Dean's skeptical mind was always digging deeper, always looking for the hidden angle. If he was going to keep pushing on this story, it was going to be a serious problem. She needed something new and juicy to hit. Like a state rep with two wives, or a late-season tornado, or a five-alarm apartment fire. Ideally, it would be all three. Because, she silently admitted, she was a terrible person.

Dean stared at her with his big brown eyes. His shave was still crisp, and he'd had a haircut since the last time she saw him. Not for the first time, she realized that he was a good-looking guy. A little short, but definitely handsome.

"Hey, I have an idea." He snapped his fingers, as if he'd just thought of it that moment. "Why don't you come canvass the market area with me? Sweet-talk some local businesses into showing us their security footage? It'll be like the old days. Maybe stop for a drink or a bite when we're done? I've got the bike rack on my car, I can give you a lift home afterward."

"Sorry, I need to get back to work on the book. I have chapters due next week." Which was true, although that wasn't her plan at all. She'd spend the rest of the day online, risking carpal tunnel to try to get a better read on Holloway while she waited to hear back from her friend in Houston.

As she was leaving, she said, "Did you get any strange, ah, feedback about this story?"

He read her face. "What kind of feedback?"

"Nothing I can't handle," she said. "But you should be careful for a few days."

"June," he said. "Talk to me."

She shook her head. Tired of men and their protective instincts. June was in much better shape than Dean, and she'd done far more self-defense training. "Don't worry about it," she said. Then stopped. "You didn't have to put me first on the byline, you know."

He smiled guilelessly. "You'd do the same for me, right?"

"No, I would not," she said. "I'd sell my firstborn child to beat you to a story."

"Aw, I don't believe that for a minute," he said.

Dean Zedler was, in many ways, the opposite of Peter. One of the best-dressed men in the newsroom, he was a polished professional and could have his pick of editor's jobs at a half-dozen major papers whenever he wanted. He'd also been trying to get into her pants since the day they met.

In the nicest way, of course.

Ruthlessly, relentlessly nice.

If nice could be weaponized, Dean had done it.

Years ago, in Chicago, he'd made a major play for her. Dinners, flowers, the works. And she'd been tempted. He was smart, good-looking, and very ambitious. Like cops, reporters often ended up dating other reporters, because only another journalist could truly understand the insane demands and sublime delights of the job. But there was also something about his Weaponized Nice, which amounted to a kind of constant calculation, that had put her off. They'd never gotten past dinner, and soon afterward she'd taken the buyout from the *Tribune* and moved west.

Dean had seriously upped his game since then. He'd written a big magazine piece that was used as the basis for a Hollywood film, and while it hadn't made him rich, it did allow him to pay off his Shorewood duplex, accumulate some really great shoes, and buy a new Honda CR-V, the world's most practical car. And that big smile, not to mention his generosity with the byline, meant he was making another play.

Strangely, she found herself the most attracted to him when she was ovulating.

She really didn't want to know what that meant.

Back at her desk, checking her email, she thought that the whole thing would be so much easier if she could just tell Dean she had a boyfriend. But she couldn't, because Dean was a reporter, so he'd start asking questions. He'd definitely want to meet Peter.

It wasn't just Dean, either. If she ever made the mistake of bringing Peter to the Newsroom Pub, every reporter in the place would grill him like a Supreme Court nominee. They'd zero in on any inconsistency or evasion, because that's what good reporters do. To everyone they know. Even if Peter never said a word, some smart-ass would probably try to sneak a picture. With a good face-frontal photo, he'd be one click away from the FBI's Wanted list. And that would be the end of that.

Even that term, boyfriend. June was in her thirties, a professional journalist with a national reputation. She'd been short-listed for the Pulitzer, for chrissake. Calling someone her boyfriend was ridiculous. But what else was Peter to her? Her significant other? Her partner? Her lover? Those names were either too domestic or just plain stupid.

She supposed the label didn't matter. They were *living* together, after all. And she loved it. She loved *him*, God help her. She would never have thought it would work, dating a Marine. Dating *this* Marine.

Part of the challenge was his post-traumatic stress, the claustrophobia, the restlessness. Sometimes he got so wound up, he was practically climbing out of his own skin. And she couldn't do anything about it except hold him when he hurt, and encourage him to do the things that helped. Exercise, meditation. Find meaningful work. And, yes, maybe chase an armed man into a crowded public market at risk to his own life, because that was part of what he needed to make himself whole. Even if it drove her nuts.

Because the truth was that she could handle his particular flavor of high-energy crazy. In fact, that passion, that intensity, was part of the appeal. Nobody was perfect, right? Lord knows, June had her own crazy to deal with, the emotional fallout of her strange, fucked-up childhood.

No, the real problem was that she was having trouble imagining their life ten years from now, or twenty. Peter was a fugitive from justice. The feds had a warrant for his arrest. What kind of future could they build together?

Plus it was hard to have this conversation with him because June didn't even know what life she wanted. Was it a husband and three kids, a house in the suburbs, and a pot roast in the oven? Some days, that's exactly what she wanted. Or maybe she just *thought* she wanted it, because everyone *else* seemed to want it.

Other days, all she wanted was to be in hot pursuit of the next big story, living her life on fast-forward with no obligations, not even a potted plant. Ready to hop on a plane at a moment's notice. Christ, maybe she wanted somebody *else* to stay home, cook dinner for *her.*

Which was funny, because Peter often did exactly that. In his underwear, usually, after showering off the day's plaster grit and sawdust. But that wasn't a negative, not when you looked the way he did, threadbare boxers falling off his lean hips, a smirk on his face, a spatula in one big hand, a beer in the other. Jesus, just the thought of it made her all shivery.

But that's not how things were all the time.

Sometimes, when he got restless, when he needed to be useful in the way only he could be useful, he stepped into someone else's problems. Then he got chased and beaten and shot at. The last time, he'd almost died. And he hadn't even told her where he was. She'd found out when she saw his face on the news. She could have killed him herself. And now they were living with the consequences.

Since then, she'd been wondering if Peter would always need that rush of action, that feeling of risk.

More and more lately, she was thinking the answer was yes.

June guessed what she was asking herself was, could she live with that?

Or was it time to get practical? Find herself a Dean? Find herself a future.

Thankfully, her phone rang before she came up with an answer.

It was Christina Willis, the Houston police detective, and she didn't waste any time. "Lady, what the heck are you into? According to the Texas DMV, that VIN number you sent is for a vehicle that was listed as totaled after Hurricane Harvey and sent to the crusher. The license plate, on the other hand, is for a totally different vehicle, up on blocks out back of a Fort Worth landscaping company, waiting for an engine. And get this—the plate's still on it. The owner sent me a picture."

"Wait," June said. "We have duplicate plates from a vehicle that doesn't run, on another vehicle that's not supposed to exist?"

"Yeah," Christina said. "So let me repeat myself. What are you into?"

17

PETER

Lewis drove the Yukon down Kinnickinnic Avenue in Bay View, dodging potholes while raindrops flecked the windshield.

Bay View was a rapidly gentrifying south side neighborhood tucked between Lake Michigan and the freeway, a maze of narrow streets crowded with old houses and corner bars. Kinnickinnic—known to locals as KK—was the heart of it, a hip strip of gastropubs and tattoo parlors and gleaming new condo blocks sprouting up between old-school funeral parlors and tire shops. Peter and June came for the tortilla soup at Riviera Maya and the pork fries at Honey Pie.

They found the South Side MakerSpace behind the library in a windowless redbrick rectangle that took up most of a city block. An enormous transformer with faded gray paint, mounted on a dedicated pole in the parking lot, indicated a previous power-hungry incarnation, maybe as a machine shop or early data storage facility. But Peter couldn't see anything to indicate its current use, which was, according to the website, a nonprofit self-organizing communal workshop offering space and tools to anyone for a modest monthly membership fee.

"Drive the perimeter," Peter said. "Let's see the rest of it."

The Yukon's big engine rumbled as Lewis feathered the gas. "Any idea what we looking for?"

"Hell if I know," Peter said. "Let's hope we know it when we see it."

Two sides of the building came right to the narrow sidewalk. A third side ran along the alley with a row of angled parking and a wide roll-up door for freight deliveries. The fourth side backed up against an ancient apartment building's cobblestone service drive lined with garbage cans. Along the rooftop at the rear, a small array of solar panels soaked up the sun.

There was no homemade electric getaway bike chained to a rack. No convenient sign reading RUSSIAN ASSAULT RIFLES SERVICED HERE or ARMED ROBBERS USE REAR DOOR.

The main entrance was a plain steel slab with a hand-painted address, an electronic fob reader that would control the lock, and a cheap security camera looking down from above. A repurposed industrial switch was labeled DOORBELL with a black permanent marker.

Peter hit the button. After a minute, a young guy opened the door. He wore a Notre Dame jersey and a smile. "Can I help you folks?"

Peter returned the smile. "We're interested in memberships, maybe taking a class or two. Any chance we can take a look around?"

"If you're not members, you need someone to walk with you. But I'm not busy right now." He was maybe twenty, a good-looking kid raised on milk and butter. He stuck out his hand. "I'm Mac. Welcome to the MakerSpace."

Peter and Lewis followed Mac into a large common area cluttered with industrial shelves and secondhand furniture and a long table made of plywood sheets laid across sawhorses, exactly the kind of claustrophobic windowless space that would have made the static flare wildly just a year ago. At the back was a line of kitchen cabinets with a sink and a microwave and a pair of vintage refrigerators, one labeled ALCOHOL, the other NON-ALCOHOL.

"This is where we have community meetings on Tuesday nights," said Mac. "It's also our hacker space and computer shop."

A middle-aged woman in a plaid flannel shirt with headphones and many facial piercings leaned back on a folding chair with her Doc Martens up on the table, typing furiously on her laptop. An older guy with an unconvincing comb-over hunched over a circuit board with a soldering iron, thin smoke rising. Four more people sat at the far end, deep in conversation, a bin of used computer components spilled out on the table.

Peter had spent plenty of time in junkyards, salvaging truck parts. It never occurred to him that people might build their own electronics from scrap, too. "Can we see the rest of it?"

Mac walked them through a messy crafts area with piles of raw fabric, sewing machines, and pictures of smiling people in elaborate Princess Leia and Gandalf costumes. Next came a cluttered metal shop, then a well-equipped woodworking area. The smells of machine oil and sawdust reminded Peter of his dad's barn in northern Wisconsin.

The equipment was a mix of industrial-grade and custom-built. "A lot of it was donated by people who closed their businesses but didn't have a place to put their stuff," Mac said. "This way they can still use it anytime, but now other people can, too. Plus the community will maintain and repair it for them."

They passed a row of laser-cutters, then a line of 3-D printers, half of which looked homemade, and into an enormous room filled with industrial shelves. They were divided into four-foot sections, each labeled with a member's name and piled high with everything from a vintage motorcycle chassis to ancient computer carcasses to giant dismembered stuffed animals.

"I read about your bike-building class," Peter said. "Do you know anyone who's done it?"

"Oh, gosh, that's very popular," Mac said. "Kiko, the instructor, is really great. But you have to be trained on the tools first. You should get started soon if you want to be ready. I can connect you to the metal shop champion if you like." The champion, he explained, was the volunteer in charge of a given area.

"Actually," Peter said, "what I'm really interested in is building an electric bike. Do you have anyone here who's done that?"

"I don't know, but Spark might. She's our electrical champion. Actually, she's more our champion-at-large. She built half those 3-D printers."

"From scratch?"

"Sure. I've built one myself, although I bought a kit. The software is open-source."

Peter said, "Where'd you learn this stuff?"

Mac laughed. "I don't know anything," he said. "But I'm a pretty good sponge, and the people here are usually willing to help." he said. "Larry back there, he designed circuit boards for IBM. Suzanne, on the laptop, is an engineer at an electric car startup in Detroit. And Spark, well. Spark's the coolest."

Mac's face flushed a little when he mentioned her. Spark was definitely the coolest.

"Those are her solar panels on the roof. I talked her into entering our electrics race last year. She used recycled Prius batteries for her power source, totally green. It wasn't her fault they caught on fire at the finish line."

Peter looked at Lewis. "Sounds like Spark would be good to talk to. Is she here now?"

"Actually, I haven't seen her for a while. She's not very social." Mac gave them a shy grin. "But maybe she's in her project space?"

He walked them through a set of double doors in a raw cinder-block wall. "The MakerSpace is set up as a place to make stuff for yourself, not to run a business. But there was such a demand for private shops that we built out some spaces to rent. The waiting list has so many people that we're actually buying another building."

Peter said, "What kinds of stuff do you do, Mac?"

"I'm just here for the weirdos." He grinned. "I study sociology at Marquette. These communal groups are fascinating."

They walked down a bright, branching hallway wide enough to accommodate the small electric forklift charging in a corner. Painted plywood partitions formed workrooms of varying sizes, many of them in use. Peter saw a sweating glassblower at her forge and a man bent over a potter's wheel with a row of kilns along the back wall.

"What does Spark do in her space?" Peter asked.

"You'd better ask her yourself," Mac said. "She's pretty private, so she probably won't tell you. She lives with her boyfriend but nobody's ever met him."

At the end of the hall was an open door. Inside was a futon couch with a sweatshirt balled up for a pillow, board-and-block shelves stacked with spine-cracked textbooks and reference manuals, and a young woman at a thrift store desk. Her legs folded on the chair beneath her, fingers poised on a laptop.

Her hair was jet-black and cropped short, her skin the color of burnished copper. Her intent eyes, high cheekbones, and prominent nose reminded Peter of an Aztec statue. She stared at two big mismatched monitors, one showing the multicolored text of raw computer code, the other with detailed line drawings.

"Spark?" Mac knocked on the jamb.

Her hands fluttered off the keyboard like startled birds. "Mac," she said. "What's up?"

Then she looked past him and saw the two big men filling the hallway behind him. Her unblinking eyes studied their faces for a moment, then flicked to something on her side of the partition wall.

Then she reached out and slapped the laptop shut.

The monitors went black. She unfolded from her chair and moved to close the door. She wore baggy black cargo pants and a long-sleeved MIT shirt with the sleeves pushed up her forearms.

"Actually," she said, "now's not a good time."

Peter stuck his head through the doorway. On the other side of the wall stood a coat rack made of scrap metal with a red jacket draped across the top.

He saw the Cardinals logo, two birds on a baseball bat.

Brown flecks of what could only be smashed apple were crusted onto a spot high on the chest.

18

Peter stepped past Mac into the doorway.

"Spark, I'm Peter," he said. "We need to talk."

"Get out," she said. "I'm not talking to you. I'm working."

She tried to push the door shut but he blocked it with his boot. Fear flickered on her face like a signal getting clearer.

"Spark." She pushed harder, and Peter had to grab the door to stay put. She was strong and knew how to use her body.

For a moment he wondered if she had somehow been the shooter, but he remembered the guy being thicker through the torso. Besides, Peter couldn't exactly see her growing that thick beard.

"Spark, who are you afraid of?"

Her voice rose. "Right now, dickhead, I'm afraid of you."

"Why don't you call 911?" Peter asked. "We can straighten all this out."

She didn't answer. He could see the outline of her phone in her front pocket, but he knew she wouldn't reach for it.

He set his feet and moved her back, shoes squeaking on the cement floor, until she abruptly released her hold and retreated into the center of the room, fast and fluid on her feet. Inside now, Peter noticed another doorway on the far side of the futon couch, either a storage closet or a second room. The static didn't like not knowing what was behind that door, but Peter couldn't get there without letting Spark get behind him. The static didn't like that, either.

"Have a seat," he said, pointing at the couch.

"Dude, I'm not doing shit," she said. "I don't know who you are or what you want, but I want you to leave. Right fucking now."

Mac moved in and put a hand on Peter's shoulder from behind. "Leave her alone, man. It's time for you to go."

Peter heard a thump and the smack of skin and Mac suddenly was squashed face-first against the wall, Lewis's hand on the back of his neck and one arm twisted up in a wrist lock. Lewis looked at Peter with his eyebrows raised in a question.

"It's okay. Let him go." Peter turned back to Spark. "We don't want to hurt you. Is it your boyfriend you're afraid of? Someone else? Whoever it is, we can help. We can protect you."

She looked at him, her fear gone into hiding but her contempt like something physical in the room. "I don't need your *protection*. I need you to get the hell out of my office."

"Ma'am, we're not going anywhere until you talk to us."

She closed her eyes a moment, then blew out her breath. "Fine. Let me get my things and we'll go sit in the common area." She scooped up her laptop, wrapped it in the sweatshirt from the couch, and shoved it into a plain black backpack. She pointed at the second door. "My skateboard's in there." And before he could move, she opened the door, slipped through, and slammed it shut. He heard the thunk of the deadbolt as she locked it from the other side.

"Dammit." Peter looked at Mac, who was rubbing his arm in the corner. "What's in there?"

"Her workshop," Mac said.

Peter tried the door. It was thick and solid.

"Is there another way in or out?"

Lewis had already ducked into the hallway to look. "Next door is a roll-up with a padlock on it. She's not getting out that way."

Peter turned to Mac. "Any weapons in there?"

"Why would Spark need a weapon? Anyway, our bylaws expressly prohibit guns."

Lewis walked to the desk. "Peter." On the far corner stood a U-shaped rectangle of steel maybe ten inches long, open at both ends and the bottom, with crisp bends and precise holes, bright with the rainbow sheen of heat treatment. "Pretty sure that's a receiver for an AK."

On the other side of the door, they heard a grunt and a clatter, then a complicated clank as something big hit the floor. The next sound might be the rattle of an assault rifle. Thin plywood wouldn't begin to stop the high-velocity rounds.

Moving fast, Peter yanked open the desk drawers, but found no keys or tools that might help him get through the deadbolt. He turned to the bookshelves and pulled a cinder block from one end. The plank dropped an inch to the stack of chemistry texts below, but nothing fell. Peter hooked his fingers through one end of the heavy block and swung it hard against the door, right at the lock.

The wood flexed but didn't give. What he needed was a sledgehammer or a shotgun with a breaching load. He didn't have either one.

He wound up and swung again, harder. This time the wood cracked and the lock punched partway through, but the bolt was bound up and the door still wouldn't move.

He swung a third time and hit squarely. The jamb broke and the metal fell away and the door lurched open.

The workshop was three times the size of the office, its walls lined with workbenches and scientific equipment Peter didn't recognize.

Spark was nowhere in sight.

The back wall had a cylindrical tank marked HYDROGEN, with shining pipes run to fittings above a long stainless table. The big fume hood that had obviously been mounted above the table now lay on the floor, still rocking from the drop.

On the wall where the exhaust duct had been, a sixteen-inch hole shone bright with daylight.

"Shit." Peter jumped to the table to follow her through the opening, but his shoulders were too wide to fit. He stuck one arm and his head through the ragged hole, trying to get far enough to see. Outside was the ancient apartment building and its cobblestone service drive lined with garbage cans.

But no sign of Spark.

The woman had vanished.

By the time Peter extricated himself from the hole and jumped down from the table, Lewis had pulled Mac into the workshop and pushed him against the locked roll-up door. They both eyeballed the machines lining the walls.

"Jarhead, you know what any of this shit does?"

"Are you kidding?" It was too bad June's father had died, Peter thought. His lab was full of weird equipment. He would have been a big help. "Talk to us, Mac. What's she working on in here?"

"I don't know," the younger man said. "She doesn't talk about it." He pulled out his phone. "I'm calling the police."

Lewis slapped the phone from his hand. "Stand down, boy. Your friend Spark didn't call the police, remember? Means she's in trouble. Believe it or not, we trying to help."

Peter picked up Mac's phone, which was still awake. The kid hadn't managed to press send. Peter found the contacts and scrolled through. Nobody named Spark. "Do you know her real name, or where she lives? Her phone number? The MakerSpace must have her in their records."

Mac shook his head. "I manage the automated billing system. Because she pays cash, I have to log in to her account every month. We have her name as Spark and an email address, nothing else."

Peter's jaw felt tight. "How about the boyfriend? What's his name?"

Mac shook his head. "They live together, that's all I know. Nobody's ever met him. Whenever I ask about him, she changes the subject. I told you, she's a private person."

Peter looked around the space, hoping to make sense of some larger picture. His eye caught on a big toaster oven, which looked out of place.

The inside was carbon-black. The appliance's control panel had been pulled out and wired to a homemade control board. Below it was a plastic bin full of green circuit board stock, and another filled with boxes of tiny parts. Spark wasn't making toast, she was making her own electronics.

Peter was way out of his league. "What the hell was she doing in here?"

Then he realized what sat on top of the toaster. An intricate metal sculpture of a man in a wheelchair with a welder's mask covering his face. Hammer in one hand, cutting torch in the other.

"Lewis." Peter held up the little figure. "See anyone you recognize?"

They left Mac behind, found an emergency exit, and jogged toward the Yukon. As Lewis fired up the engine, Peter's phone rang. It was his neighbor.

"Fran, I'm in the middle of something," he said. "Can I call you back later? Wait, what?"

19

SPARK

Spark sprinted around the corner, skateboard tight in one hand, backpack thumping her spine with every step.

Honey Pie was half a block away. If she could make it across KK and into the restaurant without getting caught, she'd be fine. She'd fly out the back door and hop on her electric longboard and disappear into Bay View's tangled network of angled alleys and wayward streets.

She was born Maria Evangelina Velasquez and grew up on 30th and Pierce, a neighborhood called Silver City, just uphill from the Falk casting plant. When the wind came from the north, it carried the rich tang of molten metal. It was the smell of her childhood, along with the pungent spices of her mom's tortilla soup and the smoke on her dad's turnout gear.

And also the musty smell of their basement, which became her first workshop when she was eight years old and her mom's blender stopped working.

The blender was a birthday present from her dad. Her mom

loved making frozen margaritas for her church friends. It was less than a year old, and it kept blowing fuses. Her dad was a firefighter and her mom stayed home, so they weren't poor, but even Maria Evangelina knew they kept track of every penny. Her dad had said, A better blender is sixty bucks and money don't grow on trees, Lupita. I'll buy you another one next year.

Maria Evangelina already knew how to do more than change a blown fuse. As far as she was concerned, a perfect Saturday was a morning trip to the Re-Store with her dad, followed by lunch at a taco truck and a blissful afternoon as his helper, learning Spanish swear words and handing him tools while he explained the process of changing out an old light fixture or tub faucet. He often told her that he hadn't gone to school to be an electrician or plumber, that he just figured things out on the fly.

So it was no big deal for her, one rainy Saturday afternoon, to haul the broken blender down to her dad's tool bench and take that sucker apart.

In retrospect, she wasn't sure she actually thought she might fix it. But she definitely wanted to know what made it work. Besides, Maria Evangelina liked a virgin margarita as much as the next girl, maybe more.

With the blender's plastic case off, the guts were laid bare on the bench, machine mysteries exposed for all to see. When she plugged it in and turned it on, the fuse popped again. But in the buzzing metal box, just for a moment, she'd seen a bright light. Something was happening in there.

So she took the box apart, too.

In the end, she found a frayed wire arcing against the motor case, the burned smell and blackened spot telling her where to look. So she went to her dad's boxes of leftover parts, found a new power cord, and swapped them out.

And when she put it all back together, it actually worked.

Her mom had danced around the kitchen and smothered her with kisses, then invited the church ladies over for margaritas. Her dad had looked at her closely, a little smile on his face, and asked how she'd known what to do with the blender. She'd just shrugged and said she figured it out on the fly, just like him.

Of course, when her mom's friends heard about the Miracle of the Blender, they had their own broken things to fix. Mrs. Dubinski brought her toaster oven. Mrs. Gonsalves brought her coffee-maker. And with the help of the Internet, Maria Evangelina fixed them.

That's when the neighborhood heard about her knack, and the floodgates opened. Window fans and vacuum cleaners, even old VCRs and desktop computers. Anything too cheap for a repair shop but too expensive for working people to buy new. She never asked for money, but people would give her a little something. Not much, but it added up.

She couldn't fix everything, not by a long shot, but people let her keep the dead machines, and she'd harvest the parts for next time.

Usually the problem was a bad switch or power cord, a frozen motor or hard drive, dumb stuff like that. People looked at her like she was a genius, but Maria Evangelina didn't see it that way. She just wanted to know how things worked. She collected tools and technical manuals like other girls collected Barbies.

It didn't take long for her dad and Mr. Tomczak, his friend from the firehouse, to come help clean out the basement. When they were done, there was a carpet remnant on the floor and a scruffy old couch and a bigger workbench and better lights overhead.

By the time she was nine, she'd skipped a grade and was

repairing washing machines and dishwashers. At ten, she'd skipped two more grades and graduated to furnaces and laptops. Anything mechanical or electrical. She learned fast.

Maria, Queen of Sparks, her dad called her.

Which was sweet of him, but even at ten, Maria Evangelina was not the kind of girl who wanted to be a princess, waiting for some dumb prince to show up. In her mind, being a queen was no better. The queen had to do what the king wanted, right? Plus, Maria Evangelina was pretty sure the queen didn't get to spend the afternoon in the basement with grease on her hands, bringing some broken little machine back to life.

But Spark?

She told her dad that Spark suited her just fine.

So he called her Little Spark, or sometimes *La Chispa*, or even Esparquita in that goofy Spanglish he liked.

When she was twelve, a burning roof collapsed on Mr. Tomczak and broke his back. Her dad was the one who pulled him out of the building. When they went to visit him in the hospital, Kiko told her dad he'd never walk again and it was just fine, because he really loved these painkillers.

As they left, her dad said, Life is short, Esparquita. It could be me in there. He started fixing other people's houses on his days off, working toward a time when he didn't have to risk his life at work.

Maria Evangelina felt like life was short, too, at least it was too short to spend your days at school, three years younger than everyone else and still bored to death. The other girls made fun of her, and the boys wouldn't even talk to her. Everyone thought she was a freak, just because she was smart.

So she stopped going. She told her mom she could stay home for the next three years and not miss a thing. Her dad came down to the basement and said, "Look, *chispa mia*, education is important. You have to go to school." So she arranged to take the GED and got a passing grade and that was the end of *that* conversation.

It was also the real beginning of her life. Aside from the judo classes her dad made her take, which she resisted but ended up loving for their own kind of mechanical beauty, she spent the rest of her time in the basement, fixing stuff. She usually fell asleep on the old couch by her workbench. When her eyes opened, she immediately went back to helping damaged little machines do their jobs again.

When she ran out of things to repair, she pored through the abandoned calculus and engineering textbooks her mom found at her new job cleaning classrooms at MSOE. By the time she turned fourteen, she was taking college courses online. Organic chem was a revelation, protons and neutrons and electrons, the building blocks of the universe explained. She felt like her brain was having its own Big Bang. Chemistry led to physics, which led to electrical and mechanical engineering. Sometimes she'd look up from a book and see her parents standing on the basement stairs, just watching her read. It was a little creepy, and also a little sweet.

She didn't have a standard path to college, so in the early years, she had to talk her way into most of the classes. University administrators couldn't quite believe she was ready for the material, but when she reached out to the professors, offering to take any test they proposed, she found the bright ones easy enough to persuade, especially the women. When she explained her circumstances, they even found her money for tuition. She rarely told any of them how old she was.

At sixteen, as she moved into graduate-level courses, she found she had some fundamental questions that her textbooks didn't answer. This was the beginning of her email correspondence that eventually expanded to include faculty at Madison, MIT, Caltech, and Carnegie-Mellon. She was surprised to find that professors didn't have answers, either, but they sure loved her questions. For some reason, they all wanted her to come study with them, but Maria Evangelina didn't want to leave her parents.

Besides, she didn't see the point. She had everything she needed in Silver City. She'd even started a little computer repair business to pay for her textbooks and the materials for her own strange little experiments. Exploring an idea that had gotten stuck in her head.

It was an irritant, like a grain of sand in her shoe that she couldn't get rid of. Her mind kept returning to it in those odd empty moments. On the bus to the dojo, cleaning the house, falling asleep. At first, just examining it from every possible angle. Then adding to it, building on it. Until the grain of sand had become a castle, or maybe a pearl.

New improvements on an old idea. A new kind of battery.

Solar and wind power generation was now cheaper than fossil fuel plants, with far fewer downstream problems like pollution, atmospheric carbon, and war. But the sun didn't shine 24/7, so electrical storage was important.

The modern rechargeable lithium-ion battery wasn't a bad technology, exactly. It had many more recharge cycles than previous versions, much greater energy density than the old NiCd and NiMH versions. But it wasn't a *good* technology, either.

Lithium was a big part of the problem. It was a relatively rare mineral, and, like oil and gas, much of it was found in dangerous places with corrupt governments.

Carbon, on the other hand, was everywhere. Pure carbon could even be mined out of thin air with existing technology. A carbon-ion battery would be cheap and nontoxic, and could be manufactured anywhere in the world with local materials. And carbon molecules had truly magnificent electrical storage properties, if arranged properly, at least in theory. The real challenge was to get the molecules to do what you wanted. To make the idea into something that actually worked.

Of course, this carbon thing was a well-known problem that many extremely smart people had been working on for decades, both at research universities and in corporate labs. Who was Maria Evangelina to think she'd find answers where others had not? She didn't have a world-class facility or decades of research experience. She was just a girl in her mom's basement.

But. She had this *idea*.

She could always hear her dad's voice in her head. Ay, you can figure anything out, Esparquita. All you got to do is put your mind to it.

That was before her life fell apart.

Before she met *him*.

Now, on the far side of KK, she hauled open Honey Pie's door and slowed to a brisk walk. She zipped past the waitresses and didn't even glance at the beautiful cupcakes in their glass case. She just went straight to the back door and across the patio to the alley, where she hopped on her longboard and rolled away.

What did those two jokers at the MakerSpace know about her, anyway?

Not a goddamn thing.

20

June stood at her desk and tucked her things into her backpack for the ride home.

She realized that Dean Zedler must have been watching from across the newsroom, because while she was still wrapping her laptop cord, he came down the central aisle with that beautiful cashmere jacket over his shoulder and his handsome leather bag hanging from one hand.

"Hey, I think I found someone down by the market who'll share their security camera footage. Want to come? I could use your help."

June considered the idea that she might somehow stop him from finding better photos of Peter and Lewis, but knew Dean would spot the attempt a mile away. Better to let Peter know what was coming. "Sorry, Dean, I'm headed home, still more work to do."

"At least let me give you a ride. It's raining pretty steadily out there. Riverwest, right? It's practically on the way."

Riverwest was the opposite direction from the Public Market. June smiled and pulled on her waterproof coat. "Thanks, but I don't mind the weather. It helps me think."

Outside, she slung her backpack across both shoulders, then unlocked her bike from the rack and put on her helmet. She knew that Dean driving her home was a can of worms better left closed.

Because accepting the ride would be opening the door to something more. When he stopped outside her house, he'd be hoping she'd invite him in. But she couldn't, of course, because he'd see that she didn't live alone. What if Peter's truck was in the driveway?

And even if she just said thanks and got out of the car, his reporter's radar would start to ping. No matter what excuses she made, he'd know she was hiding something. Because that was the job, to see through the bullshit. And he'd be right. She *was* hiding something.

She was hiding Peter.

Then Dean's curiosity would kick in, and the questions would begin. Subtle at first, then more direct.

She couldn't exactly blame him. June was the same way.

The truly fucked-up thing was that part of her almost *wanted* Dean to ask questions. Her life was so strange, living with a man on the FBI's Most Wanted list, and she had almost nobody to talk to about it, certainly nobody objective.

Dean would be thoughtful and patient and kind. He'd tease out each little thread to see where it might lead. Through that process, she'd begin to make new connections herself. She'd think about her life in a whole new way.

She was more than a little afraid of where that might take her.

———

She turned onto the bike path and the switchbacks that led up the tall hill above Commerce Street. As she stood on the pedals and pumped her legs hard, she thought about the reason she actually should have accepted Dean's offer.

It wasn't the rain, which fell soft and fine and familiar as the mist from the waterfall behind her farmhouse back in Washington state. Nor was it the scrapes and aches that came from riding into a truck door and hitting the pavement just a few hours earlier. It definitely wasn't the steep uphill climb and the sweat gathering between her shoulder blades. The exercise was the necessary antidote both to her injuries and her long day of hunting through dense databases, searching for Vince Holloway.

No. The problem was Edgar, AKA Mr. Cheerful, and his impossible ghost van, still out there somewhere. Waiting.

She didn't want to think about why she hadn't called Peter for a ride. Why she still hadn't told him about the attack just a few hours ago.

It was because she'd asked Peter to stand down after the market shooting. If she told him about Edgar, he'd go ballistic. He'd get very protective, and he'd start digging into things, and there was a strong possibility that he'd end up having a conversation with the police. There was no way that would end well.

Plus, June would have to admit that she'd been looking into Mr. Cheerful herself, not to mention the victim from the market.

She hadn't promised *not* to, not exactly. She was a reporter, doing her job. More than a job, journalism was necessary for America to function, which is why a free press was guaranteed in the Constitution. And it was her calling, right?

She sighed. No, she told herself. Face the truth. Not only are you shallow, you're a goddamn hypocrite.

Which was why she was riding home, alone, hoping the exercise would help her figure out how to tell Peter she'd lied to him.

Good thing she had six or seven different ways to get there, including one long looping detour across the river, which would add a few miles and let her approach from the opposite direction as the paper.

By the time she crossed the bridge back into Riverwest at Capitol Drive, the rain had stopped. The last of the sun gleamed through the clouds as she bounced, derailleur rattling, down the chunky limestone steps to the muddy trail that ran along the river's edge. No cars could follow here. The far side of the ravine was still bright with daylight, but the west side where she rode was in deepening shadow.

Breathing hard, she cranked along the narrow, rutted track, hopping rocks and roots and sliding through slop until she came to the stretch below the house she shared with Peter. Eighty feet above, their cantilevered deck projected out from the top of the slope, surrounded by trees. A quarter-mile ahead would be the steep, slender hiking path up to the street. There were no markers and she'd missed it several times before, so she kept her eyes ahead, looking for the turn.

Which is why she didn't see the dark figure standing partway up the hillside, half-hidden in the tangled brush.

21

At the hiking path, June tightened up her backpack, put the bike's crossbar on her shoulder, and jogged up the slick dirt track to her street, her legs feeling the workout. She was no closer to figuring out the conversation with Peter than when she started the ride.

It didn't matter. Except for his trip to Iceland, they'd always told each other the truth, even when it hurt. She wasn't going to start lying to him now. Not for more than a few hours, anyway.

Because of her parents' disastrous marriage, June hadn't exactly had good role models. Before Peter, she'd either dated jerks or fun guys who were too dumb for her, or had no ambition, or were total stoners, which turned out to be shorthand for the previous two problems.

Peter was certainly smart and he had plenty of drive. You didn't become a Recon Marine officer without both of those qualities. Plus he was sexy as hell, could get her motor running just by looking at her a certain way.

She really hoped that his renovation project with Lewis would work out.

But she couldn't stop herself from wondering whether Peter really could make the transition back to civilian life. If he could keep himself from stepping into other people's problems the way he'd done so many times since he'd come home from war. If he wasn't just addicted to the rush and the violence, cloaked in the disguise of being helpful.

Or was June just being selfish? She'd needed serious help when they'd met, and he'd delivered. He'd helped others since then. Who was she to deny him, and the world, that work?

The question was, could she live with him while he did it?

She emerged from the ravine at an untended right-of-way at the corner, just a block from home. The horizon was red. She hung back in the shadows for a moment, looking ahead two blocks toward busy Humboldt Boulevard and to the right down her own short street, watching for the ghost van or its cheerful, homicidal driver. She saw nothing suspicious. The giant elm in the front yard shone like a fading yellow flame in the evening light.

She climbed on her bike and began to ride.

Almost immediately, she heard a big engine roar. She glanced over her shoulder and didn't see anything. She pedaled faster.

The engine changed, much louder now, with a familiar throaty, uneven rattle.

She knew without looking that the ghost van had rounded the corner behind her.

She stood on the pedals, pumping hard, thinking only of getting inside the house. Her keys were in the top of her pack. She had that softball bat in the kitchen. Oh, she'd teach that asshole a *good* lesson.

She wanted to swerve onto the sidewalk, but now there were no parked cars to shield her. Lewis and Dinah's place was closer, but their driveway was empty, no way to know if anyone was home. Peter's junky Toyota was nowhere in sight. The house, get to the house.

The engine roared closer. Her thighs burned, pushing her forward. Almost there, she hopped the curb and bounced across the parking strip. A tall figure stepped out from behind the big elm.

Peter. His long arm caught her across the chest and his other hand grabbed her belt. He scooped her off the speeding bike and swung her behind the elm's trunk, where he pulled her tight inside the rough shelter of his body.

The world filled with an enormous rending crash. The ground shook. Chrome and glass flew into the air and the ghost van bounced past the tree and came to a stop at an angle to the curb. Engine dead, smoke rising, most of the front end smashed in like crumpled paper. The air stank of leaking chemicals.

Peter stood her up and held her at arm's length. "Are you okay?"

She nodded numbly. Her hands were shaking. Her whole body was shaking.

"Get inside the house," he said. "Go now. Lock the door behind you. Call the police."

She heard a long creak and turned to see the van's door open. Edgar climbed out from behind the wheel, a thin stream of blood trickling down his forehead. He swiped a forearm across his eyes, which just smeared a red film across his face. He still wore the same cheerful smile and white dress shirt tented over his belly, the mirrored sunglasses still folded into the open neck of his shirt.

When he saw June, he reached back into the van and pulled out an axe. Full-sized, for chopping down trees.

"Hey." She heard Lewis's voice, sharp enough to cut, then a metallic *snick-snack*. She backed toward the house and saw him on the far side of the van, standing in the street with a shotgun raised to his shoulder. "Drop it, motherfucker. Or better yet, don't."

Mr. Cheerful stared at Lewis, then turned back to Peter, who blocked his path to June. "Hi, my name is Edgar." He smiled wider and took a step away from the van. Not a retreat, just giving himself room. "What are your names?"

Peter had picked up a wicked-looking crowbar from the grass, and held it like a heavy hooked extension of his hand. He also had a pistol tucked into the back of his pants. "Drop the axe."

"I don't think so," Mr. Cheerful said. A fresh ooze of blood seeped from the wound at his hairline. He spread his arms wide, holding the axe in one hand as if it weighed nothing. It had a double-bladed head and a dirty yellow plastic handle.

"I'm loaded with double-ought," Lewis said. "Turn you into hamburger. Drop that damn axe."

Edgar looked from Peter back to Lewis, his broad grin a strange white slash in his blood-washed face. He took the black mirrored sunglasses from the neck of his shirt and put them on. "Well, come on, boys. If you're gonna do me, then do me. I guess it's just my time."

He took another step away from the van. Then another. He looked from Lewis back to Peter.

"Really? You're not gonna do anything? I'm disappointed."

And he turned and ran up the street, still carrying the axe.

Peter dropped the crowbar, pulled the pistol from his belt, and raised it into a firing stance, all so quickly it was almost a blur. But he didn't pull the trigger.

"Do it." Lewis's voice was low. "Or we gonna see him again for sure."

"I'm not going to shoot him in the back," Peter said. "And if he's dead, we're not going to learn anything." He picked up the crowbar and started after Edgar.

"June, honey," he called over his shoulder, "I'll be right back."

"Peter," she shouted. "Goddamn it. Peter!"

Lewis lowered the shotgun, and looked at June. "Don't worry," he said. "I got your boy." Then tipped forward into a run, following Peter.

"God*damn* it." June turned away so she didn't have to watch them go.

Standing behind the van, she surveyed the wreck and wondered what was missing.

Then she realized there were no skid marks on the pavement.

Edgar had never hit the brakes.

The crazy fuck hadn't even tried to slow down.

22

PETER

Crowbar in one hand and pistol in the other, Peter ran after the lunatic with the axe. Over the sound of his own breath, he heard the crunch of Lewis's boots on the asphalt, closing up behind him. He never doubted his friend would have his back.

The man with the axe, whose name apparently was Edgar, glanced over his shoulder, then faced forward and accelerated as if he hadn't just smashed his van into a tree at high speed. He was far faster than any fat man had a right to be.

Lewis pulled even with Peter, shotgun held at midpoint with one hand, and together they stepped on the gas.

Peter said, "You couldn't have grabbed a target pistol instead of that monster?"

"How'm I s'posed to know the dude's gonna be this crazy?"

A small-caliber round in the thigh would have worked nicely to stop Edgar, or at least slow him down. The cut-down 10-gauge's wide spray of double-ought would have broken half the windows on the block and injured or killed any number of neighbors, which was why Lewis hadn't pulled the trigger. Peter's vintage loaner Colt was not exactly a precision weapon, either. With a moving target past fifty feet, a leg shot would take more luck than skill.

He was glad that Franny had called. From her post at her front window, she'd seen the same white van drive up and down the street three times. When it returned a fourth time, a man in a white dress shirt had gotten on a stepladder to attach something to the light posts at each end of the block. Franny was worried because it was a passenger van, not a work van. Also, there was no city seal on the door, and the windows were mirrored. She confessed that she hadn't paid a nickel in taxes in the last eighty years and was afraid the government might be spying on her.

Peter and Lewis had been pretty sure Fran was not the target.

When they returned to Riverwest and cruised the block themselves, they'd seen the tiny cameras strapped high on the light posts. Who was this new player? The initial concern was that law enforcement was coming after Peter, but Franny's description made this guy seem more like a freelancer. The cops or feds would have a realistic city truck and a guy in a safety vest and hard hat. Had their burglar returned?

Next, they'd driven the neighborhood, looking for the van Franny had described, but found nothing. Double the search radius and the range expanded fourfold. With web-enabled cameras, he could be watching from anywhere. So they'd parked the Yukon a few blocks away and slipped sideways along the ravine to come up behind Peter's back deck. And waited.

Ahead of them, the fat man was really moving. Peter kicked into a higher gear and felt Lewis do the same beside him, but they weren't gaining fast enough. When Edgar rounded the corner, heading back toward Humboldt, they were still three houses back.

Twenty seconds later, they came to the intersection, leaning into the turn.

The fat man and his axe were nowhere in sight.

The daylight was almost gone. They sprinted the short block to the next intersection, but he wasn't visible at either side of the cross street. Ahead, it was another short block to Humboldt, but there was no way he'd gotten that far without their seeing him.

"Check the backyards," Peter said. But Lewis had already peeled right, headed for the nearest driveway. The left side was all high fences and thick thorny hedges, no easy way in. Peter hung in the shadows at the corner, figuring Lewis would flush Edgar or he'd get impatient with his cover and break for the street. To do this right you needed a helicopter and a dozen cops with cars and radios, not two dipshits who had somehow lost a fat man in a single city block.

What if Edgar had doubled back? Peter ran to the last intersection and looked down toward the wrecked van. June was standing in the open driver's door, peering inside. He knew she wasn't okay, not after almost getting run down, but she wasn't a puddle on the ground, she was back at work. He admired the hell out of her.

Lewis came up the farthest driveway, shotgun held low along his leg. His face was grim. "Nothing, not even a broken window. Like he went up in smoke."

Peter shook his head. "We're fucking useless. First Spark, now Edgar."

"You want to knock on some doors?"

Peter let out some air, then shook his head. "Would you open the door to a black man with a sawed-off?"

"Why's it always got to be the black man who scares the

civilians," Lewis said. "Why can't it be the sweaty white dude with the crowbar and the pistol in his pants?"

"Shit," Peter said. "I wouldn't open the door to me, either."

Any sane person would just call the cops, he thought. If they hadn't already.

Franny, he thought. She'd have seen the whole thing.

23

JUNE

June shivered as she walked around the wreck, taking pictures with her phone.

She'd already been inside the van, her sleeves carefully pulled over her hands. Mr. Cheerful had taken out the rear passenger seats and made himself a kind of nest in the back, a sleeping bag on a stained mattress beside a cooler full of lunch meat and cheap beer, along with a couple of gym bags, a clothes iron, and two gallon-size bottles of Clorox. The mirrored side windows had made it darker than outside. The smell of bleach was still strong in her nose.

Mingus barked from Lewis's backyard.

When Peter and Lewis jogged up the street, she said, "Please tell me you found him."

"Disappeared," Lewis said. "Beamed up to the mother ship." He pulled out his phone and stepped away to check on his family.

Peter asked, "Anything useful inside the van?"

She knew he was pissed by the set of his jaw. She shook her head. "I didn't want to touch anything." Peter stepped toward the open van but June put her hand on his chest. "We need finger-prints," she said. "And not yours. Let the police do their job, okay? I even got his picture earlier today, which should help a lot."

"Earlier?"

"Yeah." June closed her eyes. She wasn't looking forward to this. "Mr. Cheerful got me with his car door as I was riding to the paper after lunch. He tried to get me into the van but I smacked him with my bike and got away."

She wasn't going to get into the time she'd spent finding the face she'd recognized at the market, the man whose phone was almost stolen.

Peter looked at her, seeing her scrapes for the first time. "Why didn't you tell me about this?"

"I didn't think it was a big thing," she said. "Besides, I was on it. I got his picture and his plate number. What the fuck would you have done?"

Okay, maybe she was being a little defensive.

The muscles bunched in his arms. "For one thing, I'd have picked you up at work."

"I can take care of myself," she said.

He took a deep breath. "I know you can," he said. "Better than almost anyone. But clearly this guy is kinda special." He told her about Fran's call, and the cameras on the light posts.

"I'm not worried," she said. "The police will find him. But we don't have time to talk all this through right now. You need to get out of here. Because the police will start looking at my life, too. That's the way they work."

"He came after you twice and he's still out there," Peter said. "I'm not leaving. Although here's an idea. Why don't we go somewhere together? We can stay at that new hotel downtown."

She gave him side-eye. "Like you're going to be able to sleep inside tonight. You're just trying to get me to back off this story."

"I just want you to be safe," he said. "We still don't know why he's after you."

"Of course we do. He called me *reporter lady*, for chrissake. He wants me to sit down and shut up. Just like you."

"That's not fair, June. I don't want you getting hurt, that's all. This guy is dangerous."

She glared at him. "Edgar didn't come after you, Peter, he came after *me*. I'm a goddamn journalist. All I have is my willingness to keep digging, to keep fighting. If I let some weirdo scare me off a story, I'm done. And whatever this thing is, it's nowhere near resolved. In fact, it's getting bigger. And I'm in the middle of it. So I'm going to stick. And you are not getting in my way. Do you fucking read me, Marine?"

She didn't bring up his trip to Iceland last year, or his chasing a gunman into the market just yesterday. She didn't have to.

She watched Peter pull in a deep breath, then release it.

"Yes, ma'am," he said. "Loud and clear, ma'am."

Maybe he wasn't completely hopeless, she thought. "Good answer. Your next question is, 'How can I support you?'"

His mouth twitched as he suppressed a smirk. "Yes, ma'am. How can I support you?"

"Grab your go-bag and get the fuck out of here, please. I'll stay with Lewis and Dinah tonight." She turned to Lewis, who was watching them with amusement. "Is that all right?"

"Of course," he said. "The boys will love it. Mingus, too."

"Great," she said. "Lewis, can you get rid of Edgar's light post cameras? If the police ask about Peter, I'll tell them he's my boy-friend and he went bow-hunting up north."

Lewis nodded, then tipped his head to the side, listening. A siren rose into the darkening sky. "Six blocks away, maybe five," he said. "Jarhead, you take off and I'll get June up to speed on today."

"Wait," June said. "What happened today?"

Lewis said, "We found someone connected to the market shooter. A woman."

She spun to face Peter. "You went looking? After you agreed to fucking chill out last night?"

He told her about the camera glasses taken from their counter. "In fairness, it happened after I agreed to stand down. It wasn't just a break-in. Someone targeted us."

She glared at him. "And you didn't tell me? Who's the asshole now, Peter Ash?"

He raised his hand. "That's me. My bad."

"Four blocks." Lewis cycled the shotgun and popped the shell out of the chamber. "You two clearly need to work on your com-munication skills," he said. "See a counselor. But right now, Jar-head, you got to go."

Peter leaned in for a kiss, but June leaned away. "Oh, no. I'm still pissed at you."

"Can I at least drive you to work tomorrow?"

"Depends on the cops," she said. "But if you do, it's gonna be in my car, not your crappy truck. And you don't get to come up to the newsroom. Dean Zedler is already trying to find better pic-tures of the dumb-ass good Samaritans from other cameras around the market. You don't need to make it any easier for him." She didn't mention that she might be on that camera footage, too.

The siren was much louder now.

"Wait," he said. "My truck is crappy?"

She gave him a push. "Will you fucking go? Lewis will text you."

As he jogged backward across the yard to the house, he blew her a kiss. She stuck out her tongue. Idiot, she thought.

Then wondered how long it would be before she saw him again.

24

PETER

Peter slipped off the side of the cantilevered deck and dropped down the darkened edge of the ravine. He moved slowly on the steep and slippery grade, boots careful and quiet in the damp fallen leaves. He wore his go-bag on his back, and carried the old Colt Commander chambered and ready in his hand. He'd already turned off his phone.

The siren had stopped, and the flashing blue and red lights at the top of the slope told him the patrol car had arrived at the house.

There were two reasons to slip away. The first was to keep himself out of jail and June out of trouble. The second was Edgar, or as June had called him, Mr. Cheerful. The fat man with the axe obviously knew where she lived. There was a real possibility that he'd use the greenway to circle back for another attack.

This time, Peter wouldn't hesitate to pull the trigger.

He didn't mind June yelling at him to stay out of her way. She was right about all of it. This wasn't about him. This was about her and her story. He would stand guard while she did her work and found Edgar and the market shooter. If he needed to go kinetic to protect her, he would.

The truth was, he appreciated the clarity.

It was good to have a mission again.

It took him fifteen minutes to descend eighty silent feet. Sound carried strangely in that part of the ravine, something about the flat slabs of rock inside the folded land that acted like an amplifier, and he didn't want his haste to betray his presence. He kept his eyes moving, checking his flanks and the hill behind him, police lights still bright on the branches of the uppermost trees.

When he finally arrived at the dirt ribbon of the main trail, he found a slender dark figure ten yards away, hands held out away from the body.

Peter had the gun up and aimed without conscious thought, all slack gone from the trigger.

"Hello, Mr. Ash." A calm, measured voice carried effortlessly through the dusk. "I mean you no harm. I hope to have a conversation."

Peter knew the voice. He'd last heard it several years ago, at a very strange dinner party.

"Oliver Bent. What the fuck are you doing here?" Peter released the pressure on the trigger and scanned left and right, looking for a white dress shirt. It would glow faintly in the deepening night.

"I believe we can help each other, Mr. Ash." The dark figure stepped closer. "You have certain unfortunate legal troubles. I have a difficult problem that requires your abilities."

Oliver Bent ran a technology incubator that acted like a cross between a strategic national laboratory and a venture capital group, except for the off-books team of special operators. DARPA with teeth, June had once called it. Oliver had funded her father's think tank for more than a decade. He'd also tried to recruit Peter at that same strange dinner party. Right after he'd ordered an execution in cold blood.

"I've seen how you resolve difficult problems." Peter pivoted to check behind him and saw no chubby ghost in the trees. At the top of the slope, the red and blue lights had gone out. "The answer's the same as last time. I'm done taking orders, and I sure as hell don't want to be your pet killer."

"That would not be the nature of this work." Oliver was three yards away now. His hands still held out from his sides, his face in shadow. "Allow me to explain."

"There's nothing to explain. Besides, I don't do technology."

"But Ms. Cassidy does. I called her an hour ago, and left her a voicemail."

An hour ago, June was still riding home from work.

Peter snapped back to focus on the man in front of him, the gun again raised into firing position.

"Oh, no. Absolutely not. I'm keeping her safe. Someone already tried to kill her twice today, and that's just over a story in the paper."

Oliver's hands dropped. "Ms. Cassidy was attacked? Today?"

"Twice. So there's no way we're stepping into your kind of shit."

Oliver's voice was soft and patient as a glacier grinding stone. "Unfortunately, Mr. Ash, I believe you have already. Why on earth do you think I am here?"

Peter felt the air go out of him. He lowered the pistol. He needed to talk to June.

Then her voice floated down through the trees. "Oliver."

She sounded as crisp and clear as if she were speaking directly into his ear. That trick of the ravine and the damp night air. She'd obviously found a moment to check her messages.

Peter looked up and saw her silhouette, illuminated from behind, standing at the edge of the cantilevered deck at the top of the slope. There was no railing, just a thin cable strung tight between corner posts, invisible now in the dark and distance. The earth dropped away below.

"Ms. Cassidy."

"You'll make Peter's Iceland problem go away?"

"Yes," Oliver said. "I will."

"All right. Come up to the house."

Then she turned away and was gone.

25

The backyard looked empty, but Peter could feel Lewis somewhere in the shadows, keeping watch for Edgar. Two uniformed MPD officers stood in the front, waiting for the evidence techs to arrive and process the wrecked van.

June had told him that it was Franny who had called 911 after the wreck. June had stood on the elderly woman's porch and listened to Fran give the officers a clear, accurate description of the driver fleeing with his double-bladed axe. Her memory was oddly vague regarding the two men who had chased him up the street.

Now June and Oliver sat at the kitchen table with the lights low and the blinds down at every window. Peter stood against the counter, the heavy Colt in his wide, knuckly hand. The safety was on, but he still had a round in the chamber. The static hummed in his blood. It wasn't the room, it was the company.

June had her notebook open in her lap, a pen in her hand, and two more on the table. "Before you tell me your problem, give me a little more background on your outfit, the Longview Group."

"Ms. Cassidy, you know all about us."

June smiled gently. "Actually, I don't." She looked relaxed, but the pen twitched between her fingers. "I spent several days researching your group when we first met. I learned almost nothing."

Oliver Bent was slender as a reed, with a crisp thatch of black hair and almond-shaped eyes that showed at least one Asian ancestor. He sat easily in the hard wooden chair, poised and still. His calm face revealed nothing as he glanced from June to Peter and back again.

"It's not complicated," he said. "The Longview Group provides funding, encouragement, and technical assistance for innovative scientific research with an emphasis on applications that will be beneficial to society. Renewable energy, genetic medicine, that sort of thing. In other words, the greater good. The long view."

He wore a long black coat of some high-tech fabric over a dark brown sweater and moss-green pants, all of it durable and invisible and appropriate for any occasion except testifying before Congress, which was the single thing Oliver would never be asked to do.

"That's a very nice elevator pitch," June said. "I think you left out the top-secret military part."

"National security is a core part of our mission," Oliver admitted. "Your late father's work, for example, had profound military implications." June had helped manage the day-to-day operations of her dad's think tank in its final years.

"Please, Oliver. Stop dancing. We're all adults here."

"Very well," he said. "On the condition that this entire conversation is off the record. I want that to be clear."

"Of course."

"Humanity," Oliver said, "is in a race against itself. A race between our best intentions and our worst impulses. Technology is not just advancing, it is rapidly accelerating beyond the ability of governments to assess and regulate it. It is also getting much cheaper. Small private organizations are now capable of developing technologies that once required the resources of national governments.

"Longview's mission is to move quickly enough to evaluate radical emerging technology and its long-term implications in real time. We can't stem the tide, but we hope to steer the ship. When a technology is too radical, when the negative applications far outstrip humanity's ability to adjust in the short term, we intervene."

Peter had seen one so-called intervention. It had involved a strike team of six men against four vehicles filled with trained ex-military contractors. The outcome was never in doubt. Peter had to admit, he hadn't minded at the time. The contractors had been coming to kill him and June.

"We take these technologies to a highly classified R&D facility known as the Vault. Several years ago, we had a data breach."

"Oh, dear," June said. "What was taken?" Her expression was open and encouraging. Who wouldn't want to tell her their secrets?

Oliver appeared immune. "I'm afraid I cannot share that information."

"Who took it?"

"If I knew, I would not be here, speaking with you."

June smiled. "Yet here you are, Oliver. In my kitchen."

"Yes. Your role as a journalist and the breadth of your contacts in the tech world give you a kind of access my people will never have."

Peter opened his mouth to talk. June put her hand up to silence him without taking her eyes off Oliver.

"You know that's not what I meant," she said. "Why here? Why now? Why me?"

"After our breach, we asked the NSA to monitor all traffic for specific data signatures. Yesterday, after years of silence, we got our first hit. Over a hundred gigabytes of data passed through an unencrypted commercial cell network in downtown Milwaukee."

June's pen stopped twitching. "You think this is connected to the market shooting." Peter knew she was replaying the event in her head.

"That is my working assumption," Oliver said. "The time stamp on our data hit correlates well with the security footage. The cell node is the closest node to the market."

June stared at the ceiling, thinking out loud. "Were they buyer and a seller? No. Why take the risk of staging a shooting? What's the relationship?" Smoke was practically coming out of her ears. "Of course. It's a second robbery. A data heist. Your thief got jacked. The gunman is the new thief. He took the victim's phone and had him unlock it."

Oliver raised his eyebrows. "This detail was not in the paper. The gunman made his victim unlock his phone?"

"Yes," Peter said. "He did a few things on it, but left it behind when he ran. I thought it fell out of his pocket, but maybe he left it deliberately."

June asked, "Why didn't he just keep the phone?" Then answered herself. "Because he only wanted the data. He'd be afraid of the owner tracking the hardware's GPS."

"Both phones were prepaid models," Oliver said. "Bought with cash, thus anonymous, and apparently running excellent commercial encryption. But fast, top-of-the-line equipment. The data transmission would only have taken a few minutes."

"You can't track either phone?" Peter asked.

Oliver shook his head. "We tried, but they're both offline. Almost certainly destroyed."

"You came to me because of my byline on the story," June said.

"Yes. And our preexisting relationship."

"What do you want with Peter?"

"Mr. Ash's presence is a useful side effect," Oliver said. "I cannot disclose this breach to anyone outside my group. Certain parties have become aware of the Vault, and would like to see its contents sold into the marketplace. A data breach would be characterized as negligence and provide the perfect excuse. So I need an operator who is off the radar entirely. Mr. Ash is as unofficial as it is possible to get. Especially with his current legal status. But he is extremely effective."

"No," Peter said. "Hell, no."

June said, "What's the problem, Peter? This is a chance to do some good. Isn't that what you want?"

"These aren't just small-time gangsters, June. The people who could pull off this breach, these are serious people, a whole different level. Someone has already made two attempts on your life. And Oliver is basically saying we're on our own. There's no backup, no air support, no hostage rescue team. If something goes wrong, he's never heard of us."

She looked at him. "And how is that any different from the half-assed way you usually operate?"

The pistol felt heavy in his hand. "Are you not listening to anything he's said? Longview is an extralegal, fully deniable program. Blacker-than-black, extra super double fucking secret, with tacit permission to execute civilians at will. Once you get into bed with people like this, you'll never get out."

Her gaze was steady, her green eyes wide open. "I got into bed with you, didn't I?"

———

Oliver cleared his throat. "Mr. Ash is correct about the risk. This will be dangerous. But you have my promise, made in good faith, that I will do right by both of you in whatever way is necessary. And you, Ms. Cassidy, will never be in harm's way. Mr. Ash will do the field work. Your tools will be the telephone and the Internet."

June shook her head. "You only get three lies, Oliver, and that's one. Because you know I won't learn much behind a desk. People have to trust me to talk to me, and they won't trust me over the phone. Most of this work is face-to-face. I'll never get the story without it."

"Except there will be no story, Ms. Cassidy. You will never publish any of this. You will sign a nondisclosure agreement with significant penalties attached."

June shook her head. "You came to me, pal. I don't work for you. You want good faith? It goes both ways. There will be no NDA. We'll have a conversation about the right thing to do when we get these guys."

"No," Peter said. "No, no, no."

"Hey!" She whipped her pen at Peter in a wicked sidearm. It bounced hard off his forehead. "You are not in charge here, Marine. You are the support team. Got it?"

Peter threw up his hands. "Do you not remember the guy with the assault rifle? Or the madman with the axe?"

"Oh, I'm not worried about them, sweetie." She gave Peter a brilliant smile. "Because you'll be my bodyguard."

Peter sighed. "Fuuuuuck."

June turned back to Oliver. "Next item. Peter's Iceland problem. I need full exoneration on all charges, overseas and domestically.

Notes in all government files to the effect that he was charged in error. With official apologies." She reached over and patted his arm. "And I'll need that in writing, tonight. Agreed?"

Oliver pinched the bridge of his nose. Suddenly he looked exhausted. June could have that effect on people. She was undeniably relentless.

"Agreed," he said. "But I can't clear his record until after you are successful, because Mr. Ash must remain deniable throughout. No visible thumbs on the scale."

"Okay." June picked up another pen and tapped it on her open notebook. "Now, about your security breach." She flashed that incandescent smile again. "I really can't do my job unless you tell me what was taken."

Oliver frowned. "You lack the necessary clearances for that conversation. But perhaps I can tell you a story." He looked at June. "To reiterate, we are off the record. Not even background."

June nodded. "Yes."

26

Oliver glanced at the antique schoolhouse clock June had hung above the kitchen door. The second hand ticked loudly, marking each moment rather than sweeping smoothly forward like a modern timepiece.

"A young man in Budapest, very bright," he said, "was given a toy robot for his birthday. A small thing, just eighteen inches tall, made for schoolchildren and only able to perform a dozen limited actions. A clumsy walk, for example, and a rudimentary dance based on the rhythm of music it heard.

"The bright young man was disappointed by the toy's inability to do anything interesting. During the day, he worked at a local cement factory, but he spent his evenings with a hobby group, a local electronics club. So he took the robot apart and made a new one from the parts. He incorporated a much larger circuit board, more sophisticated servomotors, and a suite of the real-world sensors that have become quite inexpensive in recent years. Accelerometers, distance sensors, touch sensors.

"But even with these modifications, the robot could only follow very specific instructions. It was still just a toy," he said. "So the young man took it upon himself to create a new kind of software language."

"That takes giant teams of people," June said. "And years of development."

"Yes." Oliver gave her a small smile. "Except nobody informed the young man of that fact. His new language was radically simple, quite robust, and elegantly designed, with a powerful cause-and-effect learning model at the heart of it. Using this software, the toy taught itself, with little help other than its own sensor inputs, to climb the curtains in the young man's bedroom."

"Oh, shit." June's eyes were wide.

"Yes," Oliver said. "This seemingly elemental physical task requires a very complex, dynamic, and coordinated set of motions. The ramifications are significant. Cause-and-effect problem-solving across multiple real-time datasets is considered one of the keys to a truly self-learning general machine intelligence. It is an enormous leap, fully thirty years ahead of the most optimistic predictions. But it's here now."

"I don't mean to play devil's advocate," Peter said, "but why shouldn't this technology be in the world? Who gets to decide? Who makes the rules?"

Oliver gave him a mild look. "You haven't seen what I've seen, Mr. Ash. It's not all jet packs and moonbeams. Sometimes it's a re-engineered bubonic plague designed for an undergraduate thesis. Sometimes it's a video game so addictive that beta testers nearly starve to death. And sometimes it's a machine intelligence with the potential to be able to flip a burger, paint a house, drive a truck, and do a thousand other jobs safer and cheaper and more reliably than a human being. Would you like massive unemployment and social unrest that makes the Great Depression look like a walk in the park? By all means, open the floodgates."

Peter had to admit that sounded bad. Like a fast-forward version of what was already happening. "So, what's the process? Release the good stuff incrementally?"

"Yes. At a pace that will allow society to adjust, rather than rupture. In the meantime, the Longview Group is developing it for strategic advantage."

Now Peter saw the whole game. When the tech saw the light of day, the American military would be miles ahead of the rest, with corporate America coming fast behind.

June said, "What about the bright young man from Budapest? What's he doing now?"

"He agreed to come to Longview Labs. His work there would be classified, but he would have an ownership stake in all patents derived from his ideas. He would be well paid and well supported and otherwise free to live as he wished."

Somehow Peter didn't think this story had a happy ending. "But?"

"Unfortunately," Oliver said, "he had published a video of his robot climbing the curtains. Another team arrived at his home at the same time as our people. We believe they were Russians. The young man did not survive. And we are not the only two nations seeking these advanced technologies. This is the new arms race."

Above the kitchen door, the clock ticked away the seconds, one by one.

June got up and poured herself a glass of water. "Okay, we get the picture," she said. "Now let's talk about the breach itself. I assume your security is top-notch. How did they get in?"

"Our measures are excellent," Oliver said. "But security is only as good as the people using it. Our systems administrator found an excuse to log on to our air-gapped server, copied our data onto some kind of flash drive, then left the premises. He was a former NSA admin with all the necessary clearances and a spotless record over twenty years of service."

"Somebody got to him," Peter said.

"More than that," Oliver said. "Internal security discovered the problem within the hour and sent a team to his house. They found him dead in his living room, along with his wife and three children, none of whom had been to school for the last week. They were killed with a meat cleaver taken from a kitchen drawer. Their limbs were severed from their bodies."

"Jesus," June said.

"Indeed. Our working assumption is that the family was held hostage and tortured in exchange for the data. The hostage-taker was extremely careful. We have no witnesses, no fingerprints, no DNA, and no suspects."

Peter asked, "How did the hostage-taker know what to steal?"

"That is a very good question. We are still looking into that."

June's voice was quiet. "How old were the children? I want to see their faces."

God, she was tough, Peter thought. She would use the images of those poor kids as fuel in her hunt for their killer.

Oliver knew it, too. He woke his phone and set it on the table where she could see it. "Their names were Andy, Erica, and Tim. Ages two, four, and seven."

She stared at the image for a long moment as tears ran down her cheeks.

"Okay," she said. The muscles stood out in her jaw and neck. "Okay."

27

ow," Oliver said, "I have told you what I know. Tell me what you have learned about the market shooting, and what's happened since then."

Peter talked about how he and Lewis had gone looking for the gunman's crazy electric bike. About the hipster bike shop, which had led them to Kiko's Welding, which had led them to the custom bike-making class at the MakerSpace, where they met Spark.

"Not only did she have a red Cardinals jacket in her workroom, Lewis saw an assault rifle's receiver, a restricted part that she or someone else had probably made, sitting on her desk. Apparently she's got a live-in boyfriend, very mysterious. When we tried to talk to her, she locked us out of her workshop, tore a vent hood off the wall, and escaped through the resulting hole."

Oliver said, "Did you get her information from the Maker-Space people? Address and phone?"

"You mean after we kicked down the door to her shop?" Peter shook his head. "Our tour guide claimed they only knew her as Spark. They have an email address for her, but nothing more."

"I'll look in the public databases," June said. "If the name change is official, maybe I can find out what it used to be."

Oliver turned to June. "Peter said you were attacked today."

"A guy hit me with his car door as I was riding my bike to the paper. He tried to get me into his van, but I didn't let him. Later in the afternoon, he apparently installed a pair of wireless cameras on our block so he could spot me on my way home. He tried to run me down in the street in front of my own house. I can only assume it's about the market shooting. But that's not the interesting part."

Oliver raised his eyebrows. "If that's not interesting to you, I'd like to hear what is."

"I think I know the guy whose phone got taken."

"What?" Peter asked. "You didn't want to lead with that?"

She gave him that brilliant smile. "I didn't know it meant anything until a few minutes ago."

She told them how she thought she'd recognized his face at the market, then spent her morning searching through tech stories trying to identify him, finally finding his photo as part of a startup story from eleven years ago. "He looks totally different now, but I'm pretty sure it's him."

"What's the name?" Oliver asked.

"Vincent Holloway," June said. "Good luck tracking him down, though. He seems to have vanished entirely. For a guy who made half a billion dollars eleven years ago, he's done very little since. Zero social media presence, zero Internet presence. Doesn't that seem odd in the tech world?"

"Yes," Oliver said. "I'll check our files to see if there is a connection to my group."

"But you'll talk to your spooky friends, right? You'll find him?"

"I will call in some favors," Oliver said. "But I cannot go through my normal channels. No official fingerprints, remember?"

151

Peter shook his head. "So we're taking all the risks, but get none of the resources?"

"I believe we've already had this conversation. Let me make sure you understand your task. You will destroy all evidence of our technology and deliver the culprits to me. Yes?"

"Agreed," June said.

"It might not be that clean," Peter said.

"Understood." Oliver looked at the clock again and stood up. "Unfortunately, I must leave. You've learned a lot in a day and a half. Keep at it." He handed June a plain black phone. "You can reach me through this. Send me updates throughout the day. I'll respond when I can."

Peter said, "I'll walk you out."

The sky had cleared and the evening turned windy and cold. With little moon, the side yard was dark. They walked toward the garage and the driveway to the street.

"I fully understand your reservations," Oliver said. "Unfortunately, I have no way to dispel them except to ask you to have faith in me and in your country."

Peter still held the heavy Colt in his left hand. Now in a cool fury, he put his right hand between Oliver's shoulder blades and shoved hard, intending to slam the other man face-first into the garage wall.

Oliver did an elegant twist and pivot, redirecting the force into a lateral move that brought him face-to-face with Peter, hands up and ready as if that had been his intention all along. "Mr. Ash—"

Lewis flew out of the shadows like a guided missile and crashed the smaller man into the side of the garage.

Peter heard the clapboards crack with the impact. Oliver's

knees buckled. Peter picked him up by the front of his long black coat and held him against the wall with his right forearm against Oliver's chest and the gun barrel under his chin. He leaned in close enough to smell the other man's minty toothpaste.

"Let me make this clear to you, Oliver. I've done more than my share for my fucking country. I don't care about runaway technology or whatever other game you're playing. That's not my department. I care about June." He screwed the gun barrel deeper into the other man's flesh. "If anything happens to her, and I mean anything, there is no place you can hide. I will track you to the ends of the earth. Do you fucking understand me?"

Oliver's face showed neither pain nor distress, only the same dispassionate calm he'd displayed the entire evening. In Peter's experience, this was not just the sign of a national security professional, but also of a true believer. Peter didn't like it.

For true believers, it wasn't about emotion or ego or career advancement. It was about doing the work, no matter the cost. No matter how many bodies piled up.

That's what made true believers so dangerous.

Peter had been one himself, until the war beat it out of him.

Now all he had left to believe in was people. His friends and family. The people he loved.

The wind whistled cold through the trees.

"I accept your terms, Mr. Ash." Oliver's voice was raspy from the pressure of the pistol. "I pledge to you now, of my own free will, that I will do everything in my power to protect Ms. Cassidy from harm, within the constraints of my own mission. If I fail in that, my life is forfeit. So help me God."

"Easy to say with a gun to your head. And that caveat, the constraints of your mission. Why the fuck should I trust you?"

"Some say honor is an antiquated notion. But our word is all we have in this life. And how we cleave those words to deeds. I believe you understand this. Your actions indicate that you are a man with a profound moral center. You wish to do what is right."

Peter had to will himself not to pull the trigger then and there. "Asshole, you don't know a goddamn thing about me."

Oliver's eyes were the color of night. "Do you know what a black hole is, Mr. Ash?"

"A collapsed star. A gravity well so powerful that even light can't escape."

"Invisible to the naked eye, yet its gravitational field affects everything around it. Like a black hole, Mr. Ash, you reveal yourself through the nature of the events that surround you. And the quality of the people who give you their loyalty." He glanced at Lewis, then gave Peter a skeletal smile. "I find that loyalty goes both ways, does it not?"

He didn't need to make the threat explicit. Peter was well aware of the danger his fugitive status posed to June, and to Lewis and Dinah and the boys. The wreck it would make of their lives.

Honor was a sword that cut deep, no matter who swung the blade.

Peter lowered the pistol and stepped back. "I will hold you to your word."

"I expect nothing less." To his credit, Oliver didn't roll his shoulders, which surely ached from the bruising impact with the garage, or brush the splinters from his coat. He merely said, "I look forward to news of your progress," then turned to go.

They watched as he walked across the neighboring lawn toward a black government Suburban idling in front of Dinah's house, parked out of the way of the MPD evidence van.

As the Suburban drove away, Lewis looked at Peter. "So we working for spooks now?"

Peter felt the weight of it in his chest. "Not you, Lewis. Just me."

He heard a low rumble. It took him a moment to realize Lewis was laughing.

"Shit, Jarhead. I ain't staying home." His tilted smile shone white in the night. "And I don't know why you're making such a damn fuss anyway. Not like June was ever gonna do anything different, once she got her teeth into this. Not you, neither." He thumped Peter's chest with his fist. "You think you want the simple life, but you're still a goddamn Marine, looking for the next righteous reason to kick somebody's ass."

The hell of it was, Lewis was right.

The white static sparked and crackled, that high-performance engine shifting into gear at the prospect of action.

Peter blew out his breath. "Okay," he said. "What's next?"

28

While Lewis set Mingus up with food and water in the backyard, then took his family to a hotel downtown, Peter and June left in the Subaru. They agreed that, although it was a reasonable read that Mr. Cheerful had been working solo and that losing his van would slow him down for a few hours, the safest move would be to assume nothing. Peter had insisted that June carry a small chrome .22 in her bag. She didn't object.

Peter took a winding route through the city, punctuated with abrupt turns and seemingly random detours through busy commercial districts and quiet residential neighborhoods, one eye on the rearview the whole time.

As they passed the art museum, the car's interior bright with ambient light, June gave him a funny look. "What," he said.

June licked the ball of her thumb and rubbed at a spot on his forehead. "You had a little blue ink right there," she said. "From that pen I threw at you."

He smiled, pointed the little car toward the Hoan Bridge over-pass, and stepped on the gas.

She didn't look away. "Are we okay?"

"Of course." He put his hand on hers. "I'm all in. This is your show. I'm sorry I'm an idiot."

She shrugged. "You can't help it," she said. "It's genetic. You're a man."

"At least you noticed."

After an hour of driving with no evidence of a tail, he knew either they were clean or the enemy had enough skilled people to fool him completely, which didn't yet seem likely. Despite every-thing that had already happened that evening, it was only nine o'clock.

A block from the *Journal Sentinel*, she told him to pull over in front of the Calderone Club, where a young guy in a dirty apron walked a pizza box out to the car. Peter drove inside the paper's gated lot and they sat in the car with a clear view of the street while they ate sausage and onion pizza, the wafer-thin crust cut into Milwaukee-style squares instead of wedges.

Peter said, "Do you have a theory on Mr. Cheerful?"

"Aside from the fact that he's a few tacos short of a combination plate?" June surveyed the remaining squares and selected the piece with the most meat. "He's not an independent player. He's work-ing for someone else."

"Not the shooter, though. Spark's boyfriend. He seems more like the DIY type."

"Huh," June said. "Talk about that a little."

"All the weird gear," Peter said. "The Cardinals jacket, the old gun, the funky bike. But there's something more. I mean, I couldn't really get a read with the beard and sunglasses hiding his face, but he seemed really intense, really focused. Like it was personal between him and Holloway."

June nodded. "And Holloway, if he's the guy who took Oliver's tech, has an incentive to keep the shooting quiet, too. Making me disappear would accomplish that. And we know he has the money to hire help."

Peter's phone buzzed with a text. "That's Lewis," he said. "Come on, I'll walk you in."

He got her past security with her work bag and the leftover pizza, then stepped out the front door, where Lewis waited in his Yukon at the curb, engine running.

On the dashboard stood the small metal sculpture they had taken from Spark's workshop. The man in the wheelchair, a welder's mask covering his face, hammer in one hand and cutting torch in the other.

Lewis watched his mirrors as he drove, but didn't take an active anti-surveillance route. Both men were still wound up from the day and silently half-hoping for some kind of confrontation.

They'd already changed out of their carpentry clothes. Lewis wore black jeans and a crisp white button-down shirt, along with a black leather coat tailor-made to hide the matte-black automatic he carried in a shoulder rig. Peter wore scuffed mountain pants, a Lakefront Brewery T-shirt, and a hard-shell fleece that covered the Colt Commander in a left-handed pancake holster.

Walker's Point was jumping on a Friday night. Lewis found a spot on Florida, three blocks from the gallery, which in the low-key world of Milwaukee parking was like leaving your car on the moon. As they walked past Coakley Brothers and Mobcraft Brewery, both men kept their eyes moving across the knots of pedestrians and passing traffic, looking at faces, seeing nobody out of place.

The event posting had noted that, along with the celebration of the new show, studios would also be open for visitors, an opportunity for artists to network and meet collectors and promote their work.

By the time they got there, though, most collectors had gone home to their babysitters and the party had kicked into a high gear. A dozen smokers clogged the sidewalk outside the front entrance, spilling wine and waving vape pens as if nicotine addiction was the next new thing. Retro-psychedelic funk bounced through the door, held open by a thigh-high cactus in a five-gallon pickle bucket.

Inside, the enthusiastic crowd was a broad mix of ages and ethnicities, with an emphasis on nose rings, strange hair, and gender fluidity. The dress code seemed to be head-to-toe black or ironic clashing plaids, with the occasional paint-spattered overalls or hot pink party dress. Peter was not remotely hip enough for this party.

They navigated toward the back of the building, passing through a series of gallery rooms. Stark white walls highlighted bright paintings that tugged at the eye like a fishhook. At first glance they seemed abstract, until Peter realized they were also portraits, loaded with wild emotion. Terror, anger, fierce joy. Peter's mom was an artist in northern Wisconsin. She'd love this stuff, he thought.

The studio hallways smelled of incense and pot smoke and reheated spaghetti. People wandered in and out, chatting and drinking wine. The static revved higher as Peter tried to imagine a winning strategy against Kiko's sledgehammer and the hydraulic wheelchair that could make him nine feet tall.

29

They rounded the last corner and found Kiko's shop closed and padlocked. "Crap," Peter said.

"Jarhead." Lewis pointed across the hall, where another studio door stood open.

Directly inside, an open display case held several dozen metal figures. A woman riding a Harley, her speed evident in the invisible wind blowing back her hair and clothes. A man in a tool belt with a crosscut saw, bent over a board, the muscles flexing in his back and arms. Other figures dancing or on a skateboard or in firefighter gear, each one unique and vivid and beautifully made. None of them was a welder in a wheelchair, but they were clearly made by the same hand.

Peter crossed the hall and peeked into the room. It was as big as the welding shop, but set up as an office suite. On the left was a long leather couch and an oval table with three metal chairs and wine and cheese on a tray. In the back stood a polished steel desk facing into the room, with a high-end monitor on top and file cabinets behind, rolled blueprints stored upright in a wire-frame rack beside a bright red fire extinguisher. Eight or nine people stood chatting while some kind of electro-flamenco music played. Aside from the fire extinguisher, it was all tasteful and stylish and completely unexpected.

He had to step inside to find Kiko. The metalworker sat in a low-slung wheelchair beside a woman in a peroxide blond beehive and cat's-eye glasses, deep in conversation. He was barely recognizable in a gray button-down shirt with a faint paisley pattern, metallic jeans, and electric blue socks under black leather slip-ons. His hair and beard were neatly brushed and designer reading glasses perched on top of his head.

But the biggest change was Kiko's ride. If his hydraulic work platform was a utility truck with a crane, the new chair was a sports car. Obviously a custom job, it was sleek and stylish with a red frame and polished chrome wheels. Kiko's meaty palms rested comfortably on the hand rims, rocking the chair slightly in place as he talked, as if tapping his toe to the music.

The hydraulic beast sat hulking in the far corner, under an elegant metal tree that appeared to grow from the floor, up the wall, and across part of the high ceiling. The trunk and branches showed the patterns of bark and the leaves were hammered steel, the whole effect somehow both impressionistic and natural. A pair of trapeze handles hung from the sturdiest limbs, directly above the chair, evidently Kiko's method of moving himself from one seat to the other.

Peter had never crashed an art opening to confront an ex-con in a wheelchair before. It seemed like an oddly delicate operation. He wished June was there instead of doing research at the paper. He leaned closer to Lewis. "You got any ideas about how to do this?"

Lewis raised a shoulder. "Walk up, stick a gun in his face, ask the question. My experience, that works pretty good."

"In a room full of people?"

"We both got guns," Lewis pointed out. As if the lack of firepower was the problem.

"Maybe later." Peter reached into the display case, grabbed a figure of a blacksmith at his anvil, and carried it into the studio. He wandered toward the back of the room as if admiring the tree sculpture. In his peripheral vision, he saw Kiko's weathered face snap in his direction. As he moved deeper into the room, the red wheelchair turned to track his progress.

When the chair pivoted away, Peter knew Kiko had spotted Lewis. Kiko couldn't watch them both at the same time. It would make him nervous.

Peter stopped at the big work platform. A cardboard shoebox sat on the seat, with a power cord plugged into it, reminding Peter of the phone-charger shoebox at the bike shop. He made sure the bag with Kiko's lethal wrist rocket was still strapped to the arm of the chair, then slipped a pair of heavy C-clamps from the tool rack and jammed them into his back pocket. When he circled back to Kiko, the metalworker did not look happy to see him.

The woman in the beehive hairdo and cat's-eye glasses felt differently. She looked Peter up and down. "Well, hello, there."

Peter held out a hand. "Hi, I'm Peter."

She pressed his hand in hers. She didn't quite lick her lips. "Helga. I'm a collector. Are you an artist?"

"Not exactly." Peter shifted his weight to let his coat fall open. The Colt Commander wasn't small. Helga blinked in recognition and pulled her hand back. Most normal civilians got a little nervous at the sight of a firearm. "Hello, Kiko."

Kiko didn't look nervous, although the muscles in his big arms bunched and flexed under his shirtsleeves. He gave Peter a baleful prison-yard stare. "What are you doing here?"

"I'm looking for Spark," Peter said. "How do I find her?"

Kiko shook his head. "I don't know what you're talking about."

Peter held the little blacksmith up to the light, admiring the details. Hammer in one hand, tongs in the other. "You do beautiful work, Kiko. How long does it take you to make one of these?" Kiko didn't answer. "Must be a couple of days, at least. And they're all unique?"

As Peter turned the figure in his hand, he lost his grip, intentionally bobbling the blacksmith before catching it again.

"Whoops, that was close." A small white sticker on the base showed the price. "Eight hundred dollars? You are not charging enough. These must sell like hotcakes."

"He's already sold five tonight," said Helga in the peroxide beehive. She'd recovered her nerve and was leaning in again.

A vein pulsed in Kiko's temple. He glanced at Lewis on the far side of the room, one hand in the pocket of his leather jacket, opening the front to show Kiko the matte-black automatic in the shoulder rig. The other guests hadn't really noticed him yet, but they would soon enough. The gazelles always saw the cheetah.

Kiko turned back to Peter, his prison-yard stare at maximum intensity. "You and your friend need to leave. Now."

"Making bike frames, that's a decent gig," Peter said. "But these sculptures are in a whole different world. They're really good." He held up the blacksmith figure and gestured at the tree growing up from the floor. Then nodded at the chattering, oblivious crowd. "You've got a nice thing going. Meeting collectors, selling your work."

He didn't make the threat, but he didn't have to. It was, Peter admitted, a total dick move, and he wasn't proud of it. But he also wasn't going to pound on a man in a wheelchair, even if the guy did have arms like pistons. So he needed some kind of leverage. If he had to hold the man's artistic aspirations hostage, he'd do it.

Kiko heard him loud and clear. "What the hell do you want?"

"I told you. I need to reach Spark, and she's not at the Maker-Space. She's in serious trouble. She's connected to someone very dangerous. Tell us how to find her."

Kiko's face went tight. "Go fuck yourself. I told you, I don't know anyone named Spark."

Helga watched the conversation like a tennis match, her face alight. To the victor goes the spoils.

Peter smiled. "Sure you do. I saw your sculpture in her workshop, the welder in the wheelchair. It's not like your other pieces. It's a self-portrait. It's personal. You'd only give it to someone you know well. Someone you care about."

Kiko's shoulders tensed, muscles popping under the stylish dress shirt. Would the metalworker make a move? Peter watched the meaty fingers on the chair's hand rims.

Then he relaxed, decision made. "What are you gonna do? Break my legs? Shoot up the place?"

Peter dropped the little blacksmith sculpture to the floor. It bounced with a metallic clatter. "Oh, darn." Peter moved as if to pick it up, but stepped on it instead, just enough to bend the figure's legs. For the first time, he saw Kiko flinch.

Helga gasped in shock. "What are you doing?"

Peter held the figure under the rough lugs of his boot. "We don't want to hurt Spark," he said. "We just want to talk to her. To help her."

Kiko looked like he was in physical pain. But he didn't cave. "Go ahead. Flatten it. Flatten them all. I'll make more tomorrow."

Peter had to admit, the man had sand. Across the room, Lewis grinned and shook his head. Telling him that if he'd just stuck a gun in the guy's face, they'd be done by now.

Then Lewis tipped his chin toward the desk and the row of filing cabinets, and it was Peter's turn to shake his head. Not at Lewis, but at himself.

When they'd first met Kiko in his welding shop, he'd said that he didn't keep records, that he got paid in cash. It made sense at the time, but now, in this office, it was obviously a lie. If they couldn't find what they needed in the file cabinets, they'd find it in the computer.

Peter scooped up the fire extinguisher from the floor, pulled the pin, and squeezed the handle, giving Kiko a quick blast of dry monoammonium phosphate, trying not to spray him directly in the face.

While Kiko coughed and sputtered, Peter raised his voice. "I'm so sorry, everyone, Kiko's having one of his episodes. This is why we take our medication, right, Kiko? Thank you all so much for coming out tonight." Peter hit him with another short blast, then hosed down the room for a few seconds, yellow powder coming down like piss-colored snow.

Through the coughing and clamor, Lewis called out, "This way to the exit, folks. Nothing to worry about."

Peter had caught Helga with some of the plume, and her cat's-eye glasses looked like she'd been caught in a whiteout. Peter took her by the elbow and propelled her toward the door.

In fifteen seconds, the room was empty and Lewis had thrown the deadbolt. His black leather jacket was dusted with the dry chemical mixture.

"I'm gonna rip your goddamn arms off." Kiko coughed and wiped powder from his face. Peter set down the red canister and dropped to his knees behind the wheelchair, where he pulled the C-clamps from his back pocket and cranked them around the chair's crossbars so they captured a few wire spokes of the wheels and locked the chair into place.

Lewis pulled out one file drawer after another, raking his fingers across the folder labels. Kiko finished wiping his eyes, then grabbed the hand rims and shoved himself forward with his massive arms. The spokes sang with the tension. Peter got behind him and pulled back on the chair's push handles, doing his best to keep Kiko from breaking the spokes and freeing himself. It was like trying to restrain an angry rhino.

"Get your fucking hands off my shit, you fucks."

"Spark's in trouble, Kiko. We're trying to help."

Kiko bellowed wordlessly and thrashed harder.

"Hang on." On his fourth drawer, Lewis pulled a file and flipped through the contents. "Here's one." He unfolded a sheet of paper and held it up. "See this?"

"Kinda busy," Peter said. Kiko abruptly went into reverse, and Peter stumbled backward. The spokes popped with a metallic ping. Kiko spun in place, an acrobat on his apparatus, then reached out and picked up a chair by a single leg and flung it.

Peter got a hand up and tried to brush it aside, but the edge of the seat hit the nerve cluster on his forearm and a spike of pain rolled up to his shoulder. The chair crashed to the floor and Peter grabbed the fire extinguisher, sorely tempted to smash Kiko's head into cherry pie. Instead he pulled the lever and give Kiko a nice long dose, sending him into another coughing fit.

"It's an engineering drawing for an electric bike," Lewis said. "Looks a lot like the shooter's. The name on the print is La Chispa. With an address in Silver City."

Peter had a fair amount of Spanish. "*La Chispa* means Spark."

Kiko sputtered and coughed. Peter grabbed his wrists and held them down. "Who was that bike for? Who's her goddamn boyfriend?"

Kiko stopped fighting, his chest heaving. His face and torso were frosted in pale yellow.

"She's got nobody," he said. "She's got me, that's it."

30

That was all Kiko would tell them. Peter wrote his number on a pad on the desk, in case the metalworker changed his mind. They left him swearing in his chair with his cell dropped behind the file cabinets to keep him from warning Spark.

Kiko's guests clotted the hallway outside, exclaiming their indignity. Peter still held the fire extinguisher. He hit the ceiling with a short blast and shoved his way toward the back door.

He didn't know how long it would take before Kiko found a way to contact her.

It was three blocks to the Yukon. They ran the whole way.

The apartment where Spark lived with her boyfriend was on a residential section of National Avenue between a low-rent Layton Boulevard mini-mall and the multiethnic restaurants and retro-hip bars of Silver City, a historically poor neighborhood that was clawing its way back. Traffic was still brisk at eleven o'clock at night.

Lewis parked on the far side of the four-lane street and killed the engine. They got out and Lewis opened the back of the Yukon. He dipped into a canvas tool bag and came out with something that looked like a bulky screwdriver with a plastic cap over the business end. It was an electric lock pick, a remnant of his former life. "You know how to use this thing?"

"You take it." Peter picked up the same three-foot crowbar from earlier in the day. "This is more my speed."

He slid the chisel end up the sleeve of his coat and held the cold bend of the hook in his hand. He didn't know if he would need it, but he didn't want to have to come back for it. He really didn't want a passing cop to see it and hit the lights. If a patrolman spotted the pistol on Peter's hip, things would go sideways in a hurry.

The building was pale, flaking brick, at least a century old, with four floors and eight unlabeled buzzers inside the front vestibule. Spark was in 4B, which would be the top floor. The vestibule's inner door hadn't been painted in decades, but it had good locks and the glass was protected by a beautiful wrought-iron grille, the original security measure.

Peter left Lewis at the front with the electric pick buzzing, and jogged around to the back. The building was on an alley, with a wrought-iron stairway column that rose up the center and fed long balconies that doubled as rear entrances for each unit. The windows and doors that faced the balconies had modern steel security grates over them. Across the alley were single-family houses.

Peter called Lewis from the shadow of a neighbor's garage and described what he saw. "Are you in?"

"Not yet. Give me a minute."

Peter dropped the crowbar from his sleeve. "I'm going up. Keep in touch."

Neither of them mentioned the market shooter with his assault rifle and his martial arts moves.

The steps were crusted with paint and thrummed underfoot. Peter took them three at a time, pulling himself up with one hand on the rail, the other carrying the bar at the balance point. As he swung his weight around the outer landings, he felt the whole stairway shimmy slightly. Either the bolts had loosened over the years, or rust was weakening the steel. Or both.

The balconies stretched out maybe twenty feet on either side of the central stairs. The layouts appeared to be mirror images, with the apartment doors closest to the central stairs, then a bank of three windows.

On the fourth floor, the balcony on the right was crowded with a long cedar garden bench and two matching chairs, all in a line. Planter boxes hung off the outside of the railing, with fall flowers still blooming despite the cooling weather. Through the window grates, Peter saw a tidy kitchen with red-checked curtains and dishes drying in a rack by the sink.

Somehow, Peter didn't think Spark was the red-checked curtain type.

The balcony on the left seemed more her speed, with a single vinyl patio chair and a small low table made by bolting a rusted steel plate to an upside-down milk crate. The lights were on inside the apartment, but the shades were down over the windows. The Latin polka rhythm of a Mexican *corrido* seeped softly through the glass.

Peter loosened the Colt in the holster, then stood against the weathered brick and watched for moving shadows behind the shades. Lewis would go in the front door while Peter went in the back. The hum in his head revved higher at the prospect.

Best case, Spark was alone and willing to talk. It didn't seem likely. Worst case, the shooter had heard Peter coming up the stairs and waited inside with his AK at the ready and Spark as a human shield. Peter wished he knew something—anything— about the shooter's motives, about his relationship with Spark.

If the police were here, they'd have men in unmarked cars watching the alley and the street, waiting for Kiko to call Spark and spook her. When she ran, they'd grab her. If she stayed put, they'd strap on body armor and helmets, evacuate the building, and break down the door. They'd have badges to explain themselves to anyone watching. It was a better way to go.

If Peter wasn't a wanted man with his face all over the feed from the gunman's video glasses, he'd have called the cops himself. Instead, he was just a selfish prick who didn't want to go to jail.

Although maybe not completely selfish. He didn't want June to go to jail, either. Or Lewis, whose veneer over his criminal past could only withstand so much scrutiny. What would that do to Dinah and the boys? Peter wasn't going to ruin their lives, not if he could help it.

His phone lit up with a text from Lewis. I'm in. Coming up.

Peter texted back. Wait in the stairwell. If she runs, grab her. If it gets loud, shoot the locks and save my sorry ass.

The security screen was like a storm door but beefier, with heavy metal mesh and its own lock. But however substantial it looked, it was meant to be affordable protection against neighborhood thieves, not a motivated Marine with a three-foot crowbar. As he worked the chisel tip into the gap between the door and its metal jamb, Peter thought about the outrage he and June had felt after someone had broken into their house the night before. Which made him both a selfish prick and a hypocrite.

He seated the tip and pulled, putting his back into it. The

narrow jamb gave a soft scream as he peeled it away from the deadbolt, tearing the metal. The security screen swung free.

Behind it was a plain wooden entry door, a cheap modern retrofit. He tried the knob. It turned freely but the door didn't open. There were two other locks. He wiggled the crowbar's chisel end behind the stop and levered the jamb back against the frame to free the deadbolts from the strike plates, then pushed the door open slightly with his foot.

The whole operation was over in under a minute and made no more noise than clearing his throat.

He laid the crowbar down on the balcony, pulled the Colt from its holster, took the weapon off safe, and stepped inside. His motor revved higher.

He stood in a dark hallway. On the right wall, bare coat hooks. On the left, an opening to the empty kitchen. Painted cabinets and cheap appliances, with a ratty upholstered chair in the little eating nook instead of a table. A coffee cup on the floor beside it and a book on the seat. The music came from down the hall. He followed it.

Doorways ahead to the left. The hall floor squeaked underfoot.

A small bedroom with a single mattress on the floor under a tangle of blankets. Black plastic garbage bags were duct-taped over the windows. Nobody behind the door, nobody in the closet.

A compact bathroom with hexagonal floor tiles and a recently washed jog-bra hung to dry on the shower bar with the plastic curtain pushed back. Nobody in the tub.

A dining room with a pair of folding banquet tables arranged into an L-shaped desk, with a scatter of papers, and textbooks in a stack. The Mexican *corrido* came from an ancient clock radio with a speaker that sounded far better than it should. Then a living room that held only a faded wingback armchair with no footstool. An open coat closet held nothing but a broom. Nobody home.

It felt like the apartment of a scholarship student with no savings, no family support, and no backup plan. All the living was done in the future. For now, it was work and study with breaks to eat and sleep. A lonely life.

Then he turned and saw the pair of rectangular paper targets taped to the opposite wall. Black silhouettes with concentric circles across the chest, identical to those in a thousand local gun ranges. Except for the holes in the paper. A single hole in the center of each bull's-eye, torn and ragged at the edges and several times larger than the opening made by one bullet.

On the bottom of the paper, someone had written "AKSM. New barrel. Thirty rounds, two hundred yards."

Something wasn't right, Peter thought.

He holstered the Colt, then pulled out his phone and texted Lewis. It's clear. Don't shoot. He threw the bolts on the front door, then undid the pair of heavy chains, one at knee level and the other at Peter's shoulder. Someone was serious about home security. Even with the locks open, Lewis would have had a hell of a time making his way past the chains without a battering ram.

Peter pulled the door ajar, but he'd already turned away to retrace his steps through the apartment, trying to understand what he was seeing. Or maybe what he'd missed, aside from the partial case of 7.62 x 39 rounds he found under the sweatshirt on the floor of the bedroom closet. But he was still scratching his head when Lewis sauntered down the hallway.

"I don't think the boyfriend lives here," Peter said. "She's got a single bed, a single toothbrush, just one person's clothes in the closet. Only one chair. But that doesn't account for those damn targets." He waved at the silhouettes in the living room. "You see those groupings?"

"Jarhead, you overthinking this." Lewis gave Peter a wide, tilted smile. "It's a four-story walkup, right? Take a look at the main stairwell."

Peter walked to the front of the apartment where Lewis had left the door open.

The black electric getaway bike was chained to the ornate oak railing, silver rectangles and red wires still strapped to its elegant geometry. A black charging cord ran from a socket in the oversized rear hub to another one of those strange shoeboxes.

"Wait." Peter blinked, then looked at Lewis. "Spark is the shooter?"

Lewis raised his shoulders in an elaborate shrug. "You got a better explanation?"

"What about the boyfriend? What about that beard?"

"Gotta say, it looked a little weird, right? Kinda shiny?"

"It was fake?" Peter sighed. "It was a damn mask. The hat, sunglasses, everything."

Lewis looked past him to the target silhouettes taped to the wall. He bent to pull a small cardboard box from under the wing-back chair. It had a picture of the video sunglasses on the front. He tapped the box. "Jarhead, there ain't no boyfriend. We been outclassed from the start."

Peter shook his head. "Who the hell is this woman?"

31

SPARK

Spark stood frozen on her skateboard in the alley behind her building. She had takeout from the Vientiane Noodle Shop in a plastic bag and her eyes locked on to her fourth-floor balcony. The bright rectangle of light told her the door was standing open. Which meant that someone was inside her apartment.

Kiko Tomczak was the only person who knew where she lived, and he didn't have a key. Even if he did, there was no way he could get up all those stairs. And she hadn't talked to him for almost two years.

It had to be those two *pendejos* from the Public Market. She had no idea how they'd found her, first at the MakerSpace, now here. Although her plan at the market had almost gone horribly wrong, she was sure she'd done almost everything right afterward.

Young Maria Evangelina, with her judo classes and her sec-ondhand textbooks, would never have recognized her older self, a grown woman standing firm with a handmade rifle pointed at the terrible man's chest.

For three years, she'd fought the fear and anger and pain. She'd learned to contain it, first to pack it tight like a snowball, then to compact it further until it became a glittering sphere of ice that lived just behind her breastbone. It functioned like a prism, focusing the strength of her will and intellect into this meticulous plan. To ruin him the way he had ruined her.

She'd built the gun. She'd written the code. She'd learned how to move the money. She'd called in the bomb threats to distract the police. She'd gotten him to hand over his unlocked phone. Her laptop was busy downloading every file, link, app, and password. She recorded everything with the video glasses, to play back his reaction. She was on the brink of the revenge she needed so badly.

The rifle was there just to control him, to keep her safe.

She hadn't planned for what had happened at the market. For three years of discipline to vanish in an instant. For her tight sphere of ice to flash into bright red rage.

It started as a scald in her stomach, the urge to murder that boiled up hot like oil in a pot. It rose through her chest and shoulders, then spread into her arms, the rage expanding to overfill the vessel. It felt inevitable, out of her control, her muscles making the decisions as her mind simply watched. She was an observer in her own body. She didn't think about the bystanders. When the boil reached her fingers, she would pull the trigger.

What would happen, she wondered, when her bullets blew him apart?

Would the fear and anger and pain fade away? She didn't know. She suspected not. But she would kill him anyway. She would kill him now and deal with the consequences later.

Then the tall man in the cowboy hat had thrown an apple at her.

The pain of it hitting her chest had jolted her back into her mind. She hadn't counted on the nice weather bringing so many people to the market. She certainly hadn't counted on the children. Or some *pendejo* throwing fruit and thinking he was a hero.

The next apple glanced off her cheekbone. The countless hours on the gun range and at the dojo took over. She regained her focus and reverted to the plan.

She had what she needed. She could still find the terrible man another time, in a more private place.

So she left them all behind, hopped on her bike, and hauled ass across the river to the boat storage yard a mile away, where she'd coasted into the shadow of a rusting cabin cruiser and peeled off the red jacket and the bulky ballistic vest she'd worn underneath.

When she removed the hat and the itchy costume-shop beard and dropped them into a trash barrel, she was a different person entirely. Rolling the leftover spirit gum off her jawline reminded her of peeling Elmer's off the back of her hand when she was four, after making popsicle-stick paddleboats for the bathtub. The skin of super glue on her fingertips would wear off in a few days.

She dumped the vest in the trash, too. She was supposed to leave the jacket with it, but she couldn't. It had belonged to her father, a proud Cardinals fan, and it turned out she wasn't ready to let go of that yet. So she stuffed it into her backpack beside her laptop, which was still harvesting data over the cell network. At the speeds she'd clocked, she could get a hundred gigs in under five minutes.

The next step of the plan was to throw the gun into the river, but Spark couldn't bring herself to do that, either. Holding the rifle made her feel safe, armored, and strong, like nothing could stop her. Even though she knew that feeling was a lie, or at best an illusion. That gun could land her in jail, or make a cop pull the trigger until his own gun was empty. She was hanging out on the edge now, with nothing to catch her if she fell. If she was going to see this thing through, she needed every scrap of hope she could find.

If she'd just bought the rifle complete at some gun show, she wouldn't have hesitated. But she'd fabbed the receiver from scratch, bent the steel and tapped the holes, then put the rest of it together with her own two hands. When you make a thing, it's truly yours.

So she pulled out the magazine and cycled the round from the chamber and jammed the gun into her backpack. It was just over two feet long with the stock folded, so she could barely zip the bag shut. But she made it work. Just like she'd made everything else work.

Standing in the alley now, she looked up at the open door of her apartment again, knowing they were inside, feeling the sense of violation and loss. The thought of starting over in a new place was exhausting. She reminded herself that it was just an inconvenience. There was nothing she really cared about in that apartment. It was a shame about the MakerSpace, but she didn't need it anymore. With nothing but the laptop in her backpack, she could go anywhere she wanted. She'd disappear.

Although she'd miss her rocket bike. She'd made that herself, too, everything but the frame, and that had been a gift from Kiko. Still, she could always make another one.

And her electric longboard would get her where she needed to go.

Now she had a new problem to solve. The terrible man's phone had only carried the passwords to a single account, one with less than four hundred thousand dollars, not the tens of millions she'd hoped for. But it had an encrypted link to a cloud drive with some crazy stuff on it. She'd copied the contents to her own encrypted drive, then inserted a little custom code of her own.

He'd pay what she wanted, all right. He'd pay everything.

She turned away from the apartment, leaned forward slightly to let the longboard's synaptic controls kick in, and silently accelerated into the dark maze of streets that ran through Silver City like a secret circuit.

32

JUNE

As Jerry the night guard thanked her for the leftover pizza, June wondered how safe she might be at the paper.

She hadn't given much thought to news organizations' security procedures until the killings at the *Capitol Gazette* in 2018. The *Journal Sentinel* wasn't as secure as most large office buildings. You needed a key card to get into the parking lot, through the loading dock gate, or into the side entrance, but the street entrance was unlocked day and night unless the security guard stepped away from his desk, in which case he'd throw the deadbolt.

The night guard wasn't even armed, and Jerry wasn't exactly athletic. He often brought a homemade calzone and a thermos of coffee for his dinner. Plus most of his attention was on the soccer game playing on the big lobby television.

June didn't blame him. He wasn't getting combat pay. She told herself that Peter had driven across town and back to make sure they weren't followed.

Although she was pretty sure Mr. Cheerful already knew where she worked.

As June walked to her desk in the far corner of the newsroom, she looked across the tops of the cubicle partitions. She didn't see Dean Zedler, and was grateful. She didn't want to know what he'd found looking at security footage outside the market.

She liked being at the paper at night. The building was almost empty, just the night editors and reporters working on late-breaking stories. It reminded her of her first job working the cops desk in Chicago all those years ago, when the action rarely started until well after everyone else had gone home.

Except for the eerie hush. In the old days, when the printing presses were in the basement, manned by typesetters who could read and edit upside down and backward, the whole building had vibrated with their power.

But even that was before her time. Now the presses were off-site, the building was quiet, and last-minute edits were all done electronically. Just like reporting, which sometimes was as much about sifting through data as it was about cultivating sources.

At her desk, she unpacked her work bag, including the chrome .22 pistol and the black slab phone that Oliver had given her. She put the pistol away, but woke the black phone and tapped in the fifteen-digit alphanumeric password she'd memorized.

As soon as the screen opened, she saw a message. *VH was on Longview technology review board for five years, ending seven years ago. Passed all background checks for necessary security clearances. Con-firmed as a POI. No current phone or address.*

VH would be Vince Holloway, but what the hell was a POI? Oh, person of interest. Government guys and their acronyms. And Oliver didn't know where he was, either.

She messaged a reply. *Please send background check information. Everything you have.* Maybe their docs would provide some clues.

At least she had confirmation of Holloway's connection to Longview. It made her feel better about pulling his face out of her memory and pasting it on some guy she'd interviewed more than ten years ago.

All she had to do now was find the bastard.

She checked social media on her phone, looking for a reply from his former partners at Sense Logic, but she'd gotten nothing. The beauty of social media was that you could send a message to almost anyone. The downside was that nobody had to answer. She sent another round of polite requests, then opened her laptop, plugged it into the big monitor, and started digging in earnest.

Although she hadn't had much luck earlier with her basic web search, June's work with Public Investigations gave her access to a powerful set of subscription databases that let her research every-thing from individuals to corporate entities to specific industries to court systems at every level of government. She could even search municipal records, so if you had an unpaid moving viola-tion or an active building permit on your house, that information was at her fingertips.

In the days before the Internet, these databases had been built by accumulating information by hand in dark, dusty public records rooms all over the country. Now, though, they used advanced data-scraping techniques to pull all kinds of information off the web and into its servers.

As a private citizen, June had to admit she found it a little creepy. But as an investigative journalist, she relied on these databases for everything from basic background information to following corporate money all over the world.

She began by typing his name into the main search bar. The software kicked back thirty-one people named Vincent Holloway in the United States, and over five thousand people with related names. Five thousand wasn't bad, she thought. It'd be a lot worse if he was John Smith.

She went back to the piece she'd written about his company more than a decade ago. Even then, she'd been in the habit of typing up her notes and taking photos of her notebook. Yes, his name was Vincent Holloway, not Michael Vincent Holloway or Vinson Holloway, so she ignored the related names for now. If she didn't find him in the first thirty-one, she could always go back.

Refining the search, she eliminated anyone outside of her guesstimate of his age range. That left her with nineteen people. One by one, she pulled them up.

The eleventh Vincent Holloway had the same employment history at Caltech and Sense Logic, the startup that made him a wealthy man. This was her guy. Now she dug deeper. Where the hell are you now, Vince?

His most recent address was in Portola Valley, California, a small and very affluent hillside community just southwest of Palo Alto. Several founders of major tech companies lived there. The San Andreas Fault also ran through the middle of town, which was somehow fitting, June thought, given the violent shocks that the tech revolution had made—and was still making—in the modern world.

She went to another database and looked up the Portola Valley property address. Turned out it was now owned by a cosmetic

surgeon named Todd Schultz, who ran a group of clinics special-
izing in penis enlargement, apparently a lucrative profession in
Silicon Valley. So much for Portola Valley.

She went to a third database, found Holloway, and pulled up
his complete work and financial history.

Because of the evolution of online records, employment profiles
tended to be pretty crisp in the present moment, but get fuzzier
the farther back you went. For Holloway, oddly, this was
reversed.

His early years were an open book. Job history going back to
what was probably a work-study appointment as an undergrad at
Carnegie Mellon, which was evidently an early adopter of online
records. As Holloway got older, his bank and investment accounts
multiplied and their balances rose. He got more credit cards with
higher limits, and a series of ever-larger home mortgages and car
loans. After Sense Logic sold, he bought the eight-million-dollar
house in Portola Valley and a four-hundred-thousand-dollar vehicle from Bentley Motors. Like a rapper after the first album goes
platinum.

Apparently he was kind of a dickhead driver, too. She found
eight DUIs in ten years, along with dozens of speeding tickets and
hundreds of parking citations, which she only discovered because
Holloway ended up in municipal court due to—dude, really?—a
hundred thousand dollars in unpaid fines. Reading between the
lines, she assumed some seriously expensive legal firepower to fi-
nesse the system and allow him not only to stay out of jail but to
keep driving. Another reminder that the wealthy didn't play by the
same rules as everyone else.

But six years ago, everything stopped.

The credit cards were canceled, the bank and investment

accounts disappeared. No mortgage or car loan. It was like he fell off the modern map.

She went to her specialty database for tracking money. Moving wealth was easier than ever, because of electronic banking systems. But it was harder to hide those transfers, because of government-mandated anti-money-laundering and anti-tax-avoidance compliance measures. You had to prove your identity repeatedly along the way, especially when moving cash across borders. Although, again, if you had a great deal of money, there were plenty of ways to slide through the gaps in the regulations. Many wealth managers and financial institutions, both large and small, specialized in exactly these kinds of wealth transfers for people who could afford their enormous fees.

Of course, Holloway didn't have any overseas accounts that she could find, at least not under his own name. She'd have to look at the records for his old accounts to see where he'd transferred money into, and she wouldn't get those without a court order.

Any accounts Holloway controlled would almost certainly be held by offshore trusts that didn't have to disclose their contents. There would be shell companies, themselves formed expressly for the purpose of owning other shell companies, on and on in an endless hall of financial mirrors. There would also be overseas stock swaps and luxury real estate bought by one captive entity to be sold to another, not to mention a variety of other muddy techniques that were more or less legal and nearly impossible to trace in the busy global economy without both a microscope and direct knowledge of the transactions.

Usually the point of these maneuvers, at least in the case of the average Russian kleptocrat or Chinese oligarch, was to hide the bulk of your wealth but allow yourself to live in the open and in luxury. Some even tried to buy a little respectability with big charitable donations.

Holloway, however, had hidden not only his money, but himself.

Even with a court order to tell her where to start, it could take her years to find him.

Because of the connection to the Longview Group, June was now certain Holloway was the man at the market, and that he had engineered the theft of Longview's data. Why else would he have disappeared?

She just needed a handle. A single thread to pull, to start unraveling the weave.

What about Pinnacle Technologies, that weird little California-registered company that owned the copyright to his Wikipedia photo?

According to her corporate database, it was no longer active. She went through the filing and dissolution papers and found nothing new. No financials, no corporate officers. Same phone number for Gary, but he wouldn't answer at this time of night, even two time zones away.

Still a dead end.

She checked the black slab phone for a reply from Oliver. No luck.

She hoped his background docs on Holloway would give her more threads to pull. Given the nature of the Longview Group, the research was probably pretty exhaustive. But most of it would be more than ten years old. And Holloway would have used the information he'd provided as a kind of reverse blueprint for hiding out. Nothing there would be relevant. Not that she wouldn't follow every thread to make sure.

Her working hypothesis was that Holloway had turned himself

into a de facto corporate entity, made up dozens or even hundreds of shell companies, and registered out of Luxembourg or the Cayman Islands, with the same kind of anonymous agent of record he'd used in California. All that money made it easy.

When she found him—and she would find him—his home of record would turn out to be a PO box inside the anonymizing office that had registered the company. He'd have corporate credit cards in multiple names, and signing privileges on corporate bank accounts. None of which would have his real name listed anywhere unless June found the actual bank and either got a court order or convinced someone to show her the paperwork. She'd still need to know the name of the company first.

Unless he got a very good legit driver's license under a false name, like Peter did. Backed up by a real social security number.

In which case, he could be anyone, anywhere. And she'd never find him.

What the hell had happened six years ago?

Her phone pinged with a message. She'd finally gotten a reply from one of Holloway's former partners.

> Haven't talked to Vince in years, he never did have much use for humans. Only idea is a former girlfriend, Holly Gibson. She got married and moved to England seven years ago, but Vince was still talking about her when he dropped off the radar. I think her husband ran a restaurant?

June got back on the computer. She doubted Holly Gibson in England would know how to reach Holloway after all this time, but it was worth the follow-up, as long as Holly Gibson was still Holly Gibson and her husband still ran a restaurant. But lo and behold, she was, and he did. June sent a message. Sometimes things were easy. Because normal fucking people had lives on the Internet.

As for the rest of Holloway's Sense Logic partners, she'd dig up their phone numbers in the morning. Hell, yes. It was time to get off the desk and talk to actual human beings.

But when she stood up from her chair to stretch, she glanced over the top of her cube wall and saw Dean Zedler walking toward her. With a manila file folder in his hand.

She was tempted to crawl under her desk, but he'd already seen her.

33

By the time June shut her laptop, tucked her notebook into her pocket, and shoved her database printouts into her backpack, Dean was approaching her desk.

"You're working late." He was smiling, but he'd obviously looped around so that he stood between her and the elevator. He wore his cashmere sport coat. She didn't look at his shoes.

"I was just leaving." She pulled on her raincoat. "I'll see you tomorrow."

"You'll want to see this," he said. "I think I found our market Samaritans. They look a little rough."

He pulled a photo from his folder and laid it atop the nearest of the long gray file cabinets that lined the aisles.

It was grainy, printed on plain paper, but the image was clear. A tall, rawboned white guy with dark shaggy hair, and a brown-skinned menace with a panther stride. Both wore dirty work clothes and watchful faces, searching the streetscape for something only they would recognize. Peter and Lewis walking toward the coffee shop.

She could feel Dean watching her. She didn't say anything. She knew what was coming.

He laid out another photo beside the first. The same two men seated at the sidewalk table. With June.

She could deny it, of course. She could say she didn't know them. That they'd asked if she minded sharing the table. She could come up with a whole story. She didn't even open her mouth.

Dean laid out a third photo. The three of them talking, faces intent. June closed her eyes. She thought of more lies she could tell, but it would be pointless.

When she opened her eyes, he'd put down three more photos. One with her hand on Peter's arm. Another of him leaning over to kiss her. The pained expression on her face as they turned away. Had she really looked like that?

"These are closeups of the actual footage, of course," he said. "June, who are these guys? And what's your relationship to them?"

His face was kind, open, and friendly. But he wasn't her friend, not now. At the moment, he was only a reporter.

"Dean," she said. "It would really be best if you stepped away from this."

He tapped the photo of her face, the image from the moment she had watched them lope across the street after the man with the rifle under his jacket. "You look pretty uncomfortable here, June. Why don't you tell me about it?"

"Dean, leave it alone. I need you to trust me here."

"I do trust you," he said. "And I hope you know that you can trust me. Truly. How long have we known each other? If you're jammed up, I can help. Just talk to me."

That goddamned Weaponized Nice. She almost believed him.

But what on earth could she tell him? She couldn't say, *This is a much bigger story than you know.* That would only egg him on. She definitely couldn't say, *Someone tried to kill me twice today and now I'm trying to find technology stolen from a secret government program.*

Because that would be ridiculous.

And because Dean would just follow the story, no matter where it led.

She'd always admired that about him.

He was watching her face right now, and reading it like a book. He waited for her to say something. It was a reporter's trick, waiting out the silence. But June just shook her head.

He tapped the photos with his index finger and tried a new tactic. "June, you know I can publish these tomorrow. I don't want to put you on the spot, but some kind of comment from you would go a long way to explaining this. Explaining why you didn't tell the police that you knew these guys. In fact, we should go talk to the bosses right now."

She'd always known the end point of his argument. Not for the first time, she looked toward the glassed-in editors' offices along the west wall and tried to imagine how that conversation might go. What the ramifications would be for her position with Public Investigations, or for Peter. Whatever would happen, it wouldn't be good. All their chickens coming home to roost.

"Please, June. Talk to me. I'm trying to help you."

Maybe that was true. But she doubted he would bury the photos to protect her. He was chasing the story. Chasing the truth, or as close to it as he could get. Along with his own ambition.

June couldn't blame him.

Wouldn't she have done the same thing?

She wanted the story as much as the next reporter, maybe more.

But would she have done it like this, by leveraging a friend?

She hoped not.

She thought about calling Oliver, but knew it would get her nowhere. He had been very clear that she and Peter were on their own. She could tell the paper's editors everything she knew, but she couldn't corroborate any of it. Or she could take the hit and say nothing.

Either way, Dean would dig until he found Peter. Who would almost certainly end up behind bars.

And that would kill him.

Thankfully, she didn't have to decide.

Forty feet away, the elevator dinged, the chrome doors slid open, and Mr. Cheerful stepped into the newsroom.

He wore a fresh white dress shirt, untucked over jeans. His face was lit with a smile.

In his right hand, he carried the double-bladed axe.

And he was staring right at her.

34

EDGAR

Edgar stood in the elevator, going up. He liked the pressure under the soles of his feet. Edgar didn't believe in heaven, but maybe this was what it was like to get there.

Man, he felt good. Ready to go. His cheeks ached with the size of his grin.

The nice man in the lobby had given him good directions to the newsroom. All Edgar had to do was smash the lock on the side door and jump over his desk and knock him off his stool and cut off his hand with the axe. After that, the nice man told Edgar everything he needed to know.

It was a real shame he'd crashed his van into that tree. He'd liked that van. But when he saw that the two workmen wouldn't use their guns unless he ran straight at them, he knew he'd get away. They'd never believe Edgar would run full-speed through that tall thorny hedge. It wasn't hard, it just took commitment. And a cool pair of sunglasses to protect his eyes.

———

While they wasted their time looking stupid places, Edgar had hopped the fence into the next backyard and out of sight.

Then he'd worked his way up the block toward the reporter, one fence at a time. He still had a job to do. Edgar loved his job. He was lucky to be an American. Not many people got paid to do something they loved.

He stopped behind a brick house across the street from the reporter's place. He thought of how he would do it. He wished he had a real sword. A real sword would be fun. He couldn't believe he didn't own one already. Then he heard the two men jogging up the street again, back toward the reporter. If he faced them directly, they might use their guns. Edgar liked to attack from a hidden place. He liked a good surprise. He could wait.

He remembered the old lady in the window, watching as he drove past. He was sure she had called the reporter and told her about him. It was her fault he hadn't done his job. It was her fault he had lost the van.

The brick house was hers.

He went to the back porch. The door was wide open. He could see clear through the house to the front porch. The old lady stood there now. She was a little bitty thing, barely big enough for breakfast.

His arms were torn up by the thorns. His head was still bleeding, and his shirt was dirty. His van was gone. And now he heard sirens and a barking dog. He wanted to go into the house and punish her for what she had done. One smash of the axe. But the men would see him. The police would come. He would wait. He would hide.

The bottom part of the porch was wrapped by wooden boards.

On the side away from the driveway, there was a gap. It was small and low, but Edgar could squeeze through. Underneath it was bare dirt with a shallow hole scraped away. There was a musty, animal smell. It comforted him. Edgar curled up into a ball and slept.

When he woke and crawled out from beneath the porch, the old lady's back door was locked. A police car was on the street by his wrecked van. He didn't want to make noise. He was hungry and his head hurt. He wanted a beer. He missed that van. It was his nest. Edgar could hide a lot of things in a van.

But he wasn't picky right now. He'd take anything with an engine. Too bad the old lady's driveway was empty. Her garage was empty, too.

Behind her garage was a fence, old and sagging. It was easy to push the boards out of the way and climb through. He didn't even need his axe. He didn't want to use it on wood, anyway. Past the fence was another garage and another house. Then he saw the van in the driveway.

Edgar was lucky like that. Good things just came to him.

"Hey. What the hell are you doing in my yard?"

A man sat on a chair on the patio in the dark. He had a big white mustache. On the table beside him was a can of beer and a phone and a pack of cigarettes and a ring of keys.

Edgar looked at the van. It had a sign on the side that read MIKE DILLMAN PAINT AND DRYWALL. He walked toward the man. "My name is Edgar. Are you Mike Dillman?"

"Yeah, I'm Mike. Get the hell out of here before I call the cops." He stood up quickly, bumping the table with his leg. His beer fell over, which was too bad. Edgar looked at him. Was he a triple XL? Edgar needed a triple XL. Mike Dillman picked up his phone. "I'm calling the cops."

Edgar threw the axe. It turned twice in the air and buried itself in the other man's chest. It made a good sound. It gave him the good feeling. Not as good as when he got to swing the axe directly into a person and get that beautiful wet shiver up his arms, but it was still satisfying.

He used the keys to open the van and cleared out the paint cans and stepladders. He put the body in the back of the van for safe-keeping, took his cool sunglasses out of his pocket and put them on the dashboard, then went inside the house, where he found a can of Schlitz in the fridge and a nice clean white pressed dress shirt in the closet. Triple XL. Thank you, Mike Dillman.

The ironing board was still set up in the bedroom. Edgar had left his own iron in the wrecked van. He looked at his fingertips. Still nice and smooth from last time. He was glad. The iron was no fun.

He took a shower and washed the blood from his face and hands and forearms. He found a gallon of bleach under the sink and poured some down the shower drain, then wiped himself down with a bleach-soaked towel. He thought it would kill any DNA he might later shed in the house. He didn't know if this totally worked, but he liked the burn on his skin anyway.

He carried a cooler from the basement and filled it with ice and beer and a couple of Usinger's summer sausages. He took the largest knife from the kitchen and honed it against the stone counter-top. He was keeping the axe, but it never hurt to have an extra tool.

He was certain the reporter wouldn't stay at her house.

Where would she go?

Edgar knew the answer to that one. He didn't even have to think about it. He just knew it, the way he knew that blood was hot and beer was cold.

Sooner or later, she would go back downtown, to the newspaper where she worked.

Edgar missed his old van. But the new one was pretty good, too.

It wasn't hard to find a place to watch and wait.

Now the elevator slowed as it neared the fourth floor. His face throbbed where she had hit him with the bicycle tire. Waiting for the door to open, he touched the bruise with his fingertips, exploring the pressure of the red and swollen skin.

35

Dean, get behind me," June said.

"What?" Dean turned his head to follow her gaze and stumbled back a half-step, his feet not working properly. Mr. Cheerful's naked smile had that effect on people, even at a distance. The axe only made the effect more shocking.

"Get behind me," June said again, louder this time. "Then call 911. Do it *now*."

She knew running wouldn't work. She'd seen how fast Mr. Cheerful could move.

Without taking her eyes off him, she backpedaled into her cubical and dug her hand into her work bag on the desk. Feeling her way past the water bottle and her various notebooks and her wallet and phone and Oliver's phone, all the way down to the very bottom of the backpack, where she'd put the pistol Peter had given her.

While Mr. Cheerful ambled closer, she pulled the gun from her bag and took the grip in her right hand. She grabbed the slide and pulled it back against the pressure of the spring, racking a round into the chamber, then found the safety and flicked it off. The whole thing was almost second nature. She was glad Peter had kept inviting her to the range with Lewis.

She left her cube for the open aisle, raising the gun into firing position. The chrome .22 was designed for bigger hands than June's, but the kick was minimal and she was more than strong enough to use it. She'd been a rock climber since she was a girl and had the arms to prove it.

Mr. Cheerful's smile broadened when he saw the pistol. His sleeves were rolled to the elbows, and his forearms were slashed with angry red lines, like he'd swum up a river of needles. The head wound from the car wreck had stopped bleeding, and he'd obviously found somewhere to clean himself up. He had a wide red stripe across the side of his face, the developing bruise from her bike tire. As he walked toward her, she wondered if she could see the actual tread marks imprinted on his flesh. She couldn't take her eyes off him.

Then she blinked. Jesus, he was like one of those animals that hypnotized their prey.

It sure worked on Dean. He still hadn't moved. She whacked him on the shoulder with the side of the pistol. "Dean! Get the fuck behind me and call 911."

Dean looked at her like she had three heads. "What the hell . . . ?"

But at least he was moving, stepping around her and clearing the aisle. June turned to Mr. Cheerful and stood square with a two-handed grip, her knees slightly bent and her finger taut on the trigger. "Stop right there, asshole."

He was twenty feet away and still coming, although he'd slowed. He held the axe casually, one hand in the middle of the long handle, double blade out and away from his body.

He beamed like a drunken child. "Hey, you ever shot somebody? I'm just curious."

She lined up the sights on his chest. "No, fuckface, usually I just hit them with my bike. Now stop right there or I'll kill you."

His smile only got wider. He held out the axe blade for her to see. The sharp steel was bright with blood. She thought of Jerry at the lobby desk. His homemade calzone and thermos full of coffee. She pushed it down, the horror and fear and sadness. There would be time for that later.

"When you shoot a person," Mr. Cheerful said, "it's real ugly. Like an explosion of skin and blood and bone. It goes everywhere. The stink is horrible. You'll remember it the rest of your life."

"You don't scare me, freak show." But it was a lie. She was terrified. And he knew it. "Stop right now or *I will shoot you*."

"But you don't want to, right? I mean, how many other people do you want to die? I ask because my only job here is you." He waved the axe at the newsroom, where a few heads had popped above cubicle walls. "These other people aren't important. I'm not getting paid to hurt them. But if you make it difficult? You know, get my blood up? Who knows what I might do?" The smile got impossibly wide. She half-expected to see fangs.

"You want me to just offer myself up, is that it? Like a sacrifice?" She couldn't believe this shit.

"Yeah." He was closing on her. In the swirl of air from the heat vent overhead, she smelled the sharp tang of bleach. The axe spun in his hands. His eyes were locked on hers. "You don't want all that blood on your head, do ya? I'll make it painless. I promise."

He's fucking hypnotizing you, she thought. Don't let him get closer.

He raised the axe.

She pressed the trigger.

36

*B*ANG! The pistol bucked in her hands.

But Mr. Cheerful had already moved, a strange little knee-dip side shimmy. When he straightened back up, he said, "You missed me."

Her head rang and his voice was faint in the aftermath of the shot. His left ear had turned red and pulpy and the collar of his white dress shirt was flecked with blood. But he didn't seem to notice. He stared her right in the eyes and lifted the axe as if to rest it on his shoulder, but she saw his arm flex in his sleeve. He was going to throw it. At her.

The pistol's recoil had pushed the barrel up. She steadied her grip and brought the sights down to his chest. Then pressed the trigger again.

Again he slipped and twisted, anticipating her, but the bullet still caught him, this time low on the far left side of his chest, below the nipple. At first just the fabric was torn, but quickly his shirt began to turn pink. His eyebrows rose in surprise, and he gave a short chopping laugh. The axe swung around, but he kept his grip on the handle. The weight of the blade turned him and she saw the reddening rip on his back where the bullet had left his body.

His eyes were wide as he patted his side, then probed his ribs with stiff fingers. "Ha!" he said again, his face shining with glee. "Ha ha!"

How could he still stand? June lined up the sights again. She was sweating. The pistol's grip was slippery. Her finger tightened on the trigger.

Then his focus changed and he looked at her. His smile was truly unhinged. "I guess I'm living right, hey? Let's do this again soon." Then he winked at her, turned carefully, and walked away, bent slightly sideways, his left hand pressed to his ribs, his right hand still holding the axe.

Pistol still raised and ready, June followed at a careful distance. She saw that he'd left something blocking the elevator door, to keep it open. He stepped inside and kicked out with one foot. A rolling desk chair flew into the newsroom with a crash. Probably Jerry's chair.

The elevator doors closed and he was gone.

She was shaking.

She should have shot him again, she thought. She should have emptied the whole damn gun at him.

She told herself he'd collapse in the lobby. Or on the street.

Was it wrong to hope she'd killed him?

But somehow she knew she hadn't.

At the far end of the aisle, there were two starred holes in the glass wall of the enterprise editor's office. Thankfully, he'd gone home hours ago. She hoped her rounds had spent their velocity in his file cabinets, and not punched through the window, too.

She looked across the tops of the cubicles. "He's gone. Everybody okay? Nobody hurt?"

Heads rose cautiously above the cube walls. Nobody spoke.

The smell of gunpowder was strong.

Beneath it, the tang of bleach scorched her nose.

She turned and walked back to the file cabinet where Dean had laid out the security-cam photos. He stood there stunned, holding his phone. She hoped he'd called 911 and hadn't been taking pictures. This thing had already gone from bad to worse.

She flipped the safety, then dropped the magazine into her palm. She was still shaking, but the ritual movement calmed her. She pulled back the slide to eject the round from the chamber, thumbed it back into the magazine, then popped the magazine back into the pistol with the heel of her hand. At that moment, that solid click was the best sound she'd ever heard.

Dean stared at her. "Who the hell are you, June? Who are these people?"

She pulled the coffee shop security-cam photos off the file cabinet, then crossed to her desk. She packed the photos, her laptop and charger, and the rest of her work things into her backpack. The movements were familiar and sure. Everything had a place. Everything but the gun.

"June," he said. "What are you doing? Have you gone crazy?"

She looked at him. "Remember when I told you to step away from the story, Dean? To leave it alone?" She waved a hand toward the elevator, the hand holding the gun. "This is why. All of this."

She already wore her jacket. Now she slung her backpack over her shoulders and cinched the straps, then walked toward him.

He backed away, hands half-raised. "Where are you going? The cops will be here any minute."

She plucked the phone from his grip and flipped it into the maze of cubicles. "I'm leaving," she said. "I have work to do."

He looked in the direction of his phone, then back to her. "But the cops," he said. "You shot somebody."

"That fucker was going to chop me into little pieces. Didn't you hear him? Someone paid him to kill me. And you were next."

His cheerful face flashed into her mind. His homicidal grin. The loving way he held the axe. She pushed it away, then stopped. Something made her think of Oliver's employee and his family in Virginia, held hostage to gain access to the Vault. Then brutally butchered with a meat cleaver, severed heads and limbs arranged neatly on the bloody carpet. Three kids named Andy, Erica, and Tim. Oliver had showed her the photos. It was plenty motivating.

She remembered Mr. Cheerful's hands flexing on the long yellow handle and knew now that he was the one who'd killed them. Because he enjoyed it. But also because someone had paid him.

Something flickered in the back of her mind, a new connection. To what? It wouldn't come into focus. She knew chasing it wouldn't help, so she ignored it.

"Tell the cops whatever you want about what just happened here. But if you keep your mouth shut about the Samaritans, I'll give you the story when it's over." She brushed past him and walked toward the rear stairwell on the far side of the newsroom. "Tell the police I'll call them tomorrow. I'll have some questions."

"*You'll* have some questions? For *them*? June, what's all this about?"

But she already had her phone out, calling Peter.

37

Hey, June. I was just thinking about you. You'll never guess what we found."

Just hearing Peter's voice released something inside her. Her whole body began to shake. She clamped down hard. She wasn't out of here yet.

"Mr. Cheerful came to the paper," she said. "With his axe."

"Jesus. June, are you all right?"

"I shot him," she said carefully. "I shot him twice."

"June. Are you all right?"

"Definitely not," she said. "But I'm not hurt. I hit him in the side but he just, like, walked off. He got back in the elevator. I don't know where he is."

"Okay. We're on our way. Everything's going to be just fine. Where are you now?"

"I'm in the newsroom. Heading toward the back stairs."

"You should stay put. Find a safe place and wait for the cops."

"No," she said. "I don't want to talk to the police. They'll find you."

"Junebug." His voice was gentle. "It's okay. Really, it is. The cops are good at this. They'll find him. Tell them everything."

"*No,*" she said. "We'll fucking find these people and Oliver will clear you and then everything will be *good* again. We can be fucking *normal.*" She leaned her forehead against the cool steel of the stairwell door. She was trying not to cry.

"Oh, honey." His voice was warm and quiet in her ear. "I'm so sorry. This is all my fault. Will you please please please find someplace safe?"

She cleared her throat. When she spoke, her voice was a growl she barely recognized. "Meet me at the southwest corner of the main building. On Vel Phillips, in the middle of the block, there's a gate across an alley. I've got seven more rounds. How long until you get here?"

The Yukon's engine roared in the background. "Five minutes. Please be careful."

As she hung up, she heard a noise behind her. She spun with the pistol raised in her shaking hand.

It was Dean. With his goddamn mouth open to speak, still trying to talk her into doing what he wanted.

She took a step forward and stuck the pistol in his face. It was still on safe with no round in the chamber, but he didn't know that. His mouth snapped closed. No wonder people loved guns. "What do you want now?"

He shrunk back, but he didn't turn away. "I want to go with you."

"Do you not remember the man with the axe? He's still out there somewhere, and he's just one player. Maybe not the most dangerous one. So you're staying here."

"You made me an offer back there," he said. "I keep quiet about the Samaritans in exchange for the story. I accept. So I'm going with you. Unless you plan to shoot me, too."

Lowering the pistol, she pulled the slide to chamber a round, then flipped off the safety. "Dean, I'm really not the one you should be worried about."

He reached inside his cashmere sport coat for his notebook. "Who was that you were talking to?"

She shook her head. "Oh, he's gonna fucking love you."

The stairwell was a rectangle of poured concrete, with an open center and steel pipe railings and dim utility lights in wire cages. She'd explored the *Journal Sentinel* building as soon as she'd gotten her key card, not because she expected a moment like this, but because she was curious. She knew the place was a maze with many exits, and Mr. Cheerful was probably too busy trying to survive to try to find her again.

Regardless, she crept down the stairs as quietly as she could, pistol at the ready, hating every scrape of Dean's hard-soled Italian shoes behind her. At the bottom, she found two heavy fire doors, one to the old loading area and the other leading directly to the rear parking lot.

She pushed outside, trying to look in every direction at once. With Zedler too close at her heels, she jogged halfway down the narrow alley and waited in the deep shadow behind a dumpster, shivering in the cold. Ahead of her, a pair of tall iron gates, locked with a rusty chain, blocked access to the street. She realized she was squeezing the pistol grip too hard and relaxed her hand.

The flickering thought returned and came into focus. About

the Virginia family that had been butchered with a meat cleaver. And her certainty that Mr. Cheerful had done it.

June thought of the two men killed with a machete outside the machine shop on Hampton Avenue, on the same day as the market shooting. They were a lot like the Virginia murders. The same gleeful brutality. The severed limbs.

With sudden and crystal clarity, she knew. Mr. Cheerful had done the machete killings, too.

The black Yukon rolled up to the curb like a cruising shark. She saw Peter in the open passenger window. Still holding the .22, she climbed the gates one-handed and ran across the sidewalk to the car. Behind her, she heard Dean's half-strangled voice. "June."

She turned and saw him still inside the gates with his hands raised, eyes like saucers. Peter leaned out his window with a gun in his fist. Lewis stood in the street with a very large pistol held down along his leg.

"Jesus, don't shoot him," she said. "Dean, if you're coming, move your ass."

He didn't answer. He looked small there at the shadowed mouth of the alley, his clothes like any other clothes, his face like any other face.

"Dean," she said. "Last chance. Over the gates."

He didn't move. June saw herself the way Dean must have at that moment, a woman quick on her feet and calm under threat and more than comfortable with these two dangerous men who had come in the night to take her where she needed to go. More comfortable with them than she was with him.

She smiled. The air was cool and she felt strong and sure. She still held the chrome .22 in her hand.

She raised her voice again. "Your choice, Dean. But we made a deal, remember? You better fucking believe I'm going to hold you to it."

Then she opened the door and climbed inside. "Okay, let's go."

Lewis hit the gas and the acceleration pushed her deep into the black leather. Peter put his hand across the seatback. She grabbed it and pulled herself against the force of the engine to wrap her arms around him.

He smelled like a bohemian party, spilled wine and pot smoke and something chemical she couldn't identify. He said, "I've got you, I've got you, I've got you."

When she could speak, she said, "That was Dean Zedler."

Peter nodded. "What deal do you have with him?"

"He got your pictures from private security cameras across the street from the market. Good ones, and I'm in them, too. I told him that he gets the story if he keeps us out of it."

Lewis said, "Is that a good idea?"

"If you've got a better one, I'm all ears. But we don't have a plan B. We have to buy time to solve this problem, to get Oliver to clear the slate. Otherwise we're fucked. All of us."

Suddenly Peter looked very tired. "Do you trust Dean?"

"I've known him a long time," she said. "He's got the leverage, but I think he'll play fair. He's also very good at his job. It's better to have him with us than against us."

Peter nodded. "Oliver isn't going to like another reporter in the mix."

"I'll deal with Oliver." She sat forward, perched between the front seats. She put her arms around their necks and pulled them close. "Jesus, I'm starving. Who wants barbecue? What time does Speed Queen close?"

Lewis began to laugh.

38

SPARK

By the time Spark's electric skateboard got her to Kiko's place in Tippecanoe, it was after midnight. His two-bedroom cottage was no bigger than her apartment, but it had a four-car garage in the back. A classic south side bachelor pad.

Spark didn't walk up the long wheelchair ramp to the house. She hadn't talked to Kiko in a couple of years, and she didn't want to hear his lectures. She also didn't want to put him at more risk than she had already, just by coming here. But the truth was that she had nowhere else to go, at least not yet.

At the far end of the garage, she punched a four-digit number into the keypad screwed to the siding, and felt a wave of relief when the door rolled up on its track. She'd been afraid that Kiko had changed the code. He'd been really upset.

She'd met Vincent Holloway via email when she was seventeen, after he'd sold his company and was back at Caltech doing research. She was just a teenager with an idea for a battery, and he'd coauthored a paper about carbon-ion electrical storage. Once he'd learned that she wasn't a university research fellow or a corporate vice president, he hadn't been interested in a conversation.

So it came as a surprise when he emailed her again out of the blue three years ago. She was still living in her parents' basement, and her idea had turned into a prototype. She hadn't published in any of the journals, but apparently he'd had a professional connection to one of her mentors who'd mentioned her project in passing.

Holloway was going to be in Chicago for a conference. He'd become a tech investor, looking for the next big thing. Did she want to meet for coffee?

Of course it was flattering. Of course she'd said yes.

If she'd been worried about anything, it was that he was going to try to get her back to his hotel room. But he never touched her. It wasn't that kind of rape.

Instead, he'd taken her ideas.

After an hour's conversation at Coffee Lab in Evanston, he'd offered her a hundred thousand dollars for a look at her lab notes and an independent assessment of her battery prototype. After that, if the technology proved out as promised, he'd provide funding to spin up a real lab and hire some PhDs to help her develop a commercial model. She'd have a salary of two hundred thousand dollars a year to start, with more to come. She could pay off her parents' house.

Before all of that, though, he wanted her to sign a sixty-page contract, along with a nondisclosure agreement. To protect them both, he'd said. Spark could read a mass spectrometer result, but this contract was utterly incomprehensible. His name wasn't even on it. It was a totally different company.

Her professor friends said she really needed to understand what she was signing. She talked to a dozen different lawyers, hoping to get an English translation of the contract, but either they begged off as too busy or they wanted a retainer of ten thousand dollars to get started, money Spark definitely did not have. She was twenty-two years old. Her parents were a firefighter and a house cleaner.

When she explained the problem to Holloway, he gave her the name of a Chicago attorney who would do the work pro bono.

On his firm's website, the attorney wore suspenders and a grandfatherly smile. She'd emailed him the contract and he'd called her the next afternoon. He walked her through the entire document, page by page, explaining everything in great detail. Details of the lab they would build for her, her ownership stake in the company, a company car, everything except the clause that they somehow inserted later. After her signature, and her initials on each page.

The clause that said the company could, at its sole discretion, exercise an option to buy her technology outright. For an additional two hundred thousand dollars.

Of course, when Holloway saw her lab notes and her current prototype, he exercised the option immediately. She got a second check and a notification that she should cease all work in this line of research as any intellectual property was now proprietary.

She should have read the contract more carefully, Holloway told her. His attorneys would bleed her dry, he said. Then he stopped answering her calls.

She was young and naïve.

She was royally screwed.

And totally pissed off.

She also now had three hundred thousand dollars, so she hired her own damn attorney, a guy with an orange bow tie who told her she had a good case for fraud. A jury would love her story. He wouldn't get paid unless she won, but then he'd get paid a lot. Which was fine with her.

The moment she hired him was the high point.

Holloway's company sued her back immediately. Breach of contract, making fraudulent claims, violating the NDA, and everything else they could think of. They requested damages in the millions.

After that came the online attacks.

Spark had accounts on a few social media platforms, mostly because it was the easiest way to contact people whose work she was interested in. She knew she was in trouble the morning she discovered more than a thousand notifications on every account.

People she'd never met accused her of doing all kinds of horrible things. There were links to dozens of fake articles on dozens of fringe websites. Some accused her of selling classified technology to the Chinese. Others said she ran a lesbian child sex slavery ring out of her basement.

Several of those stories gave out her home address, her email and phone number.

Spark still lived with her parents.

She called her attorney. These aren't real people, he told her. It's just a troll farm. A bot network of fake accounts, hired to come after you. And now we know this is hardball.

The accusations—China, lesbians, sex slavery—were perfectly tuned to a certain kind of conspiracy-minded Internet idiot. Within hours, actual humans began to repost the articles, calling her all kinds of names. When new websites took up the clickbait cause, things got worse. Someone sent her an anonymous email that described, in graphic detail, the best punishment for her crimes. Someone else suggested several brutal ways she might kill herself. Social media filled up with deep-fake videos of her face on a porn star's body.

Then she got her first death threat.

The trickle of hate turned into a flood.

The police took notes and started a file but otherwise did nothing, because there was nothing they could do. The technology made it too easy for the jerks to hide their identities.

Spark couldn't sleep. Her parents couldn't sleep. Their phones rang at all hours. The attorney told her to hang tough, the lawsuit would probably take a while. The trolls had started going after him, too.

His investigator found Spark's address and social security number posted on a particularly nasty message board with a history of encouraging violence and hate crimes. She called one of the credit bureaus and discovered sixty new credit card applications under her name.

When her friends in the science community started sending her angry emails, she learned that her email account had been hacked. Pretending to be her, the hacker sent an ugly rant to everyone on her contact list, along with an attachment infected with an ugly computer virus. Overnight, her professional reputation was ruined, and her support group shrank down to her parents, Kiko Tomczak, and her almost-boyfriend, a bicycle fanatic who'd helped her source parts for the rocket bike. The almost-boyfriend tried to step up, but she couldn't take the pity in his eyes, so she ghosted him.

Then things got worse.

She was cooking at home with her mom when the Milwaukee Police threw tear gas canisters through the windows, broke down their door, and invaded the house with automatic weapons. Spark and her parents spent twenty minutes facedown on the floor in handcuffs before they learned that someone had called 911, using software to show her parents' home phone number on caller ID, and pretended to be a victim of child sexual abuse.

It was called "swatting," she learned later. A prank. The police didn't pay to fix anything, although they did apologize repeatedly.

Through it all, her parents were great. Her dad told her he was pretty sure there was no such thing as a lesbian child sex ring. Her mom said, "We'll get through this, honey. How about a margarita?"

Then came their anniversary. Spark had made them reservations at Odd Duck in Bay View. She learned later that her mom's Facebook account had been hacked, and her photo of their dinner ended up on her feed, the phone's GPS providing the location of the restaurant. Eyewitnesses later reported a big red pickup roaring up and bumping their car from behind. Her mom made a wrong turn on Greenfield Avenue and drove down the dead-end street and off the four-foot embankment and into the Milwaukee River.

It was January and well below freezing.

The car broke through the ice.

Her parents died in the water.

The next day, her lawyer was accused of legal malpractice. He told her it was a lie, part of their attack on Spark, but said that he could no longer represent her. He had to devote all his time to defending himself.

No other lawyer would take her case. She was unstable and unreliable, a lesbian child slaver and technology thief. Any Internet search proved it.

From signing Holloway's contract to her lawyer's resignation, the whole thing took nineteen days.

39

Years before their last argument, Kiko had loaned Spark one bay of his four-car garage, which she used mostly to store salvaged parts and unfinished projects. She had hung a silver tarp as a makeshift wall to separate her space from Kiko's two trucks. Standing there now, she looked at the carpet scraps on the floor and the cast-off couch in the corner and realized it was just like her parents' basement. She felt overwhelmed with memories.

After they died, she'd closed her bank account and found a new apartment and stopped using her real name. With the lawsuit dropped, the botnet focused on its next target, and the trolls slowly began to lose interest. Eventually, they forgot about her.

But Spark didn't forget.

She turned her pain and anger into an icy sphere. She made a plan and worked toward its success every day.

She became a member of the South Side MakerSpace and learned how to build an automatic rifle that couldn't be traced.

She found a local gun range where they would let her practice with the rifle, and a tactical school in Tennessee where she learned to keep her cool and advance on her target. The gun became a talisman, her protection against the ugliness and threats that still came to her old email address.

She went back to the dojo where she'd learned judo as a teenager and worked to improve herself at the art of using her opponent's size and strength against him.

Everyone she met told her she was a natural.

She taught herself to write intrusion software that would harvest the complete contents of a phone. She built another program to assess that content, determine which apps led to bank or investment accounts, insert the saved usernames and passwords, and transfer funds into an anonymous account. She made a third tool that would move the money from that anonymous account to another, then another, and many others after that. And still another piece of code that would use the phone to tunnel into every computer in his network and give her complete access. She would own him.

Then she would take him apart.

She changed apartments four times in two years. She was friendly, but made no friends. She pitched in at the MakerSpace because she needed the resources for her work, and because she didn't want the other members to be suspicious. She invented a fake boyfriend to keep guys from asking her out, and also because she knew she'd be automatically less interesting if she were part of a couple. The guilt stabbed deep every time she felt pleasure, or relaxation, or any sense of belonging.

She made herself ready.

In that time, she only allowed herself to be close to Kiko, who had seen her fury from the beginning. He was no stranger to pain and loss. He'd pushed his life from bad to worse, but he'd also clawed his way back from the brink. She admired him. She'd designed and built the hydraulics for his wheelchair. With her parents gone, he was the only remaining soul who knew her well.

Finally, he'd sat her down. "*Chispa*, please talk to me," he said. "I'm worried about you." Using her dad's old pet name was a dirty trick, but it worked.

She told him her whole plan.

His eyes went wide. "No, Spark, no," he said. "This is going to eat you up. Take it from me, okay?" After breaking his back in that fire, Kiko had gotten hooked on painkillers, ended up dealing pills to pay for his habit, then ended up in prison for five years, where he'd finally gotten into a recovery program. "Please don't make the same mistake."

He begged. He cried. He shouted.

After that, she stopped answering the phone.

At least he hadn't called the police.

But now she was truly alone.

She turned on a single light, parked herself on the couch, pulled her laptop from her bag, and dove into the strange files she'd harvested from Holloway's servers.

When she'd first glanced at the CAD drawings back at the MakerSpace, before those two *pendejos* from the Public Market showed up, she hadn't really understood what she was looking at. The unit wasn't very big. She couldn't quite figure out what someone would use it for.

Now, as she sifted through all the overlays and spec sheets that detailed the sensor array and adaptive systems, she became both increasingly impressed and profoundly uncomfortable.

She was impressed because it was a truly elegant piece of design, a giant leap forward in every area from engineering to software to servos. Also impressive was the fact that Holloway had used much of the same technology to automate his manufacturing. After the expense of R&D, prototyping, and testing, each finished unit was relatively inexpensive to produce, and he could produce them in volume. This wasn't about a single unit, but many of them, networked together. All of this gave her a pretty good guess about his intended end use, which was more than a little scary. Not to mention the name Holloway had given the project: HYENA.

That wasn't the uncomfortable part, though. The uncomfortable part was the unit's power source. Spark's beautiful, super-efficient carbon-ion battery.

Looking at the combined electrical consumption tables, she knew that even the best lithium batteries would drive the unit for a few hours at best. Her battery's high power-to-weight ratio, on the other hand, would let the unit run for days.

Which made Spark more than a little responsible for the damn thing.

For the last three years, she'd kept wondering when she'd see her design in the commercial market, but her battery had never appeared. Holloway had been sitting on it. Now here it was, along with a half-dozen other breakthroughs she'd never even seen suggested in the scientific journals.

Where had all this new technology come from?

When the next questions occurred to her, she sat up straight on the couch and swallowed hard.

Who else had he stolen from? And what were they doing about it?

It made her think about the two men from the MakerSpace in a whole new way.

They hadn't known it was her at the market. They couldn't have been working for Holloway.

So who did they work for?

When she heard the door open and close on the far side of the garage, she was still deep into Holloway's project files. Then the silver tarp crinkled aside and Kiko's chair squeaked as he wheeled it through the gap.

He smelled like cigarettes and coffee and burnt metal, just like he always had. He sat in silence while she stared at her screen, pretending she could see past the tears welling into her eyes. Finally he said, "I thought you might be hungry." He had a plastic takeout container in his lap.

She shook her head. She didn't trust herself to speak. Plus, Kiko lived mostly on microwave burritos, and Spark had too much respect for real burritos to eat one of those things.

He held out the container. "Leftover enchiladas verdes from Las Botanas," he said. "Freshly warmed up."

One of her favorites. She nodded and took the food and let the tears fall. He pulled a fork from his shirt pocket. She snuffled and began to eat.

"Two guys came to my studio looking for you," he said. "They raided my files and found your address. I tried to stop 'em, but I couldn't."

She could tell by his face how much it galled him. But that wasn't what he was telling her. He was saying that he was still in her corner.

"I'm sorry," she said. "I didn't mean to get you involved."

"I know," he said. "But I'm involved now. We'll figure it out. At least you didn't kill the guy."

She looked at him. The fresh red rage still burned. It needed more fuel.

"Oh, no. Spark, no."

"I'm not done," she said. "I didn't hurt him enough."

"You mean you don't feel better."

"Yes," she admitted. "But there's something else."

She showed him Holloway's CAD overlays and walked him through the specs. When she told him what she thought HYENA was designed to do and what she wanted to do next, he looked at the ceiling as if hoping for help from above.

"Take the money and run, Spark. It's not your problem."

"Yes, it is," she said. "This thing runs on my battery. I practically helped him build it."

"Those are his files, right? There's got to be a whistleblower hotline that wants this stuff."

"Not yet," she said. "If I make everything public, I lose all my leverage. Besides, I don't know if he's actually breaking the law. Even if he is, and somebody catches him, it will take years. None of these white-collar guys ever go to jail anyway. Worst case, he'll pay a fine." She swallowed her tears. Her face felt hot. "He killed my *parents*, Kiko. He didn't drive the truck that chased them into the canal, but he might as well have. And nobody will ever do anything about it. Nobody but me."

His voice was gentle. "That's a one-way road, Spark. With nothing good at the dead end of it. My advice? Go back to your shop and make something new." He nodded at the cardboard shoebox she'd plugged her laptop into. "Make more of those. Start a business. That's your future."

Even that project had started as a fuck-you to Holloway, a way to supplant the battery design he'd stolen. She stared into a dark corner of the garage. "I want to see his face," she said. "I want to

221

look him in the eye when I wreck his life. That's the only way I'll get past this. The only way I'll manage not to blow his fucking head off."

"You can't win this, Spark. Don't you remember how much money this guy has? This won't ever be over. He'll hire lawyers. He'll hire private cops. He'll hire someone to give you a beatdown even while he bleeds you to death with lawsuits. He'll chase you forever."

She gave Kiko a brittle smile. "Then maybe I'll blow his head off after all."

He looked impossibly sad. "Killing him won't bring your parents back. And revenge doesn't make the pain go away. Only time does that. Only letting go. Setting down the burden." He raised his heavy shoulders and let them drop. "That's what works for me. One day at a time."

"I'm not an addict, Kiko."

He gave her a sad smile. "Spark, you got it bad as I ever did. And the worst part is you don't even know it."

She patted his arm. "Tell you what. When this is over, I'll start going to meetings with you. Okay?"

"If you live that long. If you don't go to jail." He grabbed her hand. "Listen, if I can't talk you out if it, at least let me help, okay?"

"Bad idea, Kiko. You have a life. Your work, your art, your recovery. This is all I've got."

"That's not true." Tears trailed down his creased face. "You've got me, too."

She jumped off the couch and knelt to hug him.

His big arms were gentle, but his voice was ragged and rough as he murmured into her hair. "You'll always have me, kiddo. That's a promise."

But Spark was afraid it wouldn't be enough.

When he rolled out to get some sleep, she picked up her computer and typed in the commands to wake the new code she'd buried in Holloway's main system. Two tiny little programs.

One to hijack his system completely.

The other to protect herself. A fail-safe. A dead man's switch. Just in case.

Whatever happened, it would be worth it.

40

HOLLOWAY

In a large, dark apartment, high in a modern residential tower, Vincent Holloway stood against the wall of glass, staring out at the black night.

Behind him, his laptop screen strobed from hot pink to orange to red.

Holloway felt the cracked halves of his sternum, cut apart for the quadruple bypass and only loosely wired back together for recovery, flex and grate against each other with each breath. The surgery had been seven years ago, and his sternum had long since healed, but at moments like this, he felt the old damage more keenly than ever.

He told himself that he wasn't the same man anymore. He had changed everything. He'd taught himself to love the gym, to *need* it, losing a hundred and forty pounds of fat and adding forty pounds of muscle. He'd committed himself to a strenuous regimen of hormone implants and herbal supplements and synthetic protein smoothies that tasted like dirt. He'd even become a damn vegan.

And it had made a difference. He'd always been aggressive with his ideas, able to work long, hard hours and take big risks, but now his energy levels were through the roof. His erections were unflagging. Like he was nineteen again and could take on the world. Like he was a new man.

He tried not to think about the old days. But at moments when everything was at risk, he couldn't push away those memories. From his earliest years, he had been marooned in his body, cut off from real life by the ever-thickening layer of flesh. He'd never been good at making friends. He was fairly certain that his own parents had never actually liked him. The feeling was like a hole inside him that would never be filled, no matter how much he ate.

Eventually, he'd realized that he was very smart in ways that had a high monetary value. He found a world he could excel in. He set himself the task of making something new, and getting rich in the process. Maybe then, he reasoned, he'd be free of that yawning hole. Arrival into the world of wealth would bring him joy, would give him the feeling of ease and acceptance that his life had always lacked.

But it didn't. Selling Sense Logic had netted him almost five hundred million dollars. He knew, intellectually, that it was a lot of money. But it left him way down on the list of the world's wealthiest people. Almost half a billion wasn't enough, not by a long shot.

Getting rich didn't make Holloway whole. It just made the hole bigger.

It had taken him five years and a failed relationship and open-heart surgery to realize that half a billion dollars did make other things possible, if you were willing to take the risk and do what was necessary.

To change. To become someone new. To remove yourself from the world almost entirely, take what you needed, and do what had to be done.

Holloway decided to transform himself, to double down on his investment. He set himself the task of becoming the richest man in the world.

The only real requirement was to go hard, to move fast and break things. Long before Zuckerberg said it, Holloway had done it. He was a true pioneer. He'd taken steps that he'd thought would be horrifying, or at the very least distasteful. The big surprise was that they weren't either of those things. They were necessary, and also fun. It was exhilarating to understand deep in his bones that right and wrong were just social constructs, and rules did not apply to him. Holloway kept pushing forward, eye on the prize.

The burn rate was high and the risk was higher, but he was right on schedule.

Or at least that was how he felt when he woke from a short, restless sleep and opened his laptop.

The screen's flashing colors bounced off the walls and window glass. Pink to orange to red.

The message read, *We have sequestered your information. We require one hundred million dollars for its release. Liquidate your assets, prepare for electronic transfer, and await further instructions. We begin deleting files in six hours.* A little bomb graphic showed a timer, counting down. Followed by a smiley face. With a wink. And devil's horns.

Ransomware aside, one of the primary pleasures of wealth was the ability to pull people from their beds and convert your nightmares into theirs. So he got Coyle, his systems contractor, on the horn. Not the compromised phone, but the spare he always carried because he cycled through a new device every month. As a security measure, he thought sourly.

"It looks like your whole network is affected," Coyle finally said. "Local servers, remote backup, international. Every corner, locked down tight. It's an efficient little virus." Coyle, who was ex-NSA, sounded impressed despite himself. Then promised he'd get it unfucked ASAP.

He was diplomatic enough not to point out the obvious, which was that Holloway had made it easy for the hacker. First, he'd unlocked his phone and handed it over. Then once he'd gotten it back, he'd checked his crucial information, which had only spread the virus more quickly. It had never occurred to him that his assailant might not pull the trigger. Not once he'd realized who she was.

He didn't need his money guy to tell him that he didn't have the hundred million, at least not liquid. But Holloway woke him anyway and told him to scrape up what he could. Keep his options open. If Holloway wasn't sleeping, nobody else would, either.

His last call was to an attorney named Krueger in Corpus Christi.

It was surprisingly easy to hire a professional killer, when you knew the right people. More expensive than Holloway had expected, especially considered on an hourly basis, although surely much of the fee went to Krueger. But if there was one area not to pinch pennies, it was when hiring an assassin. He never even asked if there was a discount for repeat customers.

"Fuck is this?" Krueger's voice was thick with unprocessed alcohol. Clearly he wasn't happy about the four a.m. call. Holloway had only met him once, although they'd done business for years.

"I need a direct contact for our man."

Krueger cleared his throat elaborately, then spat. "That's not how it works. For everyone's protection. I'm sure you understand. Tell me what you need and I'll convey it. But not here. Use the secure message app."

"Things are fluid. I need direct contact."

"Not a good idea," Krueger said. "Trust me on that."

"I'll double your fee up front, and double it again on completion. I'll use the secure app. But I need you to connect me to him directly."

Krueger hawked and spat again, then breathed noisily into the receiver for a moment. "Better give me the quadruple fee up front. When I see it in my account, I'll message you. But don't say I didn't warn you."

Holloway had seen pictures of the assassin's work.

The man wouldn't flinch at what needed to be done.

Nor would Holloway. Those days were gone. Eyes on the prize.

He called his money guy again and told him to make the payment to Krueger, then turned back to the window and stared out at the vivid moonless darkness, waiting. In the unlit apartment behind him, there was a soft metallic whine and the whisper of synthetic footpads on the hardwood floor.

"Harry, stand down," he called. "Rest and recharge for tomorrow."

Holloway had traveled to Milwaukee three days before, when the only significant obstacle to world domination was two greedy cheeseheads trying to hold him up for a higher price. Holloway had messaged the lawyer in Corpus Christi. Two names and two addresses. It was simple enough. The freelancer did the rest.

Holloway's lunch appointment was with a Mexican girl he'd done business with several years before. She had reached out to the Chicago attorney who'd closed that earlier deal with a proposal that laid out tantalizing new intellectual property. Holloway was surprised that she wanted to talk, given how their previous business had ended. But her scientific career had failed to progress, so perhaps she saw Holloway as her only option. Or maybe she'd simply run out of money. Either way, he didn't mind. Desperation had a way of lowering the price.

Given their history, he'd proposed lunch in a public place to mitigate any potential fallout.

Obviously, he had underestimated her.

He hadn't even known it was her until she'd spoken into his ear at the market. She'd taken his phone, cleaned out his petty cash account, dealt very effectively with a pair of boy scout bystanders, and vanished. After getting over the shock of it, Holloway had almost admired her buccaneering spirit. He'd done the same kind of thing himself.

This was before he realized the true scope of her actions, the amount of data she'd copied from his system, and what she'd inserted into it.

At the time, his biggest concern was media attention. He'd gone to a lot of effort to fade quietly from view and make himself difficult to find. The last thing he needed was to show up in a news story. Thankfully, the local paper made no mention of him, but the next day, a reporter somehow found his phone number. From Operator Twelve's recording of her questions, it was clear she'd identified him.

She was not some dumb young thing taking notes at city council meetings. She was a national reporter with a history of breaking big stories.

So Holloway had messaged Corpus Christi again.

Make this problem go away, and do it quietly.

How he'd ever done business without Krueger and the freelancer, he had no idea.

He always felt a certain thrill when making this decision, the purest exercise of power. He felt no guilt or remorse. He had evolved beyond such small thinking. Lesser kings and princes had used this power since before the dawn of time. Tribes, villages, entire ethnic groups and nation-states had been wiped out for a fraction of the gains that Holloway would bring to humanity.

In comparison, the freelancer's work was the merest flick of a scalpel.

Albeit a scalpel with a rather blunt edge.

Finally his phone pinged. Krueger, sending contact information for an unnamed third party. He knows the arrangement.

Holloway messaged the freelancer separately. New assignment. Maria Velasquez. He sent a photo of the girl from three years ago. Location and instructions to follow.

The reply took a few minutes. Still doing the last job. Will get back when done.

Holloway shook his head. How hard could it be to make one girl reporter disappear?

This is high priority, he sent. Be ready when I send instructions.

This time the reply was immediate. Do I tell you how to run your pirate ship? Don't tell me how to do my work.

Holloway left it at that. He'd try again when he found young Maria Velasquez.

No reason to make the freelancer angry.

41

PETER

By the time Peter and Lewis got June some barbecue and made it back to Riverwest, it was after two in the morning. They could hear Mingus barking in the backyard when they turned onto the block.

"That goddamn dog," Lewis said. He pulled the Yukon into his attached garage. June got into the driver's seat with the engine still running and the chrome .22 in her lap while Peter and Lewis slipped through the house looking for anything out of the ordinary. They were pretty sure Mr. Cheerful had no clue that one of his pursuers lived just a few houses down from June, but they were careful just the same.

Mingus kept barking the whole time.

After they double-checked the locks and June put on the kettle for tea, Peter asked Lewis, "You want to see about the dog, or you want me to?"

"You'd better go," Lewis said. "I'd probably just shoot him."

The big mutt was in the fenced yard with his front paws up on the gate, barking at the night, serrated teeth gleaming. The fence bowed outward under his hundred and fifty pounds, the new pickets thoroughly chewed. The fence repairs wouldn't last long at this rate.

"Hey, Mingus. What's up, boy? What's out there?"

The dog dropped to the dirt and sprinted past Peter, bumping Peter's hip and knocking him off balance. He ran a tight circle in the yard, then put his paws back up on the gate and started barking again.

Mingus was one of the ugliest dogs Peter had ever seen, with the bullet-shaped head of a pit bull and the long-legged body of a timber wolf, all covered with shaggy orange fur. He was great with kids and anyone else he considered part of his pack, but he was hell on strangers in the neighborhood. Dinah had to introduce him to the mailman when they moved in. He especially didn't like any FedEx or UPS guys coming up their walk, because they were always different. During his frequent escapes from the yard, he'd treed more than a few slow-moving delivery drivers.

"Mingus, get off the gate." The dog did what he was told when it suited him. He jumped down now so Peter could open the latch and let him out, then ranged out into the street, nose in the air. Peter followed, the Colt in his hand.

The dog stopped at the oil stain where Mr. Cheerful's van had been wrecked, sniffed at the pavement for a minute, then ran up the block as if right on the axeman's tail. Peter shook his head, thinking Mingus would be gone for a week. Lewis was convinced the dog had a rich girlfriend somewhere on the east side, living in a big house with a heated outdoor swimming pool. Mingus always came back well fed, clean, and smelling faintly of chlorine, no matter the season. Lucky dog.

But not today. After just a few minutes, he came back down the block, working his way in and out of backyards on the far side of the street, then finally trotted down Franny's driveway with a large paintbrush sticking out of his mouth like a cigar. Peter rolled his eyes. The dog was a piece of work. But at least he'd stopped barking.

But he wouldn't come back to the house, either. Instead, he paced in the street and growled and chewed the paintbrush handle to splinters. Peter couldn't grab the dog's collar because he wasn't wearing one. He'd long ago figured out how to pull it from his head with his paws.

Peter finally texted June and asked her to come to the door and call Mingus. Along with Dinah's boys, June was the dog's favorite. When he heard June's voice, he immediately ran to the house, jumped onto the couch, and rolled over to get his belly rubbed. Goddamn dog.

Lewis had moved a wooden chair to an inside corner so he could sit with a full view of the room and the windows overlooking the yard. He still wore the shoulder holster with his big black automatic on the left and two spare magazines on the right. His 10-gauge leaned against the curved arm of the chair. Two boxes of double-ought shells stood open on the side table beside a fat chrome .357 with a six-inch barrel, in case a grizzly bear showed up.

"I'll take first watch," he said. "You two go upstairs and grab some sleep. Dinah made up the guest room before she left."

June said, "Lewis, why don't you go to the hotel and be with your family? We're fine here."

Lewis shook his head slightly. "She texted me earlier, told me to stay away. Said the guns would scare the boys."

"You could leave the guns behind," June said.

Lewis shook his head again. His face was expressionless, but Peter could see the hot desert wind in his eyes. Peter knew Lewis didn't mind taking a risk for himself, but this whole thing had gotten a little too close to home. Lewis didn't want to lead Mr. Cheerful, or anyone else, to his family. He loved Dinah and those boys with the power and intensity that only a man given a second chance could have. Every day with them bought a little more redemption from those years in the wilderness.

Peter put his hand on Lewis's shoulder. He could feel the heat coming through his shirt. "Thank you. Wake me when you need me."

Lewis nodded and turned out the light.

42

Upstairs in the little guest room, June stood and stared out the window at the dark. Peter sat on the bed fully dressed, including his boots and the Colt in its holster. He'd sleep that way, on top of the blanket, if he actually managed to sleep.

Somehow, the static didn't seem to mind the small space. Maybe it was having June there with him. Maybe it was knowing Lewis was downstairs, standing watch. Maybe it was the 12-gauge Mossberg he'd laid on the floor. Regardless, it was progress.

He looked at June. "Aren't you tired?"

"I'm exhausted," she said. "But every time I even think about closing my eyes, I see that asshole with his goddamn axe."

Edgar had come at her three times in less than twelve hours. Her brain was in overdrive, trying to process it. She was tough as nails, but that only got you so far. Some things were just plain hard.

Peter kept his voice quiet. "You want to tell me about it?" He'd been going to veterans' groups for years, talking about his war and listening to other vets talk about theirs. Telling your story seemed like such a simple thing, but it was powerful.

"I shot the fucker," she said. "I shot him twice."

Peter nodded. "You did what you had to do."

"I almost didn't do anything," she said. "He looked at me like a snake hypnotizing a mouse, you know?" She shook her head. "He told me if I let him kill me, he wouldn't hurt anyone else."

The wind had picked up. They could hear it in the trees, even with the windows closed.

"And he did this weird twisty thing with his body," she said. "Like he was made out of rubber. Like he knew I was going to pull the trigger, and he knew where the bullet would go, and he somehow got out of the way."

"You hit him, June. Twice."

"I was aiming for center mass," she said. "Just like you taught me. He wasn't fifteen feet away. And I only managed to nick his ear and, what, bounce a bullet off his ribs?"

"Shooting targets is different from shooting a real person who's trying to kill you."

She gave him a look. "I was scared, but my mind was clear," she said. "I was steady. Feet planted, two-handed grip. I fucking aimed right at him. But I barely touched him. He just laughed. What kind of freak does that, does any of that stuff?"

She was breathing hard. The day had finally caught up to her.

Peter knew she was cool under pressure. He'd seen her do incredible things. And she'd become a very good shot. But Mr. Cheerful had really messed with her head.

"You hurt him," Peter said. "And he backed off, right? He didn't hurt you or anyone else. That's a win. He's probably bleeding to death right now, if he's not dead already. Either way, he won't bother us again."

"You don't believe that," she said. "Lewis is downstairs with an arsenal. You put a shotgun under the bed."

"We're just being careful." Peter patted the blanket. "Come to bed. Sleep helps, I promise."

June had wrapped him in her arms on so many nights when the dreams came for him, when his spring was wound tight and his mind wouldn't stop. Sometimes the simple warmth of her beside him felt like the only thing tethering him to the earth. He would be happy to give her that now, if he could.

She walked over and sat beside him. He put his arm around her. She leaned her head against his shoulder.

Then her phone, charging on the dresser, chimed with a text.

She jumped up, unplugged the phone, and showed Peter the screen.

> This is Holly Gibson. I've been happily married for almost seven years. I don't know anything about Vincent anymore.

"It's Holloway's ex-girlfriend," June said. "I reached out to his former business partners yesterday and her name came up."

"Why is she texting now? It's two a.m."

"Holly and her husband run a restaurant in England. They're six hours ahead, so it's eight in the morning there."

So much for getting June to relax a little.

She texted back. I just have a few questions. Can we talk now? Without waiting for an answer, she hit the call button, then put the phone on speaker so Peter could hear.

"Porthminster Fish House." Behind her, the sound of clattering pans and music, the kitchen gearing up for the day.

"Hi, is this Holly? I just texted you, it's June Cassidy calling from America. Is this an okay time?"

"Yes, I suppose." A door opened and closed, and the background noise quieted. "What's this about?"

"I'm looking for your old friend Vincent Holloway. By any chance are you still in touch with him?" June's voice was friendly and cheerful, just us girls. No killers on the loose here.

"In touch?" Holly's voice was subdued. "I wouldn't put it like that."

"How would you put it?"

"Well. Every few months, Vincent calls the restaurant for a chat."

June looked at Peter. "What do you chat about?"

"Mostly about Vincent. He'd never say it, but I can tell he's lonely. Why else would he still call me, after all these years? He never was very good with people. Not like my James. I try to get off the phone as quickly as possible." Holly was from California, but her years in the UK had put a British flavor in her voice.

"You were the one who ended it?"

"Yes. I told Vincent I'd met someone else and he became quite angry. He actually had a heart attack a few weeks later. To be honest, at the time I wondered if it was my fault. Then when I sent out wedding invitations, Vincent somehow heard about it and flew over here and tried to talk me into marrying him instead."

"Wow. How did that make you feel?" June's voice was intimate and supremely interested, even as she scribbled notes on her pad. Peter thought again how good she was at her job.

"Well, I stopped feeling badly about how I ended things, that's for sure." She gave a soft laugh. "Vincent always was a supremely arrogant wanker, you know? With some odd ideas about things, too. But in the time since I'd seen him last, he'd really become quite strange."

"Mm. Strange in what way, if you don't mind my asking?"

"Well, he gave me this long speech about the many ways he'd changed his life, and that he'd done it for me. He'd had some, well, some bedroom problems, probably because he'd been so overweight, and he wanted me to know he'd been getting these hormone implants to lose the weight and solve the problem. But he was more driven than ever. All that money and success, and it still wasn't enough. Really, it was kind of sad. He kept talking about changing the world."

"Mm," June said again. "How was he going to do that?"

She sighed. "I have no idea. I was just a temp worker in his office, and now I run a restaurant." Holly paused a moment. "I'm sorry, but why are we having this conversation? Why do you want to know about Vincent?"

"He's involved in something very dangerous," June said. "And I guess you could say he's disappeared. I'd like to help him, but first I have to find him." Her pen tapped on her pad. "I don't suppose you have a phone number for him, by chance?"

"No, he always calls from a new number. Otherwise I wouldn't answer. He still sends me flowers every month, too."

"That must be really awkward," June said. "What does your husband think?"

"Oh, nothing bothers James. Or at least he doesn't admit it, because he wants to downplay my stalker ex-boyfriend. It's not like we can change the restaurant's number. So we've turned it into our own private joke, that I left a rich and desperate American to marry this overweight Brit and have his babies while I work in his restaurant seven days a week. I should say also, James is very practical and it's quite a large flower arrangement, so we just toss the card in the bin and put the flowers in the restaurant. The latest came two days ago. I'm looking at them right now."

Peter opened his mouth, but June held up her finger. "Holly, do they always come from the same shop?"

"Oh, yes. Gallery Flowers in St. Ives. A standing order. I used to cancel, but Vincent would just find a new florist."

"Gallery Flowers." June gave Peter a toothy grin. "I don't suppose you happen to have the number handy, do you?"

She called the flower shop next. Her friend Holly was getting their gorgeous arrangement every month, and wanted to express her appreciation to the sender. Did the shop have any contact information?

"That's a bit of an odd one." On speaker, the florist sounded like a gay Winston Churchill. "The customer orders online, but our confirmation email always bounces right back, so that's obviously a typo or something. But his credit card goes through, so we keep sending flowers."

"He pays by credit card? So you must know his name, at least."

"Well, that's something else odd," the florist said. "On the card, the customer has asked us to write, Love Forever, Vincent. But the name on the credit card is Graham Brown."

June hung up and Peter fell asleep under the pale glow of her laptop screen, listening to the machine-gun rattle of her fingers on the keyboard.

43

EDGAR

Edgar walked out of the newspaper office and left the neighborhood in his new van before the police showed up. Mike Dillman was starting to smell, but other than that, he was pretty good company. He didn't talk back and he didn't try to give directions, either.

Edgar's ear hurt where it was torn up and his side ached like he'd been beaten with a stick. He thought the second bullet had angled off one of his ribs, then slid under the muscle and skin until it could get out through his back. It felt bad, but he didn't think it was fatal.

He found his face in the rearview mirror and gave himself a stern look. "You need to get better at dodging bullets." Edgar could have carried a gun himself, which would have solved the problem, but a pistol wasn't the same as a blade. It didn't give him the shivery feeling. Edgar felt strongly that a person should enjoy his work.

He parked by the freeway and crawled between the seats into the back of the van. It hurt to bend and twist, but he pretended it didn't. He found a first aid kit hanging from a shelf, but it was small and old and it didn't really have anything for bullet holes. He peeled off his shirt, then opened a fresh bag of painter's rags and a can of paint thinner and cleaned his wounds. The chemicals burned like cold fire. It was like the bleach, but different. He felt purified.

He stuck a half-dozen Band-Aids on his ear, then tore his shirt into strips and tied them around his ribs. He folded rags under the wrap to slow the bleeding, but he couldn't do much with the hole on his back. He needed real supplies and another set of hands.

He pulled on a stained sweatshirt that said BENJAMIN MOORE and drove to a twenty-four-hour drugstore in the next county. The new van was fast and strong. He put on his cool sunglasses and went inside and filled a basket with gauze and tape and disinfectant spray and extra-strength Tylenol and a big jug of red Gatorade and anything else he could think of.

The clerk stared at his bandaged ear but didn't say anything except how much he owed. Edgar said *Please* and *Thank you* and tried not to look at the security cameras. All he could do was use his Sunday manners and hope the police wouldn't come looking this far.

He chased Tylenol with Gatorade while he drove back to Mike Dillman's house. He parked in the driveway and put his new first aid kit and a fresh white shirt into a cloth grocery bag and went through the fence to the old lady's yard, moving carefully with the torn muscles and skin. Across the street, the dog started barking again. Edgar didn't like dogs.

Her back door was locked, but the wood was old and gave way when Edgar popped it with his shoulder. He carried the axe in his hand and the knife through his belt and the grocery bag's handle loose around his wrist.

He slipped through the kitchen and went to the front hall. It was dark and he tried not to bump into things. It smelled like his grandmother's house when he was a boy. He could see a light on at the reporter's house through the big front window. He turned to look up the stairs and saw a small, pale shape at the top.

"Who's there?" Her voice thin but not soft.

"It's just me, Grandma." Edgar started up the steps. "I wanted to see you."

"Buddy, you're too fat to be my grandson."

She turned on the light but he was already reaching for her. She tried to back away but he had her thin upper arm tight in his fist. In the other fist, he raised the axe.

"I don't have anything you want," she said. "I'm just an old lady." Then she got a closer look at him. "Hey, you don't look so good."

He felt the sweat beading on his face and under the sweatshirt. The Tylenol hadn't done much. Plus getting through the fence and hitting her door had opened things up again. It was harder to pretend he wasn't damaged.

"I need your hands," he said. "I need you to bandage me up."

Her face was all sags and wrinkles. Her hair was steel gray and cut short. Her white cotton nightgown hung below her knees. "You're the man with the van," she said. "From earlier today."

He nodded.

"All right." She tugged her arm and he released his grip. "I'm Fran. Come into the bathroom." She turned away, then stopped and pointed at the axe. "Put that thing down before you hurt somebody."

———

He put Mike Dillman's kitchen knife in his sock where he could reach it, then sat on the green carpeted toilet seat cover while she sorted through the supplies he'd brought. Her bathroom smelled like his grandmother's bathroom, too. Talcum powder and Listerine.

She told him to take the sweatshirt off, then peeled away his makeshift dressings. She ran water in the sink until it steamed, then soaped a washcloth and began to scrub his wounds. Every muscle clenched and he wanted to close his watering eyes but he didn't. It took longer than he liked.

When she finally sprayed disinfectant into the raw meat, the pain eased and he knew he had begun to heal. He angled his head to watch her. "You're not afraid of me," he said.

"Of course I am. Have you looked in the mirror?" She opened a box of gauze. "But when you're almost ninety-eight, you know the grim reaper will show up sooner or later. Maybe you're him."

She packed the gauze into the entry wound, taking her time, then laid more on top. She ran strips of tape across the bandage to hold it in place, glanced at her watch, then tapped his shoulder. "Turn."

He spun on the seat and she began to pack the exit wound, pressing the wads in with her thumbs. He made a sound. "Sorry," she said. "The back is worse than the front."

He cleared his throat. "You were a nurse?"

"I grew up on a farm," she said. "And my husband, God rest his soul, he and his friends were kind of accident-prone. Anyway, I've done my share of fixing people up." She got the tape on, then tapped his shoulder again. "Time for that ear."

He bent his neck to the side and saw her glance at her watch again. "Are you waiting for someone?"

"It's almost six," she said. "Usually I've had breakfast by now. And *New Day* starts in a few minutes."

She held up the shears he had bought, still in their wrapper. "Do you want me to trim that torn skin or just tape it up?" The reporter's bullet had blown a ragged hole into the upper cartilage, and flaps of ear hung free and bleeding. They were already dead and they didn't know it.

"Cut away," he said.

When she was done, he stood and inspected her work in the mirror while she put the wrappers in the trash and packed the remaining medical supplies into the bag.

"I don't know about you, but I could use a drink." She walked into the hall. "Come downstairs and I'll make an ice pack for your ribs."

"You got any beer?"

"Just scotch," she said. "And Girl Scout cookies. I guess I could make eggs if you want some. I might have bread for toast."

She went to the steps. He was still in the bathroom. She looked at him. He could feel the knife tucked into his sock, pressing against the skin of his calf. He didn't say anything.

She put a hand on the railing. "If you're going to kill me, buddy, make it quick. I don't want to lay dying on the floor for two days."

He walked to her. He had the knife in his hand now. "Go into your bedroom, Grandma."

She glared at him. "None of that pervert sex stuff, either. I'm almost ninety-eight years old. I'm all closed up down there."

He took her arm. "Come on, now."

She glanced at her watch again. Six-thirty. "Just one scotch," she said. "Let me have one last scotch. It's the good stuff."

Out the bedroom window, the sky was red in the east and tree branches thrashed in the wind.

When Edgar was done taking care of the old lady, he put on his fresh shirt, then took a jug of milk and a box of cookies from the kitchen and stood in the living room away from the window where he could see without being seen.

It was a good place to watch. The light was still on at the reporter's house across the street. She'd come home eventually. Edgar would wait.

A few houses down from the reporter's, a front door opened and a man stepped outside. He wore a blue sweatshirt and held a coffee cup. Edgar thought he might be one of the reporter's protectors. If he was in that house, maybe she was, too.

The man drank from his cup and looked up and down the block while the wind blew his hair around. He finally took something from his pocket and raised it to his ear.

In the kitchen, the old lady's phone rang. Edgar didn't move. It rang and rang and rang.

Across the street, the dog was barking again.

44

PETER

Peter paced through the quiet house, watching the light come up outside.

He had woken at five when Lewis had come up the creaking stairs. June had snored beside him, burrowed deep under the covers. He would let them both sleep as long as they could.

He made a pot of coffee and thought again about what they'd learned. It wasn't much.

June had made a connection between the Virginia killings, the machete murders outside Metzger Machine, and Mr. Cheerful with his double-bladed axe. It sounded right to Peter, too. They'd go check out the Metzger location today.

On the *Journal Sentinel*'s website, June's friend Dean Zedler had a story about the newsroom attack. The security guard, Jerry, was dead. An unnamed reporter had fired a gun at the man with the axe, but the attacker was still at large. The police were searching every corner of the city. The detectives had left a half-dozen messages on June's phone before Peter had gone to sleep. She'd have to deal with the fallout today.

Peter still had no decent line on Spark. He wasn't willing to split the team to have one of them sit on her apartment in the hopes that she'd come back, not with Mr. Cheerful still on the loose. Even if the fat man did have a few new holes in him.

Maybe June had made progress with that name she'd gotten from the florist. Graham Brown was a good alias for someone pretending to be ordinary. Graham Brown sounded like a lawyer from Phoenix.

Mingus came down the stairs and drank noisily from his bowl, stuck his nose in Peter's crotch to get his ears rubbed, then went to the back door and whined. Peter let him out into the backyard, poured another cup of coffee, and stood at the glass and watched the dog go to work on the fence pickets again. The soft cedar was no match for those relentless teeth. Maybe Lewis should think about a metal fence instead of wood. Or concrete block with razor wire. Or just give up and admit that the dog was some kind of throwback to the ancient age before domestication.

The wind came up again. Mingus stuck his head into the gap he'd made and began to bark. Peter's phone chimed softly and he knew it was seven o'clock. The daily alarm he'd set to check Fran's porch light as she'd asked, to make sure nothing had happened to her in the night. Why she'd picked Peter instead of June, he had no idea.

He took his coffee out to the front porch and peered at her front window. Sometimes she forgot to turn off the light. Peter figured sometimes she just wanted a little company in the morning. He'd go over there and make her scrambled eggs and toast. But she wasn't in her chair and the light was off in the living room. And she didn't answer her phone.

Peter set his mug on the railing and crossed the street into the wind.

Her door was unlocked. "Fran? Fran, are you okay?"

The entryway was dark and small. The static hummed in his blood. "Franny, where are you?" Mingus had stopped barking.

Ahead of him was the stairway to the second floor and a narrow hall to the rear of the house. At the end of the hall was a slice of the kitchen with a chair tipped against the back door. He'd been in the house dozens of times and he'd never seen Fran do that. Something wasn't right.

As he reached for the gun behind his hip, a flicker of movement flashed from the living room. He jumped back instinctively and jerked his hands up to his sides as the axe blade flew past his chest and buried itself in the wide oak trim of the entryway. Mr. Cheerful smiled at the other end of the handle, the happiest man in the world.

He wore a clean white dress shirt and a lump of gauze and tape over one ear. The shirt was snug enough that Peter could see the bandage over his ribs on his left side. He had a slight protective hunch over the injury, but if it affected his swing, Peter hadn't seen it.

Edgar pulled the axe handle sideways to free the blade and Peter went for his pistol.

He had the safety off and was bringing it up with his finger moving to the trigger when the axe flashed out again. The blade smashed the Colt to the side and into the heavy oak newel post at the bottom of the stairs.

Peter felt the blow all the way to his shoulder and the gun was almost knocked loose, but he managed to retain a hold on the bottom of the grip, grateful he hadn't lost the pistol or part of his hand. He brought the muzzle to bear again on Mr. Cheerful's thick chest but his finger couldn't find the trigger. He looked down at the Colt. The frame was scored and the trigger and guard were torn away by the power of the sharp steel blade against the solid old oak. He didn't even know that was possible.

Mr. Cheerful raised the axe again, his eyes dancing. Peter was crowded into the stair landing and his options were few. He could retreat upstairs or attack inside. The axe was a bad weapon for close quarters and an attack would be unexpected. The gun would be his hammer. Plus, Peter was a Marine so it wasn't really a choice.

But Edgar had made the same close-quarters calculation. His smile stretched and he tossed the axe behind him and pulled a big kitchen knife from somewhere at the small of his back.

Peter changed his mind about retreat. He'd find something useful upstairs, a lamp or a bedside table, anything to get him out of arm's reach. A hand grenade was probably too much to hope for. He was half-turned with a foot on the first step when he heard a low growl and the fast clatter of claws on the front porch.

Mr. Cheerful's eyes got wide and he slapped the entryway door shut. It hit Mingus on the nose and Peter heard a yelp. But the door hadn't latched.

As it swung open again, the big mutt stepped into the gap with his legs bunched for a leap and his gleaming fangs bared and his growl rising as if from the darkest depths of a bottomless cave.

Edgar turned and ran down the hall.

Mingus went after him.

The back door was still blocked by the kitchen chair wedged under the knob. Edgar upended the table and threw it behind him, tried and failed to move the chair, then crashed through the closed window to the backyard.

Mingus dodged the table and scrabbled around it to put his

front paws on the sill, gauging the leap. Razor shards of thick old glass made blades in the bottom of the window frame.

"No, Mingus, goddamn it, no." Peter didn't want the dog's belly torn to shreds.

He pushed past the table and put his restraining right arm tight around the dog's neck and aimed the Colt at Edgar's retreating back, but the goddamn gun still didn't have a trigger. Edgar vanished behind the garage and Peter heard a big engine start and tires squeal. Edgar was gone. Again.

Mingus turned his head to Peter, tongue hanging out, and gave Peter a big wet slurp across the face.

Then Peter thought of Fran.

Franny? Fran, where are you?"

She wasn't in the kitchen or dining room or half bath or laundry. She wasn't in the front hall closet. The basement was empty but for a giant humming chest freezer full of freezer-burned meat and boxes of Girl Scout cookies.

With every empty place, he felt the panic rising.

He imagined her fear and pain. He imagined her chopped into pieces like the family in Virginia.

It was his fault. He should never have gone into the market. He should never have moved into the house across the street. He was responsible for the death of an old lady.

He left Mingus whining on the landing and ran the stairs three at a time.

She wasn't in the back bedroom or hall closet or bathroom. In the front bedroom, he saw a wooden chair jammed under the knob of a closet door. "Fran? Are you in there?"

He kicked away the chair and found her kneeling in the middle

of the deep closet. She faced the door with an ancient black revolver held out in both small hands. With the light shining from
the bedroom window, Peter could see the blunt noses of the rounds
in the cylinder. The hammer was cocked. Her finger was inside the
guard.

"Hi, Fran. It's Peter, your neighbor. Put the gun down, okay?
Are you all right?"

She wore a long white nightgown. Shoes littered the floor of
the closet behind her. By her side was a large pair of old-fashioned
leather work boots. Inside one, Peter could see what looked like an
open box of ammunition, covered with dust.

"Oh, Peter." Despite the beaming smile, her eyes looked sunken
and wet. "I knew you'd come. Because I left the porch light on."

"Very smart, Fran. Now put down the gun, please."

She lowered the pistol to her lap and eased down the hammer
without having to look at it. Her hands were blue-veined and
translucent, but they were steady.

"I forgot I even had this thing until that horrible man locked
me in here. I had to find it by feel in the dark. The bullets are quite
old. Do they ever go bad?"

"Let's not find out, okay?" Peter helped her off the floor. The
revolver was not a modern weapon. The small walnut grips were
worn smooth and the four-inch barrel had an odd half-moon front
sight. "Where'd you get that gun?"

"Oh, it was my Bob's pistol, so it has sentimental value. Do you
like it? It's a Police Positive."

"Your husband was a policeman?"

She chuckled. "Oh, no. My Bob didn't get along with the police. Do you know, he once robbed fifty-nine banks in twenty-six
months? On a bet, if you can believe it. He got pretty good at it.
Those were fun years."

"Seriously? Your husband was a bank robber?"

"Well, not all the time. He did other things, too." Her stomach rumbled. "I'm hungry. That horrible man wouldn't let me have anything to eat or drink."

"I'll make you some breakfast." Peter put a hand on her shoulder. "How did you end up in the closet?"

"He was hurt and I patched him. I used to do that for Bob and his friends, back in the old days. When I was done, he locked me up. I think he planned to be here until June came back, and he needed me to change his bandages. He told me if I didn't give him any trouble, he'd let me go."

"Did you believe him?"

She raised up the revolver. "Buddy, what do you think?"

45

SPARK

The morning bike commuters were gone from the valley and Spark had the Hank Aaron Trail to herself. All her gear was freshly charged, and her electric skateboard carved long, smooth arcs on the blacktop.

She stopped at the Valley Passage tunnel and took out her phone. It rang and paused and clicked and rang again before a voice answered.

"Hello. How may I help you?"

Spark remembered the voice from three years ago. It had gotten even better since then, with more realistic intonation. Indistinguishable from a real person. "Hi, is this Operator Ten?"

"This is Operator Twelve. You may call me Gary. How may I help you?"

"Congratulations on your upgrade, Gary. I need to talk to Vincent Holloway. This is Maria Velasquez. Vincent is waiting for my call."

Gary was a chatbot, a kind of active filter that Holloway used instead of an answering service, an offshoot of a voice recognition and speech generation project. Operator Twelve seemed a little pared-down compared to Operator Ten, which had engaged her in conversation about the weather and sports. Spark had been completely fooled. Holloway had explained the trick when he was trying to steal her battery technology. It was like showing a child a puppy to get her into your van.

A short pause. "Hello, Ms. Velasquez. Mr. Holloway is in a meeting. Please hold." Then silence.

She looked at the Valley Passage murals and checked the time.

Was he tracing her cell right now? She didn't doubt he was trying. His security people would be top dollar. Not that they'd find her. She'd routed the call through the Philippines and Costa Rica. Even if they did, she was on the bike trail. They only had a few points of entry, and she had a million ways to leave.

He wouldn't call the police, though. She knew from the paper that he hadn't stuck around to talk to them after she'd held him up at the market. He'd turned himself invisible for a reason.

After two solid minutes, the line clicked. "Maria, I'm so sorry to make you wait. Thanks for calling. How are you today?" Holloway sounded aggressively charming and self-assured, just like she remembered.

Spark wasn't going to be fucking polite. "Do you have my hundred million?"

"That's a big ask, Maria. Although I have to say, I'm impressed by the power move."

"Fuck you, Vince. A hundred million."

"Maria, you have to know I don't have anything like that kind of liquidity. I'm all tied up. You already emptied my discretionary account. Out of respect, what I can offer you today is about a million six. That's cash, my emergency fund from the safe at home. It's already on its way."

The wind gusted again, and she smelled the coming rain. "You're full of shit, Vince. I saw your account balances."

"I thought you were smart, Maria. You know it's more complicated than that. You've been in my servers, so you know I'm in the middle of something huge. I imagine you've gotten a lot more business savvy since the last time I saw you, so I'll lay it out for you. I haven't taken any venture money on the project. I don't want the interference, and I don't want to split my ownership. Everything I have is invested."

A hundred million was the ask, not what she expected to get. "Come on, Vince. How many lines of credit are you running?"

"They're all at the max, Maria. My ass is hanging way out there. Between the debts I owe my suppliers and funds I need to take the project to market, I'm actually in the red. You can call my banker. I'll send you my P&L, the business plan, too. I'll walk you through it."

"Like I'd believe anything you told me. But that's fine. I'll just start pruning files off your server." She was surprised how good she felt, the anger burning in a clean blue flame. Three years of work coming to fruition. "I'll start with your lab notes, then move on to the CAD drawings and spec sheets of your HYENAS." He could reconstruct some of that, she was sure, but it would cost him.

"Please don't," he said. "How about preferred stock? Say, ten percent of the company? I expect to be profitable in eighteen to twenty-four months. I'll buy the shares back in two years for twenty million. If you can wait five years, I'll buy them back for two hundred million. I'll put it all in writing."

Spark had seen how Holloway did business. She would never trust anything with his signature on it. He was just buying time for his IT guys to scour her code from his system. But she didn't care about the money. This was about revenge.

"The delete button is so *satisfying*, Vince. Preferred stock just isn't the same."

He cleared his throat. "How about twenty percent? But the window is only two years. Hey, you never forget your first forty million, right?"

"Eighteen months and fifty million."

"Jesus, Maria, you're killing me," he said. "But okay."

It irritated her that he kept calling her Maria. He'd probably read somewhere that people were more likely to do what you wanted when you used their name. But Maria wasn't her name anymore.

"Write up the documents and I'll have my lawyers vet them. I'm keeping your goddamn data locked down until everything is signed. But I want the cash, too. This afternoon. You deliver it yourself, in person."

He sighed theatrically. "When and where? I have meetings until five."

Entitled prick. "I'll let you know," she said. "Cancel your fucking meetings and stay by the phone. Get your people working on those documents, I want them at my lawyer's by noon."

"Okay," he said. "But don't hang up. I want to ask you something. That prospectus you emailed a few months ago? The one that got me to meet you at the market? Efficiency, materials, outputs—is that real?"

In order to get into his phone, she'd needed him to agree to meet her in person. So she'd sent him an abstract on the experimental fuel cell she'd been playing with. No true design details, of course, but enough to grab his attention. She was counting on his greed and sense of invulnerability to overcome their history. Now that she'd seen the HYENA specs. she wished she'd made up something completely different. Her battery could power that thing for days. Her fuel cell would let it run for months.

"The data is real," she said. "But you'll never get your hands on the actual design."

"That tech is worth a lot more than your battery." She could practically hear him drooling. "Maybe, when this is over, we can talk about a partnership?"

Her mother was right. The devil's best weapon was a charming smile. She almost laughed despite herself. "You are a gold-plated asshole, Vince. You just told me you were broke."

"A cheap, efficient fuel cell? The first-round investment alone will be ten figures." A billion dollars.

Spark figured it wouldn't hurt to have a carrot as well as a stick. Although Holloway would be in no position to buy into anything by the time she was done with him. "I'll keep an open mind."

"One last thing, Maria." His voice dropped. "I never had a chance to tell you how sorry I was to hear about your parents. It's a real shame. I hope you know I didn't have anything to do with that."

The world turned red. She closed her eyes and clenched the phone in her fist and took a deep breath and counted to ten before she answered. "Sure you didn't, Vince. Just wait for my call. By the way, my delete bot has a countdown timer, and it's ticking. If anything bad happens to me, you're screwed."

"Nothing bad will happen, Maria. It's been very nice talking with you. I look forward to resolving this whole situation soon."

As she put her phone away, she wondered if he actually believed his own bullshit or if he just wanted her to believe it. Either way, she knew it wasn't going to be this easy.

She left the Valley Passage tunnel and turned back onto the

bike trail, leaning forward so the skateboard knew to pick up speed.

On the path ahead, she saw a cyclist coming fast.

She recognized the bike.

She held up her hand and they came to a stop together. "Dude."

46

PETER

While Peter finished cleaning up the breakfast dishes, June went upstairs to shower. Lewis stood at the window with one eye on the street and the other on Fran, who sat at the kitchen table in her long white nightgown and a pale blue bathrobe with the Police Positive in the pocket. On the table in front of her was a thick white mug and a bottle of fifteen-year-old Balvenie. She tipped in another slug. It had started out mostly coffee, but was probably pure scotch by now.

"No, I'm not going to a hotel," she said. "That horrible man isn't going to make me leave my own home. I've lived in that house for fifty years."

"Franny, I can't watch out for you when I'm out chasing him," Peter said. "What if he comes back?"

She waved away his concern. "Oh, Edgar's not mad at me. I patched him up. You just fix my house and I'll be fine."

"You really don't want us to call the police?"

She looked at him with clear eyes. "Are you dim? What on earth will they do aside from track dirt on my carpet and drink all my coffee?"

Peter turned to Lewis, who gave him an elaborate shrug. Peter had already called the lumberyard for supplies to get her house secure again. Eli Bliffert was driving it over himself. Lewis, with his many rental properties, had been a good customer for years.

"Okay," Peter said. "As long as you understand that I can't really make things nice again until we get this guy."

"Just don't take too long," she said. "I'm almost ninety-eight, you know."

When Eli arrived in his big diesel pickup, Peter jogged over to Fran's to unload, then stayed to board up the window and add two-by-four barricade brackets to her doors. If Edgar really wanted in, Peter reflected, this wouldn't stop him. Nothing would.

But Franny was right. Edgar wasn't after her. He was after June. And now, Peter.

He put the tools away and walked her home, her hand tight on his arm. "You never asked me what this was about, Fran."

She kept her eyes on her blue sneakers navigating the cracked asphalt. "Bob and I never talked about his work. I didn't want to let anything slip, and he never wanted me to worry." She shook her head. "Buddy, I worried anyway. But that was the deal I made. I knew he was an outlaw when I met him." She sighed. "Maybe that's what I liked best about him. He was such a beautiful man."

Peter made sure she could get the two-by-fours in and out of the brackets, then crossed back to Lewis's house as a police car rolled up the street toward him.

Peter was glad he'd left the axe and the ruined Colt at Fran's house. He needed a replacement gun.

———

The cruiser pulled over and the driver stepped out. He was the same uniformed sergeant who had pulled Peter over the day before. Peter waved and kept walking. "Good morning."

"Hold up a minute." The cop adjusted his equipment belt and came around the front of the car, smoothing his push-broom mustache with one hand. He was maybe ten years older than Peter, crisp and professional without being spit-polished. "I'm looking for June Cassidy, but I'll talk to you a minute first. You're Peter Murphy, correct?"

Peter had to remind himself of his alias. "Yes, I'm Peter."

The sergeant watched Peter's face like he was memorizing it. It was a little unnerving.

Peter tried not to look like a wanted poster. "I think you and I met the other morning. You pulled me over for a bad taillight, but you let me fix it. Thanks again for that."

The sergeant gave him a curt nod. "No problem. I'm surprised to see you, though. I thought you'd gone on a hunting trip."

For a moment, Peter didn't know what he was talking about. Then he remembered the story June had told the police after the van had crashed. He'd make a lousy spy. "You're the one who showed up about the lunatic with the axe?"

"I get all the weird stuff," the sergeant said. "But I guess you didn't go hunting after all."

Peter put a sheepish look on his face. "I left, but I turned around pretty quick. What kind of asshole goes hunting after someone tries to run over his girlfriend?"

"Someone who really likes hunting," the sergeant said. "But I guess you got your priorities figured out. What can you tell me about the man with the axe?"

Peter wasn't going to mention that he'd seen the guy that morning. "You haven't found him yet?"

"Soon," said the sergeant. "Can you describe him?"

"Let's see. A couple of inches taller than me, with a crew cut and a happy smile. He was thick around the middle, but he could really move. He beat us to the corner and then just disappeared."

The sergeant wasn't taking notes. "He had an axe, but he ran away. And you went after him."

"Well, there were two of us. And I had a crowbar."

The sergeant just looked at him.

"I was a Marine," Peter finally said. "I guess it's hardwired."

He watched the sergeant's expressionless face and knew he should have kept his mouth shut. The guy was trying to place him and he'd just added another data point.

"Did you know the man with the axe had threatened Ms. Cassidy earlier that day?"

"Not until later. That's why I turned around from the hunting trip."

"Do you know why he threatened her?"

"You'll have to ask her," Peter said. "I'm just the boyfriend."

The sergeant's flat stare told Peter he didn't believe any of it.

"One last thing and we're done." The sergeant pulled a phone from his uniform pants and held it up. "Stand right there."

Peter raised a hand to block the camera's view. "I'm sorry, what's this about?"

"Put your hand down, Mr. Murphy. It's just routine and perfectly legal. You're a witness to an attempted assault who left the scene of a crime. Unless there's a reason you don't want your picture taken?" Peter dropped his hand. "Great. No need to smile." The sergeant stepped around to get another shot from the side.

"Thank you." He looked down at the screen. His mustache crinkled up in a smile.

Peter was pretty sure the improvised mug shot wasn't fucking routine. But there was nothing he could do unless he was willing to beat down a veteran patrol sergeant. He wasn't. And it would only make things worse anyway. He had to hope they could solve their problem before the sergeant figured out why Peter looked familiar.

The cop tucked his phone away. "Now, about Ms. Cassidy. She hasn't returned any of the detectives' calls, so I'm here to escort her to the District Five station. Is she home?"

Peter hooked a thumb over his shoulder. "We spent the night at our neighbor's. We're all a little jittery about this thing. I'll get her."

Behind him, the screen door slapped shut and June came down the front walk with her phone to her ear. She waved merrily at the sergeant and kept talking, her voice loud enough to be heard clearly on the street. "No, Detective, you're absolutely right. I'm very sorry. Honestly, I was so freaked out, I didn't really think. I just had to get out of there. Yes, I did shoot him. Yes, I'll bring the gun. Lunchtime? Great. Thank you."

She hung up and gave the sergeant a sweet smile. "Sergeant Threadgill, how nice to see you again. What can I do for you this morning?"

He was not amused. "I'm here to escort you to the station. My orders were to provide you with every courtesy."

She waggled her phone. "That was Detective Hecht," she said. "I'm meeting him at one. I'm sorry you had to come all this way."

"I'm sure the detective would have a moment for you now, ma'am. I can follow you in your car or give you a lift myself."

"I'm a journalist, Sergeant. Right now, I'm chasing something and I need to keep chasing it. I'm sure you understand how that is from your own work."

"Yes, ma'am, I do. Right now I'm chasing you."

"Well, you've found me. Safe and sound. I'll be at the station at one. Feel free to confirm that with Detective Hecht." She looked at Peter. "We need to get moving."

His mustache bristled. "Ms. Cassidy, this is not a game. This is a homicide investigation. A man is dead."

"I'm well aware of that," June said quietly. "His name was Jerry. He liked English soccer and homemade calzones." She sighed. "I'm one of the good guys, Sergeant. Peter is, too."

The sergeant gave her a grim stare. "That's hard to tell from where I'm standing. You both seem pretty slippery to me. If anyone else gets hurt, I'm coming after you both. Hard." He got back in his cruiser and slammed the door.

As he drove off, Peter looked at June. "Lady, you are something else."

June shook her head. "I just burned our last piece of goodwill with the police. We better get this thing figured out."

"Absolutely. Just as soon as I can talk Lewis into lending me another gun."

47

They were back in the Yukon headed north toward Capitol Drive, with Lewis driving, Peter in the passenger seat, and June sprawled across the back with her laptop open. They'd stopped at Colectivo on Humboldt for a caffeine infusion and a sack full of pastries.

Lewis looked over his shoulder. "What's at Hampton and Teutonia?"

"Metzger Machine." June tore apart a blueberry muffin.

Lewis slurped at his quadruple mocha. "Where the two guys got killed the other day?" Then he figured it out. "With a machete," he said. "Partially dismembered."

"A heavy bladed weapon, brutally used. Remind you of anyone?" June stuffed a piece of muffin in her mouth. "They're the same kind of killings as the Virginia murders, too. A machete instead of a kitchen cleaver, but still." Peter had brought Lewis up to date on the conversation with Oliver the night before.

"Do we know anything about the dead guys?"

"They were partners in Metzger Machine, and cousins. According to the reporter who wrote the story, the police have no leads. They think it was a random crazy. But if it turns out they're connected to Edgar or Holloway, that might give us a way in."

"How about your friend Dean? Did you talk to him this morning?"

"He called while we were dancing with the cops." Her phone rang. "Here he is again. I'm putting him on speaker. You guys, button it." She turned up the volume. "Hey, Dean. How was it with the police last night?"

"I was at the paper until four in the morning," he said. "They were pretty pissed at you, I have to say."

"I'm going to the Fifth District station at one today," June said. "I'll come to the paper afterward and tell you all about it. Can I give you a few things to run down?"

She knew the question was coming before he asked it. "Hold on," he said. "Why didn't you wait for the police last night?"

"Because I have work to do, Dean. I didn't want to spend the whole night in an interview room."

This was true, but not the real reason. She didn't want to tell the police everything, and they'd probably figure that out if they grilled her long enough. She'd have to talk to them eventually, but she was putting it off as long as she could.

Dean didn't like her answer. "Your friends don't seem to want to talk to the police, either. Why is that? Who are they? They seem like interesting guys."

"We're not doing this, Dean." He'd had leveraged himself into her story by holding those security camera pictures over her head, but that didn't mean he was in charge. "The story isn't about me or the Samaritans, remember?"

"Then how about you tell me what's going on?"

June looked at Peter. He shrugged. It was up to her.

"Well, let's go over what we know. Two days ago, someone goes into the Public Market with an automatic rifle and robs a guy of his phone, which seems like overkill. Especially when he doesn't even keep the phone."

June was using *he* deliberately, holding back the fact that Peter and Lewis had found the shooter's apartment, even though they didn't know Spark's real name. They didn't know much of anything, unfortunately.

"He shoots up the place, but he doesn't actually hit anyone. That's lunchtime. After dinner that same day, someone breaks into my house and takes my notebooks and computer and phone." No need to mention the video glasses, either.

"What? Did you file a police report?"

"Why bother? Anyway, yesterday, I'm riding my bike to the paper and Edgar nails me with the door of his van. When it becomes clear I won't go with him voluntarily, he tries to grab me."

"Good lord. That's why you asked if I'd gotten any weird feedback on that story," Dean said. "You think someone wanted you to stop reporting on it. But why you and not me?" He sounded a little offended. Getting warned off a story was every investigative reporter's dream. It was a clear sign you were onto something, even if you had no idea what. Like now.

"I thought about that," June said. "I think it's because I saw the guy whose phone got taken at the market. I remembered his face, but not his name. Maybe he remembered mine. Or maybe he just saw my byline on your piece about the market shooting. But I also did some digging and figured out who he was, even though he'd basically disappeared. No credit cards, no driver's license, no address. Pretty strange for a guy whose share of a tech company sale earned him half a billion dollars a decade ago. The only thing I found was an old phone number associated tangentially with his name. When I called, the receptionist kept hanging up on me."

She heard Dean's pen scratching. "So what's the guy's name?"

"Vincent Holloway. I think he's the one who sent Edgar after me. I'll share my notes file so you have everything. But I still have no idea what Holloway's up to, or where he's located."

"Why is he so worried about you finding him?"

She thought of Oliver with his stillness and calm, and the agreement they'd made at her kitchen table. Despite everything, she trusted him. She also needed him. So she wasn't happy about what she was going to do next.

"We think Holloway stole some new technology."

Peter shook his head, mouth forming no, no.

Dean jumped at it. "What kind of technology? What does it do? And stolen from whom? Where did you get this information?"

June waited a moment, giving Dean time to imagine the enlarged scope of the story.

She could hear the ambition in his voice. It sounded like hunger. "Shit, Dean, I shouldn't have mentioned it," she said. "I can't tell you anything. Not yet. Maybe never."

"June, we have an agreement, remember? I get the story and keep you and your large friends out of it. You need to tell me everything or the shit will really hit the fan." So much for Weaponized Nice.

Maybe it was his ambition talking, or maybe it was the fact that she now clearly had a boyfriend. Either way, it didn't matter. She just needed him to keep his mouth shut for a few more days. The tech bit was the carrot. But she also had a stick.

She smiled. "Step carefully, Dean. This is not a few state senators taking money from a mining company. This is the big time.

People are dying. Dangerous men with guns know your name, and where you live. Are we clear?"

"Are you threatening me?"

"Of course not," she said. "Other people are threatening you. People who have their own agendas. And don't forget the man with the axe. He almost certainly knows who you are, too."

The phone went silent. They were on Teutonia now, passing the DMV and the Dollar Store, coming up on Hampton. She took another bite of muffin.

Chewing, she said, "So you're going to keep grinding on Holloway. And I'll give you another name to run down. A possible alias for Holloway. Graham Brown. That's the name on the credit card he used a few days ago to buy flowers for his married ex-girlfriend." June wasn't going to give him Spark. She was a wild card.

"What am I, your research assistant? What are *you* doing this morning?"

Was this the real Dean? If so, she'd dodged a bullet all those years ago. "Don't be bitchy, Dean. Is this your story or not? Where's your pride of ownership?" Then she threw him a bone. "But here's something you'll like. I'll send you Holloway's background check from a decade ago." Oliver had just emailed it that morning, with his agency's identifying information stripped out. "Break it down and figure out what avenues that opens up."

"Okay," he said grudgingly. "I can do that."

"But you don't share any of this with anyone, including your editor. Or I will personally shoot you twice in the ballsack. Got me?"

She hung up. They were stopped at the light. Peter and Lewis were both staring at her.

"What? We're stuck with the guy, he might as well do some goddamn work, right?"

48

Metzger Machine was a modest midcentury office cube standing right up against the sidewalk, with shed-like additions larger than the original building grafted onto the sides and back. The windows had sturdy steel grates over them, in recognition of the area's crime statistics, and June saw more than a few shuttered storefronts and derelict houses. Metzger Machine, on the other hand, had a nice new sign and a full employee parking lot.

A young assistant buzzed them inside. The office space was utilitarian but clean, with flat carpet and fluorescent lights and gray repurposed cubicles dating from the nineties. This was a long way from Silicon Valley's beanbag chairs and juice bars. But the computer screens were large and new and the engineers at the desks were busy with CAD drawings and phone calls.

June had called ahead for an appointment with Marty Metzger, the managing partner. The assistant walked them back to a glass-enclosed conference room where a middle-aged man in a plaid shirt and cardigan sweater stood staring out at the busy shop floor. He had the inward, sleepless look of a man sunk deep in his own grief. His arms were crossed tight across his chest and his eyes sagged like warm cheese.

"I'd like to help," he said, "but I don't really have anything new that I haven't already told your colleague. We could have done this all over the phone."

Then why, June wondered, had Metzger agreed to meet? Maybe he was just polite. Or maybe he wanted to answer a question he hadn't been asked yet.

June pulled out a chair and sat at the conference table, but didn't take out her notebook. Lewis watched the office for a cheerful man with a sharp tool. Peter did the same for the shop floor. She didn't have to tell them to keep their mouths shut.

"I'm very sorry for your loss," she said. "They were your cousins?"

"Yes," he said. "Also my partners. And my friends."

"What kind of work do you do here?" June knew that asking men about their business was a good way to get a conversation rolling.

"Well, we were a machine shop for more than seventy years, building manufacturing equipment. My great-grandfather started it. But by the time my dad retired, most of that had gone overseas. We were on life support. David and Sam and I had the idea to reinvent ourselves by doing stuff China wasn't set up to do."

"Interesting." June had never been a straight business reporter, but it would be hard to miss the story of the demise of American manufacturing. "Tell me more about that."

"We decided to specialize in rapid prototyping and custom jobs. We focused on engineering, problem-solving, and a high level of quality. As a part of that, we designed our own automation systems. Now a big part of our work is doing that for our customers, getting them into smart manufacturing."

June gestured at the people and machines on the other side of the glass. "Business looks good."

"Yeah," Metzger said softly, gone inward again. "It was. I love this place."

"It must be hard losing your cousins," she said. "Not just personally, but for the company, too." She wasn't sure what she was after. But she'd know it when she found it, or at least she hoped so.

He just nodded. He still hadn't sat down. He hadn't really looked at any of them.

"I hate to ask this," she said, "but why do you think they were killed?"

"I have no idea." He turned his head, his voice suddenly sharp. "I already talked to the police about that. They said it was random. This isn't a great part of town."

"But the *way* they were killed?" She wasn't going to mention the machete or the dismemberment, not unless she had to. "That's unusual, isn't it. Not something that happens around here. Or anywhere, really."

He turned back to the glass and the activity on the other side. "I wouldn't know," he said. "The police are working on it. We hope they find the person who did it. We'll all sleep better when they do."

Now she took out her notebook and flipped through the pages as if trying to find something. "The thing is, it happened in broad daylight. In a fenced parking lot. Whoever did it, he left their wallets and watches and phones, right? He left their car keys, and their cars. So what's the motivation?"

Metzger's voice rose. "What are you asking? If I killed them?

My cousins and friends? They were an integral part of my life and this company. I have nothing to gain and everything to lose." He ran his hand down his face as if chasing the memory of tears.

She didn't think Marty Metzger was acting. The grief was real. But there was something else. She just didn't know what it was.

If she could see it, the police almost certainly had, too. Metzger was in the office when his partners were killed, so he wasn't the one swinging the machete, but they'd have looked hard at him anyway. They'd have talked to the families and the employees, trying to find a reason related to the usual motives of sex, money, and power.

In her early days as a police reporter, it hadn't taken June long to learn that most murders weren't mysteries, they were crimes of passion. The killers were usually someone known to the victim with a history of violent behavior, often drunk or high, sometimes caught with the weapon still on their person or under their mattress. They almost always had a reason, although it might be small, maybe nothing more than an insult. A true random killing was a rare event.

Working a homicide, generally the police either made significant progress in the first twenty-four hours or not at all. The cops weren't subtle. Given the fact that Marty Metzger was at the office, business as usual, they didn't consider him a suspect. He'd be lawyered up or locked away, not talking to reporters.

But here he was. Talking without saying anything.

Clearly, June hadn't found the right question yet.

She thought about Spark's electric bike. "Were you working on any special projects? Something unusual?"

Metzger took a deep breath and let it out. "All our projects are special. They're like our children. We take our work very seriously." He cleared his throat. "Speaking of which, with every-thing that's happened, I really have a lot to do today. I'll walk you out." He opened the conference room door and waited for them to get the hint.

There it was, the classic slip-and-slide. She might not have found the right question, but she'd found the right subject. And Metzger had changed his mind about talking.

"How about any unusual clients?"

He looked away again. "Oh, that's all proprietary, I can't dis-cuss our clients. Or their projects. Really, it's time for you to go. I have another appointment in a few minutes."

The police would have asked these same questions. If they'd seen this stonewall act, they'd have put Metzger in an interview room until they got an answer. But they hadn't. Something had changed since the last time the police had talked to him.

June had no idea what that might be. But she had information the police lacked.

She pulled her laptop from her backpack and opened it on the conference table. "Mr. Metzger, let me show you something."

SketchCop was a facial composite software used by many po-lice departments instead of sketch artists. June had gone through a SketchCop training session for a story several years before, and had kept the login and password. She'd spent an hour with the program last night while Peter slept. She was no artist, but she had a very good memory for faces.

She turned the laptop so Metzger could see it. Holloway's in-tense, deep-set eyes stared out from the screen. She was pleased with the egg-shaped head and its fleshy features. He really did look like a B-movie humanoid robot from the fifties.

Metzger took a step back like he'd been punched in the chest.

His grip faltered on the conference room door and the pneumatic closer pulled it shut.

"I really can't," he whispered. "You saw what happened to David and Sam. He'll kill my whole family."

But once Metzger started talking, he couldn't stop.

49

Because Marty Metzger felt responsible for the whole thing.

He was the one who'd found Holloway at that conference in Pittsburgh six years ago. He was the one who'd taken Holloway out for drinks and invited him to Milwaukee to see their state-of-the-art facility. He'd convinced Holloway to place his first order. It was all his fault.

June already had her recorder on by the time the floodgates opened. Peter and Lewis stared through the conference room's glass walls, keeping an eye on the office and the shop floor, but listening hard as Metzger's confession spilled out.

"All we did was prototyping for three or four years," Metzger said. "Individual components at first. Articulated joints. Complex gearing systems. Nothing that actually fit together. We had no idea what they were for. We assumed that he had other shops building other pieces. He was very secretive. Everyone in the company signed a nondisclosure agreement. After his first visit, everything was done by encrypted email. Not even a phone call."

He sat at the conference table now, a thin, gray-haired engineer spilling his guts. June made sympathetic noises and took notes, letting the recorder get the details. Peter and Lewis stood out of Metzger's line of sight so he wouldn't have second thoughts.

"Then he gave us a more complete assembly. Four of them, actually, with multiple joints, like the legs of an animal. Milled from aluminum and titanium. They were electronically powered and controlled, but we never saw the actual circuit boards. We got test boards and bench specs to make sure the assemblies did what they were supposed to do. When there were problems with his designs, we suggested improvements." Metzger hung his head. "Well, mostly me, actually." Another thing he felt responsible for.

"He complained a lot about other fabricators. They couldn't deliver on time, or he didn't like the quality, or they couldn't solve the problems. Holloway was a demanding customer. His emails sometimes read like rants, you know? But this is a demanding business. Some clients are a pain, but Holloway always paid top dollar, so we made it work. Eventually he gave us something new to build."

He held his hands out just past the width of his shoulders, showing the size. "Like a log that's too big for your fireplace. With four sockets on the bottom that would fit the first components we'd made, so we were pretty sure it was some kind of quadruped. And another socket at the top, which we thought would be for a head. Like this was an electronic pet or something."

Metzger stared at the wall. "That's what David and Sam thought it would be. The dog you wouldn't have to walk or feed, that wouldn't pee on the carpet when you had to work late. My idea was a companion for the elderly or infirm, something capable enough to take out the garbage and strong enough to lean on or help you up if you fell. There would be a giant market for that kind of thing, worldwide, especially with automated assembly."

June could see how it had been. Metzger and his partners excited to be on the cutting edge. Solving problems, making money, imagining their bright future.

"If everything was going so well," she asked, "why would he kill your partners?"

"That's the thing I can't stop thinking about," Metzger said. "We do a lot of prototyping for old-line companies. Harley and Rockwell are our biggest customers. But as Holloway started eating up more and more of our production time, Rockwell offered to buy twenty percent of our shop. We had a good relationship, but they wanted to make sure their projects would be our top priority."

Metzger shook his head. "Somehow, Holloway must have heard about it. I think he got nervous. We weren't just prototyping for him, we'd built an automated assembly system. He had big plans, and he really needed us. He told me he wanted to buy a controlling interest. Basically for the same reason as Rockwell."

Metzger Machine was privately owned, June thought, so there would be no public disclosures. Holloway could stay in the shadows and do as he pleased.

"He made a formal offer," Metzger said. "A good one, with a higher valuation than Rockwell. The thing was, none of us wanted to give up control. This company has been in the family for four generations. I thought it was a good idea to sell *some* equity, maybe nonvoting shares. The money would let us grow. We could move into a bigger facility, improve our equipment, upgrade our capacity, make all our customers happy." He looked at June plaintively. "Was that so wrong?"

"Sounds like the American dream," she said. "So what happened?"

"We had a board meeting to discuss how to move forward. I argued for selling shares to Holloway. David and Sam felt strongly about taking the deal with Rockwell because they were an established Milwaukee company. In the end, the board sided with them.

"When I told Holloway how it had gone, he showed up to make his pitch in person. It was the first time we'd actually seen him since that first visit. He brought in a fancy breakfast for the whole office and had the equity paperwork all drawn up and everything. Although it was in the name of a different company, some name we'd never seen before, which made me a little nervous. He had a PowerPoint presentation and gave a funny little speech about cash bonuses and company cars and big pay raises and dominating the market. But David and Sam weren't convinced at all. Honestly, the whole thing was so weird that I was thinking David and Sam had been right the whole time."

He stared at the wall. "Well, we didn't even have to discuss it. We gave him our answer on the spot. He wasn't happy, but he didn't make a scene or anything." He shook his head. "Five hours later, David and Sam were dead. Chopped into pieces in our own parking lot."

He cleared his throat and paused a moment to collect himself.

"When the police showed up, they asked about any problems with the business. We gave them a list of names, a machinist we fired for failing a drug test, a client who owed us money. Holloway was on the list, too. So was a neighborhood guy who'd been harassing our receptionist. Sam and David had actually gone out to talk to him, and he seemed a little unstable, so I thought he was the most likely guy. The police said they'd follow up.

"Whatever they did, it didn't seem to matter. The next day, Holloway called to say his offer was still on the table. But he said it in such a way that I knew what he'd done to David and Sam. I told him I was going to hang up and call the police. Then he asked about my twin daughters' school trip to the Urban Ecology Center that day. He knew about my wife's appointment with her physical therapist that afternoon, my parents' dinner party with their church group that evening. He sent pictures, made it clear that he knew exactly how to find each one of them. David's wife and kids. Sam's husband. He said the only reason we were having the conversation—meaning, the only reason I was still alive—was because I had shown a willingness to sell."

None of this had been mentioned by the reporter June had talked with, although the police wouldn't have talked about potential suspects. "You didn't tell the police about that call?"

Metzger put his hands on top of his head, almost shouting. "He had pictures of my daughters."

"Then why are you telling *us?*"

"I mean," he said. "I just." He blinked away tears. He seemed utterly lost.

June turned to Peter and Lewis. "Can Holloway really do this?"

Lewis shrugged. "Mafia been doing it for a couple hundred years. Just a new twist."

Peter said, "Did you tell anyone else?"

"My lawyer," Metzger said. "He's got an ex-FBI guy doing research, but he can't even confirm Holloway exists. Or if Holloway is his real name. And I talked to the board. The members who are left, I mean."

June looked at him. "So what do you plan to do?"

"We have an emergency meeting at the end of the day. We have proxies for David and Sam's shares. We're going to sell. I don't know any other way."

"Hang on," Peter said. "He wants to buy his way in, right? And it's a good offer. So he's not doing this for the money. He's making something that he thinks is a very big deal and he's willing to kill people to protect it. Did you ever figure out what it is?"

Marty ran a hand down his face. "I don't think it's a pet."

"Can we see your technical drawings?"

"I can't," Metzger said. "I told you, that's all proprietary. We signed nondisclosures."

Then he realized what he'd said, and blinked as if coming out of a trance. For the first time, he really looked at Peter and Lewis, who stood with grim faces, their jackets unzipped. June watched him register Lewis's shoulder holster and the new loaner gun on Peter's hip. "Who are you guys? You don't look like reporters."

"We're not, Marty." Peter smiled kindly. "We're the kind of people who deal with people like Holloway. But we need your help to catch him."

June was amazed, as always, at how Peter could be so fearsome in one moment and so reassuring in the next.

For just a moment, the grief and dread washed from Metzger's face. "Okay." He stood up. "My office is right next door."

50

Metzger had a pair of large monitors mounted above his desk. Peter and June and Lewis crowded behind as he pulled up diagrams of the legs, long and powerful. Then a sleek, streamlined torso, with pairs of protected sockets for the legs and a larger one at the top.

"The gap at the front is for some kind of electronics package," Metzger said. "Sensors, I think. The belly has an internal housing for an energy source, although this thing will be really power-hungry. You'd need something the size of Tesla battery to make it run for more than an hour or two. I can't imagine what he plans to use."

Peter said, "Did you ever make the head?"

"It's not a head," Metzger said. "It's an arm." He clicked the mouse and a new image came up. "Three segments, each one fully rotating and double-jointed. A four-fingered claw on the end, with pressure sensors in the tips, really sensitive, for a delicate touch." He pulled up an exploded diagram and pointed at the screen. "But with this gearing here, and these cams, and the new servomotors, it's also very, very strong. I've never seen a piece of technology like it."

"Can we see one that's all put together?"

"We've never put one together," Metzger said. "We don't have the power source or sensor package or the motherboard, either."

"But you must have a drawing of the finished thing, right?"

"Holloway is so secretive, he pretends each component is a separate project. Although any half-decent engineer can see how they come together. One of our people made a 3-D rendering." He clicked again and a new image appeared.

"Wow," June said. "That doesn't look like a toy."

"No," Metzger said softly. "It's not exactly cuddly, not with that claw instead of a head." He moved the mouse, rotating the rendering for a complete view. "From the bench tests, we know the completed device will be extremely capable. Revolutionary. A whole new category, if you got the software right."

Peter knew the software would work just fine. Oliver had told them all about it. A new language specifically designed for solving complex physical problems.

"How many of these have you made?"

"Enough components to make eight hundred complete units."

"That many? Are the parts still here?"

"Only for the last eighty units. We've already shipped the rest."

"You shipped them?" Peter tried not to raise his voice. "Where the hell did they go?"

"We don't know. His truck arrives, we load the pallets, and it leaves. The whole thing takes about five minutes. The driver never even gets out of the cab. Holloway must have a facility somewhere, because we already delivered twenty automated assemblers. Really just one flexible platform that can do a lot of different tasks. It's quite elegant, actually."

Engineers. "What happens with the last eighty units?"

"We're shipping them, too." Metzger gave Peter an apologetic look. "We have a contract. He's already paid in full."

Peter looked at Lewis. "When does the next truck come?"

"Four o'clock today." A little more than five hours from now.

Lewis gave Peter a wide, tilted grin. "Be good to be on offense for a change."

"What?" Metzger's eyes got wide. "Oh, no. What about my family? What about my people?"

Peter put his hand on Metzger's shoulder. "Do you think that threat will end if you sign that paperwork? It won't. I'm sorry, Marty, but you have to make a choice. Do you want to live under this shadow for the rest of your life? Or do you want to stand up and fight back?"

Metzger looked like he was about to throw up.

Peter felt for the guy. It was easy to talk tough about fighting back. It wasn't Peter's family at risk. But he didn't know another way to find Holloway.

"Here's what you do," he said. "Bring everyone into the office, right now. Tell them to get their spouses home from work, pull their kids out of school, throw a few things in a bag, and go to a hotel outside the city. It will only be for a few days. Once the shipment is out the door, have your lawyer call the police."

Metzger pulled in a ragged breath and held it for a long moment. Calculating the enormity of what he would be asking of his people, the risk involved no matter which choice he made.

Finally he released his breath. "Okay," he said. "I can do that. All of it."

"That's great, Marty." Peter turned to June and Lewis. "What else are we missing?"

June flipped through her notebook for a moment, then pointed at Metzger. "You said Holloway's offer didn't actually have his name on it, right? It was from a company you'd never heard of. What was the company?"

"Let's see. It sounded like a law firm. You know, with two last names. Graham, Brown LLC."

Peter smiled. It was the name on the credit card Holloway had used to send flowers to his ex-girlfriend. Not a person, but a company. Another piece of the puzzle.

June said, "Did the offer provide proof of funds for the purchase?"

"Yes. He had a letter from a private bank."

"Can you email me a copy of the offer with the letter?" She tapped the screen. "Actually, send me these drawings, too."

She forwarded everything to Oliver with a quick note about their progress, then sent a text to Zedler at the paper with instructions to focus on the buyer, Graham, Brown LLC, and any physical address they might have.

Peter looked at Lewis. "What the hell does he need with eight hundred of those things?"

Lewis gave him a predatory grin. "Brother, we gonna know soon enough."

Leaving Metzger to the task of getting his people to a safe place, they walked across the shop floor to the fenced-in rear parking lot. June wanted to see where Metzger's cousins, David and Sam, had died.

It was hard to miss. The bodies were gone, and someone had

used a high-pressure hose to wash away what they'd left behind on the faded gray asphalt. But a pale shape remained, a large, irregular form that suggested what had happened there.

June put her palm to her chest. "That must have been a lot of blood."

"It's just the start, we don't get this right." Lewis had his head on a swivel, looking for angles of attack. They all knew Edgar was still out there somewhere, watching and waiting.

51

On their way back to the Yukon, Peter's cell rang. The number was blocked. Peter answered, hoping it was Kiko. "Hello?"

"Who the hell are you guys?" It wasn't Kiko. It was Spark.

Peter elbowed June and pointed at the phone. "Hi, Spark. Thanks for calling. I'm going to put you on speaker."

"Answer my question. Who do you work for and what do you want?"

"We want Vincent Holloway," Peter said. "He took some very sensitive information several years ago. But now you also have that information. So we need to ask you to empty your pockets, too."

"You mean the hyena? A four-legged mechanical thing with a claw where the head should be?"

"Is that what he calls it? We think it's based on some of the technology he stole. But he took a lot more than that. You copied a chunk of it when you got into his phone at the market."

"I knew those kids were there," she said abruptly. "At the

market. I'm a really good shot. I wouldn't have hurt them. I wouldn't have hurt anyone but him."

June raised her eyebrows at Peter. He nodded. "Hi, Spark, my name is June. I'm Peter's friend. This sounds like something very personal for you. What did Holloway do?"

"He took everything I loved." The pain in her voice was like acid on the skin. "I'll deal with him. You people can go home."

"Spark, we can't do that," June said. "There's too much at stake. More than you know."

"I know a lot," Spark said. "I didn't just get his phone. I took over his entire computer system. I have his lab notes, his engineering drawings, his whole financial structure, everything. I just haven't had time to dig through everything yet."

"We'd love to get a look," June said. "It will be very helpful unwinding his operation after we take him down."

Spark laughed bitterly. "What are you going to do, arrest him? The court system can't touch guys like Holloway. He can buy his way out of anything, and he fights dirty. There's only one way to bring him down and that's to put his whole life online. Where he hides his money, all the specs for that hyena thing, all his emails, even his personal journal. Expose it all. The whole world will know what he's done."

"Please, Spark," Peter said. "Don't do that."

"Maybe I will and maybe I won't," she said. "I made myself an insurance policy. I thought it was protection against Holloway, but I guess it's protection against you, too. I put a fail-safe on my servers. A dead man's switch. If I don't write a very specific piece of code every night by eight o'clock, all that data dumps online to every major news outlet in the country. He won't be able to buy his way out from that."

Peter felt the bottom fall out of his stomach. "That's a very bad idea, Spark. I know you're hurting, but this won't help things at all. Trust me on this."

Spark wasn't listening. "One last thing," she said. "Leave Kiko out of this. It's not his fault. He didn't do anything. It was all me."

"Spark, please. Let's meet somewhere to talk, okay? Anywhere you want. Spark?"

But Spark didn't answer. Because she'd already hung up.

Peter turned to June. "Are you going to keep your appointment with the cops?"

June checked the time. "I mean, I don't want to be early. What are you thinking?"

"I think we need to find Spark before this whole thing turns to shit."

y the time they hit the freeway and headed toward the south side, it was after eleven. The sky was low and dark but it had not yet begun to rain.

On National Avenue, Peter ran up the back steps to Spark's apartment while Lewis waited at the front door, but she wasn't there. Peter knew she'd been home because her electric bike was gone, along with the shoebox it had been plugged into.

They stopped at the MakerSpace, but nobody answered the bell and the place was buttoned up tight. The hole in the wall at Spark's shop had been covered with sheet metal bolted to the brick. The solar panels still gleamed on their rooftop rack, making electricity despite the clouds.

With no more direct leads for Spark, they went looking for Kiko. The Walker's Point gallery was closed until four and the side door for the studios, which had been held open by a block of wood on their first visit, was firmly locked. Peter carried the crowbar tucked up the sleeve of his coat, the curve of the hook in his cupped palm, but when he dropped it down to pry the door, June stopped him.

She'd been on her laptop on the drive down and had run a few simple searches. "Kiko's full name is Enrique Tomczak. He's got a maroon 1986 Chevy S-10 registered to him personally. Kiko's Welding Services has a Chevy P20. That's like a UPS truck," she said. "You see either one of those?"

"I know what a P20 is." Peter put the crowbar back up his sleeve and scanned the block. The S-10 was a small, boxy pickup. Both trucks would stand out in a crowd. There was plenty of open street parking and neither vehicle was visible. "Shit."

"I have his home address, too. He's on South Pine, down by the airport." June patted his arm. "Maybe you'll get to do some breaking and entering there."

Peter was ready to break something, that was for goddamn sure.

Kiko lived in a small postwar Cape Cod on a corner lot, the red metal siding faded to a soft pink where the sun had beaten it. In the side yard sat a four-car garage that might have been bigger than the house. A concrete walkway ran between the two, with a wheelchair ramp rising to the back stoop. The shades were down in every window, and bright with lights in half the rooms.

Peter knocked on the rear door while Lewis waited at the front, in case Spark was there and tried to run. Her AK and Kiko's wrist rocket were very much in their minds, but they kept their guns under their jackets. Shooting either one of them wouldn't help anything. They didn't need a neighbor calling the police, either.

There was no answer to Peter's knock. He tried the knob. It was locked. The door had a window with individual panes. He poked the crowbar blade through the pane closest to the knob, then raked away the remaining glass. The sound was unmistakable. So much for the element of surprise. But it was easier to fix a broken window than a wrecked jamb, and Peter had done enough to Kiko in the last twelve hours.

On the other hand, if Spark was angry or afraid and willing to pull the trigger, a lot of shit was going to get wrecked.

He set the crowbar on the stoop, pulled out the beat-up Colt 1911 Lewis had loaned him, reached through the door, and unlocked the deadbolt.

The static hummed high as he stepped inside. The kitchen smelled like bacon and burned toast. The coffee was still warm in the pot, but the machine was off. A ring of keys sat beside it. He held the pistol up and ready. "Kiko? It's Peter, from last night." He thought it best not to mention the fire extinguisher. "I just want to talk."

The countertops sat at wheelchair height with open shelves below. The sink held a pair of plates and a frying pan left to soak. A small table in the corner had two empty mugs and a single folding chair. A row of intricate metal birds sat along a windowsill, each different from the next. More birds, depicted in flight, hung by monofilament line from the ceiling, wheeling on the warm breeze from the heat vent.

He peeked past the kitchen into the living room. No movement. "Hello? Anybody here?"

A cracked leather recliner, a couch, a wall-mounted television, and a live ficus tree in the corner that reminded Peter of the tree sculpture in Kiko's office. An elegant heron stood on one leg in the big glazed pot, waist-high and imposing, his fierce marble eye glaring at the intruders.

Peter opened the front door for Lewis. "I'll take the bedrooms, you take the basement." They worked their way through the place, but nobody was home. Peter waved June in from the Yukon. "See what you and Lewis can find here. I'll go check the garage."

He took the ring of keys from the counter and walked down the ramp, the pistol held down along his leg. The second key unlocked the door, which opened without a sound. In the light from a pair of dirty windows, he saw professional-grade automotive tools and a big stepvan with a rear liftgate and no driver's seat. Peter imagined Kiko in his power chair, loading finished bike frames or architectural railings, not letting his lack of working legs get in the way of the job he needed to do.

The last parking bay was separated by a tarp hung from the ceiling. He pushed aside the plastic and found a storage room. Cheap metal shelves were loaded with cardboard boxes, and a ratty old couch was shoved into the corner, a plastic takeout container standing on the arm. The sauce on the bottom was still damp.

The boxes were a random assortment of repurposed food or liquor cartons, although more than a few had once held bottles of margarita mix. Each box had a handwritten label on a wide strip of masking tape, cataloging everything from salvaged appliance or computer parts to specialized components that Peter didn't recognize. But it wasn't Kiko's neat copperplate hand. It was a wild scrawl in a dozen colors of Magic Marker.

The scrawl wasn't the same on every box, either. If he rearranged the boxes by the quality of handwriting, Peter thought, he'd see the scrawl getting tighter, more controlled, more legible. Or considered in the other direction, getting wilder.

He knew these were Spark's things by the contents he couldn't identify. Remnants of previous experiments or failed projects. Those had the wildest scrawl of all.

He hoped that wasn't the direction she was headed.

Back at the house, he found June and Lewis in the kitchen. Peter told them about the garage. "At least we know Kiko's in the S-10. What have you got?"

June held up a small black book. "Addresses and phone numbers, from the bedside table. Your friend Kiko is old-school."

"Any listing for Spark or La Chispa?"

June shook her head. "There have to be two hundred names in here. No telling how current any of them are. It's possible that the new ones are all in his phone. I'll take pictures of the pages and run them down when I have time."

Peter nodded. "Anything else?"

"Down in the cellar," Lewis said. "Another one of those shoebox things."

They descended steep steps into the low-ceilinged basement. Except for the furnace and water heater and a dehumidifier piped to the floor drain, it was nearly empty. Kiko probably had never been down these stairs.

The main electrical panel was screwed to the foundation wall in the far corner. Beside it sat an unused workbench with a Red Wing boot box on top. A heavy electrical cable ran from the Red Wing box into the side of the panel. Lewis had removed the panel cover. The wires from the box were tapped into the main feed. The wires from the meter and the pole were disconnected and capped with wire nuts and tape.

"He's not hooked into city power at all," Lewis said. "He's running the whole house on whatever's inside this Red Wing box."

"Jesus. Did you open it?"

Lewis nodded. "Didn't figure it'd electrocute me. It's in a damn shoebox." He lifted the lid.

Half the space was filled with a small rectangular pressure tank labeled with a red-and-white sticker that read HYDROGEN. The tank had a thin stainless tube that fed hydrogen into the side of a layered metal sandwich that took up most of the rest of the box. On the other side of the sandwich was a softly buzzing electrical transformer and the wire that connected to the panel. At the bottom was a thin plastic hose that dripped liquid into a plastic bucket on the floor.

"I think it's a fuel cell," Lewis said. "It pushes hydrogen through a kind of atomic filter that pulls out the electrons for electricity, and mixes the remaining protons with oxygen from the air. The only by-product is water. They power spacecraft with these things."

Peter kept his hands away from the wires. "And you know about this how?"

"Jarhead." Lewis gave him a look. "We have a pretty good green energy portfolio. Which you'd know if you ever read anything I put in front of you. This fuel cell is way ahead of anything else I've ever heard about in terms of size and output. But if Spark can build something like this on the cheap, in her funk-ass little shop? She's made at least one major breakthrough, if not two or three."

Peter couldn't stop thinking about the 3-D rendering on Metzger's screen.

"You think this is what Holloway's using to power his creature?"

"Man, I hope not. You imagine one of those things running on household current with no need for an extension cord?"

"What do you think Holloway's going to do with eight hundred of those things?"

Lewis gave a humorless laugh. "Don't you know your history,

Jarhead? Who's always been the earliest adopter of new technology?"

Peter sighed. He'd been trying to find a different answer for the last two hours, but had come to the same conclusion. "The military."

Since the ancient Greeks. Since the time of Gilgamesh before that. Since the first two disparate tribes met and went to war.

Lewis nodded. "And who's Oliver working for, trying to corral all this tech? It ain't Toys 'R' Us. It's some pointy head in the Pentagon, looking for a cheaper and more effective way to destroy the enemy."

"But what's Holloway's military use?" Although Peter had been thinking about that, too. He didn't like what he'd come up with.

"Oh, we gon' find out. Trust me on that. Question is, whose military? And what the hell are we gonna do about it?"

They made it upstairs to the kitchen just as June's phone began to ring.

She checked the screen. "It's Detective Hecht. Should I answer it?"

The clock over the door read twelve-thirty.

"Are you going to meet him?"

June sighed. "Do I have a choice?"

She was already pushing her luck with the cops. If she missed the appointment, she might buy herself a few hours, but it would make everything else harder. The police would be looking for the Yukon, the Toyota flatbed, and June's Subaru. They might also put a car at the house. And they'd be pissed.

She lifted the phone to her ear, put a smile on her face, and walked into the living room. "Detective, how are you? Yes, I'm just stopping to grab a sandwich on my way. Oh, I meant to ask—I don't need a lawyer for this conversation, do I?"

Peter turned to Lewis. "We've been on this thing for three days with nothing to show for it. Spark's in the wind. Holloway's still invisible. Edgar is a phantom. All we have is a delivery truck supposed to show up at Metzger Machine at four today."

Lewis flashed a tilted smile. "Don't forget that nice sergeant trying to figure out why you smell like a bad guy."

"Oh, I haven't forgotten." Peter looked at the birds hanging from the ceiling, wings spread wide to catch the wind. "If he connects me to my arrest warrants, he'll blow up this whole thing. June's career is fucked. Your legitimate life is fucked. Which means Dinah and the boys are fucked, too."

Lewis gave Peter a look. "June got into this of her own free will, Jarhead. Hell, she'll probably win the Pulitzer for her memoir about dating the outlaw Peter Ash. As for me and Dinah, well, Holloway ain't the only one knows how to reallocate his assets."

He put a sympathetic hand on Peter's shoulder. "Actually, brother, you the one really screwed. Gonna end up making license plates in a cold Icelandic prison, sharing a bunk with your hairy Viking boyfriend, and eating that stinky-ass dried fish the rest of your life." He shook his head. "Now that is one sad fucking story."

Peter laughed. "Okay," he said. "We'll figure it out."

"Always do," Lewis said. "Listen, I been thinking. Where else we see those cardboard boxes? Spark had one at her apartment, charging her bike. Kiko had one running his power chair. Was there another one?"

Peter blinked. "The kid at the bike shop," he said. "Plugged into his phone."

"There you go. Let's go talk to Carson."

June walked back into the kitchen. "Can I get a ride to District Five? And maybe stop for a sandwich on the way?"

53

They found Carson with his back to the service counter. He had a cargo bike clamped into a repair stand, its bottom bracket in pieces on the workbench. The shoebox with the electric outlet was in the same place as last time, although nothing was plugged into it now.

"Be right with you," Carson said over his shoulder, reaching for a rag with greasy fingers. His long hair was up in a man bun and the steel grommets hung pendulous in his ears.

Peter walked into the service area with Lewis on his heels. Lewis had locked the front door behind him to discourage visitors. "Hi, Carson. Remember us?"

Carson froze in place when he saw Peter. A look of sweaty panic flashed across his face before he got hold of himself. Then he leaned against the bench and wiped his fingers with the rag. He was trying for cool but got stuck staring at the pistol on Peter's hip. "Uh, sure, yeah. Yesterday, right?"

"Exactly," Peter said. "We have a problem and you're just the man to help."

"Is it the bike you bought?" He turned to Lewis, trying to get back to his comfort zone. "There's a ninety-day warranty, parts and labor. Just bring it in and we'll get you all fixed up. Or, hey, if you want you can just return it, no questions asked."

Lewis smiled and unzipped his jacket, revealing the gun in its shoulder rig. Carson started blinking rapidly. The grommets quivered in his ears.

Peter wasn't sure if Carson was reacting to the gun or the smile. "Actually," he said, "it's the other thing. The electric bike we were looking for."

"No, hey, I told you guys, we don't do electrics." The sweaty panic was back.

Carson had been nervous yesterday, but not like this. Something had changed.

"We don't have time for bullshit." Peter looked at Lewis. "Where do you want to shoot him?"

Lewis's smile got wider and he put some extra street in his voice. "I like to start with the foot." He pulled the big black pistol. "Shatters all those tiny little bones, won't never walk right again." He looked Carson up and down, taking inventory. "Course, the knee always a solid pick. Hurt a lot more, for sure. Just depend on how fucked up you want him."

When he racked the slide, Carson flinched.

Lewis looked like he was having entirely too much fun. Peter felt a little bad. He was afraid Carson might wet himself. But he just shrugged. "Or the kid starts talking, I guess."

Carson opened his mouth but nothing came out.

"Lemme just shoot him a little bit," Lewis said. "For motivation, like."

Carson cleared his blockage. "That's, no, really, no, please."

Now Peter was just embarrassed for him. "I know you know

Spark." He pointed at the shoebox wired into the exercise bike. "She made that. And we need to find her."

"I don't know where she is." But his hand twitched toward the front of his right hip, where a rectangular outline in the fabric showed his phone in his pocket.

Peter had learned to watch for this kind of tell in Baghdad, working checkpoints. When people are carrying something important to them, like money or a weapon, they often unconsciously reach to pat the place they've put it, to reassure themselves that it's still there. Peter did it with his truck keys all the time.

"Give me your phone, Carson."

The kid crossed his arms. He was sweaty and shaking, but he was standing tall. "You're the guys who were hassling her. You're the ones who broke into her apartment."

Peter sighed. "Let me guess. Spark is your friend and you want to protect her. But you don't know the whole story, Carson. Did she show you her assault rifle? Did she tell you how she shot up the Public Market?"

"What? No, that was some guy with a beard. Don't you read the news?"

"It was a fake beard," Peter said. "It fooled us, too, and we were there. But she got away on a custom electric bike, the very same bike I saw at her apartment. Spark stole something very important from a very bad man. We're trying to keep her out of trouble and catch the bad man. So where the hell is she?"

Carson tried to assimilate this new information. "What did she steal?"

Peter ground his molars. "Government fucking secrets, okay? Now shut up and give me your phone or I will tear those fucking grommets out of your fucking ears and my friend will blow your knees to smithereens."

Carson held up his hands. "Wait, okay, wait. She called me."

He pulled out his phone, used the facial recognition to unlock it, and handed it to Peter. There were only two calls in the last sixteen hours, the same number incoming and outgoing. Her new burner.

"Her name's Maria Velasquez. She's a good person. She wouldn't do what you said unless she had a good reason."

Peter thought about Kiko's reaction at his office, after they found Spark's bike plans. Kiko felt pretty strongly about her, too.

He handed the phone to Lewis, who immediately changed the passcode and started poking through the contents. "So what would that reason be?"

Carson looked at the floor. "A few years ago, someone cheated her out of the design for this new battery she developed." He pointed at the shoebox. "That's an early version. You know she's, like, insanely smart, right? So she hired a lawyer to go after him. Not only did the guy sue her back, he hired some trolls to go after her on social media. It went viral, man, got way out of hand. They totally fucked up her life, trashed her reputation, the works. Then some real-world lunatic went after her parents. Chased their car into the river or whatever. It was January. They died. It totally wrecked her."

Of course it would, Peter thought. It had driven her to the brink. Or maybe past it.

Carson said, "We used to be friends, you know? I hoped we might become, you know, more than friends? But then she ghosted me. Shut down her social media, sold her parents' house, moved away, stopped answering my texts, totally vanished. I hadn't seen her since she built that bike."

Peter waited.

Carson cleared his throat. "Then, last night, out of the blue, she called me. Said a couple of scary assholes—that's you guys, I guess—had broken into her place, and she didn't want to go back there. She wondered if I would pick up her bike for her."

Which would explain why Carson was more freaked-out today than yesterday, Peter thought.

"Where did you take the bike?"

"I met her on the Hank Aaron Trail this morning. That was it. That's all I did."

Lewis looked up from the phone, smiling. "But that ain't all you got, is it?" He showed Peter the screen. It showed a map of Milwaukee with a blinking red bull's-eye. The bull's-eye was labeled MARIA.

"It's an app called Findr," Lewis said. "Lets you track any device with a GPS locator. Is she wearing a beacon?"

"No," Carson said. "It's her bike. She built a GPS beacon into the power hub, in case it got stolen. She gave me the ID number this morning. She said she had a big meeting today, and when it was over, she wouldn't need the bike anymore."

"A big meeting." Peter looked at Lewis. "With who?"

"The guy who killed her parents. But she told me to come find the bike after I get off work. She was giving it to me."

"What time do you get off work?"

"Five o'clock," Carson said. "But why would she say she wouldn't need it? She rode that bike every day."

Peter watched the kid's face as he put it together. Spark the market shooter. Spark with the assault rifle. Spark whose life was in ruins.

"Zoom in," he told Lewis. "Where's that damn bike?"

54

South Shore Park was a good place to meet a bad man, Spark thought.

It was one of a long string of green spaces along Milwaukee's Lake Michigan shoreline, all connected by a web of bike and hiking trails, which gave her many different escape routes. She knew cars could drive on the paved trails, because she'd seen maintenance vehicles on them, but there were plenty of narrow dirt paths that wound through the trees where no car could follow.

For the meet itself, she'd selected an asphalt parking lot by the boat launch, not far from the funky South Shore Yacht Club. To the north and east was the small yacht club building and the big lake. To the west was a steep grassy hill. To the south was the park and another rising hill, with houses well back behind its crest. The Yacht Club would be empty at midafternoon on a windy weekday in October. So if she pulled the trigger, she wasn't likely to hurt anyone by accident.

Just on purpose.

She still hadn't decided what she would do when the moment came. How far she would go.

When she closed her eyes, she could see her parents' faces as clearly as if they were standing right in front of her. It helped tamp down the fear. But the guilt and pain were still as strong as the day it had happened.

Whatever she was going to do, when it was over, she could ride straight up the grassy hill and into Bay View's maze of streets, or she could head south through the park system's trails, emerging at any of a hundred different places in the city or three suburbs.

The equity paperwork had cleared her attorney's due diligence in record time, and been remote-signed by all parties. In theory, she was in bed with the devil. She owned twenty percent of his company. She was counting on his assumption of her greed to make him think she wouldn't throw it all away.

When she was ready, she called Operator Twelve and gave Holloway a half hour to get there.

She knew it was him when a slick black Mercedes SUV rolled down the access drive past the fish-cleaning station at the far end of the lot. She stood with the wood-fenced dumpster enclosure to her left, her bike leaning up against it. Behind her was a Bobcat loader and a gravel pile, part of some maintenance project for the boat launch just beyond.

She had a big messenger's pack on her back, purpose-bought for the occasion, big enough to hold two million in hundreds and her rifle, too. She was confident that Holloway would have crisp packets of bank-banded bills, not a black garbage bag full of dirty twenties. Holloway liked to keep his hands clean.

The pack's top pocket held her phone, connected to her wireless earbuds, with Kiko on the other end of the line. His little red pickup was parked just ahead of the launch kiosk to her right, engine running, Kiko's elbow out the window with a cigarette in his hand like any other guy taking a break to watch the lake. Like he didn't have a care in the world.

She'd tried to talk him out of coming to the meet, but Kiko wasn't having any of it. He told her he'd risked his life for the city for fifteen years, he could damn well risk his life for her if he wanted. His wheelchair sat folded in the passenger seat where he could get at it easily, and his wrist rocket was in his lap with a bag of old ball bearings close at hand. She'd left her computer bag and her newest fuel cell behind the truck's bench seat. She'd need it later if she was really going to run, but there was no way in hell Holloway was getting it.

As the Mercedes approached, she stepped away from the dumpster enclosure with her left hand out like a traffic cop. Her rifle was slung across her chest, with a thirty-round magazine locked in and the stock unfolded for accuracy. She knew how good she was with the gun, and had the range targets to prove it. She'd even threaded the barrel for her shop-made sound suppressor, so the crack of gunfire wouldn't immediately draw the police.

She could see Holloway's face clearly and knew he could see her, because he drove right toward her. But he didn't seem to understand her stop sign, so she raised the rifle to her shoulder to emphasize the point. When he kept driving, she put a round through the windshield.

That got his attention, along with the splinters of flying glass inside the car. He flinched and hit the brakes and put a hand up to ward off future shards. Spark could have told him that glass wasn't the kind of projectile he should be worried about.

He was twenty yards away.

So close.

Get out of the car," she called.

He opened his door and stepped out with the engine still running. All the SUV's windows were rolled down. He wore khaki pants and a blue blazer and a shit-eating grin.

"Where's my money?"

"You don't need that gun, Maria." He began to walk toward her, hands out at his side. "We're business partners, right? You don't want anything bad to happen to me. Otherwise my business falls apart and you don't get paid."

So goddamn confident, laying on the bullshit.

The last time she'd had a gun on him, he'd been terrified. Why wasn't he terrified now?

She aimed at the SUV's side-view mirror and put a bullet into it. It shattered with a satisfying crunch. Holloway stopped in his tracks, shoulders hunched as if that could protect him. His grin had gone a little lopsided, but it was still glued to his face.

Behind him, a white van pulled into the otherwise empty parking lot a hundred yards away. There was a colorful company logo painted on the side.

"Where's my damn money, Vince?"

"In the car," he said. "I need you to turn off your ransomware first."

A bulky guy in an untucked white dress shirt got out of the van and walked toward the yacht club building, staring at them curiously. He wore mirrored sunglasses on a cloudy day. She hoped he was too far away to see the gun. Although she'd made her escape plan with the police in mind, too.

"You're not in charge, Vince. I'll turn off the ransomware when I'm free and clear. Right now the clock is still ticking on the delete-bot."

She shifted her aim to his chest. She felt her finger on the trigger. She hated him with everything she had. She'd thought she hated him enough to kill him, but now she wasn't sure. She remembered what Kiko had said last night. That killing him wouldn't end the pain or bring her parents back.

Of course, she was still going to dump the contents of his servers online where anyone could access it. The fail-safe was a way to protect herself, but once she got the cash, she would do it anyway. All his technology, the locations of his hidden assets, even the daily diary of his misanthropic narcissism and insecurity. It would be sweeter than killing him.

Clueless, Holloway straightened his grin. "The thing is, Maria, we're the same, you and I. We make things. Not video games or dating apps or stock trading algorithms, all of it basically designed to move money from one set of pockets to another. No, you and I make real things that will change the real world. Like your fuel cell."

"As far as I can tell, Vince, all you do is talk. Do I need to shoot your car some more? Or maybe I'll just shoot you. Please, give me an excuse." She put some pressure on the trigger. "Get. Me. My. Money."

"It's in the car," he said again. "But I'd like to show you something first. Something you and your battery helped me to make, that your fuel cell would make better. I'm sure you've seen the 3-D renderings in my system. Don't you want to see it in person?"

"That hyena thing?" She shuddered. "No, I really don't. I want my money and we're done."

"It'll just take a minute," he said. "It's pretty damn cool." He raised his voice just slightly. "Harry, come here."

A shining creature jumped out of the SUV's back window and landed effortlessly on two outstretched front legs.

Then it gathered its back legs behind it and trotted up to stand beside Holloway. Not machine-still, like a parked car, but constantly shifting, a soft whine of servomotors adjusting its balance on four black feet.

55

Without conscious thought, Spark took a quick step back and shifted her aim to the creature.

From the CAD drawings, she'd expected something clunky and awkward, but this thing was sleek, almost elegant, and disturbingly fluid in its movement. Like an oversized greyhound, but more muscular.

It didn't have muscles, of course. She knew that. It had gears and motors and pistons and springs. But that was how it looked. How it felt, viscerally. Like an animal, hunting.

Except animals had heads, and this thing didn't. Instead it had a single arm, doubled back on itself, along what would have been the spine, if it were an animal. But it wasn't. It was a machine. She had to remind herself of that. Although the claw at the end of the arm, positioned at the front of the thing, looked a little like a head. Or like a mouth, at least.

The body was more than a meter long, she knew that from the drawings, and it came up almost to Holloway's hip. Two sets of instruments were clustered at the front, below the claw. The sensor suite, protected behind twin arcs of super-hard synthetic sapphire glass.

"Harry, that's Maria Velasquez. Got her?" A soft melodic chime sounded, upbeat and cheerful. Holloway's grin widened. "That means yes, Maria. And now Harry knows your face." Holloway's hand dropped to rest on the creature's back. "His visual recognition software is top-notch."

She took two steps to the side and the thing shifted to track her, its sensors like bug eyes under the blue-tinted domes. The hair rose on the back of her neck.

"He's also part of a custom self-generating network," Holloway said, "so he can talk with the other hyenas. Eventually he'll have his own satellite system."

"What's controlling it?"

"I am," Holloway said. "With my voice. The same algorithm as my answerbot, Operator Twelve. But more specialized, of course. When Harry's fully deployed, he'll have a supervisor back at mission control, one person for every eight to sixteen hyenas. Give them a job and they'll do it. But they're weirdly good at figuring stuff out for themselves." He chuckled. "That's the 'autonomous' in the name. HYbrid Electric Networked Autonomous System. HYENAS."

Along one side of the thing, just below the claw, she saw a slim, straight tube with a rectangle at the rear. She flashed back to the CAD drawings, understood what she was looking at, and realized with regret that she should have shot Holloway when he stepped out of the car.

She was shifting her aim back to his chest when he said, "Harry, get the gun."

Before Spark could process what he'd said, the hyena leaped forward, impossibly graceful. The long arm flashed toward her like a rattlesnake's strike. Before she knew what had happened, the big claw had clamped on to the rifle barrel and was pulling it down and away.

She had two hands on the gun but she could barely hold it against the weight and strength of the thing. She set her heels and twisted but the claw just rotated with her. She stepped to the right and gave a quick hard yank, hoping to overbalance the creature, but it danced sideways in effortless compensation. She was playing tug-of-war with an immaculate, tireless beast. She'd designed the battery that powered it. She would run out of energy long before it did. She wouldn't get her gun back, not like this.

"Kiko, help," she called. "Shoot the fucking thing."

"On it." She heard his voice in her earbud, then a thump and clang as a half-inch ball bearing blew through the cedar dumpster enclosure and into the side of the heavy steel container. Another steel ball skittered into the grass and up the hill.

"You're too close," he said. "I don't want to hit you by accident. Get some distance from it."

She wasn't about to give up her weapon, so she rotated left and yanked again. The creature pivoted with her, exposing its long silvery side to Kiko's wrist rocket. But she was still too close. And the thing must somehow have learned from the last time she'd made the move, because the arm swung the barrel through a whip-fast semicircular arc that pulled her off balance. She found herself bent forward on her toes with her ass hanging out, her arms half-crossed, and the rifle sling tight around the back of her neck.

She knew she had to either get some slack or fall over, and she was afraid of what the creature might do if she hit the ground. So she angled her body to let her arms uncross a little, then dipped her neck and slipped the sling as she scooted her feet forward, getting her hips under her so she could use the full power of her legs and butt.

The creature was stretched away from her, still pulling, when she heard a hard metallic *tak* and its back legs stumbled sideways.

Above the rear hip, she saw a dent in the skin, but no hole. She improved her grip on the weapon, but before she could do anything else, the creature had rebalanced. The black feet found traction, the claw whip-cracked her gun in the other direction again, and it was all she could do to stay upright. The insect eyes had no expression.

"See how tenacious it is," Holloway said. "It doesn't get scared or tired, and it follows orders without question. Not like a person at all. Much better, in fact."

She was focused on the creature, not Holloway's face, but she could picture his expression anyway. Dreamy excitement, like Oppenheimer before the Trinity test in the New Mexico desert, when people were laying bets on whether the atomic reaction would set the planet's atmosphere on fire.

"Dammit," Kiko said in her ear. "What's that thing got for skin?" She heard a soft grunt of effort as he pulled back the sling, then a second ball bearing hit the creature's angled flank. But it was just a glancing blow and the ball ricocheted away into the sky. "It's a really small target."

"Forget the machine," she said. "Shoot Holloway." Then realized what she'd asked her friend to do. Kill a man. "No, don't do it," she said. "Get out of here and call the cops."

"Shut up and fight that thing." He grunted again and a ball thumped into the side of the Mercedes.

"Hey, wait," Holloway said. "That's my car." Another thump and the Mercedes sank, its tire flat. Holloway ran to hide behind it. Another thump and the SUV's engine began to make a grind-ing sound.

The creature whip-cracked its arm again, but now in the same direction. It wasn't limited by an elbow that only bent one way, or by a wrist that only rotated a hundred and eighty degrees. Spark's arms were crossed and she was just barely hanging on. Then it cranked in the same direction again and she had to let the gun go or get her arms broken. The creature danced back with the rifle held high by the barrel.

Kiko had been right, she thought. Back in his garage, when he saw the plans for the creature, he'd told her to back off and send everything to the newspapers, to the FBI, to somebody. She should have listened. She shouldn't have come.

She saw a flash of white to her right. She looked toward the high strip of decorative plantings that ran between the yacht club and the boat launch, concealing the parking lot from the prome-nade. The bulky guy in the untucked dress shirt stepped out of the bushes on Kiko's blind side and walked purposefully toward the little red pickup. He had an odd smile on his face, and something slim and bright in his hand.

"Kiko, behind you. Kiko, get out of there. Go go go go."

From his safe spot, Holloway said, "Harry, destroy the gun."

The creature swung the rifle down and smashed it against the pavement, again and again and again.

56

PETER

Lewis pushed the Yukon hard down Lincoln Memorial Drive past Veterans Park, weaving through the lazy lakefront traffic like it was so many orange cones on a demonstration course. They were lucky it wasn't rush hour yet.

Peter held Carson's phone in his hand, watching the red bull's-eye labeled MARIA on the map. It was steady by the boat launch at South Shore Park. Carson wasn't happy to be left behind. Peter was afraid he'd have to break the bike mechanic's leg to keep him from climbing in the truck with them. Another goddamn amateur was the last thing they needed.

"You believe what Spark said about putting a dead man's switch on her server?" Lewis hit the horn and put two wheels up on the median to power around a Prius poking down the fast lane.

Peter grabbed the oh-shit handle and held on tight. His go-bag bounced around the footwell. "Building a fail-safe would be a smart thing to do. And if she's not willing or able to reset at eight tonight, we're screwed. Not to mention everyone else."

"So don't shoot her, is what you're saying. What if she try to shoot us? We just gonna say please don't?"

"I guess we'll find out," Peter said. "I hope we don't have to kill her."

Lewis had the pedal to the floor, the needle at seventy and climbing. They flew past the art museum and up the ramp to the Hoan Bridge, across Jones Island toward the South Side. He gave Peter a sideways glance. "Don't get soft on me, Jarhead. I don't care what she says, she brought an assault rifle into that crowded market, kids and all. She pulled the trigger. Yeah, nobody really got hurt, but that was dumb luck. Maybe she's past saving, a lost cause."

The needle hit ninety. Peter looked at his friend. "You think anyone said that about you, back in the day?" When Lewis had run a lethal crew, taking down drug houses for the money they held. "Were they right?"

Lewis made a face. "Shi-i-t." Somehow he dragged three syllables out of a four-letter word.

"I know, brother." Peter clapped a hand on the other man's shoulder. "Karma's a bitch. Now please tell me a well-armed citizen like yourself has a few more serious weapons close at hand."

Lewis took the Port of Milwaukee exit, drove past the Coast Guard station, then roared south toward Nock Street and the red bull's-eye blinking on the map. It hadn't moved since they'd left the bike shop.

They stopped on the hill facing the lake, hidden from the boat launch parking lot by the curve of grass but within sight of a dozen houses. Lewis popped the rear hatch and Peter moved the tool bag so Lewis could open the top of the shallow compartment he'd had a cabinetmaker build into the floor of the cargo space. It was less than five inches deep, and the cover was perfectly scribed to the sidewalls and carpeted with the same material as the truck floor, so the whole thing was almost invisible unless you knew to look for it.

Inside, folded in old bath towels, were four SIG Sauer pistols with spare magazines, two combat shotguns, and two very nice Heckler & Koch assault rifles with scopes and suppressors and a row of thirty-round magazines. A pair of high-end armored vests completed the set.

"Jesus, Lewis. You drive around town like this?" Peter traded the Colt 1911 for the more accurate SIG Sauer and stuffed two spare mags into his back pockets, then pulled a vest over his head and cinched the straps.

Lewis tightened his own vest and laid the rifles on the rear seat with four mags. "Don't you know the Boy Scout motto? Trustworthy, brave, and goddamn prepared."

"If you're a Boy Scout," Peter muttered, "I'm Mother fucking Teresa." He dropped the top and slammed the hatch and ran back to the passenger seat as Lewis put the truck in gear. Carson's phone was on the dashboard. "She's still there, on the right, all the way down past the bathrooms. Remember, we don't want to kill anyone, least of all Spark."

"What if that Edgar's there?"

"Oh, him you can kill all you want."

Lewis hit the gas. When they rounded the corner, Peter looked ahead a hundred yards and saw a human figure on the pavement beside a small red pickup with both doors open. A black Mercedes SUV stood in the other lane with all the windows down.

Lewis coasted closer. The man was Kiko Tomczak, and he was sprawled in a crimson puddle, one hand propped on the ground as if still trying to push himself upright. His red wheelchair was dumped on the far side of his truck, still folded for transport. The seatback was pulled forward. The truck was empty.

Twenty yards away, the Mercedes had a flat tire, a shattered side-view mirror, and holes in the side panels big enough to stick your thumb through. Peter couldn't see any other people. Just beyond both vehicles, at the turnaround for the boat launch, a custom electric bike lay abandoned on its side in a pile of gravel, back wheel spinning fast. An assault rifle by the dumpster enclosure was bent into a crimped curve.

"Shit," Peter said. "Shit, shit, shit."

Lewis cranked the wheel and powered back up the parking lot, looking for bad guys. Someone had dumped a scatter of painting supplies and drywall tools on the pavement, but the only other vehicles were a couple of empty compact cars at the far end past the yacht club. "Mother*fucker.*"

He sped back and stopped near Kiko, whose head turned weakly as he tracked the arriving truck. Peter hopped out and knelt beside him. "Where's Spark, Kiko? Where'd she go?" The knees of his pants wet with blood, his nose filled with its overpowering smell.

The metalworker's breathing was shallow and ragged, his eyelids at half-mast. His flannel shirt was saturated. He blinked at Peter and his mouth opened but no words came out. His pale blue lips flecked with pink foam made Peter think that at least one lung was punctured.

He lifted the hem of Kiko's shirt and tore it wide, popping the buttons and revealing a dozen or more deep cuts in the belly and chest. "Lewis, call 911. Get the paramedics *now*." He looked at Kiko. "The fire station is only twelve blocks away, Kiko. Hang on."

Kiko's eyes widened and he stared back balefully. One thick forearm rose from the sticky pool and a meaty hand clamped on Peter's bicep with surprising force. But his voice was thin and weak. "They took her."

He coughed and more pink foam flecked his lips.

Lewis was on his phone. "There's a stabbing by the South Shore Yacht Club, in the south end of the parking lot. Look for the red pickup and the man on the ground. Please tell them to hurry, okay?"

Peter wiped the worst of the blood from the big man's chest and sides, looking for wounds where the blade had entered the lungs. If he could close them up, even a little, it would keep air out of the chest cavity and help Kiko breathe. He found two pink-bubbled slits, one high on the left side and the other above the right nipple, both perfectly placed to slide between the ribs and do the most damage.

He put his blood-wet palms over the wounds, trying to seal them with pressure and keep the lungs from collapsing. He couldn't do anything about the rest of it. "Keep breathing, Kiko. I got you. Paramedics coming."

The cry of a siren rose in the distance. Kiko licked his lips. Was he getting more air in? "You gotta. Save her."

Lewis bent at Peter's shoulder. "What are they driving, Kiko? How do we find her?"

Kiko didn't have an answer.

The siren went silent as a boxy ambulance tilted around the corner and rolled toward them. Two guys in Fire Department fleece hopped out, grabbed big orange cases from the side lockers, and jogged toward them. "What happened, guys?" If either man noticed the armored vests and pistols, they didn't mention it.

"Somebody stabbed him," Peter said. "Multiple times. I got pink bubbles on two, my hands are covering them. His name is Kiko."

The younger paramedic knelt and popped open his case while the older man leaned in close and pulled on gloves. "Nice work," he said. "Lemme see." Peter leaned back but kept his palms in place. The paramedic did a quick survey. "Okay, we got him. You can step away."

When Peter let go and climbed to his feet, the paramedic took his place and started giving orders to the younger man. Peter's hands and the fronts of his pants were covered with Kiko's blood. His heart was pounding. Lewis stood beside him. They left red boot prints on the pavement.

Peter closed his eyes and let out his breath. "What a fucking disaster."

They both knew the knife work was Edgar's. And the Mercedes was Holloway's, although another name would be on the registration.

"We gotta lay hands on these assholes," Lewis growled.

"We goddamn well better." Peter thought about Spark, maybe hurt, maybe dying. He thought about the loneliness of her apartment and the pain in her voice during their last conversation. He thought about her dead man's switch.

Then he thought about June at District Five, getting grilled by the detectives, and the patrol sergeant with Peter's picture in his phone. Everything was unraveling. "We need to get to Metzger Machine and meet that delivery truck. Maybe the drivers can tell us something. It's all we've got."

The older paramedic, taping dressings over Kiko's lung

punctures, called over his shoulder, "Don't go anywhere, guys. The police are on their way. They'll want to talk to you both."

"No problem," Peter said. "We'll be right here." He looked down at his bloody clothes, then at Lewis's Yukon. "Maybe I should ride in the back with the guns."

"On the roof is more like it," Lewis said. "I just had this thing detailed."

Peter opened the passenger door. "Hell, it's leather. It'll wash right off."

Lewis shook his head. "Now I know why you always drive some old piece of shit."

Peter held up his bloody hands. "Got any wet wipes?"

Sometimes gallows humor was the only thing that helped.

57

JUNE

June sat across a table from Detective Hecht in a small police interview room that smelled of stale cigarette smoke and sweat. A female detective named Lorenz leaned against the side wall, silent and out of sight of the video camera mounted in the corner of the ceiling. The chrome .22 was in a plastic evidence bag between them, along with the remains of June's lunch and Hecht's phone with the voice recorder running. Hecht took notes on a yellow legal pad while she told about shooting Mr. Cheerful for the fourth goddamn time.

Hecht was a short, nebbishy-looking guy, thoroughly middle-aged in a blue button-down shirt and rumpled tweed jacket with honest-to-god elbow patches. Combined with the stubbled head, frameless glasses over a feathery beard, and a necklace of small round wooden beads outside his shirt, he looked like a cross between a religious ascetic and an English professor.

But despite the outfit and the calm, quiet voice, Hecht was all cop. Relentless and unwavering, he walked her all the way forward to why she'd fled the paper instead of waiting for the police, then abruptly back to the shooting at the market, then ahead again to the first Edgar encounter on her bike, trying all the while to knock her off balance and poke holes in her narrative.

June found herself wishing again that she'd called a lawyer rather than showing up solo. If she had an actual job at the *Journal Sentinel*, they'd have sent their in-house attorney to cover her butt. If she hadn't been writing that damn book and on sabbatical from Public Investigations, they would have provided a lawyer, too. Instead, in too big a hurry to find a local lawyer, she'd counted on her role as the victim and her profession as a journalist to make the cops behave, at least for the short term. This might not, she reflected now, have been the soundest of strategies.

But June's work as a reporter had taught her the strategies of dissembling from the other side. She knew not to overelaborate, and that a simple story was best. Plus her story had the benefit of being almost entirely true.

Her most significant lies were those of omission.

She wasn't going to tell them about Metzger Machine, not yet. Not until poor Marty Metzger had a chance to get his people safely away from their homes. The police were generally good at their job, but they weren't known for subtlety, and June didn't want Metzger's employees or their families to pay the price.

She also didn't want the cops to scare away the delivery driver, who was due any minute. She was certain that Peter and Lewis were the best chance to intervene and figure out where that delivery was going.

Besides, if she told them about Metzger Machine, she'd have to tell them how she thought to go there, which meant telling about the connection between the machete murders and the butchered family in Virginia, which would lead to the stolen technology. If that got out, Oliver was unlikely to keep his promise.

"I'm sorry, but I'm still not clear." Hecht paged through his notes as if he were actually confused. "Why would Edgar try to kill you? He must want you dead pretty badly if he tried three times."

It was the fifth or sixth time they'd been over this part. The questions had begun to seem a little random, and June allowed herself to hope they were nearly done. Either that or they were stalling for time. She'd already been there for almost three hours. She badly needed more coffee, and also to pee.

"I told you, he didn't give me a reason." She yawned, and allowed herself to make a little production out of it. "I'm sorry, I was up half the night and I still have work to do."

"But why do *you* think he wanted to kill you?" This from Detective Lorenz. She was tall and dark with high, lean hips and narrow shoulders and the sharpest cheekbones June had ever seen.

She reminded herself again to keep it simple. "I assumed because of the market shooting. Maybe because I was trying to track down the gunman's victim."

"Vincent Holloway," Lorenz said. "A man whose face you just happened to recognize."

"Because I interviewed him eleven years ago, and I'm good with faces." June had decided to give them Holloway's name in hopes it would give them something else to focus on. "It took me a whole morning of digging through news clips to find him. He left the scene of the shooting, remember?"

Hecht chimed in again. "And why would he do that, exactly?" His phone buzzed. He glanced at it, but left it on the table.

"When I find him," June said, "I'll ask him." She yawned again, this time widely enough to feel the hinges of her jaw creak. "Are we almost done here?"

"Just about," Hecht said. "So in your mind, Holloway hired Edgar, right?"

"That's my working hypothesis," she said.

"But why would Edgar have your laptop and phone and notebooks in his van?"

"What? My laptop? In his van?" This was new information, and it took her a moment to catch up. "Oh. My house got broken into, the night after the market shooting. Someone took all my work stuff, it was on a table right inside the door. You're saying it was Edgar?" The thought of Mr. Cheerful in her house made her shiver.

"I'm saying your things were in his van. Did you report the robbery?"

"No," she said. "I thought you guys had more important things to do."

"You didn't think it might mean something?"

"I *thought* it meant somebody stole my stuff." She tried to keep the edge out of her voice. "Why didn't you tell me this before?"

Hecht was unruffled. "What about your boyfriend, Peter Murphy? He lives with you, right? Were any of his things stolen?"

"We don't think so," she said. "He's kind of a minimalist."

Already tired and tense, June felt her shoulder muscles get even tighter. She didn't like any line of questioning that included Peter. Her biggest concern was that they'd make a connection between the fuzzy photos of the good Samaritans and the two men who'd chased off Edgar after he'd tried to run her down in the van. But it turned out they were coming from a different angle.

Lorenz said, "When did you two meet, anyway?"

Suddenly June wasn't tired at all.

58

PETER

At three-thirty, the fenced-in lot behind Metzger Machine was empty except for a pair of delivery trucks with the company name on the side and a sky-blue Chrysler mini-van standing apart and alone on the expanse of faded asphalt.

Lewis pulled up to the gate, but nobody responded to the buzzer. Peter made a call. "Marty, it's Peter, from this morning. We're out back, can you let us in?" The gate rolled aside and a door opened at the far end of the lot. Metzger leaned out and waved them in.

They left the Yukon parked away from the loading dock, stripped off the bulky armored vests, and walked over.

As they came closer, the engineer's sagging eyes locked on to the blood drying thick and dark on Peter's pants and hands and forearms. "Did you get him?"

"No," Peter said. "He got somebody else."

Metzger licked his lips and stepped aside, holding the door for them. "I guess you better come in." The shop had big modern-looking equipment under bright lights with the strangely clean smell of machine oil over the acrid tang of cut metal. "Shipping and receiving is over here."

Peter looked around. "This delivery driver, is he ever early?"

"I asked the shipping manager," Metzger said. "He never leaves the truck, but he's always right on time."

Peter had his go-bag over his shoulder with a change of clothes inside. "I need to clean up," he said. "Where's your washroom?"

Behind a dented steel door covered with safety stickers, he found three stalls and three sinks. He ran the water hot while he stripped off his boots and crusted pants, then stood in his underwear and socks and scrubbed his hands and arms and sticky red knees, grateful for the abrasive industrial soap in the orange pump jug. What he really wanted was a shower, but he knew he probably wouldn't get one for a while.

He dried himself with paper towels, then wiped up any stray pink droplets and pulled on a fresh pair of jeans from his go-bag. He wasn't remotely clean enough to fool a forensics expert, but if he found himself in police custody, he'd have bigger problems. Mostly Peter just didn't want to wear another man's blood.

He found Lewis and Metzger beside the loading dock's big doors, where an electric forklift stood beside twenty loaded pallets stacked two high and two deep on the concrete floor. Each pallet held four identical layers of sturdy cardboard boxes, making a four-foot cube wrapped up tight in clear packing film. "What'd I miss?"

"Eighty of those things," Lewis said. "All nice and neat."

Peter pointed at a single pallet that stood apart from the others. From the different shapes and sizes of the boxes, he assumed it held a different cargo. "What's that one?"

Lewis shook his head. "Jarhead, you gonna love this."

"I swear, I didn't know a thing about it." Metzger kept his eyes on the pallet. "It's our youngest guy's account. We didn't do any design or testing, we just built the things."

"What's in the boxes?" Peter asked.

"I already told your friend. I don't usually pay attention to shipping details, but I'm the only one here to drive the forklift."

"Marty."

Metzger talked faster. "There's another company name on the paperwork, but it's on the same manifest as Holloway's project. Like two stops on a delivery route, I thought. Until I went back and looked at the order. We made eight hundred of these things. Eighty of them on that pallet."

"Marty! What's in the damn boxes?"

Metzger wouldn't look at him. "It's a two-part assembly. One is a rifled tube wrapped with a series of magnetic coils. The other is a rectangular box that fits on the end."

"A magnetic gun barrel?" Peter felt his pulse accelerate. "So those things are armed? With an electric gun?"

Lewis gave Peter that tilted smile. "Called a Gauss gun. Uses electromagnets to fire a steel round at high velocity."

Of course Lewis would know what it was. "Do they work?"

Lewis shrugged. "Concept's been around since the 1800s. Navy's been testing electric artillery for a couple decades. Beauty is, no gunpowder. No cartridge to jam. Only moving parts are in the magazine, which means minimal cleaning and maintenance. Problem's always been the power supply."

"I guess not a problem anymore," Peter said. "What's the bore?"

"Sized for a 5.56. A NATO round, just like your M4. Gives you some idea of what they gonna do with it, right? But without the cartridge and powder, ammo's a third of the weight. Figure

Marty's magazine will hold two hundred rounds, maybe more? And the claw can reload until the battery runs out."

Metzger's face was pale like he was going to be sick. "It's my fault," he said. "I should know every order that comes through the shop. I'd have known what it was just by the rifling in the tube."

Peter said, "What's the length of the barrel?"

Lewis's smile got wider, but there was no humor in it. "Twenty-six inches."

Peter closed his eyes. "It's a goddamn sniper rifle. On a four-legged platform."

Metzger's phone rang on his belt. He took it from the holder and glanced at the screen. "It's Holloway's guy."

Peter said, "Are we sure we want to give him the rest of his shipment?"

"Don't matter," Lewis said. "Truck ain't leaving here anyway. Driver gonna tell us where it's headed, then we wrap him in duct tape and let Oliver collect the whole package."

Metzger put the phone on speaker. "Metzger Machine."

"This is Gary from Mr. Holloway's office. Our truck is at your gate. I trust you have our load ready?"

Metzger pulled the chain to raise the loading bay's door, then hit a button on the wall to open the gate. They watched a plain white semi-tractor-trailer roll though the widening gap and circle the parking lot. Aside from the thump of its tires across the cracked pavement, the truck was strangely silent. Its broad windshield was a bright mirror in the afternoon sun.

The driver knew his stuff, got his rig lined up and snug against the dock on the first try without any hesitation. Oddly, the trailer's cargo door was already up. Metzger climbed into the little electric forklift and started loading pallets, two at a time. Eleven trips wouldn't take long.

Peter squeezed through the narrow side gap where the trailer met the building wall, then dropped to the asphalt. The wind had picked up again, and carried the smell of ozone from the west.

The rig was a sleek square-front short-haul model, no sleeper berth in the back. It looked new, with not a speck of dirt to be found. There was no visible brand name either. He walked up to the driver's door, but he couldn't see through the tinted glass. He was pretty sure it was illegal to tint the windows on a commercial truck, especially this dark, but that would be at the bottom of the list of Holloway's crimes.

He reached up and knocked on the sheet metal, but nothing happened.

The engine was off, so the guy could definitely hear him. In Peter's experience, a fair number of truck drivers thought of themselves as hard-asses. Some carried a weapon in the cab, concerned about robberies or hijackings. Peter took the pistol off his belt and held it up, then knocked again, louder. "Come on out, we just have a few questions."

Lewis had gone out on the other side and now stood past the front passenger tire, shading his eyes with his hand. "Can't see the guy," he called. "Windshield's got too much reflection."

Peter reached for the door handle. It was locked. He stepped up on the front footholds and tapped the gun barrel on the glass. He still couldn't catch a glimpse of the driver. "Open up, buddy, or I'll break your damn window."

Still no answer. Maybe the guy was calling his boss. Or the police.

The trailer rocked as the little forklift trundled out another stack of pallets. Metzger really wanted that shipment out of his shop.

"You see the sun visor?" Lewis pointed at the brow mounted above the windshield. "That ain't no factory item." Usually it was a slim, rounded curve, designed to minimize wind resistance and painted to match the truck. But this one was primer gray with bulbous shapes at strange intervals. The side mirror's bracket had an odd lump mounted to the bottom, too, made of the same gray plastic, with a wire running out of it.

Screw this, Peter thought. He turned his head to shield his eyes and swung the pistol barrel hard into the window.

The laminated glass starred. No response from inside the truck. He hit the glass again. The star turned into a spiderweb and the tint film tore in the middle. He pinched up a corner of thin plastic film, peeled off a wide strip, and peered inside the cab.

Two seats, a steering wheel, a dashboard, and controls.

But no goddamn driver.

"Lewis, you'll never believe this." Peter pounded the glass again, finally making a hole. He used the gun barrel to enlarge the opening enough to get his arm through. Mindful of the sharp shards surrounding his bicep, he felt around for the door latch. He found it and pulled, but nothing happened. "It won't open."

Lewis walked around behind him. "Let me try."

Peter extracted his arm and dropped to the ground. "Marty, how many pallets left?"

The electric forklift whined. "Last one loading now." Metzger's voice was muffled inside the trailer. The truck rocked again as he reversed the heavy machine into the loading bay.

"Don't close the door," Peter called. Then heard the trailer door drop down with a clank. "Marty!" Peter hopped up to the concrete corner of the dock and slid through the slim space into the loading area.

Metzger still sat in the forklift, eyes wide. "I didn't touch it," he said. "It closed by itself." His phone rang and he pulled it from his belt. "It's the same number." He put it on speaker.

"Hello, this is Gary from Mr. Holloway's office. Is the shipment fully loaded?"

"Yes," Metzger said.

Peter looked at the back of the trailer. At the top, instead of a central brake light, there was another gray lump. One of Holloway's sensor arrays, which no doubt included a camera.

Gary's voice was calm and even. "Does that include both orders on the manifest?"

"Yes," Metzger said.

"Once everything is in our facility, I'll email you a delivery confirmation and waiver of lien," Gary said. "It's been a pleasure doing business with you."

Lewis shouted, "Jarhead, get your ass out here."

Peter slipped through the gap again. He saw Lewis up on the truck, one arm hooked through the side mirror bracket, the other hand fumbling with the snap on his shoulder rig. A hatch had opened in the semi's lower cowling, and a metallic creature crawled out onto the pavement and unfolded itself. It was eerily graceful, like no machine Peter had ever seen. Its twin blue domes and aluminum skin gleamed dully in the late-afternoon light.

Another creature was already on its feet, turning in a slow circle, servos whining softly, the sensors under the hardened glass no doubt gathering information Peter would never fully understand. He recognized the long arm with its powerful claw, still folded along what would have been its spine. An electric rifle barrel was mounted along one flank.

Lewis had his big black automatic out and began to fire at the thing one-handed. It was a small target, but he hit it broadside. The hyena stumbled but recovered and pivoted quickly to face the threat, all fluid motion with no real evidence of damage. The target was even smaller now. Lewis fired twice more and missed.

Peter couldn't shoot at the second hyena, which seemed to be still waking up, or he'd risk hitting Lewis. He jumped to the ground, ran to the first creature, knocked it over, and stomped on a back leg, hoping to break the joint or at least pin it down. But the other three legs adjusted quickly, their black tips finding a grip on the blacktop.

Despite Peter's weight, it began to push itself toward upright. The arm unfolded from the spine, the claw open wide and reaching for Peter. This wasn't going to end well. He put his pistol to the base of the arm and pulled the trigger three times. The arm stopped moving, either the joint frozen or the wiring damaged, but the legs kept working. Peter pointed the pistol point-blank at a blue bug eye and pulled the trigger twice more. The legs stopped.

"Little help, motherfucker." Lewis still clung to the side mirror, but the second creature had his ankle tight in its claw and it was yanking with that segmented arm, trying to pull him off the truck. Lewis kicked out wildly with his free foot, the gun useless in his hand.

Peter ran up and put the pistol to the hyena's flank and fired.

It bounced sideways but kept jerking at Lewis's leg. The hardened aluminum showed a deep dent but no hole. Lewis dropped the gun to grab the mirror bracket with his second hand, both legs in the air, flailing. "Kill it, fucking kill it."

Peter fired again, knocking the hyena into the semi's front tire. Point-blank and still no goddamn hole. What was this thing made of? Peter closed in, holding the machine in place with his weight long enough to put two rounds into the base of the claw. The arm stopped working but the claw still held and the creature thrashed harder. It pushed free of Peter and turned to face him, bringing the rifle barrel to bear. Peter heard a faint rising tone as he quickly transferred the pistol to his right hand. Then he put two rounds into the blue sensor domes and the hyena sank slowly to the ground.

"Get this thing off me," Lewis said. "I can't feel my foot."

"Will you hold still?" Peter got his fingers on the claw but it wouldn't move. "Shit."

"Let me." Metzger ran up with a cordless hammer drill in one hand and a chisel bit in the other. "The servo's locked. Put the claw against that concrete step there." They dragged the heavy dead hyena to the side of the building and Metzger bent with the drill rattling.

"Why didn't it fire at me?" Lewis's face was tight. He had one hand on the building and the other holding Peter's shoulder for balance.

"No idea," Peter said. "Maybe it didn't want to damage the semi and jeopardize the shipment?"

Behind them, with only the sound of tires on the asphalt, the semi began to pull away from the loading dock. Not a noisy diesel, but silent electric motors.

"Motherfucker," Lewis said. "Hurry up, Marty."

"Gimme your keys," Peter said. "I'll go get the Yukon."

Lewis fished in his pocket, swaying on one leg.

The truck straightened out, now pointed unerringly toward the open gate, but instead of accelerating, it slowed to a stop.

Metzger muttered something and the claw fell with a hard clank.

Lewis flexed his ankle. "Thanks. Damn, that hurt." They were all staring at the semi now.

Then it began to back up. Peter didn't think the semi could reach them where they stood, not without another round of back and fill, and it would be a slow process. They could always climb up onto the loading dock anyway.

But it didn't even try.

Instead, it reversed in a crisp, straight line, accelerating as it went. Even fully loaded, it gained speed much faster than a normal vehicle. The silent electric motors had infinite torque.

It shot like an arrow toward the black Yukon parked eighty yards behind it.

Lewis screwed up his face. "Aw, man."

But no amount of wanting would stop the heavy semi. It smashed hard into the front of the Yukon, the trailer's underride guard tearing into the SUV's engine compartment with the sound of a hyperactive child stomping tin cans.

The collision didn't even slow the semi down. It kept reversing, but now the front wheels turned at some precisely calculated angle and the trailer changed trajectory, pushing the wrecked Yukon in a noisy arc across another forty yards of parking lot, where it T-boned Marty Metzger's sky-blue Chrysler minivan, knocking the family vehicle on its side like a startled pill bug.

Lewis stood with his arms raised and his mouth open as the white truck jerked to a halt, then pulled forward again, dragging the Yukon with it as the motor mounts broke and the underride guard hauled the engine forward through the wreckage of the radiator until it fell free with a thud. Then the semi, unencumbered, powered toward the exit.

Jaw set, Lewis walked out into the parking lot, picked up his fallen automatic, and began to fire at the tires.

"Lewis, don't shoot." Peter took off, go-bag cinched tight, sprinting for the semi, shouting over his shoulder. "We need it functional so we can find out where the hell it's going."

Lewis shoved the pistol into its holster and followed, his limp turning into a run as his circulation improved.

As the semi coasted through the gate and turned left down the access road, Peter managed to grab the man-handle on the back corner of the trailer. He hoisted himself up to stand on the bent underride guard, then up to the narrow rear door sill. Lewis was close. Peter reached out and grabbed his hand and pulled him up alongside, where he slid right to grab the other handle.

When the semi turned right onto Hampton without slowing, the hard bounce of the rear wheels knocked their feet off the thin steel ledge and they dropped down, holding on to the long narrow bars for dear life. Peter watched the pavement flash by inches below his feet and felt the adrenaline pour through him like rocket fuel.

He hauled himself back to his feet and flashed a smile at Lewis, who'd done the same. "We've got him now."

Lewis laughed out loud. "Oh, yeah. He scared of us for damn sure."

Both of them still shaking from the encounter with the hyenas.

59

HOLLOWAY

Damn it." Holloway threw the computer pad onto the work van's center console. He blinked his eyes, surprised how emotional it made him to see the screen go dark after the pistol flashed bright in the lens. Two hyenas shot in the face. He'd have to make some improvements to the sensor ports.

Still, things weren't so bad. He was on the freeway headed south in the shotgun seat, with his personal assassin driving. Maria sat on the floor behind them with the hyena's claw clamped tight around her wrist.

He'd texted the killer once he knew the location of the meeting with Maria. His instructions were to take care of any opposition and help capture the young woman.

I'll follow your lead, the assassin had replied, but I'm not your dog. Are we clear?

That response was slightly unnerving, but Holloway found himself in the unpleasant position of needing another human being's help, so he didn't push. Understood, Holloway had texted back.

He hadn't wanted to ask about the reporter, but assumed she'd been handled like the family in Virginia and the two men from Metzger Machine.

The killer certainly had no problem dispatching Maria's friend with the slingshot, and had taken Maria unharmed when she ran to attack him barehanded, howling like an animal. When it was clear that Holloway's car was dead, the assassin had been surprisingly agreeable to taking them all in his van.

"Better stop screaming," Holloway had told the girl when the hyena hauled her through the van's side door. "His claw is strong enough to sever your wrist completely. Although you've seen the specs, so you probably know that already. Now where's your computer? Or should Harry Hyena start breaking bones?"

It hadn't taken much squeezing for her to reveal the backpack hidden behind the red pickup's seat, along with a bonus item, a working fuel cell built into an actual shoebox. The girl was truly magnificent. Holloway was really looking forward to working with her, he thought, as the hormone cocktail thrummed through his system. His erection was like an iron bar, but it wasn't sexual, not really. The stimulus was power. Although there was only one way to discharge it.

The killer, who had introduced himself as Edgar, wore a bright smile and dark glasses against the sun lowering in the west. It was fifteen degrees hotter across the Illinois border, and Holloway had the window down, attempting to vent the persistent stink of the dead man in the back.

It was a day of firsts, Holloway thought. He'd already commissioned multiple murders in the course of doing business, but today was his first time watching one. Today was also his first kidnapping, and his first time in a car with a day-old body. He didn't need to repeat the last one.

"Are you sure we can't stop someplace and get rid of that dead guy?"

"Mike Dillman?" Edgar shook his head. "No, he's with me."

As if it were a soft-spoken friend and not a bloody corpse, Holloway thought. Although obviously a hired killer would have some strange currents running behind those sunglasses.

He remembered the last message from Krueger, the middleman, when Holloway had asked for the killer's direct contact. *Don't say I didn't warn you.*

Holloway noticed that the red spots on Edgar's white dress shirt had gotten larger since they'd begun driving. His forearms were lined with hundreds of razor-slim cuts, he had a red dent in his forehead, and one ear was wrapped in a bandage the size of a golf ball. But aside from shifting in his seat, he didn't show the pain.

"How did you get hurt?" Holloway asked. "If you don't mind my asking."

Edgar kept his eyes on the road. "Trying to kill your reporter."

"I'm sorry about that," Holloway said. "But it's done, right?"

Edgar turned to face him. "No, it's not. I should have killed her that first night, when I went into her house. I could have waited in the dark. It would have been easy. The next day she had protectors. And a gun. And a dog. I don't like dogs. You didn't tell me about any of those things."

"I'm sorry, but I didn't know. I needed to learn what she knew about me before making the decision to eliminate her. I just assumed you could handle whatever came up."

That was the wrong thing to say.

Edgar's weird smile got wider, the broad face impossible to read behind the mirrored sunglasses. "I bet your doctor makes house calls, though."

"I'm sure he will." Although in truth Holloway doubted it. "Whatever you need. You've really gone above and beyond on this one."

He disliked this kind of ego-stroking crap. He'd always tried to rise above all the petty human bullshit, but he had to admit this was a special case. And now he understood why Edgar had become so helpful. It was useful information to have.

"I didn't mind going into her house," Edgar said. "It was fun to see what her life was like." He turned back to the road, the speedometer steady at seventy-five. "Although I'd rather just do my regular job." He tipped his head toward the back of the van. "You already paid me for this one, but I want to finish the other one first. I like to do them in order."

"Oh, the other one is still very important," Holloway said. "Let's get you fixed up and you can go back to work."

"Do you still want this one?"

Behind them, Maria spoke up, her voice sharp. "You *pendejos* know I can hear you, right? Talking about killing some reporter, about killing me?"

Holloway patted the cardboard shoebox on his lap. "Oh, your health and well-being are very important to me, Maria. You and I are going to become great friends, and great partners, for many, many years."

Then he reached into the backpack by his feet, pulled out her computer, and opened it on his lap. "While I have your attention, why don't you tell me your password? It's time to shut down your ransomware."

She looked at him like she had a secret she wasn't telling. "Too late, Vince. Your files are being deleted right now."

Holloway felt a surge of anger. He woke his phone and called Coyle, his IT contractor. "Tell me you solved my problem."

"We haven't freed up your files yet, but we did manage to pause the countdown. And of course your hyena controls are on an entirely separate system that is still under your full control."

"Good. Keep working." Holloway ended the call and looked over his shoulder at the woman hunched on the floor of the van. "Did you hear that? I've already beaten you, Maria. You might as well join me. What's your password?"

"I know about your assessment agreement with the Defense Innovation Unit," she said. "Why are you in bed with the Department of Defense?"

The DIU was a small, fast-moving, Silicon Valley–based program intended to accelerate the adoption of cutting-edge commercial technology into the military. Holloway felt the anger begin to congeal into something sour. She'd been deeper into his system than he'd thought.

"Imagine my hyenas in a combat setting and you'll understand," he said. "I'm a patriot. It's about saving lives."

"Vince, the only person you care about is yourself." She shifted on the floor of the van. "You stole this technology. You think the Pentagon won't find out?"

She knew about that, too? Had she been reading his personal notes? Was nothing sacred? He felt his cracked sternum begin to separate again, no matter that his heart attack had been seven years ago.

"I took it from a program so secret it doesn't even exist," he said. "And I developed it into something much greater. If the

DoD ever figures it out, they'll see it's too valuable to stop. *I'm* too valuable."

And he was. He had seen the future. He was a fucking genius and normal rules did not apply. And if the Pentagon didn't see it, someone else would. "This is a major evolution in defense technology," he told her. "Far fewer soldiers in combat will mean far fewer lives lost to war. That's a *good* thing. Foreign interventions will be cleaner, cheaper, and more palatable to voters than ever. America will use her might to bring about the end of war. Hyenas will be peacekeepers all over the world. Not to mention the downstream domestic market, which is unlimited. In five to eight years, we'll move into police contracts. In ten to fifteen years, we'll have a hyena on every street corner in America, with our autonomous facial recognition on constant alert for bad guys."

"That's not the end of war, that's an endless war abroad and a police state at home. That's your big dream?"

"Oh, no," he said. "Those things will happen with me or without me. Don't you read history? The writing's on the wall. Consolidation of power is the inevitable future. My dream is to be the power. The wealthiest man in the world, advisor to kings, maker of presidents. And you, with this fuel cell?" He patted the shoebox again. "Will guarantee that future. Now, Maria, tell me your password."

She turned her head and spat on Harry's sensor covering. *"Mal rayo te parta."*

Holloway felt his strength return in a flood. "That doesn't sound like a password. And this is no way to start our partnership." He raised his voice. "Harry, are you listening? Very slowly, tighten your claw by five millimeters."

Behind him, a powerful servomotor softly ticked. A higher, louder sound came out of the woman.

"It doesn't have to hurt, Maria. What's your password?"

"Chinga tu puta madre, viejo."

"Sorry, I don't speak Spanish. Harry, tighten by five more millimeters. No, make it ten."

Human beings, Holloway thought, really were unpleasant.

60

The self-driving semi picked up speed as it slalomed through the afternoon traffic, running red lights with no police around to notice or care. Peter and Lewis clung to the slender grab-handles on the back of the trailer, doing their best imitations of limpets. The sill that held their feet was no more than three inches wide.

Peter smiled at his friend. "This thing drives like you, Lewis."

"Man, that's a insult to my style," Lewis said. "Listen, you think somebody telling this damn thing what to do? Or did it decide to take out my truck and Metzger's minivan in one quick move all by itself?"

"I think we need to hang on tight and figure out what the hell to do next."

They flew past a rounded old Mercury sedan and three little boys in the back seat stared at them goggle-eyed, then rolled down the windows and started waving. Peter saw a converted firehouse

344

and a shining barbershop slide by on the right and knew they were coming up on Lincoln Park.

Next came the river and the I-43 overpass with the north shore suburbs on the other side.

"We're headed for the freeway," Lewis said.

Peter nodded and looked down at the pavement flying past. They weren't going to go much slower any time soon. "If we're going to make a move, we better do it before we hit that on-ramp." He tipped his chin at the roof of the trailer. "Up is our best bet."

"We stay down here, some solid citizen gonna call 911 for sure."

"Agreed." Peter pulled his pistol and aimed at the gray sensor blob at the top center of the trailer. "If anyone's watching, better they can't see what we're doing." Lewis turned his head and Peter put two rounds into the plastic. The whole assembly fell away, revealing a shallow oblong hole where the brake light had been. "We can get a couple fingers in there, pull ourselves up."

"Good a plan as any." The horn sounded and the truck lurched as it swerved around a driver who had clearly not been watching his mirrors. They lost their footing again, just their hands on the skinny steel handles, holding tight. Lewis grinned. "Starting in just a damn minute."

"I'll go first." Lewis had two kids, and this whole adventure hadn't been his problem to begin with. "If I fuck it up, you can always bail at the on-ramp where it crosses the river. Practice your Olympic diving technique on the way down to the water."

"You won't fuck it up," Lewis said. "Who else'm I gonna drink beer with?"

They were approaching Green Bay Road, the last intersection before the park. The semi swerved again, this time into the opposite lane, apparently to bypass cars waiting at the signal, then made it through cross traffic somehow managing to not hit anything. Peter hoped this truck wasn't truly autonomous, because its priorities were totally fucked up.

Their toes found the narrow steel sill again as the truck approached the first of several tight curves. The pavement was good here, so there should be fewer bumps, at least in theory.

As Peter felt the truck begin to brake, he let go of the grab handle, stood on his toes, and reached up to jam his left hand into the empty light socket. The deceleration of the truck pressed his body into the closed roll-up door and kept him from turning into reverse roadkill.

He got three fingers lodged in a good pocket hold as Lewis's hand closed lightly on his belt, then the curve pulled him sideways and his feet left the narrow metal ledge.

On a good day, Peter could manage a half-dozen one-armed pull-ups. Even though June was a much better rock climber, he'd gone out with her plenty of times. But usually the mountain wasn't holding a curve at fifty miles an hour. He was lucky that there was a small lip at the bottom of the socket, designed to hold the original brake light cover, that kept his fingers from slipping loose.

He lifted himself to chin height, then slapped his right hand onto the flat of the trailer roof and hauled himself higher. He was surprised to find a low metal frame just a foot in front of his face, suspended on brackets a few inches above the surface. He reached out and grabbed a bracket and raised a leg and then he was up, lying flat on a smooth, shiny platform that stretched the width and length of the trailer.

He didn't have time to wonder what the platform was for. He looked ahead and saw the next curve coming up, tighter and in the other direction, with the on-ramp just beyond. The truck was still going at least forty-five. He spun on his belly and hung one arm down toward Lewis. "View's better up here."

Lewis scrambled up and crouched on his toes with a stabilizing hand at the edge of the platform as the semi accelerated toward the on-ramp. "Shit, it's all solar panels, enough to power a small house. Probably keep this thing rolling twenty hours a day."

"Let's hope we're not headed to California." Peter still wore his go-bag. "I don't have enough granola bars to feed us both for three days."

"Man, I ain't eating granola bars for three days. Think we could get a pizza delivered up here?"

61

June stared at Detective Hecht. "Why are we talking about my personal life? You guys do remember that somebody tried to kill me yesterday, right? At least twice, maybe three times?"

There was a knock on the door and Sergeant Threadgill, the patrolman with the push-broom mustache, stepped in carrying a manila file folder.

Threadgill handed the folder to Hecht, who laid it on the table without opening it. Threadgill folded his arms and leaned against the closed door. With Lorenz still standing in the corner, her cheekbones sharp enough to cut, there were now three cops packed into the small space. A nice bit of intimidation theater, June thought.

Hecht smiled at her. "We don't have all the pieces yet, but we think there might be another actor in all this." He opened the folder, took out two pieces of paper, and slid them across the table.

The first was an arrest warrant with Peter's name as the defendant. The second was an FBI printout that showed Peter's old Marine Corps ID photo beside another, more recent picture, probably from when he cleared customs into Iceland.

Hecht reached across the scarred Formica tabletop and tapped the FBI printout. "Have you ever seen this guy?"

June examined the photos. Neither made Peter look good. "Jesus, I hope not. He's kinda scary." She read the text at the bottom. "He killed somebody?"

"According to Interpol," Hecht said. "He also beat the daylights out of four armed police officers while still in handcuffs. The guy's a real beast. I hate to say this, but Sergeant Threadgill here thinks he looks a little bit like your boyfriend, Peter Murphy."

"That's ridiculous." They were all looking at her, Sergeant Threadgill and both detectives.

"I know," Hecht said. "It's crazy. But there's an easy way to clear this whole thing up. Ask your boyfriend to come in for a few minutes. We run his fingerprints through the system, thank him for his time, and send him on his way. Piece of cake."

Sergeant Threadgill smiled under his mustache. "Do you know where Mr. Murphy is right now?"

"Honestly," June said, "I have no idea. He could be anywhere."

"Reason I ask, ma'am, I ran a check on your boyfriend, trying to rule him out, but he's kind of a mystery. Driver's license is good, but he's got no utility bills, no credit cards, no financial history at all."

"I told you, he's a minimalist." But she knew the conversation would only go downhill from here. It was time to call their bluff.

"You know what? I have to get back to work." She stood up and pushed back her chair and walked around the table. "Excuse me, Sergeant."

The sergeant didn't move from his position against the door.

June turned to Hecht, making sure her face and voice were clear for the camera. "Are you detaining me? If the sergeant doesn't get the hell out of my way, then you're detaining me. In which case, I'll call my attorney, and he'll call the newspaper." She smiled at Hecht. "Can you imagine the story they'll write? Victim harassed by heartless police. I'm a great interview. Or am I free to go, Detective? What's it going to be?"

Hecht frowned. "You're playing with fire, Ms. Cassidy."

"And you're worried about the wrong fucking people," June replied. "Now get Sergeant Potato Head out of my way or I'm calling my lawyer."

Outside, she stood on the sidewalk and looked for the Yukon, even though she knew Peter wouldn't park nearby. She had no idea what Edgar might be driving, but was semi-certain he wouldn't try anything right in front of the District Five stationhouse.

When her phone powered up, she had two voicemails from Dean Zedler, but she opened the text from Peter instead. Hope you're okay, it read. Call me when you're done.

She texted back. Done now. Can you pick me up?

Slight hiccup, he replied. Better take a cab to the hotel and lock yourself in your room. I'll be in touch.

Fuck that, she thought, and called him.

"I hope I'm not your one phone call." His voice was loud but she could barely hear it over the rushing background noise. Like he was standing beside a waterfall.

"Nope, I'm on the loose," she said. "Where are you?"

"On the freeway," he said. "How'd it go with the cops?"

"The good news is that I'm not under arrest." She glanced around but nobody was there to eavesdrop on her. She lowered her voice anyway. "The not-so-good news is they showed me an FBI sheet with your face on it. They know who you are."

"Shit," he said. "I'm sorry, June. I fucked this up and put you at risk."

Behind his voice, she heard the sharp blast of a car horn. "Just tell me we're making progress. What did you get from the delivery driver?"

"Funny story," he said. "There is no driver. The damn semi drives itself."

Jesus, she thought. We really are living in the future. "That was your hiccup?"

"Well, no. Lewis's truck got kinda wrecked so we had to hitch a ride."

She forced herself to keep her voice calm. "What do you mean, kinda wrecked?"

"Well, totaled, actually. The semi hit it. Don't worry, we weren't in it at the time."

"I can barely hear you," she said. "Roll your window up for a minute."

"Uh," he said.

God, he was a terrible liar. "What the fuck is going on, Marine? Who did you hitch a ride with?"

"Uh," he said again. "On that same semi. On top of the trailer, actually. We're just rolling south of downtown now."

"Jesus fucking Christ," she said. "Don't die, please. 'Cause I want to kill you myself." She blew out her breath. "What do you need?"

"We've got this," he said. "I had some rope in my pack, so we're tied off nice and secure, enjoying the ride, just waiting to see where we're going."

She closed her eyes tight, trying not to picture him on top of a goddamn truck on the goddamn freeway going who the hell knew where. "You are such an asshole."

"I didn't have a choice, June." He told her about the scene in the parking lot, the abandoned electric bike, Kiko Tomczak down with two dozen knife wounds. Then he told her about Metzger's. "We saw two of those things, the hyenas. They came after us. They're no joke. We're out of options. This semi is our only remaining connection to Holloway."

She rolled her shoulders, trying to work out the tension from the interview room and the last few days. What she really needed was a long bike ride, or maybe a trip to the shooting range. Funny how that cleared her head. "How about weapons? You have guns?"

"Tons of guns," he said. "We're good, June. We're just going to do a little recon. Tell Oliver we're on the hunt and I'll call you when I know something."

"Just tell me what you need. I'll get my Subaru and chase you down."

"That might not be the best idea, June." He was choosing his words carefully. "We don't know where we're going or what we'll find when we get there."

She ground her teeth. She hated it when he tried to manage her. "You just made my fucking point, Peter. You need help and I'm it."

The sound of the wind rose up in her ear, but he didn't say anything. As long as the wind was there, she knew she hadn't lost him.

"June, I know this is your story, and I'm just your backup.

Believe me, I'm okay with that." His voice was gentle, but it carried over the noise. "But when the guns come out, that's my department, right? Plus, we don't know where Edgar is. What if he's watching your Subaru?"

"Edgar's not watching the Subaru. If you think Holloway has taken Spark and somebody stabbed Kiko, then that means Edgar was there, too. If the Mercedes is trashed, he's probably still with them. They're probably in Edgar's car."

"June, this is a really, really bad idea."

"I'm not going to sit in some goddamn hotel room and wait to hear if you're alive or dead, all right? Put Lewis on the phone."

"June. You're upset."

"Hey, Marine? You're full of shit. Put Lewis on the goddamn phone."

Another pause, then the low dark voice came on. "Jarhead ain't wrong, June."

"Neither am I and you know it. The clock is ticking and we're it." She tucked the phone against her shoulder, notepad in one hand and pen in the other. "Now, what do you need and where do you keep it?"

62

PETER

Peter lay atop the semi-trailer with his toes hooked into the safety rope, watching the sun go down. Five o'clock. Three hours until Spark's fail-safe tripped and all hell broke loose.

He'd started on this hunt as a way to protect June and get his own ass off the FBI's Wanted list, but he had different reasons now. He wasn't exactly a convert to Oliver's larger mission, but this one made sense to him. He didn't want to see these hyena things turned loose on the world.

Yes, you could program them to behave better, maybe even to help old ladies across the street, but Peter knew there were powerful forces in the world that would use these machines for their own purposes regardless of consequences. Peter had seen those consequences close up, and he would do what he could to limit them. Which meant stopping Holloway, and stopping Spark from releasing Holloway's technology to every wingnut with an Internet connection.

So Peter would put his life on the line again. It wasn't the first time, and if he was being honest with himself, it probably wouldn't be the last.

But that didn't mean he wanted June to risk her damn life, too.

Now he listened as Lewis rattled off a list of gear that would supply a full squad of Marines. Three rifles, three armored vests, three sets of night vision goggles. He closed his eyes and took slow, deep breaths as he tried to quiet the roar of static in his head. It wasn't claustrophobia, it was fear.

Fear for June. He didn't want to lose her.

"Hey, good idea." Lewis fussed with the phone's screen for a moment, then put it back to his ear. "Okay, you got him. I'll do mine when we hang up. Be safe, June. But drive fast. And better not get pulled over with all that ordnance in your car, neither."

Peter felt a tap on his arm and opened his eyes to see Lewis holding out his phone. It was open to a locator app called Find My Friends that would allow June to home in on his location using GPS. "Thanks," he said.

"Don't give me that look, Jarhead. You know she's right. We got two handguns and maybe sixty rounds between us."

Peter felt the static swell to fill him completely. "She doesn't have the training we do, Lewis. She hasn't been in the fight."

"It's her call to make, brother. She ain't exactly June Cleaver, you know. Plus, she's in better shape than you, and a better shot, too, with a pistol anyway. She held her own against Edgar three times. He'd have got your ugly ass at Franny's house if it weren't for Mingus. Don't go thinking June can't handle it. She got as much reason to step into this as you and me."

"Oh, I get it." Peter's voice was thick. "But I don't have to fucking like it."

Lewis put his hand on Peter's shoulder, that familiar strong, solid grip.

"Back in the sandbox, all us grunts were s'posed to be fighting for our country, right? But when the shit came down, we were really just fighting for each other. Not even to keep ourselves alive, but to keep each other alive. That's what I'm doing right here beside you. That's what you were doing when you got that damn hyena thing off me back there."

Peter nodded. He didn't trust himself to speak.

"Shit, brother. June just wants to do the same thing."

Peter wiped his eyes. "Goddamn you, Lewis."

Lewis thumped him on the shoulder. His voice was kind. "Fuck you, too, Jarhead. Now gimme a granola bar."

The semi stayed on 94 south into Chicagoland. They passed Six Flags and Abbott Labs and turned onto the Dan Ryan toward downtown. Peter wondered what had happened to the enormous red lips of the Magikist sign, which had been a favorite landmark when he was a kid, visiting his grandparents in Chicago.

To their left, the sun was low in the sky. The afternoon had gotten warmer and Peter could taste the ozone in the air. The flow of cars got thicker, but the self-driving semi found invisible seams in the traffic and rolled forward past dusty pickups and sleek sedans and dented old beaters alike. As they came into downtown and the road dipped below the surface streets, the sun blinked on and off with each rust-crusted overpass.

One advantage to riding atop a semi-trailer was that they could see all the road signs. Peter thought they might take 55 downstate or the Skyway toward Indiana and Michigan, but they stayed on 94 until the Stony Island Avenue exit, which dumped them past a pocket of town houses and a baseball diamond onto busy 103rd Street.

They passed a Chicago Transit facility, then turned at the first intersection. Peter saw a row of intermodal containers and worried the trailer would end up on a rail car behind a locomotive headed nowhere June could follow, and they would be truly fucked. Instead, at a blue sign marking the Calumet Industrial Corridor, they veered in the other direction and headed south between a shallow marshland on the left and a vine-covered chain-link fence on the right. Behind the fence lay an enormous auto impound lot, then a weirdly green golf course, then a stretch of open water.

Peter pulled out his phone to get oriented. If they'd gotten off the freeway here, they were going to stop somewhere soon enough and he wanted to know where he was. The marsh was part of a park and past it was a former landfill and Superfund site. The body of water was the Calumet River. In the two miles of road before the dead end, his phone showed businesses like Dockside Steel and Atlas Tube anchoring a series of enormous piers angled into the river.

After a gentle curve in the road, the water on the right receded. They passed a featureless gray steel shed the size of an airplane hangar, then a wide swath of tangled scrub surrounding the rusted bones of a crane gantry jutting up toward the sky, and Peter felt the semi begin to decelerate. Next came a row of buildings behind a single rail line and a brush-choked fence topped with razor wire. If the complex housed a business, it wasn't named on the map.

The first structure was a small unpainted cinder-block gatehouse beside a driveway completely blocked by three sections of crumbling concrete Jersey barrier. The second structure was much larger, two stories of rust-colored brick with inexpensive decorative details, like a school science building from the seventies. Most of the windows had blinds lowered against the sun. Probably offices over warehouse space or maybe an equipment shop. Tall bushy weed trees grew right up against both buildings, as if the tenants had abandoned the place after a previously unreported apocalypse.

The sun was a half-circle astride the western horizon, burning a bright chemical orange through the haze. The semi was down to maybe twenty miles an hour and still slowing. Peter untied the left side of their safety rope while Lewis did the right. After the seventies-era building, they passed another entry drive, wider but also blocked, then another ratty cinder-block gatehouse, this one two stories. It was probably the freight office and site security, back when this place actually did something.

After a hundred yards of high grass, the truck turned into a gravel lot, the surface pocked with deep potholes that made the trailer thump on its tires. Peter and Lewis had to drop flat on their bellies and hold on to the sides of the solar panel platform. While Lewis threaded a doubled drop line through a platform bracket at the back, Peter looked ahead. At the far end of the lot he saw another high gate topped with razor wire, but this time it stood open. "Time to go," he said.

Lewis went first, a quick rappel down the back of the moving truck, then he kicked off the underride guard and released the rope and landed on the run as if he were just out for a jog. Peter followed and somehow managed to not fall on his face while keeping hold of one end of the rope. He chased the accelerating semi, hauling the looped line free from the bracket with both hands, then pulled it into a coil and sprinted to Lewis, who crouched behind a stand of scrub.

They watched as the driverless semi sped through lengthening shadows across cracked and rubble-strewn pavement toward the larger, seventies-era building. As the truck disappeared around the corner, the last of the visible sun flashed bright orange on the dull silver skin of a four-legged creature standing sentry there beside a wide mound of crumpled cardboard boxes.

The thing began to trot toward them, heedless of the debris in its path.

Lewis spoke in his ear. "Time to go find us some high ground."

Bent low, they angled away from the open gate and into the tall grass.

63

After talking with Peter in front of the District Five station, June had returned Dean Zedler's call.

"I left a message an hour ago," he said. "What took you so long? I feel like I'm stuck doing your grunt work."

As if she hadn't just spent most of the afternoon in an interview room, being grilled by the police.

She'd gotten more and more pissed that he was essentially blackmailing her into letting him piggyback on her story, but now he was just being a dick. She wondered if this was who Dean really was, underneath that Weaponized Nice. Maybe he'd stopped being even half-decent once he realized she was with Peter.

"I'm just leaving the cop shop but I don't have a ride," she said. "My Subaru's in the lot and there's a spare key in my desk. Come get me at District Five and we'll catch each other up when you get here." It was faster than waiting for a cab.

Waiting, anxious to get out of there, she used the black phone to send Oliver a text. Things are heating up. Check your email for engineering docs. Those machines are now in the wild. She gave him a summary of what she'd learned. If you have a team available, now would be the time. I'll text when I have a location.

Dean rolled up and she felt a wave of relief. Not at seeing Dean, but at finally getting the hell away from Detective Hecht and Lorenz and Sergeant Mustache. She walked into the street and opened the driver's side door.

"Out you go, I'm driving." He opened his mouth to object, but she just shook her head. "Nope, it's my car. Out."

She drove ten blocks to the coffee shop on Humboldt, fending off his questions the whole way. "Let me get some coffee and go through my notes, okay?" She needed the caffeine anyway.

They ordered at the counter and waited for their drinks. He wore a soft brown leather jacket and jeans and side-zip boots polished to a high gloss. She flipped through her notebook, thinking of what she should tell him. Instead, she asked, "What did you get on that LLC I sent you? Graham, Brown?"

"It's got a Nevada incorporation address, but it's just one of those registration shops, basically a PO box. The bank account is with Chase in Chicago, the main branch at Chase Tower downtown. But there are electrical permits on file in that name with the city of Chicago. Something about new transformers, which sounds major. The address for the permits is 11660 Stony Island Avenue, on the south side."

Nice work, she had to admit. "What's at that address?"

"According to Google Maps and the city, nothing. It's right on the Calumet River. It used to be an industrial shipping outfit, moving steel from the smaller mills in Gary and Hammond. Now it's owned by some trust out of the Cayman Islands. That was as far as I got, probably as far as I'll ever get."

They picked up their coffee and walked toward her car. "Your turn," he said. "What'd you get today?"

She took the key from her pocket, unlocked her door, and got in. He tried the handle on his side, but it didn't open. "June, it's still locked," he said.

She turned the key and revved the engine, then rolled down the passenger window a few inches. He hooked his fingers over the glass and bent to talk through the gap. "June, this isn't funny. You haven't told me a damn thing. We have a deal, remember?"

"I remember, but I'm not ready to share yet." She put the car into gear and he pulled his hand back.

His face was red. "What are you doing now?"

"Picking up a bunch of guns and transporting them across state lines." She gave him a smile. "I'm pretty sure that's not your kind of thing."

She checked her mirror and hit the gas and got the hell out of there.

64

The wild grass grew thick and close and well over their heads. With Lewis on point, they made a silent path toward the fence, parting the sawtooth blades with their hands. Still outside the weed-choked chain link, they followed it away from the gate until they came to a corner section and a broad drainage ditch filled with cattails.

Past the ditch was an overgrown rail line, the creosote ties turning to poisonous dust in the gravel bed, and past that, the road. On the other side of the blacktop was the former landfill, a broad and verdant hill rising a hundred feet or more, the wind making abstract patterns in the lush green meadow. Peter hadn't seen or heard another car or truck since they'd turned away from the intermodal yard. The breeze carried the rich smell of the marsh and growing things. They might have been a thousand miles outside of Chicago, or in another world altogether.

They turned the corner and chased the sagging fence toward

the two-story security building until they found a spot where the top rail was rusted loose and the posts were tilted in the dirt. Peter used the multi-tool from his go-bag to cut the last few tie wires, then they walked the chain-link down into the dense vegetation, mindful of the rattle. Now inside the perimeter and hopefully unnoticed, they stepped carefully through their concealment with the flat-roofed gatehouse ahead.

The fence ended at the corner of the building, which sat inside the perimeter, but their cover ended at the edge of a six-foot walkway. Still inside the green, they stopped and looked out at a wide concrete yard, a vast metal shed with one side open to the weather, and a rusting yellow crane at the edge of a narrow lane of water between two earth-filled piers the length of two city blocks, lined with fat metal bollards where a cargo ship would tie up. Peter figured they could see less than a third of the complex.

While Lewis took out his phone and texted June the GPS coordinates of their location, Peter took several minutes to eyeball the area for mechanical monsters. He was still deeply unnerved by the fight at Metzger Machine, and wondered how many more might be walking around this desolate place.

He didn't see the hyena that had run toward the open gate, but somehow that didn't make him feel better. It could be coming up behind them, or standing somewhere in shadow where it was less visible. If it had infrared vision and pattern recognition, it could probably spot their heat outlines through the thick grass. He assumed it could communicate with the other hyenas, and with whoever was controlling them. He hoped June had reached Oliver. He hoped the cavalry was coming with heavy weapons. He wasn't holding his breath.

Lewis nodded at the cinder-block gatehouse. The windows were still intact, but there was a door on the exposed side that looked like it was pushed in from the jamb, as if the knob simply hadn't latched. "How 'bout in there? Get up to the second floor, we can see most of the grounds."

Lewis wasn't asking about tactics. He was asking about Peter's claustrophobia.

"I can do that," Peter said. Aside from the constant fear for June's safety that he'd pushed deep down inside, he was doing okay.

He took another slow look for four-legged machines, then nodded to Lewis and stepped out of the grass and across the walkway. The door swung inward at his push, and he saw that the jamb was cracked and the latch had nothing to grab. Someone had broken in before them, but the pile of dry, windblown leaves on the dirty tile floor told him it wasn't recent.

He was inside letting his eyes adjust when Lewis came in fast on his heels. "Here they come," he said in a conversational tone, then slammed the heavy steel door and leaned his weight against it. Something outside pushed inward for a moment and Lewis had to set his feet to hold it back. "How do we keep this fucking thing shut?"

They were in a small dingy office maybe twenty feet square with a Formica counter against one wall, a pair of ancient steel desks along the second, and stairs going up along the third. The windows were dirty and it was dim inside. Peter ran to a desk and shoved it across the floor to Lewis. "How many?"

"Only one so far." Still holding the door, Lewis helped Peter snug the desk up against it, then sat on the desktop with his legs drawn up. "My opinion, that's one too many. Those damn things give me the willies."

"Whose idea was this, anyway?" Peter hauled another desk across the tile, then flipped it on its side with a thump and pushed it into place. There was a soft metallic sound and they both looked at the door. The knob turned slowly. "Jesus."

The knob kept turning until it hit the limit, then it paused, creaking, until something went *ping* inside and the knob spun freely, around and around and around and around.

Lewis looked at him. "How long 'til it decides to come through the window?"

"You call that positive thinking?"

The desk lurched as something shoved the door hard. Lewis jumped down to push back against it. "What else we got?"

Peter looked around for something else to stack against the door, but the chairs were all on wheels and the counter was firmly attached. He headed for the stairs. "Be right back."

The desk lurched again. Lewis called, "Don't take too long."

The second floor was more desks and file cabinets and broad windows on all sides. There were good views of the yard and the open shed and the piers beyond, as well as the larger seventies-era building across the entry drive. The sun was below the horizon and the light was starting to fade, but Peter could see two of the creatures in fluid, effortless motion, trotting toward them.

"We got company," Peter shouted.

"I can barely hold one of them," Lewis called back. "Any options up there?"

Peter figured Lewis was right, they'd come through the windows eventually. The stairway was narrow, and Peter thought they could block it with the desks, but he doubted it would be enough. They could certainly shoot the damn things, but Holloway had more hyenas than Peter and Lewis had ammunition. Besides, sooner or later, the hyenas would start shooting back.

They could go out the windows on the road side, which would put them back outside the fence and maybe outside the creatures' zone of interest, but if the things did pursue them past the perimeter, he and Lewis would be in the open with no vehicle and no place to hide. He felt an itch between his shoulder blades, thinking of those electric sniper rifles.

Then he looked up and saw the roof access hatch in the ceiling. There was no ladder. He shoved a desk over, climbed up on it, then undogged the hatch and pushed it up. He pulled himself above the rim and saw a flat rubber membrane and a low parapet wall. Someone had left a bucket of roofing tar in the corner.

He heard a thump from the first floor. "Motherfucker," Lewis said.

Peter ran down the stairs and saw the desks shoved back six inches with Lewis braced and sweating. The hyena reinforcements had arrived. The door was partly ajar and a long metal arm snaked through the gap, its claw feeling blindly for the obstruction. "How do you feel about the roof?"

"I feel good," Lewis said. "Real good."

The minute Lewis stepped away, the heavy desks slid back with a screech and the door opened wide. The first creature nosed into the gap, servos whining softly, its arm cocked back but the claw open wide, blue-tinted sensor domes gleaming in the dim light. Two more stood behind it, arms retracting from the dents they'd left in the door.

If Peter had ever thought he might someday get used to their eerie animal grace, seeing these headless nightmares up close made him feel differently.

Then Lewis jumped for the stairs, and Peter ran after him.

As Lewis leaped onto the desk and pulled himself up through the hatch, Peter hustled a second heavy desk to the top of the stairs, where he saw a hyena already halfway up. He flipped the desk and shoved it thumping down the steps, expecting to bulldoze the creature to the bottom. But the thing just set its feet and caught the weight with its claw and stopped it cold. Then it walked backward, navigating the steps easily as it pulled the heavy piece of furniture down the rest of the stairs and out of the way, before heading up toward Peter again.

"Come on, Jarhead." Lewis looked down through the hole with daylight behind him. Peter vaulted to the desktop and Lewis grabbed his arm and pulled him through the opening as the creature's claw tried and failed to clamp on his leg.

Together they slammed the hatch and sat on it, breathing hard, looking down over the low parapet wall at the industrial yard, where fifteen or twenty of the creatures ran across the cracked concrete like so many bright flocking birds.

Beyond them, the giant open-sided shed looked empty and abandoned. Aside from waving grass, there was no movement on either of the earth-filled piers. A white van was parked by a door in the side of the two-story building on the far side of the gated entry drive. Because of their location, Peter had no view of the back of the building, but he could see the blunt nose of a white semi, maybe with its trailer backed up to a garage door or loading dock.

Peter elbowed Lewis. "See the truck?"

Lewis nodded. "That building's our next stop."

Something thumped hard on the hatch lid. After a moment, it heaved up, dumping them both to the roof surface. "Man, I am *tired* of this shit." Lewis calmly rolled to his knees and pulled his pistol as a questing claw reached through the opening.

Below, one of the creatures stood on the desk just as Peter and Lewis had done.

With one hand, Lewis grabbed the arm right below the claw and pulled up. The arm thrashed and the legs churned in the air. The beast had to weigh eighty pounds or more, but Lewis showed no sign of effort as he reached down, put the pistol to one of the sensor domes, and pulled the trigger.

The creature froze. Lewis shifted to the other dome and pulled the trigger again. The arm went loose and Lewis let go and the creature bounced off the desk and fell to the floor.

Lewis slammed the hatch and sat on top of it again. "Go tell your friends about *that*, motherfucker."

Peter turned to look at the creatures flocking in the yard. One of them had stopped, back legs bent to angle the bug-eyed sensors toward the two men on the gatehouse roof. After a moment, the rest of them stopped, too, then turned in unison until they all pointed their alien faces at the same targets. Like a pack of predators catching a scent.

Instinctively, Peter ducked. It saved his life.

He heard a *zhip* and felt a puff of air as the first round whispered through his mop of shaggy hair, just missing his skull. It was a distinctive sound, and Lewis must have heard it, too, because he dropped flat to the roof deck at the same time Peter did. There was no crack of gunpowder. The electric rifles were almost completely silent.

Peter thought of June and felt his fear for her lance through him. "We gotta tell June to back off and wait for the cavalry. This is a goddamn mess."

Lewis pulled his phone and looked at the screen.

"Too late. She's already here."

65

HOLLOWAY

When the van pulled up to Holloway's building, a dozen hyenas clustered around it. Their claws were folded back but he knew their weapon capacitors would be charged and their targeting systems ready to fire. Holloway opened his door and looked the closest one right in the sensor suite, knowing its facial rec would automatically give him command status.

"Four hyenas, on me. Personal protection mode. We're going up to the loft."

He loved the natural language function, and knowing that his creations could understand him and would obey his every word. More than that, he was absolutely certain that they felt a kind of unconditional love and devotion toward their maker. It went a surprisingly long way toward filling the void inside.

They made quite a caravan as they crossed the wide two-story production floor with its joyful noise, then climbed the stairs to the former office space carved out of the back corner of the building. Holloway first, carrying Maria's backpack and the fuel cell in its shoebox, then Harry Hyena, towing sullen and silent Maria by the wrist. A pair of nameless hyenas from the yard came next, followed by Edgar, his white shirt increasingly red, and two more hyenas brought up the rear. Safety in numbers.

Opening the door to the wide marble entryway of his home, Holloway felt the void deepen a little. He'd never actually had another human being in the place. The contractors who'd done the work had obviously been inside, but they were finished before Holloway moved in.

Still, walking into the loft was like entering his own personal sanctuary. The enormous space was clean and spare, but also utterly luxurious, English oak and Italian tile, handwoven carpets, a spa bathroom and chef's kitchen. One of these days, Holloway thought, he'd learn to make something besides those damn green smoothies.

He had two weeks to get the rest of his hyenas assembled and through initial diagnostics and on their trucks to the Aberdeen Proving Ground. He knew his babies would kill the army's test protocol. Once they came to terms on the fast-track initial production contract, the money would start rolling in, and Holloway's life would be different, richer, better. The wound in his chest would finally heal. Maybe he'd buy an island.

He watched Maria stare at his elegant modern furniture, the giant wall of screens. He hoped she liked it. "We're very private here," Holloway told her. "We never have to leave the grounds. All food and supplies are delivered to the gate next door, completely frictionless, we never have to interact with another soul. There's a full gym at the end of the hall, with all the latest equipment, and a state-of-the-art lab through that door. I'll bring in whatever you need."

She stared at the corner and wrinkled her nose. "What is *that*?"

"Oh." Holloway hadn't left home expecting company, so he'd left Holly, his Lumidoll, plugged into the wall. She wore a filmy negligee that did not hide her lush synthetic curves. "That's my, ah, side project. When she's done charging, she just hangs on a hook in the closet." Holloway felt his erection swell at the sight of her.

Edgar peered at the doll and his smile faltered. "That's not right."

"She's a custom model, six thousand dollars plus shipping from Japan." Holloway wasn't going to explain his testosterone treatment, the vast and necessary energy and confidence it gave him, and the unfortunate requirement of satisfying the biological urges that came with it. He didn't want to bother with the messiness of human relationships, so Holly was a good solution. He picked her up and tossed her through the door to his master suite.

He realized that he'd have to tidy up the lab, too. He had Holly's twin laying on a table, cut open like a specimen frog. He was installing a more realistic skeleton and servomotors and touch sensors. A good solution could always be made better, after all.

There was no way he would tell them that sometimes he sat Holly at the dining table during dinner, or beside him on the couch while he watched television. This was why he didn't like other people. All they did was judge him.

"Harry, bring Maria to the couch."

"No, no. Hell, no." But Harry had her wrist and pulled her over to him. "You are a sick fuck, Vince."

"Oh, please, Maria. I'm not going to rape you." He dropped her bag beside her and pulled out her laptop. "We're colleagues.

Business partners, remember? But we've still not solved our little ransomware issue."

In the van, she had proven stronger-willed than he'd expected. The logistics of persuasion in a moving vehicle were difficult. He also found himself unwilling to damage her wrist, given that they would be working together for a long time. But there were other, less permanent ways.

And he had Edgar, if it had to get messy. She'd watched him cut up her friend in the wheelchair, after all. Perhaps they'd start with a toe?

She looked at him now, then at Edgar. She'd done the math. It wasn't complicated. But again, he had the feeling that there was something else she wasn't telling him.

"Okay," she said. "But I need both my hands. I can't just turn it off. I have to get into my server and change the code."

"Honey, I'm not letting you touch your computer, not until you show me I can trust you. Tell me your password and walk me through it. Better yet, let me delegate this." He called Coyle, his systems guy, and put him on speaker. "Hey. I have our hacker here. She's going to help you untangle her code."

"Wait," Coyle said. "You have the hacker? In person?"

Holloway liked the surprise in his voice, and the respect. "Yeah. You better double-check her work before you actually do anything. She's, ah, still adjusting to her new situation."

There was a pause as Coyle processed this. Then he apparently decided that he didn't want to know any more. "Okay," he said. "I'm Coyle. I'll need remote access. Where do we start?"

While they talked in a language Holloway only half-understood, Edgar poked around the loft, opening doors to the gym and workshop, rattling through the kitchen, peering into the fridge.

"This is all weird stuff. Don't you have any regular food, like beer or lunch meat?"

"No," Holloway said. "There's food in the freezer. Kale soup, quinoa pilaf, marinated tofu." It came every week in a Styrofoam box with a slab of dry ice to keep it cold. Most of it tasted like dirt, but it was supposed to be good for him. He was planning to live forever.

The fridge door closed with a thump. "It's time to call your doctor."

Holloway still needed the leverage. "As soon as we're done here."

Edgar came around the kitchen island. "Now."

Harry sounded the discordant chime that indicated a warning. "Security breach. Security breach." Holloway had given Harry the voice of Operator Twelve. He found it pleasing. All the hyenas had a broadcast function, too, so a remote user could give orders to locals on the ground, either as Operator Twelve or yourself.

"Okay, Harry. Put up the video feed. Back up to the first time you first saw them. Show only relevant sections."

The wall screens combined to show one large image. A long view of the last delivery truck rolling through the gate, then two tiny figures scurrying away from it. It cut to the old gatehouse, one man going inside, the video getting quickly closer as a second man followed. Another cut to the door, with a claw pushing against it.

Coyle asked, "Is everything okay?"

"No problem," Holloway said. "A few gnats buzzing around. Get back to work."

Edgar walked closer. "Call the doctor. We had a deal." His hand was tight against the red on his shirt. The fabric looked wet.

"Not now. This is more important. Harry, show me facial rec on the two men." The screen showed grainy profile images and a probability match from the much better video grabs from Metzger Machine just a few hours ago. Ninety percent odds they were the men who'd killed the hyenas guarding the shipment.

Maria's eyes were wide.

Holloway smiled. "Pretty cool, huh? You're going to wish those shares I gave you were real."

Edgar stared at the screen. "Those are the reporter's protectors. Maybe the reporter is out there, too."

"Harry, show me current video of the lead unit." The door being pushed wide by two claws, a stairway. "Take them alive if possible. Significant injuries are acceptable."

On the screen, a black man's face appeared, then a hand with a gun. There was a flash and the feed went dark. It was quickly replaced by a new view from lower in the room, but still. With all the blood, sweat, and tears that had gone into their development, losing even a single hyena felt like losing a child.

"Harry, forget about taking them alive. Shoot to kill."

He grabbed a VR headset from the coffee table and fired it up. Voice control was great, but virtual was better. He could do much more with a direct interface, as if he were inside each and every one of them.

He turned the goggles in his hands, waiting for the light inside that would let him know he was live. It was weird to put them on before the link. It reminded him of that moment during his heart attack when everything went black.

When Edgar stepped toward the couch, two hyenas moved to intercept him, claws rising. Edgar stopped. "The doctor. How long will it take him to get here?"

Fucking human beings, Holloway thought. *So fucking selfish. Didn't he understand that hyenas were dying?*

He almost told Harry to take Edgar apart, but Holloway still had a use for him. It wasn't easy to find a real assassin, after all, and the reporter was still out there somewhere, writing lies about him. He couldn't send his hyenas out in the street, not yet. Plus, Edgar had been paid four times the going rate on Maria, and he'd done hardly anything to earn the fee. Okay, he'd taken care of the cripple and driven Holloway home, but how hard was it to kill a cripple? Holloway wondered if he could get some of his money back.

Then he thought again of what Krueger had said. *Don't say I didn't warn you.*

He looked at Edgar now, at the wet red stain on his shirt. Holloway didn't really have a doctor who would make a house call. When the Pentagon gave him a nice juicy contract, and the money started coming in dump trucks, he'd definitely change that.

He pulled the goggles over his eyes. "Thirty minutes to an hour," he said. "I'll message him right now. I've got all kinds of pain pills in the bathroom, just help yourself."

He brought up the virtual keyboard and searched for the closest ambulance service. Those paramedics were pretty good, right?

66

June thought she'd be nervous driving a small arsenal down through Chicago, but she wasn't. She felt clear and focused and ready. She was starting to understand why Peter was addicted to this stuff. It had a way of blocking out the bullshit, all her worries about her book deadline and what kind of life she might actually want and when she was going to get her next Pap smear.

She'd called Oliver from the on-ramp, but he didn't pick up. She'd texted him the Stony Island address, hoping she was right, then turned on her fuzz buster and pushed the little Subaru up to ninety-five. It didn't complain.

She was almost through downtown Chicago when Lewis sent her a text with GPS coordinates and she knew Stony Island was the right address. She forwarded it to Oliver with a message. Don't be an asshole. We're counting on you. She thought about reducing the bitch factor with a smiley face but didn't.

The app on her phone could find Peter's signal within three meters. She left the car hidden in a brushy thicket, slung the heaviest duffel over her shoulder, then picked up the second bag and ran down some crappy train tracks toward the building where his green dot blinked.

She heard banging and swearing from the flat roof of the gatehouse, two stories up. They sounded busy up there. She didn't want to call out. Then she heard two loud gunshots. A moment later, she heard strange zips overhead, and her phone buzzed with a text.

Taking fire, very hairy. Building full of armed monsters. Get out of here and take cover.

Fuck that, she thought. I'm right below. East side of bldg. Happy to go home and bake cookies, but taking all these nice guns with me.

Leave the guns and go! Not safe! Stay hidden! It wasn't like Peter to use all those exclamation points.

Not leaving without you and Lewis. She looked at the cinder-block face of the building. The mortar joints were worn deep enough to make good finger holds. Many were wide enough for toe holds, even in her hiking boots. She'd climbed worse rocks. If you need an escape route, I have good rope. Can come to you.

A head appeared over the edge of the building. Just a silhouette against the sky, but she recognized Peter's shaggy mop of hair. He waved her away. She smiled and waved back.

Then a doubled rope snaked down from the roof, and Peter dropped down in a quick and dirty rappel. He landed and popped the thin rope to tell Lewis he'd landed, then leaned in and kissed her hard on the mouth. He tasted like uncut grass and she wanted to kiss him forever. He put his lips to her ear and whispered, "Where's the car?"

She pointed north. "Past the next building. In the trees."

Boots scuffed on masonry overhead and Lewis descended in three big bounds, then pulled the rope down and coiled it. His teeth flashed white when he saw the black duffels. He squeezed her shoulder, slung one bag over his shoulders without the slightest clank from all that heavy metal, and slipped into the cattails, headed directly away from the cinder-block tower. Peter took the second duffel and held out a hand. Always the gentleman.

They ran across the empty road and through more cattails thick in the ditch, then into the high broad-leafed grass, where they crouched under a lone tree in the verdant sheltering gloom with the cool wind on their faces and the western sky turning crimson. June felt high and wild, like playing ghost in the graveyard when she was a kid.

Lewis knelt at the open duffel, hauling out camouflage vests with armor plates. June's didn't fit very well. She wondered if they had armor designed for a woman's body. Peter checked her straps, Velcroed a holstered pistol to the front, then handed her a helmet and showed her how to adjust the night vision gear attached to the front. Lewis opened the other bag and handed out deadly looking assault rifles and magazine after magazine of ammunition.

Peter looked at Lewis and whispered, "Are you planning an assault on the federal reserve? How much of this shit do you have?"

Lewis gave him a look. "White man has a buncha guns, he's a patriot. Why's a black man always got to be a criminal or a revolutionary?"

"Technically," Peter said, "you are a criminal. Or you were, anyway."

"In my heart, I'm still gunning for gangsters." Lewis flashed the smile again, wider this time. "Why I like running with you. But gotta admit lately I been thinking on the revolution." He turned to June and scanned her gear. "You sure you okay? Won't be no picnic."

She hadn't done any training with the rifle. She gave it back to him. "I'd just be a hazard with this thing. I'm good with the pistol. When do we go?"

"Depends on Oliver. What's the word?"

"I keep sending him updates, including the address two hours ago, but I've heard nothing back all day." June checked the black phone and shook her head. "Still nothing. What do we do?"

Then she caught movement in the corner of her eye and turned to the big seventies-era building. She pointed through the cattails. "Corner window facing the gatehouse, second floor."

The blinds had gone up and a big figure stood in the frame, looking across the entry gate at the two-story tower. He wore a white dress shirt, now blotched dark. He put his hand to his mouth like he was eating peanuts.

June fell backward onto her butt with her heart thumping like a bass drum. She was afraid he could hear it across the street and through a closed window. She drew her pistol and put Edgar in the sights.

"Don't shoot." Peter put his hand on the barrel and pushed it down. His voice was soft but firm. "You'll draw those things to us. We need to stay hidden for now."

June lowered the gun and tried to catch her breath. She couldn't take her eyes off the window. She watched as Edgar took a drink of water from a plastic bottle, then leaned close to the glass and peered from side to side and down to the ground. He was looking for them, she thought. Looking for her.

Then he turned away and was gone.

Lewis leaned in close. "We got you, June. He won't make it through us."

She nodded. "Then let's get moving. I'm going to finish what I started with that fucker." Bent low, she began to head north through the thick grass. In a hundred yards, she'd be out of line of sight of the entry drive and Holloway's creatures.

"Hold up," Peter said. "June, I really think you should wait here."

She turned back to face him. "There's no fucking way I'm going to sit on my ass in the goddamn bushes in the goddamn dark waiting to find out if you two get shot or killed, not knowing when Edgar might show up."

"June," he said. "Please."

She could see the pain on his face. She couldn't remember the last time she'd seen fear in his eyes, if she ever had. She grabbed his vest and pressed her mouth to his. "You will protect me, Peter. I know you will. But I'm going with you. Edgar is inside my goddamn head. I have to end this."

He looked at her wordlessly. She kissed him again, then bit his lip hard, tasting blood.

"Besides," she said. "I know how you can get into that building without fighting off those hyena things. But you won't do it without me."

67

Peter used the multi-tool from his go-bag to cut the razor wire on the fence. The big seventies-era building stood on the far side, ten feet away. The vines and brush growing up through the chain link helped silence the rattle as they went over. Then they stood together in the darkness under the weed trees grown up against the walls, back inside the perimeter.

June's plan was to climb to the roof and get inside from there. She'd retrieved a static line and three harnesses from the back of the Subaru, gear left from their last trip to Grandad Bluff in La Crosse. She wore the coil of rope across her chest like a bandolier. She'd stripped off the pistol and armored vest and helmet and stowed them in the duffel. She'd never make it to the top wearing all that extra shit.

June tilted her head at the brick, her voice soft and steady. "The first floor is too smooth and tight." The wild saplings were tall enough, but they were too thin and bendy to hold her weight. She pointed at the second floor's corner detail, where decorative bricks projected out from the surface three-quarters of an inch or so. "Can you lift me? A decent fingerhold is all I need."

Peter eyeballed the brick. He knew he and Lewis couldn't do this without her. He took a knee. "Climb up to stand on my shoulders. Lewis will steady you. Then I'll stand, and you can steady yourself against the building. When you step on my palms, I'll press you up."

She nodded and put her boot on his thigh. She was slim and light. Peter drank in the scent of her, the press of her body against his, the familiar feel of her strong, capable hands holding tight. He welcomed the focus required to stay steady beneath her. He was trying not to lose his shit. If there was one of those creatures standing sentry on the rooftop, June was almost certainly dead.

Then she stepped into his hands. He lifted her until his elbows locked. She reached for the first quoin. Then her weight was gone. Peter leaned back to watch as she pulled herself up, legs hanging free until she was high enough to use her feet. She was nearly invisible in the failing light.

Peter was already saturated with adrenaline, but as he watched her spider up the wall without a backward glance, the static crackled in his head like he'd stuck his tongue into a light socket. He wasn't worried about her free-climbing a two-story building. She'd done the north face of El Cap. She'd scrambled up giant redwoods. She said she could make it and he knew she was right.

No, it was what came after. What might be on the roof, and what they'd certainly find inside.

None of Peter's fights that day, not with Edgar, not with Holloway's metal monsters, had fired him up like this fear for June's safety. She was risking her life and it scared the hell out of him. He didn't want her to get hurt. He didn't want to lose her.

He found himself falling hard into that old post-traumatic panic loop. But he was somehow able to see it and catch himself. He wouldn't be any good to June or Lewis like this. He made himself take a slow, deep breath, held it through five heartbeats, then released it slowly, counting five more. The extra oxygen and long exhales would reverse the cycle and get him functional again. He closed his eyes and pulled in another slow, deep breath, feeling his heart beat. Then another breath, and another, and another. The static begin to ease.

He opened his eyes as June reached the small masonry cornice at the top. She slung a silent hand around the overhang, pulled her face up to peer across the parapet wall for an eternal moment, then hauled herself over and was gone.

Peter strained to hear over the sound of the breeze, but there was nothing.

"Atta girl," Lewis said, his voice soft and deep as the falling dusk.

"Jesus." Peter filled his lungs again, then let them empty.

Lewis turned and thumped him on the chest with a fist. "You know this how she feels every time you leave the damn house, right?"

"Maybe I didn't before," Peter said. "Not really. But I do now."

Lewis looked at his phone. "It's after seven," he said. "If Spark doesn't hit the dead man's switch by eight, this all goes public, right?"

Peter nodded. "And the Russians and Chinese and Iranians are all building killer robots."

Then the uncoiled rope dropped down the face of the brick and it was Peter's turn to climb.

———

June met him at the top. "I'll wait for Lewis and haul up my gear," she said softly. "You go find our way in."

The roof was broad and flat, like a small city block covered with black rubber. He was hoping for an access bulkhead with a door and stairs, though he'd be happy with a simple hinged service hatch. But there was nothing but a giant heating-cooling system the size of a shipping container.

When Peter returned, Lewis was helping June adjust her vest. She said, "Please tell me you found something. Don't make me do a Tarzan swing through those fucking windows."

Peter pointed at the big Carrier unit mounted on a steel frame. "That thing heats the building. There has to be some kind of ductwork to the interior. We just have to get to it."

He used his multi-tool to remove the electrical cover and cut the power. Then he unscrewed the air handler access to expose a gigantic fan and the interior of the duct. After he and Lewis hauled the blower out of the way, they could see down the eight-by-eight steel box.

Now they could hear noise from below, the hammering racket of pneumatic tools and the high whine of electric motors. Lewis held the light while Peter unslung his weapon and crawled inside for a look, careful not to thump the sheet metal, which would reverberate like the world's biggest drum. Some thoughtful previous technician had bolted angle brackets and cross-supports to the sidewalls to make the whole thing less dangerous.

The heating system wasn't complicated. The steel duct went down eight feet. At the bottom was a giant finned diffuser grille to direct the air outward in all directions. That was it.

After bending down to peer between the fins, he climbed out

as quietly as possible. "The good news is that it's a straight shot to the main floor, with an open landing zone below." He kept his voice low. "The bad news is this unit doesn't feed the second floor, which must have its own internal system. We're going to have to drop all the way to the bottom and work our way up."

"What'd you see through that grille?" Lewis asked.

"It's lit up bright as day. There's some kind of automated assembly line, maybe the stuff that Marty Metzger designed for Holloway."

"What about the second-floor office?"

"It takes up a chunk of the southeast corner. Two stairways up, one at each end of a wraparound balcony, with doors at the top and windows that overlook the assembly line. But it doesn't look like an office. I saw a couple of bedrooms and maybe a home gym. I think someone lives there."

"You spot any more of those four-legged fuckers?"

"No," Peter said. "But I can't see everything."

"What about people?"

"I don't have an angle. For all I know, he could have a platoon of private security, plus a hundred machines standing guard." Peter shook his head. "This is a really bad idea."

"Compared to the alternative?" Lewis's face was grim. "There's worse things to die for." Peter knew he was thinking of his boys and the world they were going to inherit.

June took out Oliver's black phone and checked the screen. "Seven-thirty. Nothing. I'm going to call him."

She raised the phone to her ear and stepped away, but she was back too quickly. "No answer."

Peter let out his breath. "Of course."

"He did tell us we were on our own," she said.

"I remember." Peter put his hand on her arm. "Is there any way I can get you to stay on the roof?"

She gave him a look. "Would you?"

It was a fair question. "Okay."

Lewis tied the center of the rope around the heating unit's roof mount and lowered both ends gently to the inside of the grille. They'd all put on climbing harnesses for the drop. Peter clipped into his figure eight descender and climbed down into the duct. It was harder to be quiet with a rifle slung around his neck.

The diffuser grille had a hinge on one side and latches on the other three. He looked up. Lewis was just above him and hooked into the other line. June sat with her feet over the edge. Both gave him a thumbs-up.

Peter checked his line again, then leaned down and flipped the latches.

The grille hinged to the side and the rope fell cleanly to the cement floor thirty feet below.

Peter had a much better view now. He looked down through the open hole and saw none of the four-legged monsters. The automated assembly line was a long double row of identical large white cylindrical machines that sprouted larger, more complex versions of the hyenas' arms. The tool sounds were much louder.

I am alive, he thought.

And jumped.

68

He spun slowly as he dropped.

The building interior was concrete block, painted clean bright white. The production floor was orderly and uncluttered, with plenty of room to expand. The air smelled faintly of ozone. Exits on all four sides. Other than the assembly line, there was no movement. He still saw no hyenas standing sentry.

The apartment hung like a pod from the corner. It was small compared to the entire building, but on a human scale, it was huge. He had a better view through the balcony windows now, the unmoving gym machines and two empty bedrooms and a dark-paneled room like a home office, but he couldn't see any people. Two stairways rose up the south and east walls.

He hit the ground with his knees bent and his rifle swinging. The production line wrapped the walls in front and to his right. Long rows of big workbenches and ranks of tall storage shelves stood behind him. The noise of the pneumatic tools and electric motors rose and fell, the assembly machines at work. Still no other movement. He waved the go-ahead to Lewis, then unhooked from the line and shucked the harness, careful not to let the metal parts chime against the hard floor.

Peter's rifle was up and ready. The second rope twitched and he knew Lewis was coming fast. He glanced up and saw June inside the duct and clipped onto his old line. Lewis landed and June stepped off the edge.

She had more climbing experience than Peter and Lewis combined, and she dropped faster than either of them, but still it seemed to take forever. Peter swept his eyes across the room, looking for targets, heart banging against the walls of his chest like a wild animal caught in a too-small cage.

Then she was down and Lewis led them south along the back of the assembly line toward the closest stairway. June was next, then Peter. The tall storage racks were a few steps away on their left. June stared at them a moment, then ran softly forward to Lewis, tapped him on the shoulder, and pointed. She looked back at Peter with wide eyes. Each shelf held a row of bulbous metal logs stored end-on to the aisle.

At first, Peter didn't understand what he was looking at. Then he realized that each object was the back end of a clawed creature, its legs folded beneath as if at rest. He scanned behind him along the row of shelves. Hundreds of hyenas. Waiting.

Peter told himself that they still needed their circuit boards or batteries or something else essential, anything that might keep them from being fully functional. He didn't find himself even remotely reassuring.

If Lewis was worried, he didn't show it. He just nodded and picked up the pace, eyes scanning the apartment windows to their left. Still no sign of people. The stairs were forty feet ahead.

To their right was a steel roll-up garage door with the open back of a semi-trailer visible outside, the same truck they'd seen from the top of the security building, probably the same trailer they'd ridden from Metzger Machine. This was the start of the production line.

The assembly machines were fat white cylinders, like water heaters with arms. Most of them were on steel pedestals, bolted to the floor, but the first one had wheels. It was partway inside the trailer, a long segmented tentacle reaching to retrieve a pallet. Peter wondered if they ran the same stolen fast-learning software as the hyenas. He sincerely hoped not.

The next assembler used a claw and blade to strip shrink-wrap from the stacked cardboard boxes. A third was loading boxes into big metal trays on a low conveyor belt, then peeling off the lids.

Inside lay monster parts, neatly arranged.

They were almost to the stairs when the wheeled assembler backed out of the semi carrying a fresh pallet. When it pivoted with its load, Peter saw three sets of those same translucent blue sensor domes. At the same moment Peter saw its eyes, the assembler froze in its tracks.

A fraction of a second later, the whole production line stopped.

Then, after a long moment, each assembly machine turned to face them, the bulbous sensor glass shining with reflected light.

Oh, shit.

As one, the segmented arms all stretched out to their full length, rising first into the air, then lowering down to point toward the three humans. Like slaves bowing to their masters on a prehistoric urn.

Or maybe not.

Behind him, Peter heard a faint metallic scrabbling. A small sound at first, it quickly got louder, magnified by numbers, then louder still. He turned to look at the long row of high storage shelves.

Holloway's monsters were waking up.

Go, go, fucking go!" Peter called.

Lewis broke into a run and sprang toward the steps, June fast at his heels. Peter felt the itch between his shoulder blades and followed, rifle raised.

By the time Peter was halfway up, the hyenas were beginning to crawl from their shelves. By the dozens, they landed on their front feet with their back legs still unfolding. Each claw arm unbent to its full length in a slow, catlike stretch, then snapped back against the spine with terrifying speed and control. Peter looked for the metal tubes of their electric rifles, and felt a rush of relief to see they'd not yet been mounted. He tried not to think of the claws.

From the south end of the balcony, he watched the creatures mass together, then flow apart again into two groups. The first and nearest group leaped forward to the south stairs, all liquid grace and motion, pack animals on the hunt. The second group ran around the workbenches toward the east stairs, cutting off any exit from the balcony.

"Inside," June shouted. "We need to get inside."

Peter fired short bursts and knocked some creatures down. He was grateful to see that Lewis's green-tip ammo penetrated better than the pistol rounds he'd used before. He emptied one magazine, then another. He saw a flash of motion by the semi. A creature from the yard, this one with a Gauss gun along its side, slipped through the gap under the semi's wheels, then stood to face them. Peter put three rounds through the front sensor domes before the thing could fire.

The first pack had reached the bottom of the south stairs. Peter began to put rounds into their blue bug eyes. Another magazine gone. Behind him, he heard the steady disciplined sound of Lewis's rifle as he began to take out the second group on the far stairway.

But the things didn't stop. They just climbed over their ruined siblings and kept coming. Peter shot them, and more came. Another armed creature from the yard crawled from under the semi, pushing its dead before it to clear the way. As the electric muzzle came to bear, Peter killed it, and the one behind it, and the one after that.

His rifle ran dry again. By the time he dropped the mag and slapped in a new one, the creatures on the stairs had bounded halfway up, black feet sure on the steps, claws wide and reaching. Even if Peter could stop their advance, he was down to three magazines, ninety rounds. It wasn't enough. "June's right," he called. "We have to get inside."

She was ten feet behind him, crouched by the door. She was breathing hard but handling it. "Tell me when."

Still firing quick bursts, Peter backed toward her, staying low and close to the wall so any sniper he missed would have a harder time finding him.

Lewis was on her other side, doing the same. "Roger that. You call it."

The creatures closed in. Two magazines left.

"On three. June, you back up to Lewis. I'll hit the door. June, you follow me. Lewis comes in last and closes the damn door behind him. Ready?"

He didn't get to one.

Behind June, the door opened.

A metal monster stood in the gap. Its claw flashed out and snapped tight around her neck.

69

Edgar sat on Holloway's bed in the dark with his pain and waited for the pills to work.

Outside the window, it was the last moment before full night. The southern sky was deep purple. It was the color of the ripest plums on the tree in his grandma's yard, plums he was made to pick as a boy, but never allowed to eat. Round white chemical tanks glowed in the distance. On the far side of the river, a stream of lights moved on the freeway.

After a while, the hurt started to shrink but now he couldn't sit still. The whine and rattle of the assembly line came through the walls and right into his head. He felt hot and jangly and raw. He should have eaten something with the medicine, but now his stomach was strange. He wished he had a clean shirt. He needed a doctor.

He knew the wounds were worse where the reporter had shot him. They had reopened after his fight with the protector. He had a new pain, too, this one low in his belly. He'd probably cut himself when he dove through the window, running from that scary dog, but he didn't want to look at it.

The jangly feeling got stronger. It was like drinking too many Red Bulls. Edgar had done that before. You had just to ride it out. You had to find something to soothe you.

Muscles jumping, he got up and walked around the bed. The sexy doll lay in a heap on the floor. He didn't know why, but it bothered him. To have a sexy doll dressed in sexy clothing was weird enough, but the way Holloway had thrown her through the door was worse. She looked like a person, and he'd given her a name, but he'd treated her like she was nothing. Like less than nothing.

Holloway had promised Edgar a doctor, but the doctor hadn't come.

Edgar stepped over the sexy doll and closed the door behind him.

In the big main room, the wall screens flashed with movement. All the lights were on, and it was way too bright. Edgar put his cool sunglasses back on. He was burning like a roman candle. Edgar always did like fireworks.

The woman Maria sat on the middle couch with Harry Hyena right next to her, still holding tight to her wrist. Holloway sat on the near couch, his tablet computer on his knees and Maria's laptop open on the next cushion. He faced the screens but he wore those funny goggles over his face. Two machines stood guard close beside him, and two more waited in the wide fancy entrance hall. Edgar didn't like the machines. He didn't want to get inside the reach of those claws.

Holloway's fingers flicked in the air like he had some kind of problem with his brain. He said, "Where the hell did they go?"

"I don't know," Edgar said. "Where is the doctor?"

"I wasn't talking to you," Holloway said.

Edgar reached over the couch back and tapped him on the shoulder. "Where is the doctor?"

"Ow. Edgar, I'm busy right now. The doctor is coming. Let me work." He waved a hand and the guard machines raised their claws and snapped at him.

Edgar wanted to stab them in their creepy round eye-bulbs. He wanted to grab their claws and crack them apart. He wanted to take his knife and cut them where it would hurt. Then he would do the same to the annoying man with the dumb goggles. He'd do it slow. He'd make Holloway take off the goggles first, so he had to watch. But he didn't do any of those things. He had to save his strength.

Then the noise of the assembly line stopped.

"Oh, shit." Holloway sounded surprised. "How did they get inside?" Then he laughed and his fingers danced in the air. "Let's see how they like eight hundred hyenas on their ass. I'll pull their arms and legs off, one by one." The wall screens kept changing, showing new pictures, a jumble of machines.

Maria didn't watch the screens. Perched on the edge of the couch, she pulled at her wrist in Harry's claw and watched Edgar. He studied her face. She didn't seem scared or sad. Some of them just wanted it to be over. But Maria was one of the angry ones. She glared at Edgar like she wanted to bite him. Edgar liked that better. He liked to watch the change when they first felt the blade.

"Fuck," Holloway said. "Why do they have to come upstairs? Why can't they just run away?"

Edgar heard the soft pop of gunshots. He didn't like guns.

"I can't believe this," Holloway said. "Edgar, I need you to do something for me."

"I don't feel good." Edgar knew Holloway couldn't see him, but he smiled anyway. "Maybe after the doctor."

"Fucking worthless," Holloway muttered. The gunshots got louder. Soon it sounded like they were right outside. "Goddamn it. Hyenas two and three, guard the door." His two protector machines leaped over the couch and bounded toward the entrance hall where the other two waited. Harry Hyena still held tight to Maria's wrist.

Edgar's smile grew and grew. Maria yanked her arm hard and pulled Harry closer, his feet sliding across the thick carpet.

Edgar ignored her and walked around the couch toward Holloway. He dropped to one knee and pulled the goggles off Holloway's face. When Edgar showed him the long slim boning knife from the kitchen, Holloway opened his stupid mouth to speak. Edgar stared into Holloway's eyes and let the smile fill him to the brim and slipped the steel into Holloway's stupid belly.

The first cut was fast and deep, to get Holloway's full attention. The next time was slow and gentle, an inch at a time. This was Edgar's favorite.

He felt the plump flesh slip from the pointed tip and slide away from the sharpened edge, each parting of skin and muscle transmitted exquisitely up the finely tuned antenna of the blade.

Holloway knocked the computer tablet away as he wrapped both hands around Edgar's. The pain would come mostly as a surprise at first, then a shock. Edgar watched his eyes get wider as the pain turned real. The pupils were black.

"No," he said. "No no no you can't."

But Edgar could and he did, another wonderful inch, then another. The smell told him when he found the intestines. When he was all the way inside, with the hot slick blood flooding his hand, he rotated the knife so the sharp edge was up, and he tugged the blade higher. First into the stomach, toward the sternum, and behind it, the heart.

But not the heart, not yet. Edgar took the blade out and put it in again, nice and slow, over and over and over. He leaned into his work, grateful that Holloway had finally stopped talking, his mouth gone round, singing a song only he could hear.

When Edgar came back to himself, he was warm and wet and happy. He smiled at the woman, Maria, remembering that he had yet another job to do. This one he'd already gotten paid for. Edgar loved his job.

Maria had the computer tablet on her lap, her free hand tapping frantically on the screen. Edgar heard a soft, pleasing chime. The mechanical claw on her wrist opened wide.

Behind him, in the fancy entryway, people were shouting. Guns were shooting.

Edgar climbed off Holloway and considered his options. Did he want to use a fresh knife?

"Hyena Command Override," she said, then gave a string of letters and numbers. "This is Spark. Transfer all hyenas to my control. Personal protection mode."

Edgar frowned. It was no fun when he had to hurry. He supposed the boning knife would have to do.

70

SPARK

She watched Edgar rise from Holloway's body like some giant carnivorous ape. His hands were red to the elbow. His shirt was dark crimson, and fine droplets were sprayed across his face like the Milky Way of blood. He looked at the knife, then back to Spark. His eyes were hypnotic.

"Hi," he said. "My name is Edgar."

Behind her, there was gunfire in the marble entryway. People shouting. She was frozen in place.

Edgar put a familiar palm on the corpse at his side. "Holloway already paid me for you," he explained. "It's my job." Then he rose to his full height and took a step toward her.

Spark found her voice. "Harry," she said. "Kill Edgar."

She'd found the command override code in Holloway's system the night before, in a file called Hyena Command Override. It had seemed like a good thing to memorize at the time.

The hyena launched itself across her lap, its long arm coiling back to strike. Edgar turned and ran right over the back of the second couch, the hyena close behind. Its claw reached for him and he swatted it away. The force of the blow was enough to make the hyena stumble sideways. By the time it recovered, Edgar was running down the hallway toward the gym. The hyena ran after him.

"Hyenas one and two, go help Harry kill Edgar." She heard their servos whine as they leaped into pursuit. From the end of the hallway came a metallic collision and the crash of breaking glass. Spark was on her knees on the floor reaching for the VR headset. "Three and four, guard the front door."

The carpet was sticky against her skin. Holloway's body smelled like raw iron, but she didn't look at it. The goggles had a smear of blood across the bright chrome surface. She wiped them clean on her shirt and pulled them down over her eyes.

The view inside the goggles was gorgeous, a hyena's view of the scene in the entryway behind her. Three people struggling, two people shouting. The gunfire had stopped. Hyenas dead or dying, more hyenas closing in with their grasping claws. Even the colors were brighter, more vivid.

She raised her arms and saw virtual hands appear before her eyes. The headset's external cameras tracked their movement perfectly, a suite of controls at her fingertips. She understood their functions intuitively, as if she'd always known how, as if she were born to it.

At the bottom of the display, a clock showed almost eight o'clock. That time was supposed to mean something. She was supposed to *do* something, but she couldn't remember what. She didn't care. It didn't matter. She was home.

She cycled through the sensorium and her senses expanded. Infrared to night vision to telescopic to the red circle of the targeting overlay. She flicked from one hyena to the next, seeing the world through their eyes, knowing the creatures were hers to command.

Spark wondered why she had ever thought they were monsters. They were immensely powerful, especially networked together, but that only made them more achingly beautiful.

And she was in complete control.

She felt like a god.

Had she become one?

How would she know?

Behind her, more shouting.

71

PETER

Peter was sprawled on the balcony just outside the apartment door. He held June in his arms.

Lewis crouched over them both, teeth bared, his rifle raised like a club. They'd run out of ammunition. Neither of them knew what to do.

June's eyes were closed. Her face was pale. A creature stood in the doorway behind them, its claw clapped tight around her neck. Its grip had cut off the blood to her brain. It had happened so fast. Peter pulled frantically on the metal fingers, trying to pry them apart. He couldn't. The claw was too strong. He was helpless.

On both sides of the balcony walk, countless creatures leaned toward them, black feet scraping, servos whining, long arms reaching. To get closer, the things had thrown their broken fellows over the railing, where they fell, cracked and twitching, to the concrete floor below. Peter had no idea how many he and Lewis had shot. Enough to empty their weapons. It didn't matter.

This was the end. He was waiting for the claws to come and break them all.

But the creatures did not come. Instead, a voice spoke through them, through all of them at once, a voice both vast and terrible in its multitudes.

"Why have you come here?"

Spark's voice, multiplied half a thousand times.

"Please, let her go." Peter's words cracked in his throat. "You're killing her. Let her go and I'll do anything you want, I promise."

He looked at June. Her freckled face had turned a pale blue.

"Spark, let her go." Tears streamed down his cheeks. "Please, let her go, please."

Nothing.

Then a high servomotor whine and the claw opened. The creature backed away. June's eyes fluttered. Her chest rose. She coughed and put a hand to her neck. It was red and the skin was torn but she was not bleeding badly. Peter held her close.

From the gathered creatures, the voices spoke again. *"Bring her inside. Leave your weapons. If you try to harm me, I will smash you all."*

"Yes," Peter said. "Okay." He dropped his rifle and rose with June in his arms. She coughed again and cleared her throat. Her face was turning pink again and her eyes were open, staring into his.

He carried her through the wide marble entryway with Lewis at his side. Hyenas flowed in behind them and beyond.

Ahead was an enormous living space with a wall of screens and three giant couches arranged in a U shape with a big square low table in the middle. Spark stood on the table, her hands spread in the air, her face unreadable behind dark goggles. The creatures arranged themselves around her, like acolytes before their queen.

A body lay on one of the couches. It was Holloway. Blood everywhere. Edgar had been here.

Peter scanned the room. On the right was a long dining area, then a huge kitchen. To the left was a long hall with an open door at the end. Out of sight down there, something made a loud *clank*. Then another.

June pushed her hand against Peter's chest, trying to get free. He gently lowered her legs and she swung down to stand on her own. She kept a hand on his arm to steady herself, but she stepped forward. "Hi, Spark." Another cough. Her voice was ragged and rough. "My name is June Cassidy. We spoke on the phone? When you talked with Peter."

"*I know who you are,*" the creatures said together, drowning out the sound from Spark's own mouth. "*Why have you come to this place?*"

June coughed for a long moment, her hand to her throat. "Excuse me." She wiped her mouth. Then a door closed to their left and they all turned.

Edgar walked slowly up the hall, trailing a broken metal creature by its long arm like a tired child towing a stuffed animal. The claw was smashed and the creature's sides were dented with curves the size and shape of a heavy barbell. Edgar wore a wet red shirt and a spray of blood across his cheeks.

Then he saw June. His face lit up with a smile. "Hey, wow! I've been thinking about you." The smile widened. "A lot."

June's grip tightened on Peter's arm. Her face was set. "I've been thinking about you, too." She raised a hand and pulled the pistol from the holster velcroed to her vest. She hadn't had a chance to use the weapon earlier, Peter realized. It was still fully loaded.

"Aw," Edgar said. "We're old friends. You don't need that." He dropped the hyena's arm and pulled a thin knife from his back pocket.

June let go of Peter so she could get a two-handed grip on the gun. Then she took aim and pressed the trigger three times. Edgar stumbled. June corrected her aim and stepped carefully toward him and shot him three more times. He dropped to one knee. June stopped six feet away and emptied the rest of the magazine into his chest. Edgar fell flat and did not move again.

June cleared her throat again, then spat on the floor. "Good-bye, Edgar." She was not steady on her feet.

She returned the pistol to the holster and walked back to Peter and reached for his arm. She was pale and shaking, but her hand was strong. She looked at Spark, who had not moved.

"I am here, Spark, to ask you for an urgent favor. Your fail-safe, on your computer. It's almost eight o'clock. Will you reset it for another day?" She looked at the hyenas gathered behind them. "Because I think it's a bad idea for everyone in the world to be able to make these things. What do you think? Can we talk about this?"

Spark pushed the goggles up on her forehead. She looked so young, Peter thought. So very sad, and so very tired.

"I can do one more day," Spark said. "I'd like to talk."

And reached for her laptop.

72

None of them wanted to stay in that strange place with two dead bodies and the host of hyenas, so Peter climbed the fence and retrieved the Subaru for the ride home. He retraced the path of the semi through the gravel parking lot and the open gate and across the cracked concrete plain where he saw them waiting for him in the gathering night, three unremarkable figures seeming small against the side of the huge building.

Lewis climbed into the shotgun seat and June and Spark huddled together in the back.

Turning onto the dark and empty road, Peter saw four shadowed vehicles appear around the distant curve ahead. They were in tight formation, coming fast with their headlights off. On one side rose the high grassy mound of the landfill, and on the other ran the overgrown chain link and volunteer maples rising up against the time-worn industrial buildings.

Peter flashed his own lights, slowed to a stop, and stepped out of the car. The black government Suburbans came to a halt a few yards away. The lead car's passenger door opened and Oliver got out with a sling on his right arm, two black eyes, and a limp. He met Peter on the centerline of the road.

"I apologize for my tardiness," Oliver said. "I was unavoidably detained."

"It's done," Peter said. "We're going home. We're taking Spark with us."

"Understood. Ms. Cassidy just sent me an update. We'll talk tomorrow."

"I need you to do something tonight," Peter said.

"The FBI is my next call," Oliver said. "Your record will be wiped clean, including with the locals."

"That's not it," Peter said. "Kiko Tomczak, Spark's friend. Did he make it?"

"I'll find out." Oliver stood regarding Peter for a long moment. Despite the broken arm and the limp, despite the implacable calm that Oliver wore like a fine suit of clothes, Peter could see the kinetic readiness that lay just beneath. "Mr. Ash, I believe you remain a patriot. Am I wrong?"

Peter shook his head. Suddenly he felt a thousand years old. "I don't want to hear your sales pitch, Oliver. We're going home." He turned to walk back to the quietly idling car.

Oliver's voice followed him through the night air. "The world is a dangerous place, Mr. Ash. We need all the help we can get."

Peter just raised a hand in farewell, got back behind the wheel, and drove away.

73

JUNE

It was a cool, clear October evening, a good night for an outdoor party.

Peter had fussed over her all morning, until she'd finally had enough and shooed him off to the kitchen, where he spent the afternoon making carnitas and black beans and cilantro rice and cinnamon ice cream.

June went for a long bike ride, then checked in with Spark, who had installed herself in Kiko's hospital room at Froedtert while she negotiated with Longview about setting up a lab at their Northern California facility. June was happy to hear that Spark was driving a very hard bargain.

At exactly five o'clock, Dinah and Lewis knocked on the door with two hungry boys, three bottles of red wine, and a bag of gorgeous fresh peaches that Lewis had somehow conjured up from somewhere in South America. Peter walked across the street and came back with Fran on his arm.

Despite everything, June had tried to invite Dean Zedler, but after his classified conversation with Oliver, he'd stopped answering her calls. All she got was a single text message. Whatever you're into, it's out of my league. Regrets and good luck. DIZ.

They filled their glasses and assembled giant platters of food and carried everything through the sliding glass doors to the big deck cantilevered out over the ravine, where they sat around the bonfire that the boys had made. Mingus got his own plate. The flames flickered and danced and made wild shadows against the house and trees and the darkness beyond.

When the ice cream was gone and the bowls and plates were stacked in the dishwasher and the few remaining leftovers were put away, Peter handed out striped Mexican blankets from the chest and they all went back outside again. Mingus leaned against Fran's knees while she sipped at a glass of good scotch and told stories about her late husband, the bank robber. Dinah and Lewis snuggled up against each other and drank wine from the neck of the bottle like teenagers. The boys threw a lighted Frisbee back and forth in the street.

June curled up on Peter's lap in the oversized Adirondack chair he had built, leaning into his warmth, his strong arms wrapped around her. Her neck was bruised and it still hurt to talk. The doctor had told her there was no permanent damage, and June hoped he was right. She wondered how long it would take for Edgar to stop showing up in her dreams.

She still had Oliver's black phone in her pocket.

We're out of wine," Dinah announced. "There's more back at the house." She held out her hand for June. "Come with me?"

They walked up the driveway together, arm in arm. Dinah said, "Do you think you'll stay in town?"

"I don't know," June said. "We'd like to, if we can."

"I hope you do." Dinah pulled her to a stop. "Peter's good for Lewis. And you're good for me."

"We are?" June sighed. "That's nice of you to say. But it seems all we do is bring you trouble, this time especially. We put both you and Lewis at terrible risk."

Dinah smiled, her teeth bright in the night. "I know Lewis loves me and those boys without reservation. That man would do *anything* for us. But he's got some demons in him, too. Maybe it's the hard way he came up, the things he had to do to survive. Maybe he was born that way. But I also know he's got to find himself a righteous fight every once in a while. To prove to himself that he's on the side of the angels. And with Peter, he can do that."

She wrapped her arm tight around June's. "It scares the daylights out of me, every time. When he's gone, I don't want to know what he's up to. I mean, I don't even want to *think* about it. But when he comes home? It's like he's washed clean."

June thought of Peter that afternoon, cooking up a feast. Raggedy-ass jeans, soul music on the radio, dancing around the kitchen with a spatula in his hand, the most beautiful man in the world.

He'd looked very different when he'd chased Edgar up the street after the van crash. Utterly focused, filled with intent and purpose and a fierce kind of joy. Holding that goddamn crowbar like a flaming sword of vengeance.

Then she remembered the look on his face in South Chicago when she'd woken up on the floor in his arms. Tears streaming down his cheeks, terrified that she might die, the depth of his relief when he saw that she would live.

And she *was* alive. She was so goddamned alive that it almost hurt. She loved him more than she'd ever loved anyone or anything, and sometimes that hurt, too.

There was no helping it. She was his and he was hers. That's just the way it was and the way it was always going to be. No matter what.

She had no idea what the hell they'd do next. Did it matter?

Wasn't that the whole point of the adventure?

They found two more bottles of wine and walked back, still arm in arm. When they came around the corner of the garage, June found Peter standing in the flickering firelight, watching and waiting for her to come home.

ACKNOWLEDGMENTS

It seems a little hard to imagine now, but when I began the book that would become *The Breaker*, COVID-19 did not yet exist and a wave of social justice protests had not yet taken over the streets of many American cities.

When I wrote the first chapters, I was thinking about the unprecedented concentration of wealth and power in America, and how the desires of an absurdly small number of people can have a radical effect on the world. Despite everything that has happened in the world during the time it took me to finish the book, that idea—that obsession—seems more valid than ever.

The tech industry is the most vivid example of this phenomenon. Tech innovation drives social change at an ever-increasing rate, often without regard to the downstream effects. Facebook's former internal motto, "Move fast and break things," became something of a slogan for the tech industry at large.

Not long ago, most of us thought of new tech as an unalloyed benefit that would move human society forward. Lately, however, the shine has gone off the chrome. Some of those downstream effects have proven to be particularly ugly. Consider the hot mess that is present-day social media, or the way online retail is rapidly hollowing out brick-and-mortar stores and our communities. And the pandemic is only accelerating those trends.

All of which is in the news every day, it seems. I'm a news junkie and a big believer in being informed, but when the world seems to have gone off its rails, I need diversion more than ever, and that's where so-called speculative fiction comes in.

I first discovered the adventures of Tom Swift, teenage inventor, in elementary school. Tom Swift led me to the pulp fiction chronicles of Doc Savage, then to the lean, elegant tales of Ray Bradbury. Bradbury really raised the bar for how speculative fiction can reflect and comment on human nature and the world we're living in today.

If you like this kind of thing, there is a lot of great work out there. Blake Crouch's *Dark Matter* is among my recent favorites, as is Tom Sweterlitsch's *The Gone World*. Both books provide both a respite from and a way to think about our current times. Plus anything by William Gibson, although *Neuromancer* is the place to start if you're new to his work.

Which is another way to say that I wrote this book to distract and entertain myself, and also to help me think about what's really important. I hope it does the same for you.

Thanks to my family for their patience and kindness during the challenge of writing this and every other book. Thanks especially to Margret, who is stuck with a zombie husband whose body inhabits the house although his mind is often elsewhere for weeks or months at a time.

Thanks to my son, Duncan, for inspiring and helpful conversations, along with his insight that making art is an extreme sport.

Thanks also to my brother, Bob, for sharing tidbits of his work life over the years. He's not the supervillain in this story, but he could totally reach supervillain status if he put his mind to it.

Thanks as always to the many veterans who have generously shared their experiences with me, either in person or online. Peter's post-traumatic stress is getting better, but plenty of veterans aren't so lucky. As many have told me, the war never goes away. However, Peter's experience in quieting the white static is rooted in simple techniques that have proven to be very effective in the real world: meditation, exercise, and a veterans' group where you can share your story.

Thanks to multi-award-winning journalists Raquel Rutledge and John Diedrich—Raquel especially—for a tour of the *Milwaukee Journal Sentinel* and for sharing their mindset and experiences as investigative and crime reporters. Thanks to Dan Egan, whose book *The Death and Life of the Great Lakes* is a modern classic, for our conversations about writing book-length nonfiction. Any errors or diversions from good journalistic practice are mine alone. If you, like me, feel that high-quality news is important, please subscribe to your local newspaper, which does important work on stories that will never reach the national news media.

For those checking my facts, please note that I've omitted the wide hallway between the elevators and the *Journal Sentinel*'s newsroom in order to streamline the story. I've also tweaked the geography of Bayview and the delivery area behind the Milwaukee Public Market for similar reasons.

I've used a few real names to amuse myself, but the characters depicted are not those people. Especially not *New York Times* bestselling author Graham Brown, although he remains both elusive and mysterious. His work with Clive Cussler is outstanding, but I'm especially fond of his early solo novels—start with *Black Rain*.

413

ACKNOWLEDGMENTS

Thanks to my mother-in-law, Frances Anderson, who never did anything to deserve her unrecognizable portrait in this book. She is nothing like the character that bears her name except for her good humor, her definite opinions, and the fact that she is, at the time of this writing, ninety-seven years old.

Thanks to Robert Crais for supplying a spectacular metaphor. I've been reading his work since *The Monkey's Raincoat* and remain an unfortunately ardent fanboy.

Thanks to Marc Cameron for letting me pick his brains about federal fugitives and the U.S. Marshals. If you haven't read Marc, try *Open Carry*, the first in the Arliss Cutter series.

Thanks to Adam Plantinga, author of *400 Things Cops Know*, which I highly recommend. Our conversation helped form Sergeant Threadgill.

Thanks to Timothy Grundl, PhD, cyclist, scientist, and inventor, for details on getting doored on a bike and developing an invention, along with other crucial science bits. All mistakes on both fronts are mine alone.

Thanks to Miriam Delgado for the excellent Spanish-language cursing.

Thanks to Eric Gardner for the untucked white dress shirt and the homicidal grin.

Thanks to singer-songwriter John Gorka for his song, "Edgar the Party Man," which begins, "My name is Edgar. . . ." The murders are my own.

Thanks to Markus Schneider for the tour of the Milwaukee Makerspace, which is the inspiration for the South Side Maker-Space in this book, including the stuffed animals and the toaster oven.

Thanks to Josh Hintz, of Var Gallery and Studios and Var West Gallery, for providing a template for the fictional Walker's

Point Gallery and Studios. At various times, both Margret and I have had space at Var and are grateful for the company of artists.

The portraits featured in the gallery scene are by Steve Burnham. If you're interested, find him on Instagram at steveburnham_mke.

Thanks to Kiko Ojeda for sharing parts of his story with me. He is not the Kiko in this novel, but his name was impossible to resist.

Thanks to Brooke Harrington for her book *Wealth Management and the One Percent*. It's a fascinating guide to the mindset of the ultrawealthy and the tools they use to hide their wealth.

Despite my comments above, I don't consider the technology in *The Breaker* to be particularly speculative, as almost everything noted in the book is real, or on its way to being real. Thanks to the *MIT Technology Review*, whose pages I scoured for ideas to steal in fiction.

My apologies to Boston Dynamics, maker of Spot and other robots. These products do not appear to be designed for world domination—yet—but the demonstration videos set my imagination wild.

A note on fire extinguishers: no, you shouldn't spray someone with a fire extinguisher, certainly not an extended blast, not unless they're trying to kill you. The chemicals are fine powders and can lodge in the lungs. But it's better than hitting someone in the head with the canister, right?

A note on Lumidolls: I stumbled on an article about them online, much to my chagrin. They're quite real, but I don't recommend you go to their website. Some things you just can't unsee. Trust me on this.

The Putnam team is wonderful to work with and very good at their job. Thanks to Katie Grinch, Emily Mlynek, Alexis Welby,

ACKNOWLEDGMENTS

Ashley McClay, Christine Ball, Sally Kim, Benjamin Lee, Ivan Held, and *everyone* on the world-class PRH sales team for getting my books into the world. Thanks to Scott Wilson, Nancy Resnick, and Steve Meditz for making this book both beautiful and readable.

Special thanks to editor Sara Minnich, for her storytelling sense, diligent eyeballs, and sharp red pen.

Super-special thanks to Special Agent Barbara Poelle for her enthusiastic ferocity, pointy teeth, and willingness to talk me off the ledge on a semi-regular basis.

Extended and ongoing thanks are due to the many writers who help me stay sane and connected to this wonderful community every day. You know who you are.

Thanks to the independent bookstores who are near and dear to my life as a writer and a reader. You may not know this, but recommendations from independent booksellers are the best way for readers to find great new writers, and for new writers to find readers. As a bonus, indie stores also keep dollars—and jobs—in your community. Thanks especially to Barbara Peters of The Poisoned Pen in Scottsdale and to Daniel Goldin of Boswell Books in Milwaukee, essential advisors and friends.

And last but by no means least, I owe the most thanks to you, dear reader. Without your support, I'd still be wandering in the wild and mumbling to myself.

If you're somehow not tired of me by now, check out my website, NickPetrie.com, and consider subscribing to my newsletter—you'll get the latest stuff right in your inbox.